Ethel Lillian Voynich, Paul Frenzeny

The Humour of Russia

Ethel Lillian Voynich, Paul Frenzeny

The Humour of Russia

ISBN/EAN: 9783337346652

Printed in Europe, USA, Canada, Australia, Japan

Cover: Foto ©Andreas Hilbeck / pixelio.de

More available books at **www.hansebooks.com**

THE
HUMOUR OF RUSSIA

TRANSLATED BY E. L.
VOYNICH, WITH AN
INTRODUCTION BY
STEPNIAK
ILLUSTRATIONS BY
PAUL FRÉNZENY

LONDON
WALTER SCOTT, LTD
1895

NEW YORK
CHARLES SCRIBNER'S SONS
1895

CONTENTS

— ••• —

INTRODUCTION.

OF all manifestations of literary genius humour is the rarest, and I am not sure that it is not the highest. Laughter is immortal. The sentimental novels over which our grandfathers and grandmothers shed floods of tears—the "Corinnas," the "Clarissas," and the "New Heloises"—have become for us soporifics of an almost irresistible strength. But the world still laughs, and will laugh for ever, over the masterpiece of Cervantes and the burlesques of Voltaire. Who nowadays can read from beginning to end Francesco Petrarca, and who can put down Giovanni Boccaccio when once begun?

Then again, whilst the demand for refreshing, invigorating laughter has been in all times the greatest, the number of authors who have come forward to dispense it is surprisingly small, even in the richest literatures. The Italians, for example, have had only one master of immortal laughter—the above-mentioned Boccaccio. The great Manzoni possessed the deep intrinsic qualities of a humorist but had not the pungency. In the long list of Italian authors of our century there is only one humorist of first magnitude — Carlo Porta, who wrote not in literary Italian but in the Milanese dialect.

Of all races the stern, sad English are by far the richest in the beautiful gift of genuine humour. The melancholy Slavonians come, I think, next to the English. Melancholy does not exclude humour. On the contrary, the richest pearls of humour are gathered at the bottom of the sea of sadness. The greatest humorists have never been men of cheerful mood, and this seems to be as true of nations as of men.

From the time when Russia first possessed a literature worthy of the name, we have always had eminent humorists, some of them, like Gogol and Shchedrin, belonging to those makers of divine laughter who so rarely appear among the nations.

But although justly popular in their own country, the Russian humorists are hardly known abroad. This is certainly due not to want of opportunity of knowing them. Gogol's masterpieces, "Dead Souls" and "The Inspector," were translated years ago into English. But he is not half so well known in this country as any of the three great Russian novelists. Humour is so eminently national, it is so closely bound to the soil where it is born, that it can rarely be transplanted to other climes and skies. It certainly loses more in translation than ordinary fiction, and it requires a peculiar gift on the part of the translator that its distinctive characteristics should not be lost altogether. However, translators have had the courage to try their skill upon Gogol, who is not only the greatest but the most comprehensible of Russian humorists.

With him the comical effect results neither from the peculiar manner of description nor from the contrasts presented, but from his unique gift of bringing to the surface the comical traits of men's characters. His is the deepest and the most artistic form of humour, which on this account becomes sometimes international. Gogol's heroes—some of them at least—are as comprehensible to the English as Charles Dickens's Mr. Micawber and Mrs. Nickleby are comprehensible to the Russians.

The present volume contains two beautiful examples of Gogol's art, which has not been yet translated into English—"A Madman's Diary" and "Marriage."

The "Diary" is a fanciful sketch, presenting perhaps the most typical sample of "Humour," as distinguished from other forms of the comical, which can be found in any literature. It is an intensely pathetic, and at the same time irresistibly droll, bit of autobiography of a poor wretch of an official whose life has been one of insufferable humiliation, and whose mind, upset by a fatal passion for a fashionable girl, seeks refuge in the dream of greatness ending in total madness. "Laughter through tears," that was Gogol's own definition of the character of his muse, and in no other work has he shown so palpably what he meant by that expression as in "A Madman's Diary."

"Marriage," although bearing the author's heading, "an utterly incredible story," and viewed by him as a mere joke, is recognised by all Russia as one of Gogol's truest and finest works. It contains two of the best conceived and most delicately drawn characters of our great character-maker, that of the hero, the old bachelor Podkolyòssin, an amusing type of irresolution and pusillanimity, and of his friend Kochkaryòv, the meddlesome busybody, who, just after he has abused the professional matchmaker Fèkla for having married him to a fool, becomes fired with an irresistible longing to confer upon his bosom friend Podkolyòssin the blessing of an alliance with another fool of exactly the same type. As a comedy of customs "Marriage" reproduces a patriarchal life so remote from the modern English that some explanations are necessary. Among the uneducated part of the Russian middle-class, as well as among the peasantry, marriages are arranged by the parents. The young people being considered too ignorant to be consulted upon a matter of such importance. In the villages, among the peasantry, where everybody is known by everybody else, no special intermediaries are needed to arrange these matches. But it is different with the middle-class living in large cities. Here a class of professional matchmakers and go-betweens exists. Naturally enough, it lends itself very much to ridicule, and two samples of it appear in the present volume—one in Gogol, the other in Ostròvsky's comedy.

Gogol, who was born in 1810 and died in 1852, is the oldest of our great prose writers. To him we can trace the origin of the Russian realistic novel as well as drama. Ostròvsky, who is his successor in the dramatic art, is our contemporary. He was born in 1824, and died four years ago. To him the Russians owe their theatre: he left us thirty-seven dramas and comedies, varying in merit and popularity, but all keeping their place upon the stage.

"Incompatibility of Temper"—one of the two of his comedies that are given in the present volume —is a sample of that pure and deep humour which we admire in Gogol. Serafima, the heroine, with her extraordinary stupidity, sentimentality, apparent whimsicalness, and practical pigheadedness, is as living and striking a creation of Russian humour as the best of Gogol's types. But in the next comedy the sunny, sympathetic humour changes into the harsh laughter of the satirist.

The "Domestic Picture," the second of Ostróvsky's dramas, is anything but a picture of Russian domestic life. It is a bitter and merciless satire, exposing the commercial dishonesty, the result of ignorance, which prevailed in the bulk of our middle-class two generations ago, and the shocking immorality nestling secretly in those families where despotism has destroyed all natural ties of affection and uprooted all sense of honour.

With Shchedrin (Saltykóv) we are in presence of the greatest satirist the Slavonic race has produced. He is a man of our time, Russia having lost him only a few years ago. For about fifty years he was the moral leader of liberal Russia, having devoted his life to the awakening of the national conscience by all the ways and methods which his incomparable genius could suggest. He was the political chronicler of his time, reproducing in rough caricatures, which made the whole of reading Russia roar with laughter, the principal events which took place in the country. At the same time, in his more elaborate works, as the "Story of the Golovlevs," and others, he equals Dostoyèvsky in the power of creating weird, gloomy, strikingly original figures, as well as in the subtle delineation of the whole man from the inner side.

When the boldness of some idea or the virulence of some attack rendered it impossible for Shchedrin (on account of the censorship) to speak plainly, he resorted to what he himself used to call the "slave's language," employing the Oriental form of the fable, the allegory, the fairy tale.

The best of Shchedrin's works are not translated into English, and probably will never be. His unrivalled wit and humour are untranslatable, because they depend chiefly upon the marvellous skill in using the Russian language. This is not inferiority, but difference in the quality of the talent. Rudyard Kipling's military stories, to quote an English example, are certainly very fine samples of genuine humour. But what would remain of them if stripped of their racy idiom? And how many second and third-rate authors are just as good (or as bad) in any decent translation?

Our great satirist stands at the head of those authors who must be read in their own tongue. The translator has shown much discernment in choosing as samples of Shchedrin's art three minor works of his, in which the language is of lesser importance. One is a burlesque, "The Recollections of Onésime Chenapan," which is an amusing caricature of the Russian "administrators." The other two are fables—"The Self-Sacrificing Rabbit," in which the satirist boldly ridicules nothing less than *the feeling of loyalty under a régime which consists of brutal violence erected into a system*, and "The Eagle as Mecænas," a skit on the Tzar himself.

The gloomy author of *Crime and Punishment* once relieved his mind with a queer, semi-fantastic little story, " The Crocodile," which amuses by its incongruities and contrasts. It has not been before translated, so far as I know, into any foreign language, and the English admirers of Dostoyèvsky will be the first to read it.

But the object of the translator was not merely to make a collection of the best humoristic works of the best Russian authors. She wanted to give samples of all kinds of Russian humour, and her list includes the two Uspènskys, Glyeb and Nikolai, V. Slyeptzòv, and even some sketches by Gorbounòv. There is hardly a name worth mentioning that could be added to these. As to translation, it is as good as it possibly could be. Only a person with the translator's exceptional knowledge of the Russian language could have overcome the difficulties inherent in a work of such a kind. Yet, with all that, I doubt whether the English will make a fair estimate of the above-mentioned authors, though among them there is one—Glyeb Uspènsky —who enjoys an enormous and well-merited popularity among the very exacting and discriminating Russian public.

What has been said about the untranslatableness of Shchedrìn applies *à fortiori* to the minor humorists. Their charm depends in a still greater degree upon the language. The unique flexibility, richness, and freedom of the Russian idiom allows those few who have got the mastery over it to obtain with it truly wonderful effects. Some authors do this at the expense of more substantial qualities. With our younger humorists the language runs riot.

They are like those injudicious painters who, having a great command over the colouring, neglect to give the necessary correctness and fulness to the *lines*, which alone know of no decay and are preserved through time and space. The translation is like the plain black and white reproduction of a picture. Only the substantial, unperishable part of the work is preserved, the rest being lost almost entirely. And in regard to the examples taken here from our minor humorists,—if English readers enjoy the humour of " A Trifling Defect in the Mechanism," or " The Porridge," it will be as high a compliment to the translator as to the authors.

A trifle of my own—" The Story of a Kopeck "—has been kindly included by the translator in the present collection. It is quite a youthful production, and will not, I am afraid, be of much credit to Russian humour. But in view of the catholicity of the translator's choice, which includes even Gorbounòv, I thought it might stand where it is.

Whatever be the reader's opinion of the merit of separate stories, the translator, as well as the publishers, deserve the thanks of the lover of Russian literature for bringing out this collection.

The smile is the most characteristic trait of a human face. We do not really know what a face is like before we have seen it smiling. Now with a nation its humour is what a smile is with an individual.

S. STEPNIAK.

THE HUMOUR OF RUSSIA

DRAMATIS PERSONÆ.

AGÀFIA TIKHÒNOVNA, *marriageable girl of the merchant class.*

ARÌNA PANTELÈYMOVNA, *her aunt.*

FÈKLA IVÀNOVNA, *professional matchmaker.*

PODKOLYÒSSIN, *aulic counsellor.*

KOCHKARYÒV, *his friend.*

YAICHNITZA, *usher.*

ANOÙCHKIN, *retired infantry officer.*

ZHEVÀKIN, *seafaring person.*

DOUNIÀSHKA, *a girl in the house.*

STARIKÒV, *shopkeeper.*

STEPÀN, *Podkolyòssin's servant.*

AN UTTERLY INCREDIBLE INCIDENT.

IN TWO ACTS.

ACT I. SCENE I.

(A bachelor's apartment. PODKOLYÒSSIN, alone, lying on the sofa smoking a pipe.)

Pod. Really when a man's alone, and thinks about it at his leisure, it does seem after all as if one ought to get married. Indeed, if you think of it, here one goes on, living and living ; and one ends by getting quite disgusted with everything. There, I've let the time slip by once more; and it's holy season [1] again. It's too bad! Everything's ready, and the matchmaker's been coming for the last three months. It makes me feel quite ashamed. Hi! Stepàn ! (*Enter* STEPÀN.) Hasn't the matchmaker come?

Step. No, your honour.

Pod. Have you been to the tailor?

Step. Yes.

Pod. Is he making the dress-coat?

Step. Yes, sir.

Pod. How far has he got on with it?

Step. He is making the button-holes.

Pod. What do you say?

Step. I said he's begun to make the button-holes.

Pod. And didn't he ask you what your master wants with a dress-coat?

Step. No, sir; he didn't.

Pod. Perhaps he asked you whether your master wasn't going to get married?

Step. No; he didn't say anything about it.

Pod. Did you see any other dress-coats in the workshop? I suppose he makes for other people too?

Step. Yes; there were a lot of coats hanging up.

Pod. But I'll be bound the cloth of them isn't as good as mine!

Step. No, sir; the stuff of yours looks nicer.

Pod. What do you say?

Step. I say the stuff of yours is nicer, sir.

Pod. That's all right. Well, and didn't the tailor ask why your master wants a dress-coat of such fine cloth?

Step. No.

Pod. Didn't he say anything about whether your master thought of getting married?

---

[1] In Russia marriages cannot be solemnised during the weeks appointed by the Greek Church as fasts.

Step. No ; he didn't talk about it at all.

Pod. But I suppose you told him what my position is, and where I serve ?

Step. Yes, sir.

Pod. What did he say to that ?

Step. He said, " I'll do my best."

Pod. That's all right. Now you may go. (*Exit* STEPÀN.) I am inclined to think that a black dress-coat is the most decorous. Coloured coats are all very well for secretaries, and clerks, and all that small fry—they look just fit for milksops. People higher up in the service ought to observe what is called a—a—a—a—— There ! I've forgotten the word ! It's a fine word ; and I've forgotten it ! It's all very well to put on airs, little father, but an aulic counsellor takes the rank of colonel too ; the only difference is that he has a uniform without epaulettes. Hi ! Stepàn ! (*Enter* STEPÀN.) Did you buy the blacking?

Step. Yes, sir.

Pod. Where did you buy it ? In the shop I told you about, on the Voznesènsky Prospect ?

Step. Yes, that was the shop.

Pod. And is it good ?

Step. Very good.

Pod. Did you try it on the boots ?

Step. Yes, sir.

Pod. And does it shine ?

Step. It takes a beautiful shine, sir.

Pod. And when you bought it, didn't the man ask you what your master wants with such good blacking ?

Step. No.

Pod. Perhaps he asked you whether your master was going to be married ?

Step. No ; he didn't say anything.

Pod. All right ; you can go. (*Exit* STEPÀN.) One would think boots were a trifling thing ; and yet if they are badly made, or not properly blacked, no one will respect you in good society. It makes a great difference, somehow. . . . Another horrid thing is, if one has corns. I'd be ready to put up with almost anything rather than have corns. Hi! Stepàn! (*Enter* STEPÀN.)

Step. What's your honour's pleasure?

Pod. Did you tell the shoemaker that the boots musn't give me corns?

Step. Yes, sir.

Pod. And what did he say?

Step. He said, " All right." (*Exit.*)

Pod. The deuce take it all! It's a difficult business, this getting married. What with one thing and another— first this has to be set right, and then that—the devil take it all! it's not half so easy as people say. Hi! Stepàn! (*Enter* STEPÀN.) There's another thing I wanted to say——

Step. The old woman's come.

Pod. Ah! she's come? Send her in. (*Exit* STEPÀN.) Yes; it's a sort of thing—a sort of—a hard matter. (*Enter* FÈKLA.) Ah! good-morning, Fèkla Ivànovna! Well? What have you got to say? There's a chair; sit down and tell me about it. I want to hear all about her. What's her name? Melània——

Fèkla. Agàfia Tikhònovna.

Pod. Yes, yes, Agàfia Tikhònovna. I suppose she's some old maid of forty?

Fèkla. Well, then, you're just wrong. I can tell you, if you marry her, you'll come to thank me and praise her up every day of your life.

Pod. I suppose that's a lie, Fèkla Ivànovna?

Fèkla. I'm old to tell lies, little father; lying's a dog's work.

Pod. But the dowry? What about the dowry?

Fèkla. The dowry? Well, there's a stone house in the

Moscow borough,[1] two-storied ; it brings in such a profit that it's a pleasure to think of: one corndealer pays seven hundred for his shop ; then there are wine vaults that attract plenty of customers ; two wooden wings, one entirely wooden and the other with a stone basement : they bring in an income of four hundred roubles each. Well then, there's a market-garden on the Vỳborgskaya[2] side. The year before last a merchant took it for cabbage-farming ; and such a good sober fellow—never touches a drop of drink—and he's got three sons ; he has married two of them, "but the third," says he, "is too young ; he can stay in the shop and see after the business. I'm getting old," says he, "so it's time for my son to stay in the shop and see that the business goes on all right."

Pod. Well, but tell me what she's like to look at.

Fèkla. Like sugar-candy ! Pink and white, like roses and cream. . . . Sweeter than honey ; sweeter than I can say ! I tell you, you'll be over head and ears in love with her ; you'll go about to all your friends and enemies and say, "I've got something to thank Fèkla Ivànovna for."

Pod. Well, I don't know ; she's not a staff-officer's daughter.

Fèkla. No ; but she belongs to the third guild. And then she's one that even a general needn't be ashamed of. Why, she won't even hear of a merchant. " I don't care," says she, "what my husband's like ; I don't even care if he's ugly, but he must be a noble." There's a real lady for you ! And you should just see her on Sundays, when she puts on a silk dress. Dear Lord ! How it rustles ! Like any princess.

[1] The district of St. Petersburg in which stands the terminus of the Moscow railway.

[2] The north-east district of St. Petersburg.

Pod. Well, you see, that's why I asked you, because I'm an aulic counsellor; and so—you understand. . . .

Fëkla. Of course I understand. There was an aulic counsellor that tried for her already, but she refused him; she didn't like him. But then he had such a strange way with him; he was all right to look at, but he couldn't speak a word without telling lies. It wasn't his fault, poor fellow; the Lord made him so. He was sorry enough himself about it, but he just couldn't help lying; it was God's will, that's clear.

Pod. And is she the only girl you've got on hand?

Fëkla. Why, what do you want with another? She's the best you could possibly have.

Pod. You don't really mean that?

Fëkla. If you look all over the world, you won't find another like her.

Pod. Well, little mother, we'll think it over, we'll think it over. You'd better come again to-morrow. I'll tell you what: you come again, and we'll have a comfortable time; I'll lie on the sofa, and you shall tell me about her.

Fëkla. Come, little father, that's too much of a good thing! I've been at your beck and call for more than two months, and nothing's come of it yet; all you ever do is to sit in your dressing-gown and smoke a pipe.

Pod. I suppose you think to get married is no more than to say " Hi! Stepàn, bring my boots!" and just put them on, and go out. No, no! one must think it over, and look about one.

Fëkla. Oh! there's no harm in that. If you want to look, who minds your looking? The goods are in the market to be looked at. Call for your coat, and go off now, without wasting the morning!

Pod. Now? Why just look how dull the weather is. If I go out, I may get caught in the rain.

Fëkla. Dear me! What a misfortune! Why, little

father, the grey hairs are coming on your head already. If you wait much longer, you won't be a marriageable man at all. A fine prize! An aulic counsellor! I can tell you, we can get hold of such grand suitors, that we shan't care to look at you!

Pod. What rubbish are you talking? What's put it into your head all of a sudden that I've got a grey hair? Where's a grey hair? (*Feels his hair.*)

Fèkla. Why shouldn't you have grey hairs? Most people do, when they live long enough. Take care, though; you won't have this girl, and you don't like that girl—but I can tell you, I've got a captain in my eye that's a head and shoulders taller than you, and he talks just like a brass trumpet. He serves in the ammaralty. . . .

Pod. It's not true! I'll look in the glass: you're only pretending there are grey hairs! Hi! Stepàn! Bring the looking-glass! . . . No! wait—I'll go myself. What next? Heaven defend us! that's worse than small-pox! (*Exit into adjoining room. Enter* KOCHKARYÒV, *running.*)

Koch. Where's Podkolyòssin? (*Seeing* FEKLA.) *You* here! Ah! you! . . . Look here! What the devil did you marry me for?

Fèkla. What's the harm? It's right and lawful.

Koch. Right and lawful! What do you suppose a man wants with a wife? Did you suppose I couldn't get on without one?

Fèkla. Why, it was you yourself that wouldn't let me alone. It was always "Granny, find me a wife!"

Koch. Yah! . . . You old rat! . . . And what are you here for, I should like to know! You don't mean to say Podkolyòssin wants to get married?

Fèkla. And why not? God has blessed him.

Koch. No! really? What a rascal! he never told me a word about it! Now what do you think of that, if you please? Isn't he a sly rogue? (*Enter* PODKOLYÒSSIN, *holding a mirror, and gazing into it intently.* KOCHKARYÒV *slips up behind, and startles him.*)

Koch. Booh!

Pod. (*cries out, and drops the mirror*). Ah! you crazy fellow! Now what is the use of doing that? Now what a silly thing to do! You just brought my heart into my mouth!

Koch. There, I was only joking!

Pod. Fine sort of joke! I can't get my breath yet; and there, you've smashed the looking-glass! And it was an expensive one—I got it in the English shop.

Koch. There, never mind! I'll buy you another looking-glass.

Pod. Yes, I dare say! I know what those other looking-glasses are like! One's face comes out crooked, and they make one look ten years older.

Koch. Look here! it's I that ought to be angry with you, not you with me. You hide everything from me, your friend. You think of marrying?

Pod. What nonsense! I never thought of such a thing.

Koch. My friend, you're caught in the act! (*Points to* FÈKLA.) There she stands; everybody knows what sort of bird *she* is. Ah, well! never mind; there's nothing to be ashamed of; it's a good Christian action—indeed, it's necessary for the good of the State. I don't mind; I'll take the whole responsibility of it. (*To* FÈKLA.) Well, tell me who she is, and all about her. What class does she belong to?—noble, official, merchant? And what's her name?

Fèkla. Agàfia Tikhònovna.

Koch. Agàfia Tikhònovna Brandakhlýstova?

Fèkla. No, no! Kouperdyàgina.

Koch. Ah! she lives in the Shestilàvochna, doesn't she?

Fëkla. No, she doesn't, then ! She lives near Peski, in the Mýlny Row.

Koch. Oh, yes ; in the Mýlny Row ; a wooden house, next door to a shop, isn't it ?

Fëkla. No, it isn't. It's beyond the wine-vaults.

Koch. Beyond the wine-vaults ! Then I don't remember.

Fëkla. Well, when you turn into the Row, you see a stall ; and you pass the stall and turn to the left ; and there, straight in front of you, just right before your eyes, there's a wooden house, where a dressmaker lives; you don't go into the dressmaker's, you go on to the next house but one ; it's a stone house, and that's where she lives—Agàfia Tikhònovna.

Koch. All right, all right ! now I can manage it all. You can go now ; we don't want you any more.

Fëkla. What's that ? Do you mean to say that you mean to settle a wedding yourself ?

Koch. Yes, yes, myself—only don't you interfere.

Fëkla. Oh, for shame ! for shame ! That's not a man's business ! Little father, keep out of it.

Koch. Be off ! be off ! you don't understand anything about it ; don't interfere ; mind your own business, and get along with you !

Fëkla. All you care for is to take the bread out of people's mouths ;—you're no better than an infidel ! A man ! and to mix up in things like that ! If I'd known, I wouldn't have told you a word. (*Exit sulkily.*)

Koch. Now, my lad, this business musn't be put off—put on your hat and come along.

Pod. Well, but I—I—I haven't decided—I was only thinking ——

Koch. Fiddle-de-dee ! Only don't be bashful : I'll get you married as finely as you like. We'll go straight off to the lady now, and you'll see how fast we'll get it all settled.

Pod. What, go off now! What next will you want?

Koch. Bless my soul, man, what would you have? Now, just think yourself what comes of not being married. Look at the condition of your room—there's a muddy boot—there's a washing basin—there's a heap of tobacco on the table; and here you lie on your side, the whole day long, like a regular stick-in-the-mud.'

Pod. It's quite true; I know myself everything's in a muddle in this house.

Koch. Well now, when you have a wife everything 'll be so different that you'll hardly know yourself. Here there'll be a sofa, there a lap-dog, then a birdcage, and fancy-work lying about. . . . And just imagine—you sit on the sofa, and suddenly a little woman comes and sits down beside you, a pretty little girl . . . and puts up a little hand——

Pod. Ah! the devil take it! when one thinks of it, what beautiful hands there are—just as white as milk!

Koch. How you talk! Anybody would think women had got nothing but hands! . . . My lad, they've got—— in fact the deuce knows what they haven't got!

Pod. Do you know—I confess it to you—I *do* like to have a pretty woman sit beside me.

Koch. There now! there you see! Then all that's wanted is to make the arrangements. You needn't take any trouble about that, though; I'll manage the wedding and the dinner, and all that. . . . You can't possibly do with less than a dozen of champagne—that there's no question about. We must have half a dozen of Madeira too; I expect the lady's got a whole tribe of aunts and cousins and all the rest of it, and they won't want to be done out of their share. Then there's the Rhine-wine—what the devil do you call it, eh? And as for the dinner, I'll tell you what, old chap: there's a butler I know of that'll settle it all for us; the dog will give you such a feed as you never saw in your life.

PODKOLYÒSSIN: "DO YOU KNOW—I CONFESS IT TO YOU—I *DO* LIKE TO HAVE A PRETTY WOMAN BESIDE ME."

KOCHKARYÒV: "THERE NOW! THERE YOU SEE! THEN ALL THAT'S WANTED IS TO MAKE THE ARRANGEMENTS."

Pod. But my dear fellow ! you set about the business as if I were going to be married at once !

Koch. And why not ? What's the use of putting it off ? You've decided ?

Pod. Me ? Oh, dear no ! I haven't decided at all !

Koch. Well I never did ! But you just said you wanted to marry.

Pod. I only said it wouldn't be a bad idea.

Koch. Well now, really ! And we were just settling up everything. . . . What's come to you ? Don't you like the idea of a married life ?

Pod. Oh, yes, I like it.

Koch. Well then, what's it all about ? Where's the difficulty ?

Pod. There isn't any difficulty; only it seems so strange. . . .

Koch. What's there strange about it ?

Pod. Of course it's strange. One's always been a bachelor, and now to be a married man——

Koch. Tut, tut, tut ! I wonder you're not ashamed of yourself. No, my friend, I see I must talk to you seriously. I'll be quite frank with you, like a father with a son. Now just look at yourself—look at yourself attentively and seriously, just as you're looking at me now—what do you think of yourself? What are you like? You're no better than a log; you're a mere cypher. Tell me what you live for? Now just look in the glass and tell me what you see—nothing but a very stupid face. Well now, suppose that you've got children round you, not just two or three—you know, but a whole half-dozen—and every one as like you as two peas. Here you are alone, an aulic counsellor, or a head of a department, or director of some kind—what do you call yourself? But now just suppose yourself surrounded with little directorkins, and tiny rascals and small fry generally ; and there they hold out their chubby little fists and tug at your whiskers; and you'll play doggie with them: Bow—wow—wow! Now, can you imagine anything more delightful?

Pod. Ye-e-s, only you know they are such mischievous little monkeys; they'll spoil everything, and pull all my papers about.

Koch. Oh! that doesn't matter! But just think; they'll all be like you—that's the beauty of it.

Pod. After all, it really is a deucedly funny notion—a little white puff-ball of a thing—no bigger than a puppy-dog —and yet it's like you!

Koch. Of course its funny, tremendously funny; there, make haste and come along!

Pod. All right; I don't mind.

Koch. Hi! Stepàn! Come and help your master dress.

(Enter STEPÀN.)

Pod. (*dressing before the glass*). I almost think, though, that I ought to put on a white waistcoat.

Koch. Oh, nonsense! What does it matter?

Pod. (*putting on his collar*). Confound that washerwoman! How badly she's starched my collar! It won't stand up a bit, Stepàn! You tell the stupid woman that if she's going to do her work that way, I shall find another washerwoman. I expect she spends her time philandering with sweethearts instead of ironing clothes.

Koch. There! there! man, make haste! What a dawdle you are!

Pod. All right—all right! (*Puts on coat, and sits down.*) Look here, Ilia Fòmich, do you know what? I think you'd better go alone.

Koch. What next! The man's gone daft! *I* go? Why, which of us is going to get married—you or I?

Pod. The fact is, I don't feel inclined for it to-day; let's go to-morrow.

Koch. Now, have you got one single grain of sense? Now, are you anything in the world but a moon-calf? You get ready, and then, suddenly, don't want to go! Now be so kind as to tell me, don't you call yourself a pig and a camel after that?

Pod. Look here—what's the use of bad language? I haven't done you any harm.

Koch. You're a booby, a perfect booby, any fellow will tell you that. I don't care if you *are* an aulic counsellor—you're nothing in the world but a fool. What do you suppose I'm taking all this trouble for? Only for your good. Don't I see that you'll let the prize slip through your fingers? And there you lie, you confounded old bachelor! Now just have the kindness to tell me, what do you call yourself? You're a dummy, a milksop, a nincompoop, a— I'd tell you what you are if I could only find a civil word for it. You're worse than any old woman!

Pod. Look here, that's too much of a good thing. (*Softly.*) Are you gone off your head? There's a serf in the room, and you let him hear you say bad words! Can't you find another place to quarrel in?

Koch. I should like to know who could help quarrelling with you! Bad language! What else could anybody turn their tongue to? You begin by behaving reasonably, and arrange to get married, as any sensible man would; and then, all of a sudden, without why or wherefore, you must get a bee in your bonnet, and there's no more sense in you than in a wooden post. . . .

Pod. There, that'll do! I'll come; why, you needn't fly at me like that!

Koch. Come? Of course you will—what else should you do? (*To* STEPÀN) Give him his hat and cloak.

Pod. (*at the door*). What a queer fellow it is! There's no making him out at all. All of a sudden he sets to work and abuses you without rhyme or reason. Doesn't understand how to speak to a fellow.

Koch. There! I'm not going to scold you now. (*Exeunt.*)

SCENE II.

(*A room in* AGÀFIA TIKHÒNOVNA'S *house.* AGÀFIA TIKHÒNOVNA *spreading cards for fortune-telling,* ARÌNA PANTELÈVMOVNA *looking over her shoulder.*)

Agàfia. Why, auntie! there's a journey again! Some king of diamonds takes an interest in me; then there are tears, and a love-letter; on the left-hand side the king of clubs expresses great sympathy—but there's a wicked woman that stands between.

Arìna. Whom do you think the king of clubs stands for?

Agàfia. I don't know.

Arìna. I know who it is.

Agàfia. Who?

Arìna. A good, honest cloth merchant, my girl—Alexièy Dmìtrievich Starikòv.

Agàfia. That I know it isn't; I'm positive it isn't he.

Arìna. You can't get out of it, Agàfia Tikhònovna; I can tell by the fair hair. There's only one king of clubs, you see.

Agàfia. Then you're just wrong; the king of clubs here means a nobleman—there's a good deal of difference between a tradesman and a king of clubs.

Arìna. Ah! Agàfia Tikhònovna! you wouldn't talk like that, my girl, if your poor papa, Tìkhon Pantlèy-monovich, were alive. I remember how he used to bang his fist on the table and shout out—"I don't care a rap for any man that's ashamed to be a merchant; and I won't give my daughter to an officer. Other people can do that if they're fools enough! And my son shan't be an officer, neither," says he; "isn't a merchant as good a servant of the State as any one else?"　And he'd bang his fist on the table again, and, my girl, he *had* got a fist of his own!　Indeed, if the truth must be told, your poor mother would have lived longer if he hadn't had such a heavy fist.

Agápa.　There you see!　And you think I'd put up

ARÌNA: "BUT WHERE ARE YOU GOING TO GET HOLD OF ANY NOBLE THAT'S WORTH HAVING?"

with such a brute of a husband?　I won't marry a merchant for anything in the world!

Arína.　But Alexièy Dmitrievich isn't one of that kind.

Agáfia.　No, no! not for the world!　He's got a beard! And when he eats soup, it'll all run down his beard.　No, no, no! I won't, I won't!

Arína.　But where are you going to get hold of any

noble that's worth having?   You can't go and pick him up in the street!

Agáfia.   Fèkla Ivànovna will find me one ; she promised to find me a splendid one.

Arìna.   But, my precious one, she's a liar.

(*Enter* FÈKLA.)

Fèkla.   Oh no, Arìna Pantelèymovna ; it's a sin to give people a bad name for nothing.

Agáfia.   Ah! Fèkla Ivànovna!   Now then, tell me quick, have you found any one?

Fèkla.   Yes, yes ; only don't hurry me.   I've been tearing about so—let me get my breath!   I've been all over everywhere on your business—at the Departments, at the Ministries, running all over the place. . . .   Why, do you know, little mother, I nearly got beaten on your account—it's true!   That old woman that arranged the Aferov's marriage — you know — she just flew at me. "What are you after here?" says she, "taking the bread out of other people's mouths.   Keep to your own quarter!" says she.   And I told her right out, " I'll do anything for my young lady," says I, " so you needn't put yourself out about it."   However, I don't mind the trouble ; I've got you a fine set of suitors.   I can tell you there never were such fine ones since the world began, and never will be. Some of them will come to-day—that's why I ran in to tell you.

Agáfia.   To-day!   Oh, Fèkla Ivànovna, I'm afraid!

Fèkla.   There's nothing to be afraid of, little mother. It's a thing that's got to be.   They'll only come and take a look at you—nothing more.   Then you can take a look at them, and if you don't like them they can go away.

Arìna.   I hope you are bringing good, respectable gentlemen?

Agáfia.   And how many are there?

Fékla. Let me see—there are six of them.

Agáfia (screams). Oh!

Fékla. Dear heart, you needn't jump like that! It's best to have a choice; if you don't like one you can take another.

Agáfia. Are they of noble birth?

Fékla. Every one! The very noblest birth that ever was.

Agáfia. Well, what are they like?

Fékla. Oh, regular good ones—nice and neat, all of them. First there's Baltazár Baltazárovich Zhevákin—a splendid gentleman—he used to serve in the fleet—he would just do nicely for you. He wants a wife with a nice plump figure—he hates bony women. Then there's Iván Pávlovich—he's a Court usher, and such a grand gentleman, that one's afraid to go near him. Big and stout, you know; just grand to look at. And you should have heard him shout at me—"I don't want to hear any nonsense about what the girl's like; just tell me plainly how much moveable and real estate she's got."—"So much and so much, little father."—"That's a lie, you old hag!" and, a—a—he said another word, little mother, that I don't quite like to repeat. I saw in a minute that he must be a *real grand* gentleman!

Agáfia. Well, and who else is there?

Fékla. Then there's Nikanór Ivánovich Anoúchkin—he's a nice, fair, pretty gentleman; and oh! little mother, such sweet lips, like cherries! "All I want," says he, "is that my bride should be pretty and refined; and that she should be able to talk French." He's a gentleman with a lot of breeding, and all sorts of fine Frenchified ways. Oh! he's mighty particular! And he's got such slim little legs.

Agáfia. N—n—no; somehow or other these over-particular people ... I don't know ... I can't see anything much in them

Fekla. Well, if you want a more solid husband, you'd better take Iván Pàvlovich; you couldn't make a better choice; he's a gentleman . . . what you may call a *real* gentleman; he could hardly get in at that door, he's so big and grand.

Agàfia. And how old is he?

Fekla. Oh! he's a young man still—about fifty, or not quite fifty even.

Agàfia. And what's his name?

Fekla. Iván Pàvlovich Yaìchnitza. [1]

Agàfia. Do you mean to say that's a name?

Fekla. Of course it's a name.

Agàfia. Goodness gracious! What a funny name! Why, Fèkloushka, supposing I were to marry him, I should have to be called Agàfia Tikhònovna Yaìchnitza—it sounds like I don't know what!

Fekla. Eh-h-h! little mother; there are such names in Russia, that all you can do when you hear them is to spit and cross yourself. But if you don't like the name you may as well take Baltazàr Baltazàrovich Zhevàkin—he'd be a fine bridegroom.

Agàfia. What sort of hair has he got?

Fekla. Very nice hair.

Agàfia. And his nose?

Fekla. H-m-m . . . his nose is all right; everything's in its right place, and he's a very nice gentleman. Only you musn't mind one thing: there's no furniture in his rooms, only a pipe and nothing else at all.

Agàfia. And who else is there?

Fekla. Àkinf Stepánovich Pantelèyev—he's an official, a titular counsellor.[2] He stutters a little; but then he's such a very modest gentleman.

Arìna. You always keep on "official" and "official" you'd better tell us whether he doesn't drink.

____

[1] Literally, "Omelette" or "Custard."   [2] Government clerk.

Fëkla. Yes, he does drink; I wouldn't tell you a lie—he drinks. But then, you see, he's a titular counsellor. And then he's so quiet and gentle.

Agàfia. No, no; I don't want to have a drunkard for a husband.

Fëkla. As you like, little mother. If you don't care for one you can take another. But after all, what does it matter if a man takes a drop too much sometimes? He's not drunk the whole week round, you know; some days he'll come home sober.

Agàfia. And who else is there?

Fëkla. There is one more, only he's not quite the sort. . . . Never mind him, the others will do better.

Agàfia. Well, but who is he?

Fëkla. Really, it's not worth while talking about him. He's in a good position—aulic counsellor and all that—but such a slow stick-in-the-mud, there's no getting him out of the house.

Agàfia. Well, and who else? You have only told us about five, and you said there were six.

Fëkla. Surely you don't want any more? Why, a minute ago you were frightened at so many, and now they're not enough!

Arìna. What's the use of all your noblemen? Even if you have got half a dozen of them, one shopkeeper's worth the whole lot.

Fëkla. Oh, no, Arìna Pantelèymovna, a noble is more distinguished, somehow.

Arìna. What's the use of being distinguished? Just look at Alexièy Dmitrievich—what a beautiful sledge he can drive in, and his cap is real sable! . . .

Fëkla. Yes, but a nobleman with epaulettes on can drive past and call out, "Out of the road, counterjumper!" or, "Show me your best velvet, shopman!" and then the merchant will have to say, "Certainly, little father!" and

the nobleman will say, "Take off your hat, you clown!"
That's what he'll say.

Arìna. And if the merchant likes, he won't give him
the stuff; and there's your nobleman in rags without a thing
to put on.

Fèkla. Then the nobleman will give the shopkeeper
a black eye.

Arìna. Well then, the shopkeeper will go and complain
to the police.

Fèkla. Then the nobleman will complain to the senator.

Arìna. And the merchant to the governor.

Fèkla. And the nobleman——

Arìna. Fiddlesticks! Fiddlesticks! You and your
noblemen! The governor's grander than any senator!
You're just off your head about noblemen! Don't tell me
—a nobleman can take off his hat as well as any shopkeeper, when there's a reason why. . . . (*Door-bell rings.*)
There's some one at the door.

Fèkla. Bless me! It must be they!

Arìna. Who?

Fèkla. They . . . Some of the suitors.

Agàfia (screams). Oh!

Arìna. Holy Saints! Have mercy on us sinners! The
room's in such a muddle! (*Catches up all the things on the
table, and runs about the room.*) And the table-cloth!
Just look at the table-cloth! It's perfectly black. Douniàshka! Douniàshka! (*Enter* DOUNIÀSHKA.) Bring a
clean table-cloth—quick! (*Pulls off table-cloth and rushes
about the room.*)

Agàfia. Oh, aunt! What shall I do? I'm half undressed!

Arìna. Little mother! Run and dress, quick! (*Rushes
frantically about room.* DOUNIÀSHKA *brings table-cloth.
Door-bell rings.*) Run! Make haste! Say "Directly."
(DOUNIÀSHKA *exit, and calls without* "*Directly.*")

Agáfia.   Auntie, my dress isn't ironed!

Arìna.   Oh! Merciful Heaven! Spare us! Put on another.

Fékla (*running in*).   What are you standing about for? Agàfia Tikhònovna! Little mother! Make haste! (*Door-bell rings*).   There! there! he's waiting all this time.

Arìna.   Douniàshka! Let him in, and ask him to wait. (DOUNIÀSHKA *runs into hall and opens door. Voices without:* "At home?"   "At home; come in, please." *All stoop down and try to look through keyhole.*)

Agàfia (*screams*).   Oh! what a fat man!

Fékla.   He's coming! he's coming. (*Exeunt in a headlong rush. Enter* DOUNIÀSHKA *and* IVÀN PÀVLOVICH YAÌCHNITZA.)

Doun.   Wait here, please. (*Exit.*)

Yaìch.   It's all very well to say "Wait," but I can't spend much time waiting about for her; I only got a few minutes' leave from the Department. Supposing the General were to ask, "Where's the usher gone?" "Gone to look for a wife!" Tut, tut, tut! The general would give her what for, I know. . . . I may as well look through the list again. (*Reads.*) "Two - storied stone house." (*Looks up and examines room.*) Yes! (*Reads.*) "Two wings—one wooden, one with stone basement." . . . H'm.
. . . The wooden one is not up to much. (*Reads.*) "Carriage; carved two-horse sledge, with large and small rugs." . . . I daresay they'll be only fit to break up. However, the old woman declares they're first-rate; well, let's suppose they are. (*Reads.*) "Two dozen silver spoons." . . . Of course one must have silver spoons for the house. . . . "Two fox-fur cloaks." . . . H'm . . . "Four large feather-beds; two small ones." (*Compresses lips expressively.*) "Twelve silk dresses; twelve cotton ditto; two dressing-jackets; two . . ." H'm . . . those are trifles. "Under-linen; table-cloths. . . ." All that's

her business. However, I shall have to verify it all. It's very likely they'll promise a house and carriage and all sorts of things now, and when once you're married, you find there's not a thing but feather-beds and pillows. (*Door-bell rings;* DOUNIÀSHKA *runs hastily through room into hall, and opens door. Voices without,* "At home?" "At home." *Enter* ANOÙCHKIN *and* DOUNIÀSHKA.)

Doun. Wait here, please; they'll come presently. (*Exit.* ANOÙCHKIN *and* YAÌCHNITZA *bow to each other.*)

Yaìch. Your servant, sir!

Anoùch. Have I the honour to address the papa of the charming lady of the house?

Yaìch. Certainly not, sir, I have not the pleasure of having any children.

Anoùch. Oh! I beg your pardon! I really beg your pardon!

Yaìch (aside). That man's face looks to me very suspicious; I shouldn't wonder if he's come about the same business that I have. (*Aloud.*) You doubtless have some . . some . . . business with the lady of the house?

Anoùch. N-n-no. . . . Oh, no! I have no business. . . . I just came in as I was taking a walk.

Yaìch (aside). He's a liar! taking a walk, indeed! The scoundrel wants to get married! (*Door-bell rings,* DOUNIÀSHKA *runs through into hall and opens door. Voices without:* "At home?" "At home." *Enter* ZHEVÀKIN *and* DOUNIÀSHKA.)

Zhev. (to DOUNIÀSHKA). Just give me a brush, will you, my dear? One gets so dusty in the street. And take off that cobweb, please. (*Turns round.*) That's right; thank you, my dear. Just look on the other side; I fancy there's a spider running up me. Are you sure there's nothing on the back of my collar? Thank you, child. There! I'm sure there's something! (*Smooths coat-sleeve with his hand, and looks at* ANOÙCHKIN *and* YAÌCHNITZA.)

It's real English cloth. In '95, when I was only a midshipman, and our squadron was in Sicily, I bought it and had a uniform made; in 1801, under his late Majesty, Paul Petròvich, when I was made lieutenant, the cloth was as good as new; in 1814, I went on an expedition round the world, and it only began to get a little worn at the seams; in 1815, when I retired from the service, I just had it turned; and now I've worn it ten years, and it looks almost new still. Thank you, my dear! My little beauty! (*Kisses his hand to her, goes up to mirror, and arranges his hair.*)

Anòuch. If I may take the liberty to ask, Sicily. . . . You were just mentioning Sicily—it is a fine country, is it not?

Zhev. Oh, beautiful! We spent thirty-four days there. I can assure you it's a most charming place—such mountains; and the most beautiful trees . . . what they call *granite* trees. And the loveliest Italian girls—perfect little rosebuds, . . one can hardly refrain from kissing them.

Anòuch. And are they well educated?

Zhev. Magnificently; as highly educated as any countess here. I remember, when I used to go along the street, —well, of course you know, a Russian lieutenant, epaulettes here (*points to his shoulder*), gold embroidery, and all that, —well, and these little black-eyed beauties,—I must tell you, they have verandahs to every house, and roofs as flat as this floor—well, you look up as you pass, and there sits a little rosebud; and of course one must keep up one's reputation (*makes a salute and waves his hand*), and she just answers like that (*makes gesture with his hand*). Of course she's always beautifully dressed little silk cords, and taffeta stuff, and earrings, and all sorts of feminine trifles, . . . in a word, the daintiest little sugar-plum——

Anòuch. Allow me to ask you one more question. In what language do people converse in Sicily?

Zhev. Oh, always in French, of course.

Anoúch. And do all the young ladies speak French?

Zhev. All, without exception. You perhaps will hardly believe me; but we lived there thirty-four days, and in all that time I never heard one of them speak a single word of Russian.

Anoúch. Not a word?

Zhev. Not one. And mind, I am not speaking of the nobles, and what they call the Signors—those are their officers, you know—but just pick out any common peasant that brings loads on his head, and try him; just say: "Dai, bràtetz, khlyeba," [1] he won t understand—I assure you he won't understand. But if you say in French : " Dateci del pane," or " Portate vino," he'll understand you, and he'll run and bring it at once.

Yaìch. This same Sicily must be a very interesting country, I think. You were talking about the peasants. What are they like? Do they have broad shoulders, and plough the land like our Russian peasants?

Zhev. That I can't tell you; I didn't notice whether they ploughed or not. But about the question of taking snuff, I can inform you that they not only smell snuff, but even put it in their mouths. The carriage of goods is very cheap there, too; you see there's water everywhere, and gondolas. . . . and in the gondola there'll sit a sweet little rosebud of an Italian girl, beautifully dressed, with the daintiest little kerchief and camisole. . . . There were some English officers with us—sailors like ourselves. . . It seemed so strange at first; we couldn't understand each other. But after a bit, when we got to know each other well, we began to understand all right. You just point to a bottle or a glass, you know, and the Englishman knows at once that that means "Drink;" then you put your fist up to your mouth, and just do so with your lips—" Puff, puff," and he knows you mean "Smoke a pipe." Indeed, I

[1] " Bring some bread, my man."

assure you, its rather an easy language ; the crews got to understand each other in about three days.

Yaìch.   Life must be very interesting in foreign parts. It is a great pleasure to me to become acquainted with a travelled gentleman.   Allow me to ask whom I have the honour of addressing ?

Zhev.   Zhevàkin, retired lieutenant.   Permit me, on my side, to ask with whom I have the pleasure to converse.

Yaìch.   Ivàn Pàvlovich Yaìchnitza, government usher.

Zhev. (not hearing well).   Thank you, I have already lunched.   It's cold weather, and I knew I had a long walk before me, so I had a marinated herring.

Yaìch.   You have not quite understood me, I think ; I said my name is Yaìchnitza.

Zhev. (bows).   Oh ! I beg your pardon ; I am a little hard of hearing.   I . . . really . . . understood you to say . . . that you had lunched on an omelette.

Yaìch.   Yes ; it's very unfortunate.   I thought of asking the General to allow me to change my name to Yaìchnitzyn ; but my friends dissuaded me ; they said it would sound like Sobachi Syn.[1]

Zhev.   Yes, there are such cases.   All our squadron, both officers and crew, had the most extraordinary names : Pomòykin,[2] Yarỳzhkin,[3] Lieutenant Pereprèyev ;[4] and there was one midshipman—a very good midshipman too—whose name was just Dỳrka ;[5] it was so odd ; the captain would call, " Come here, Dỳrka ; " and we all of us used to tease him, and call him stop-gap, and bung-hole, and all sorts of things. (*Door-bell rings,* FÈKLA *runs across stage.*)

Yaìch.   Ah ! Good-morning, little mother !

Zhev.   Good-morning ! How are you, my dear ?

Anèùch.   Glad to see you, little mother, Fèkla Ivànovna.

Fèkla (hurriedly).   Thank you, thank you ; same to you.

---

[1] Son of a dog.   [2] Pomòy—dish-water.   [3] Yarỳzhnik—rake, roué.
[4] Pereprỳelyi—stewed too long.   [5] Dỳrka—any little hole or gap.

(*Exit into hall; opens door. Voices without :* "At home?" "At home." *Then several half-inaudible words;* FÈKLA'S *voice answers angrily :* "Just you take care !" *Enter* KOCHKARYÒV, PODKOLYÒSSIN, *and* FÈKLA.)

Koch. (*to* PODKOLYÒSSIN). Now just keep up your courage—that's all that's wanted. (*Glances round, and salutes the company with a surprised expression.*) (*Aside.*) Oho ! What a lot of people ! What's the meaning of this ? They can't all be suitors. (*Nudges* FÈKLA, *and speaks to her softly.*) Where did all these crows come from, eh ?

Fèkla (*softly*). There are no crows here ; they are all honest people.

Koch. (*to her*). There are plenty of them, but they're precious draggletailed.

Fèkla (*softly*). I doubt they'll fly better than yours, for all he's so grand. 'Tisn't fine feathers make fine birds.

Koch. (*softly*). Yes, every crow thinks her own children the fairest. (*Aloud.*) What's she doing now ? I suppose that door leads to her bedroom ? (*Approaches door.*)

Fèkla. For shame ! I tell you she's dressing.

Koch. Well, dear me ! there's no harm in that ! I'll only just look in—nothing more. (*Peeps through keyhole.*)

Zhev. Permit me to satisfy my curiosity too !

Yaìch. Let me have one little peep.

Koch. (*continuing to look*). There's nothing to be seen, gentlemen ; there's something white, but I can't make out whether it's a woman or a pillow. (*They all crowd round door and try to peep through key-hole.*)

Koch. There's . . . some one coming ! (*All start back. Enter* ARÌNA PANTELÈYMOVNA *and* AGÀFIA TIKHÒNOVNA. *All bow.*)

Arìna. To what are we indebted for the honour of this visit ?

Yaìch. I read in the newspapers that you wished to enter into a contract to supply timber ; and therefore, as I hold the post of usher in a Government Department, I called to inquire what kind of timber you can supply, what quantity, and at what date.

Arina. We don't take contracts ; but we are very glad to see you. Allow me to ask your name.

"ALL BOW."

Yaìch. Iván Pávlovich Yaìchnitza, collegiate assessor.

Arina. Be so kind as to take a seat. (*Turns to* ZHEVÁKIN *and looks at him.*) And may I ask——

Zhev. I . . . you know . . . I saw an advertisement about something. . . . I thought I might as well look in.

. . . It's such fine weather to-day, and the grass is growing so nicely along the road. . . .

Arìna. And your name, if you please?

Zhev. Retired naval lieutenant Baltazàr Baltazàrovich Zhevàkin, Number 2. There was another Zhevàkin in the service, but he retired before I did; he got a wound in the knee, and the ball went through it such an odd way— it didn't touch the knee itself, but it injured a vein, and drew it all up, so that, if you were standing near him, it always seemed as if he were going to kick you.

Arìna. Be so kind as to sit down. (*To* ANOÙCHKIN.) May I ask the reason——

Anoùch. As a neighbour . . . as I live so very near . . . you see——

Arìna. Perhaps you live in widow Touloùbova's house opposite?

Anoùch. No—n—no; I live at Peskì just now, but I have the intention of moving to this quarter of the town sooner or later.

Arìna. Be so kind as to sit down. (*To* KOCHKARYÒV.) Allow me to ask——

Koch. Why, surely you recognise me? (*Turns to* AGÀFIA.) And you, madam?

Agàfia. I—I— don't remember ever seeing you.

Koch. Why, think a minute; I'm sure we've met somewhere.

Agàfia. I don't know, really. Was it at the Biriòushkins'?

Koch. Of course it was!

Agàfia. Oh! do you know what's happened to her?

Koch. Of course I do—she's married.

Agàfia. Oh no! that would be nothing; but she's broken her leg.

Arìna. And very badly too. She was coming home late at night in a *drozhki,* and the coachman was tipsy and overturned it.

Koch. Ah! yes; I remember, of course; I knew she'd got married, or broken her leg, or something of that kind!

Arina. And your name?

Koch. My name? Why Ilia Fòmich Kochkaryòv. We're

ARINA: "WHAT IS THE GENTLEMAN'S NAME?"
KOCHKARYÒV: "PODKOLYÒSSIN—IVÀN KOUZMÌCH PODKOLYÒSSIN.

almost relations, you know. My wife is always talking about— but allow me, allow me. (*Takes Podkolyòssin by the arm and leads him forward.*) My friend Ivàn Kouzmich Podkolyòssin, aulic counsellor, sub director in a Department.

It's he that does all the business and manages everything in the most admirable way.

Arìna. What is the gentleman's name?

Koch. Podkolyòssin—Ivàn Kouzmìch Podkolyòssin. The director is simply put there as a figure head: all the business is done by Ivàn Kouzmìch.

Arìna. Indeed? Be so kind as to sit down.

(*Enter* STARIKÒV.)

Star. (*bows to the company in a rapid, off-hand, business manner, with one arm akimbo*). Arìna Pantelèymovna, how do you do, little mother? The lads on the Arcade told me that you had some wool to sell.

Agàfia (*turning her back contemptuously and speaking under her breath, but so that he hears*). This isn't a stall in a bazaar!

Star. Oh, oh! Seems I've come at the wrong time! I doubt you've settled your business without me.

Arìna. Sit down, sit down, Alexièy Dmitrievich; we've no wool to sell, but we're glad to see you; please sit down. (*All sit down; silence.*)

Yaìch. It's very strange weather to-day. Early in the morning it looked quite like rain, but now it seems to have gone over.

Agàfia. Yes, indeed, this weather is quite extraordinary; sometimes it's bright, and then again it gets wet and rainy —it's very disagreeable.

Zhev. Ah, little mother! When our squadron was in Sicily it was spring-time—with us it would be February— they have the new calendar, you know—when we went out into the street it would be quite sunny, and then it would begin to rain, and it would be just like real ordinary rain.

Yaìch. The most disagreeable thing is to sit alone in such weather. It's all very well for a married man—that's quite another thing—but when one lives alone it's really——

Zhev. Oh! it's more than any one can stand!

Anoúch. Yes, indeed, one may say——

Koch. Oh yes, it's altogether unbearable—life's not worth having. Heaven defend anybody from such a position!

Yaìch. Now supposing, madam, that you were asked to choose who should be the object of your affections. Allow me to ask, what would be your taste? You will excuse my directness. What . . . occupation . . . do you consider . . . most . . . worthy of respect in a husband?

Zhev. Would you choose, madam, a husband acquainted with the storms of the ocean?

Koch. No! no! In my opinion the best sort of husband is a man who has almost the whole management of a Department in his hands.

Anoúch. Why anticipate? Why treat with contumely a man capable of appreciating the social intercourse of high-class society?

Yaìch. Madam, it is for you to decide! (*Silence.*)

Fèkla. Speak up, little mother! Tell them something.

Yaìch. What have you to say?

Koch. What is your opinion, Agàfia Tikhònovna?

Fèkla (aside to her). Make haste! say "Thank you," or "With the greatest pleasure," or something. . .   It's not proper to sit like that!

Agàfia. I'm ashamed, I'm ashamed, really. I shall go away. Auntie! stop here instead of me!

Fèkla. No, no, you musn't go away; it's improper, it's disgraceful. They'll think . . . I don't know what!

Agàfia (aside). No, no, I can't stand it, I can't—I can't! (*Runs away. Arìna and Fèkla follow her.*)

Yaìch. Well, that's a good one—everybody's gone away. What's the meaning of that?

Koch. I expect something's happened.

Zhev. Oh, no doubt it's some little matter of feminine toilet. . . . They want to pin something, or to put the camisole straight, or—— (*Enter FÈKLA.*)

All (crowding round her). What is it? What's the matter?

Koch. Has anything happened?

Fèkla. Of course not! What should happen?

Koch. Then why did she go away?

Fèkla. Why, you made the poor girl bashful, all of you —frightened and upset her till she couldn't stand it. She sends you her excuses, and asks you to come in for a cup of tea in the evening. (*Exit.*)

Yaìch. (aside). Oh! now they're going to begin with cups of tea! That's what I hate about all this match-making business—it's such a worry. To-day won't do; and come again to-morrow; and the day after to-morrow a cup of tea; and then they have to think it over, and can't make up their minds! But dear me! the matter's simple enough; there's nothing to rack one's brains over! Confound it all! I'm a busy man, I've no time for this sort of thing!

Koch. (to PODKOLYÒSSIN). She's a nice-looking girl, isn't she?

Pod. Yes, she's nice-looking.

Zhev. I think the young lady is pretty.

Koch. (aside). The deuce take it, if that idiot hasn't fallen in love! He'll be getting in the way! (*Aloud.*) I don't think she's pretty at all, not at all.

Yaìch. Her nose is too big.

Zhev. Now, there I don't agree with you : she's a regular rosebud.

Anoùch. I quite agree with you. The only thing is, she's not quite— I am inclined to doubt whether she is acquainted with the manners of high-class society. Do you think she knows French?

Zhev. If I may take the liberty of asking, why didn't you speak French to her yourself, and try?—very likely she knows it.

Anoùch. You think I speak French? No, I did not

enjoy such educational advantages.   My father was an
eccentric personage, he never even thought of having me
taught French.   I was a child in those days; it would have
been easy to teach me—a few good whippings were all that
was needed, and I should have known it perfectly well.

Zhev.   Well, but as you don't know French, why do you
particularly want——

Anoùch.   Ah! no, no; it's quite another matter with a
woman.   It's quite necessary that she should know it;
otherwise, one thing and another—(*helps himself out with
gestures*)—nothing is as it should be.

Yalch. (*aside*).   Well, those that like can care about that.
For my part, I shall go round the house and look at the
wings from the courtyard; if everything's all right, I'll settle
the matter this very evening.   I'm not afraid of all these
suitors; they're nothing but milksops, all the lot of them.
Girls don't like that sort of men.

Zhev.   I think I'll go and have a smoke.   Perhaps our
way lies in the same direction.   May I ask where you live?

Anoùch.   At Peskì; in the Petròvski Row.

Zhev.   Yes; it's a bit out of my way; I live on the
Island,[1] in the Eighteenth Line.   But all the same I'll walk
with you.

Star.   No no; they're getting too proud for me here.
Ah! you'll remember your own folk some day, Agàfia
Tikhònovna!   Your servant, gentlemen.   (*Bows and exit.
Exeunt all but* PODKOLYÒSSIN *and* KOCHKARYÒV.)

Pod.   What are we waiting for?

Koch.   Well, what do you think?   She's a charming girl,
isn't she?

Pod.   Do you think so?   I'm bound to confess that she
doesn't take my fancy.

Koch.   Come now, that's too much!   You agreed with
me yourself a minute ago that she was pretty.

[1] " The Island," in the singular, means the Vasìlyevsky Island.

Pod. Yes; but, you see . . . her nose 's too long ; and she doesn't know French.

Koch. What next ? What do you want with French ?

Pod. After all, a girl ought to know French.

Koch. What for ?

Pod. Why, because . . . really I don't know why. But it isn't the same if she doesn't know French.

Koch. Well, you're a simpleton ! Somebody makes a remark, and you get it into your head, and there it sticks ! She's a beauty ; she's a downright beauty ; you won't find another such a girl anywhere.

Pod. Well, I thought she was very pretty. But afterwards, when they began to talk so much about her nose being long, I thought it over, and I see she really has a long nose.

Koch. Oh, you blind bat ! Can't you see through that trick ? They talked like that on purpose to get rid of you ; and I abused her too ; one always does that. My lad, she's a splendid girl ! Just you look at her eyes ! There's the very devil in eyes like that ; they can talk, and breathe, and anything. And as for her nose, it's an exquisite nose ; it's as white as alabaster ; there's plenty of alabaster that wouldn't come up to it. You should look with your own eyes, my man.

Pod. Yes ; when I think of it, she really is pretty.

Koch. Of course she's pretty. Look here—they've all gone away now ; let's go to her and propose, and settle it all up.

Pod. That I certainly sha'n't do.

Koch. Why not?

Pod. It would be downright effrontery. There are a lot of us ; it's for her to choose.

Koch. What's the use of taking any notice of them ? You're not afraid of rivals, surely ; if you like, I'll get rid of them all in one minute.

Pod. How can you get rid of them?

Koch. That's my business. Only give me your word that you won't wriggle out of it afterwards.

Pod. I've no objection to that; I'm willing.

Koch. Your hand on it!

Pod. (*gives hand*). My hand on it!

Koch. That's all I ask of you. (*Exeunt.*)

ACT II. SCENE I.

(*Agàfia Tikhònovna alone.*)

Agàfia. Really, it is a very difficult thing to have to choose. If there were only one or two of them—but to choose out of four! . . . Nikanòr Ivànovich is very nice-looking, though he's rather thin. Ivàn Kouzmìch is not bad-looking either. Indeed, to say the truth, Ivàn Pàvlovich is a very fine-looking man, too, although he's fat. I should just like to know what I am to do! Then Baltazàr Balta-zàrovich has great merits, too. Indeed, it's so difficult to decide that I simply don't know what to do. If one could put Nikanòr Ivànovich's lips on to Ivàn Kouzmìch's nose, and then take a little of Baltazàr Baltazàrovich's easy way, and just a bit of Ivàn Pàvlovich's stoutness—I'd make up my mind at once; but now one keeps on thinking and thinking . . . really my head has begun to ache! I think the best thing would be to cast lots. It must be as God wills—whoever comes out shall be my husband. I'll write all their names on bits of paper, and roll them up tight, and then, what must be, will be. (*Goes up to table, takes out of a drawer paper and scissors, cuts little slips, writes, and rolls them up while speaking.*) A girl's position is a very trying one, especially if she's in love. No man can ever enter into that; indeed, they don't care to understand it. There! now they're all ready! I've only got to put them in my reticule, shut my eyes tight, and what must be will be. (*Places slips in reticule, and shuffles them with her hand.*) I'm afraid. . . . Oh! if God willed that Nikanòr Ivànovich should come out! No; why? Better Ivan Kouzmìch! They're all so nice . . . No, no; I won't decide . . . I'll take whichever one comes out. (*Thrusts hand into reticule, and takes out all together.*) Oh! oh! they've all come out! And my heart beats so! No; it won't do; I must have one! (*Replaces slips in reticule, and shuffles again.* KOCH-KARYÒV *enters softly and stands behind her.*) Oh! if it were Baltazàr. . . . No; I mean Nikanòr Ivànovich. . . . No, no; I won't think; it's as fate decides!

Koch. Take Ivàn Kouzmìch; he's the best.

Agàfia. Ah! (*Screams, and hides face with both hands, not daring to look round.*)

Koch. Why do you start so? Don't be afraid, it's I; you'd much better take Ivàn Kouzmìch.

Agàfia. Oh! I'm ashamed! You've been listening.

Koch. Never mind; never mind; I'm like one of your own family, you know; you needn't be bashful with me. Come now, let me see your pretty face.

Agàfia (*half uncovering her face*). Indeed I'm ashamed!

Koch. There now! Take Ivàn Kouzmìch.

Agàfia. Oh! (*Screams, and hides face again.*)

Koch. Really, he's a splendid fellow; he manages that Department wonderfully. . . . In fact he's a marvellous fellow!

Agàfia (*gradually uncovering her face*). Well, but what about the other one, Nikanòr Ivànovich? He's very nice, too.

Koch. Oh! he's not fit to be mentioned in the same breath with Ivàn Kouzmìch.

Agàfia. Why not?

Koch. The reason's plain. Ivàn Kouzmìch is a man. . . . Well, what you may call a man . . . such as you won't find again.

Agàfia. And Ivàn Pàvlovich?

Koch. Ivàn Pàvlovich! He's a regular good-for-nothing; they're all good-for-nothings.

Agàfia. Not all, surely?

Koch. Just look yourself; just compare them; there are all sorts of people; but really, such a set—Ivàn Pàvlovich, Nikanòr Ivànovich—they're like, Heaven knows what!

Agàfia. Well, but really, they're very . . . modest.

Koch. Modest, indeed! They're regular bullies and roughs. I suppose you don't want to be beaten the next day after the wedding?

Agàfia. Oh, dear! Oh, dear! That's such a dreadful misfortune that there couldn't be anything worse!

Koch. I should think not! One can't imagine anything worse.

Agàfia. Then your advice is that I should take Ivàn Kouzmìch?

Koch. Of course you should take Ivàn Kouzmìch. (*Aside.*) The business seems to go pretty smoothly. I'd better run to the confectioner's and fetch Podkolyòssin.

Agàfia. Then you think . . . Ivàn Kouzmìch?

Koch. Certainly, Ivàn Kouzmìch.

Agàfia. And must I refuse all the others?

Koch. Of course you must.

Agàfia. But how am I to do it? I'm ashamed to.

Koch. What's there to be ashamed of? Just tell them that you're too young to marry yet.

Agàfia. Well, but they won't believe me; they'll begin asking why, and how, and all that.

Koch. Well, if you want to put an end to it at once, you can simply say, "Get along with you, blockheads!"

Agàfia. But how am I to say that?

Koch. Well, just try. I assure you that, after that, they'll all run away.

Agàfia. But . . . but it sounds . . so rude.

Koch. Well, but you'll never see them again, so what does it matter?

Agàfia. Even so it doesn't seem nice ; . . . they'll be offended.

Koch. What in the world does it matter if they are? If they could do you any harm that would be another thing ; but the worst that can happen is for one of them to spit in your face—that's all !

Agàfia. There ! you see !

Koch. Well, what harm? Why, some people are spat at over and over again ! There's a man I know—such a handsome, fresh-coloured fellow—he was always coaxing and teasing his director to raise his salary, till at last the director lost all patience, and turned round and spat in his face. "There's your salary !" he said ; "let me alone, you demon !" But for all that he raised the salary, and the man was none the worse for having been spat at. What's there to mind in that? It would be another matter if you hadn't got a handkerchief near, but you have one in your pocket—you've nothing to do but to take it out and dry your face. (*Door-bell rings.*) There's some one at the door—one of them, I expect. I shouldn't care to meet them just now. Isn't there another way out ?

Agàfia. Oh, yes, down the back stairs. But, indeed, I am trembling all over !

Koch. Only keep your presence of mind ; everything will be all right. Good-bye ! (*Aside.*) I'll run and fetch Podkolyòssin. (*Exit. Enter* YAÌCHNITZA.)

Yaìch. I purposely came rather early, madam, in order to find you alone and talk with you at leisure. As regards my position, madam, you are, I presume, acquainted with it : I serve as collegiate assessor, I enjoy the good-will of the authorities, and my subordinates are obedient . . . only one thing is wanting—a partner to share my life.

Agàfia. Y-yes . . .

Yaïch. I have at last found that desired partner. It is—yourself. Answer me plainly—yes or no? (*Looking at her shoulders; aside.*) She's not like those scraggy foreign women; there's something of her.

Agàfia. I am still very young. . . . I do not wish to marry yet. . . .

Yaïch. Don't wish! . . . Why, what do you employ a matchmaker for? Perhaps, though, you mean something else—explain to me . . . (*Door-bell rings.*) Confound the people! They won't let one settle one's business in peace!

(*Enter* ZHEVÀKIN.)

Zhev. Pardon me, madam, if I have come too early. (*Turns round and sees* YAÌCHNITZA.) Ah! there's one already. . . . Ivàn Pàvlovich, my compliments.

Yaïch. (aside). You be hanged with your compliments! (*Aloud.*) Well, madam, your answer? Say only one word —yes or no? . . . (*Door bell rings;* YAÌCHNITZA *spits on the floor.*) Damn that bell!

(*Enter* ANOÙCHKIN.)

Anoùchkin. Perhaps, madam, I have arrived earlier than is becoming and consistent with good breeding. (*Sees the others, utters an exclamation, and starts back.*) My respects, gentlemen!

Yaïch. (aside). Keep your respects and be damned to you! The very deuce brought your spindle-shanks here— if you'd only tumble and break them! . . . (*Aloud.*) Well, madam, how is it to be? Decide. I am a man in office; my time is valuable—yes or no?

Agàfia. (confused.) Oh, no, please, . . . I don't want . . . (*Aside.*) I don't know a bit what I'm saying!

Yaïch. You don't want? . . . In what sense do you mean that?

Agàfia. Oh, I didn't mean . . . I . . . Oh, indeed!

. . . (*Gathering up her courage.*) Get along with you. . . . (*Aside, clasping her hands.*) Oh, dear! Oh, dear! what *have* I said!

Yaìch. "*Get . . . along* with you"?!. . . What does "get along with you" mean? . . . Permit me to ask, what do you mean by this? (*Places arms akimbo, and advances towards her threateningly.*)

Agàfia (*stares at him; then screams*). Oh! oh! he's going to beat me! (*Exit running.* YAÌCHNITZA *stands open-mouthed;* ARÌNA PANTELÈYMOVNA, *hearing the noise, runs in, looks at him, and screams.*)

Arìna. Oh! he's going to beat us! (*Exit running.*)

Yaìch. What's it all about? What can have happened? (*Door-bell rings; voice heard without.*)

Koch. (*without*). Go in; go in! What are you stopping for?

Pod. (*without*). You go first; I'll come in a minute; I'll just fasten my strap; it's come undone.

Koch. (*without*). I know you'll sneak away again.

Pod. (*without*). No, I won't; I won't, indeed!

(*Enter* KOCHKARYÒV.)

Koch. What next! wants to set a strap right!

Yaìch. (*to him*). Be so kind as to tell me,—Is the young lady an idiot?

Koch. What do you mean? Has anything happened?

Yaìch. Her behaviour is most extraordinary. All of a sudden she ran away, screaming out, "He'll beat me! he'll beat me!" It's enough to mystify the devil!

Koch. Yes; she gets like that sometimes; she's weak in her head.

Yaìch. May I ask if you're a relative of hers?

Koch. Oh! yes; I'm a relative.

Yaìch. What is your relationship to her, if I may inquire?

Koch. A—a—a, really, I don't know. Let me see—my mother's aunt was some relation to her father; or else her father was related to my aunt; my wife knows all about it; that's a woman's business, you know.

Yalch. Has her mind been affected long?

Koch. Ever since she was a little child.

Yalch. A—a—a, yes — of course it would be better if she had more sense. But, after all, it's not bad to have a foolish wife—once the other considerations are all right, you know.

Koch. But, my good sir, she hasn't a sixpence!

Yalch. What! But the stone-house?

Koch. Oh! it's only called stone; but if you knew the way it's built! It's just coated over with stucco outside; but the walls are made of all kinds of rubbish—chips, and splinters, and rubble, and what-not.

Yalch. You don't say so!

Koch. Of course. Why, don't you know the way houses are built nowadays? They only build houses so as to be able to mortgage them.

Yalch. But this house isn't mortgaged, surely?

Koch. How do you know that? It's a good deal worse; it's not only mortgaged, but the interest hasn't been paid for the last two years. Then they've got a brother in the Senate, who has his eye on the house. He's the most pettifogging hair-splitter that ever was born; the rascal would fleece his own mother of her last petticoat!

Yalch. But the old matchmaker told me . . . Oh! the old hag! A monster in human . . . (*Aside.*) By the bye, though, he may be making it all up. I'll submit the old woman to a strict interrogation. And, if it's true, . . . oh! I'll give her something she won't forget in a hurry!

Anoùch. (*to Kochkarjòv*). Permit me, too, to trespass on your time with a question. Not being myself acquainted with the French language, I have great difficulty in discovering whether a woman knows French or not. Does the lady of the house——

Koch. She doesn't know A from B.

Anoüch. Is it possible?

Koch. Oh! I know that very well! She was at boarding-school with my wife; and she was the idle one of the school —always in the dunce's cap. And as for the French master, he used simply to beat her with a stick.

Anoüch. Just imagine! The first minute that I saw her I had a sort of presentiment that she doesn't know French.

Yaïch. French be hanged! But that confounded matchmaker . . . Oh! the old hag! the old brute! If only you knew the way she described it all! Like a painter; for all the world like a painter! "A house, wings, base-ments, silver spoons, sledges, nothing to do but to get in and drive!" One hardly ever comes across such a page in a novel! Oh! you old harridan! once I get hold of you! . . .

(*Enter* FÈKLA. *All crowd round her and begin to speak at once.*)

Yaïch. Ah—h—h! There she is! Just come here a minute, you old ——! Just come here a minute!

Anoüch. How could you deceive me so, Fèkla Ivànovna?

Koch. Now then, my beauty, stand up to the scratch!

Fèkla. I can't make out a word you say when you deafen me like that.

Yaïch. The house is just built of stucco, you old hag, you! And you told me lies! It's nothing but garrets, and the very devil knows what.

Fèkla. I don't know; I didn't build it. I suppose if they built it with stucco it's because they liked stucco.

Yaïch. And it's all mortgaged too, is it? May the devils eat you up, you damned old hag! (*Stamps his foot.*)

Fèkla. Oh! for shame! using such words! Anybody else would say " Thank you " for all the trouble I've taken.

Anoùch. Ah! Fèkla Ivànovna! and you deceived me too ; you told me she knew French !

Fèkla. So she does, dear heart, so she does! And German ; and all that outlandish gibberish. She can talk all the ways you like.

Anoùch. No, no; I'm afraid she talks nothing but Russian.

Fèkla. And what's the harm of that? Of course she talks Russian ; because Russian's easier to understand. And if she could do all that heathen jabber, it would be the worse for you, because you wouldn't be able to understand a word. What have you got against anybody talking good, plain Russian ? It's the proper way to talk; all the saints talked Russian.

Yaìch. Just come here a minute, confound you! Just come here to me !

Fèkla (backing towards the door). Not I! I know you too well ! You've got a heavy hand ; one never knows when you may strike !

Yaìch. Ah, my dove ! I'll pay you out for this ! When I take you to the police-station you'll get a lesson how to deceive honest people. I'll let you know! And tell the girl from me that she's a beast ! Do you hear? Be sure you tell her. (*Exit.*)

Fèkla. Well, I never did! He's in a fine fury ! Just because he's fat, he thinks there's no one like him in the world. And supposing I say that you're a beast yourself, what then ?

Anoùch. I am bound to say, my good woman, that I did not expect you to have deceived me so. If I had known that the young lady is so uneducated, I . . . I simply would never have set foot inside the place. That's the truth ! (*Exit.*)

Fèkla. Is the man drunk or daft? These fine folk are over hard to please! All that foolish learning has just turned his head! (KOCHKARYÒV *points to* FÈKLA *with his finger, and bursts into a roar of laughter.*)

Fèkla (angrily). What's all that guffaw about? (KOCH-KARYÒV *goes on laughing.*) Well, you needn't go into a fit!

Koch. Matchmaker! matchmaker! She knows her business! she knows how to arrange marriages! (*Continues to laugh.*)

Fèkla. You're a wonderful one to laugh; I should think your mother went daft the hour that you were born. (*Exit angrily.*)

Koch. (continues to laugh). Oh! I can't! . . . I can't really! . . . It's too much! . . . I shall die of laughing! . . . (*Continues to laugh.* ZHEVÀKIN *looks at him and begins to laugh too.*)

Koch. (throws himself into a chair exhausted). Oh! . . . Oh! dear! . . . I'm half killed! . . . If I laugh any more I shall simply die! . . .

Zhev. I admire your merry character. When I was in the navy, there was a midshipman in Captain Voldyrèv's squadron—Pyetoukhòv his name was, Antòn Ivànovich—he was very merry too; sometimes, if you'd just lift up one finger—so—he'd set off laughing, and he'd laugh the whole day long. Really, just to look at him was enough to put one into a laughing mood; and at last you'd begin to laugh yourself.

Koch. (recovering his breath). Oh! Lord! have mercy upon us sinners! What has the idiot got into her head? As if *she* knew how to arrange a marriage! She, indeed! Now, if I arrange a marriage, it's another matter!

Zhev. Do you seriously mean that you can get people married?

Koch. Of course I do. I can marry anybody to anybody.

Zhev. In that case, marry me to the lady of this house.

Koch. You? What do you want to be married for?

Zhev. How "what for?" Allow me to remark that is rather a strange question. What do people want to get married for?

Koch. But you heard that she has no dowry.

Zhev. That can't be helped. Of course it's unfortunate; but with such a very charming girl, so well brought up, one can live even without a dowry. A modest room (*gesticulating*), here a little entrance-hall, there a small screen or some kind of partition, you know——

Koch. What's there in her you like so much?

Zhev. To tell you the truth, she took my fancy because she is plump. I'm a great connoisseur in feminine plumpness.

Koch. (*looking askance at him; aside*). The old mummy may give himself airs; but he's for all the world like a pouch with the tobacco shaken out. (*Aloud.*) No; you have no business to be married at all.

Zhev. Why so?

Koch. It's plain enough why. Look what your figure's like! Between ourselves, you've got a leg like a chicken's.

Zhev. A chicken's?

Koch. Certainly. Just see what you look like.

Zhev. What do you mean, though, about a chicken's leg?

Koch. Just simply a chicken's.

Zhev. It appears to me, sir, that this approaches to a personality. . . .

Koch. I say this to you because I know you're a sensible man. I shouldn't say it to everybody. However, I'll get you married, if you like, only to another woman.

Zhev. Thank you, no; I must ask you not to marry me to another woman. If you will be so kind, I should prefer this one.

Koch. As you like. I'll arrange it for you, only with one

condition—you musn't interfere at all ; you musn't even let the young lady see you ; I'll manage it all without you.

Zhev. I don't quite understand. How "without me?" Of course the young lady must see me.

Koch. Not at all ; not at all ! Just go home and wait ; it'll all be done by this evening.

Zhev. (rubbing his hands). That'll be splendid ! That'll be capital ! Don't you think I ought to have my certificate, though—my list of service? Perhaps the young lady would like to see it ; I'll fetch it this minute.

Koch. You needn't fetch anything ; only go home ; I'll let you know this very day. (*Exit* ZHEVÀKIN.) Yes ; and don't you wish you may get it ! . . . I wonder why on earth Podkolyòssin doesn't come ! It's very strange ! He surely can't be setting his strap to rights all this time. I'd almost better run and find him.

(*Enter* AGÀFIA TIKHÒNOVNA.)

Agàfia (looking around). Have they all gone ? Is there no one here ?

Koch. There's no one here ; they've all gone.

Agàfia. Oh ! if you knew how I shook and trembled ! I never felt like that in my life before. But what a dreadful man that Yaichnitza is ! What a tyrant he would be to his wife ! I keep fancying every minute that he's coming back !

Koch. Oh, no ! he won't come back. I'll lay my head on it that neither of the two will show his nose here again.

Agàfia. And the third?

Koch. What third ?

Zhev. (Poking his head in at the door ; aside). I'm simply wild to know what she'll say about me with that little rosebud of a mouth !

Agàfia. I mean Baltazàr Baltazàrovich.

Zhev. (aside). Ah ! that's it ! that's it ! (*Rubs his hands.*)

Koch. Oh! that creature! I was wondering who you could be talking about. My dear lady, the man's a complete idiot—Heaven knows what!

Zhev. (*aside*). What's that? That I confess I don't understand.

Agàfia. Do you know, he seems to me a very nice person?

Koch. A drunkard.

Zhev. (*aside*). I really don't understand this!

Agàfia. You don't mean to say he's a drunkard too?

Koch. Oh! dear me! yes; a thoroughpaced scoundrel.

Zhev. (*aloud*). Allow me; *that* I did not ask you to say. If you had said something to my advantage, or in my praise—that would be another matter; but to speak of me in such a manner, to use such words—you may find some one else who will consent, but not your humble servant.

Koch. (*aside*). Whatever has brought him back again? (*Softly to* AGÀFIA.) Look! look! he can hardly stand on his feet. He's as drunk as a lord; and it's the same thing every day. Send him about his business and make an end of the whole affair. (*Aside.*) Podkolyòssin doesn't come, and doesn't come, the scoundrel! Oh! I'll be even with him! (*Exit.*)

Zhev. (*aside*). He said he was going to praise me, and instead of that he began abusing me! Very queer man! (*Aloud.*) Don't believe him, madam.

Agàfia. Excuse me, I am not well; my head aches. (*Going.*)

Zhev. It cannot be; there must be something about me that displeases you. (*Points to his head.*) I hope you don't mind my having a little bald place here; it's nothing, really; it's from fever; the hair will soon grow again.

Agàfia. It is all the same to me whether it grows or not.

Zhev. Madam! indeed. . . . If I were to put on a black coat, my complexion would be much lighter.

Agáfia. So much the better for you. Good-afternoon. (*Exit.*)

Zhev. (*Alone ; calls after her.*) Madam! tell me the reason! Say why! What is your objection? Is there any defect in me? . . . She's gone! It is a most extraordinary thing! This is the seventeenth time it has happened to me ; and always just in the same way. At first everything goes all right; and then, when the critical moment comes, they always refuse me. (*Walks up and down the room, meditating.*) Yes, I believe this is really the seventeenth girl. And what in the world is it that she wants? I should like to know why . . . on what grounds . . . (*Meditates.*) It's mysterious, very mysterious! Now, if there were anything to object to in me! (*Inspecting himself.*) I think nobody can say that of me, thank Heaven! It's very strange! I wonder if I hadn't better go home, and hunt about in my trunk. I used to have some verses there that no woman could stand against. . . . There really is no understanding it! Everything seemed to be going all right. . . . I see I shall have to alter my tack. It's a pity ; it really is a pity. (*Exit.*)

(*Enter* PODKOLYÓSSIN *and* KOCHKARYÒV, *looking behind them.*)

Koch. He didn't see us. Did you notice what a long face he went out with ?

Pod. She surely hasn't refused him as well as the others !

Koch. Point blank.

Pod. It must be dreadfully embarrassing to be refused !

Koch. I should think so !

Pod. I still can't believe she really said straight out that she prefers me to all the others.

Koch. Prefers indeed ! She's simply off her head about you. If you'd heard all the sweet names she gave you— why, she's over head and ears in love !

Pod. (*sniggering contentedly*). And you know, really,

when a woman likes, she can say such words to you as no man would ever think of—"piggykin-snout," "my own little cockroach," "blackie." . . .

Koch. Oh, that's nothing! Once you're married you'll find out before two months are over what words a woman knows how to use—enough to melt you all away, my lad !

Pod. (*laughing*). Really ?

Koch. Word of honour ! Look here, though, we must get to business. Lay your heart bare before her this very minute, and ask for her hand.

Pod. This very minute ! My dear fellow, how can you !

Koch. This minute, certainly ; and here she' comes. (*Enter Agàfia.*) Madam, I have brought to your feet the mortal whom you see. There never was a man so desperately in love—poor fellow, I wouldn't wish an enemy to be in such a state. . . .

Pod. (*nudging his arm ; softly*). I say, old fellow, don't lay it on too thick. . . .

Koch. (*aside to him*). All right. (*Aside to her.*) Help him out, he's very shy ; try to be as easy as possible. Make the most of your eyebrows, or keep your eyes down and then flash them at him suddenly—you know how !—or bend your shoulder somehow and let the dog look at it ! I'm sorry, though, you didn't put on a dress with short sleeves ; however, it's no matter. (*Aloud.*) Well, I leave you in agreeable company. I'll just look into your dining-room and kitchen a minute ; I must make arrangements—the man I ordered the supper from will be here in a minute ; perhaps the wine has come already. . . . Good-bye ! (*Aside to Podkolyòssin.*) Out with it ; don't be afraid ! (*Exit.*)

Agàfia. Will you sit down, please ? (*They sit down ; silence.*)

Pod. Do you like the water, madam ?

Agàfia. How do you mean—the water ?

Pod. I mean—to go boating in summer, in the suburbs.

Agàfia. Yes, we sometimes make an excursion with friends.

Pod. I wonder what sort of summer we shall have?

Agàfia. It is to be hoped it will be fine. (*Silence.*)

Pod. What is your favourite flower, madam?

Agàfia. The carnation; it smells so sweet.

Pod. Flowers are very becoming for ladies.

Agàfia. Yes, they make an agreeable occupation. (*Silence.*) What church did you go to last Sunday?

Pod. To the Voznessénsky, and the week before to the Kazansky Cathedral. But it is all the same—one can pray in any church. (*Silence. Podkolyòssin drums on the table with his fingers.*) The Ekaterinhof excursions will soon begin now.

Agàfia. In a month, I think.

Pod. Even less than a month.

Agàfia. I expect there will be some pleasant excursions.

Pod. To-day is the eighth—(*counts on his fingers*)—ninth, tenth, eleventh—in twenty-two days.

Agàfia. Dear me, how soon!

Pod. I don't count to-day in. (*Silence.*) What a daring race the Russians are!

Agàfia. How so?

Pod. The working men. They will stand right on the top of anything. . . . I passed a house to-day that was being plastered; and there stood the plasterer afraid of nothing.

Agàfia. Indeed? And where was this?

Pod. On my way, where I always have to pass, going to the Department. I attend regularly every day now. (*Silence. Podkolyòssin again drums on the table; at last takes his hat, rises, and bows.*)

Agàfia. Going already?

Pod. Yes. . . Pardon me, I have perhaps bored you.

Agàfia. How could that be! On the contrary, I ought

to thank you for causing me to pass the time so pleasantly.

Pod. (*smiling*). Really, I am afraid I have bored you.

Agáfia. Oh no, indeed !

Pod. In that case, allow me to come in some other time—some evening.

Agáfia. With the greatest pleasure. (*They bow. Exit Podkolyóssin.*)

Agáfia (*alone*). What a superior person ! I have only now learned to know him well ; it would be difficult not to love him ; he is at once modest and judicious. Yes, his friend spoke truly of him ; I am only sorry that he went away so soon—I should have liked to hear him talk some more. How delightful it is to talk with him ! The best of all is that he doesn't talk small-talk. I wanted to say two or three words to him, but I suddenly felt so timid, and my heart began to beat so. . . . What an excellent gentleman ! . . . I'll go and tell auntie. (*Exit.*)

(*Enter* PODKOLYÓSSIN *and* KOCHKARYÓV.)

Koch. Why go home ? Whatever nonsense do you want to go home for ?

Pod. What should I stop here for ? I've said all that's proper already.

Koch. Then you have made her an offer ?

Pod. N—no, that's the only thing—I haven't done that yet.

Koch. Well you really are—why didn't you ?

Pod. I should like to know how you expect me, without talking about anything else first, to plump the question that way—"Will you marry me, madam ? "

Koch. And *I* should like to know whatever nonsense were you talking about for a whole half-hour ?

Pod. Oh, we talked about all sorts of things ; and I acknowledge that I'm delighted. I passed the time most agreeably.

Koch. Look here, man, think yourself; when are you going to get it all done at that rate ? It will be time to go to church and be married in an hour.

Pod. Are you gone mad? Be married to-day! . . .

Koch. Why not?

Pod. To-day!

Koch. But you gave me your word ; you said that as soon as the other suitors were got rid of, you were ready to be married at once.

Pod. I'm quite willing to keep my word—only not at once. I must have at least a month breathing-time.

Koch. A month !

Pod. Of course.

Koch. Are you gone right off your head ?

Pod. I can't do with less than a month.

Koch. But, you wooden block, you, I've ordered the supper ! . . Look here, Iv·an Kouzmich, don't be obstinate, there's a good fellow ; get married at once !

Pod. My good man, what are you thinking of? How could I do it at once?

Koch. Iv·an Kouzmich, I ask it of you. If you don't care to do it for your own sake, do it for mine.

Pod. I tell you I can't.

Koch. You can, my dear fellow, you can, perfectly well ; there now, don't be so whimsical, don't, please !

Pod. But indeed I can't do it ; just think how odd it would seem !

Koch. What is there odd about it ? Who's been putting that into your head ? Now just be sensible and think it over ; you're a clever fellow—I don't say that to flatter you, or creep into your good graces ; I don't say it because you're an aulic counsellor—I say it out of sincere affection for you. . . . There now, dear old chap—make up your mind—look at the thing as a reasonable man should.

Pod. If the thing were possible I would ——

Koch. Iván Kouzmìch! My dear friend, my good fellow! If you like I'll go down on my knees to you!

Pod. But why?

Koch. (*kneeling*). There! I'm on my knees before you! There now, you see, I entreat you! I'll never forget it if you'll do me this one favour—give in, please; please give in!

Pod. I tell you, man, I can't.

Koch. (*rising angrily*). PIG!!

Pod. Oh. you can rant if you like!

Koch. Idiot! Blockhead! There never was such an ass!

Pod. Rant away; I don't care!

Koch. Who have I taken all this trouble for? Who have I been working for? All for your good, you nincompoop! I declare I'll just throw it all up and leave you in the lurch; what's it to me?

Pod. Certainly, throw it up if you like. Who asked you to give yourself so much trouble?

Koch. But you'll come to grief altogether—you can't manage anything without me. If I don't get you safely married, you'll be fooled for the rest of your days.

Pod. What's that to you?

Koch. Oh, you dunderhead! It's you I'm trying to help!

Pod. I don't want your help.

Koch. Then go to the devil!

Pod. Very well, I will.

Koch. That's the right end for you!

Pod. All right.

Koch. Be off with you! Be off! And I wish you may break your leg! With all my heart I wish a tipsy cabman would drive his shafts down your throat! You're an old rag, not an official! I give you my word that everything's over between us. Don't you dare to show your face in my house again!

Pod. I shan't. (*Exit.*)

Koch. (*alone*). Go to the devil—your old friend! (*Opens door and bawls after him.*) Fool! (*Walks up and down in great agitation.*) Now, did anybody in the world ever see such a man? The blockhead! Indeed, to speak the truth, I'm a precious fellow, too! Now just tell me, please —I appeal to you all—am I not an ass and a dolt? Why should I toil and moil for him and argue till my throat aches? What's he to me, please? He's no kin of mine! And what am I to him—nurse, maiden aunt, mother-in-law, sponsor? Why, why, *why* the devil should I take all this trouble and give myself no rest? And all for him— may the foul fiend carry him away! The deuce take it all! Sometimes there's no making out what a man does a thing for! What a scoundrel! What a sneaking, miserable cad! Oh! you pig-headed brute, you! Wouldn't I just like to punch your nose and box your ears, and knock out your teeth and—— Ah! (*Strikes at the air with his fist.*) This is the provoking thing about it—he just goes off, and doesn't care a rap; it all runs off him like water off a duck's back; that's what I can't stand! He'll just go home to his lodgings and lie on his back and smoke a pipe. Confounded sneak! There are plenty of ugly brutes to be seen, but such a hideous mug passes any man's power to imagine; you couldn't invent anything worse if you tried— you couldn't, really! And he's just mistaken. I'll go and fetch him back on purpose, the scoundrel! I won't let him give the slip like that; I'll go and bring the sneak back! (*Rushes away. Enter* AGÀFIA.)

Agàfia. Really, my heart beats so, I can't make it out! Whichever way I turn, Ivàn Kouzmìch seems to stand before me. It seems as if one couldn't escape one's fate. Just now I wanted to think of something altogether different, but it's all the same whatever I take up. I've tried to wind off some silk and make a reticule, but Ivàn Kouzmìch keeps getting under my hand. (*Silence.*) And so now, at last, a change of condition awaits me! They will take me, lead me to the church. Then they will leave me alone with a man—oh! I shudder from head to foot when I think of it. Farewell, my maiden life! (*Weeps.*) All these years I have lived in peace. I have just gone on living, and now I must be married! And to think of all the cares of marriage : children, boys—they always quarrel and fight— and then there'll be girls, and they'll grow up, and one must get them married. And one is fortunate if they find good husbands. But supposing they marry drunkards, or people that may any day gamble away anything they have! (*Gradually begins to sob again.*) I haven't had time to enjoy my girlhood ; I haven't lived even twenty-seven years unmarried. (*Changing her tone.*) I wonder why Iván Kouzmìch is so long coming! (*Enter* PODKOLYÒSSIN. KOCHKARYÒV'S *hands are seen at the door, shoving him forcibly on to the stage.*)

Pod. I have come, madam, to explain a certain matter —only I should wish to know beforehand whether you will not think it strange——

Agàfia (*dropping her eyes*). What is it?

Pod. No, madam; tell me first, will you think it strange?

Agàfia. I can't. What is it?

Pod. But confess ; I am sure what I am going to say will seem strange to you.

Agàfia. How is that possible? It is a pleasure to hear anything from you.

Pod. But you have never heard this thing from me. (AGÀFIA *drops her eyes lower.* KOCHKARYÒV *enters softly, and stands behind* PODKOLYÒSSIN.) It is about—— But perhaps I had better tell you some other time.

Agàfia. What is it?

Pod. It is—— It's true, I wanted to explain to you now, but I still feel a little doubtful.

Koch. (*folding his arms, aside*). Oh! Gracious heavens! What a man! He's an old woman's flannel shoe, not a man. He's a parody of a man, a burlesque of a man!

Agàfia. Why should you feel doubtful?

Pod. A sort of doubt keeps coming over me.

Koch. (*aloud*). Oh! how stupid! Oh! how stupid! This is what it's about, madam: he asks your hand, and wants to tell you that he can't live, can't exist without you; he wants to know—do you consent to make him happy?

Pod. (*half frightened, excitedly nudging him*). I say! don't!

Koch. Can you decide, madam, to render this mortal happy?

Agàfia. I do not presume to think that I can give happiness—— However, I consent.

Koch. Of course, of course; ought to have been settled long ago! Give me your hands!

Pod. In a minute. (*Tries to whisper in his ear.* KOCH- KARYÒV *shakes his fist and frowns at him.* PODKOLYÒSSIN *gives his hand.*)

Koch. (*joining their hands*). Well, may God bless you! I consent, and I approve your union. Marriage is a kind of thing—— It's not like just taking a sledge and going for a drive; it's of quite a different character; it's an obliga- tion—— I haven't time now, but I'll tell you afterwards what sort of obligation it is. Well, Ivàn Kouzmìch, kiss your bride; it is your right to do that now; it is your duty to do it. (AGÀFIA *drops her eyes.*) Never mind, madam, it is quite right and proper; let him kiss you!

Pod. No, madam, you must permit me now. (*Kisses her, and takes her hand.*) What a lovely little hand! Why have you such a lovely little hand? Allow me, madam. I wish that the wedding should be at once—at once, with- out any delay.

Agáfia. At once? Perhaps that will be too soon.

Pod. I won't hear of anything! I should like to have it this very minute.

Koch. Bravo! That's good! That's a noble fellow! I always had great hopes of you in the future! Indeed, madam, he's quite right; you'd better go and dress at once. To tell the truth, I've sent for the carriage already, and invited the guests; they're all gone straight to the church. I know your wedding-dress is ready.

Agáfia. Oh! yes; ready long ago. I'll dress in a minute. (*Exit.*)

Pod. Well, I thank you, friend! Now I appreciate all your kindness. My own father wouldn't have done for me what you have done. I see now that you acted from pure friendship. Thank you, old chap! I'll remember it all my life. (*With emotion.*) Next spring I'll certainly go and visit your father's grave.

Koch. It's nothing, old man; I'm glad myself. There now; let's embrace. (*Kisses him, first on one cheek, then on the other.*) May God give you happiness and prosperity (*they kiss*), peace and plenty; may you have many children.

Pod. Thank you, friend! Now, at last, only now, I know what life is; a new world has opened before me. Now I see, as it were, that everything moves and lives. I feel, I seem to go off into a mist—I don't know myself what has come to me. Up till now I never saw or understood all this; I was just like a man that knew nothing; I never thought, never pondered over things; I lived just as any ordinary man does.

Koch. I'm glad, very glad! I'll just go and see how they've set the table; I'll be back in a minute. (*Aside.*) All the same, I'd better take away his hat, in case of anything. (*Exit, taking hat.*)

Pod (*alone*). Indeed, what have I been, until now?

PODKOLYÓSSIN: "WELL, I DON'T KNOW; IT ISN'T SO HIGH; ONLY ONE STORY."

Have I understood the meaning of life? No, I have
understood nothing. What has my bachelor life been
worth? What have I done? Of what consequence have
I been? I have lived and lived, served, gone to the
Department, dined, slept—in a word, I have been a quite
ordinary and frivolous man. It is only now I see how
foolish are all the people who do not marry. And yet, if
you think of it, what a number of people are in that state
of blindness! If I were a king anywhere, I would command that everybody should marry, every single person,
that there shouldn't be one bachelor in all my kingdom.
Really, to think of it, in a few minutes I shall be married!
Suddenly I shall taste such bliss as one only hears about in
fairy-tales—bliss that there is no describing, there are no
words to describe it. (*After a short silence.*) All the same,
put it how you like—but there's really something almost
dreadful in it when you think it over. For all one's life,
for ever—you can't get over the fact that you're tying yourself. And once it's done, no excuse will help you, no
remorse, nothing, nothing—everything's finished; all is
over. Why, even now there's no way out of it; we shall be
before the altar in a few minutes. I couldn't go away if I
wanted to—the carriage is at the door; everything's ready.
I wonder, though, couldn't I go away? Why no, of course
not; there are heaps of people at the door, and everywhere, and they'd ask me why. No, no, it won't do! By
the by, there's the window open; what if I jumped out.
No, no; oh, no; it wouldn't do; it wouldn't be proper—
and then, it's so high. (*Goes to window.*) Well, I don't
know; it isn't so high; only one story, and that a low one.
Why, no, no, of course I can't; I haven't even got my hat;
I can't go without a hat, it would seem so queer!
Couldn't I manage without a hat, though, after all? What
if I were to try? H—'m. I might as well try. (*Clambers
on to window-sill and crosses himself.*) Lord, give Thy bless-

ing!¹ (*Jumps down into the street. Heard grunting and groaning without.*) Oh! oh! It's a good height though! Hi, *drozhki!*

Cabman's voice (without). Drozhki, sir?

Pod. (without). To the canal, by the Semyònovsky bridge.

Cabman (without). I don't mind going for ten kopecks.

Pod. (without). All right! Make haste!

(*Drozhki is heard to drive away. Enter* AGÀFIA *in her wedding-dress, walking timidly and hanging her head.*)

Agàfia. I really don't know what is come to me. I feel ashamed again, and I am trembling all over. Oh! I wish he weren't in the room just this minute; I wish he'd gone out! (*Looking round shyly.*) Why, where is he? There's no one here! Where can he be gone? (*Opens door into hall and calls.*) Fèkla, where is Ivàn Kouzmìch gone?

Fèkla (without). He's there.

Agàfia. Where?

Fèkla (entering). But he was sitting in this room!

Agàfia. Well, he isn't here, you see.

Fèkla. He certainly hasn't gone out of the room! I was sitting in the hall.

Agàfia. Then where is he?

Fèkla. I'm sure I don't know. He can't have gone out by the back door. I wonder if he's sitting in Arìna Pante-lèymovna's room?

Agàfia. Auntie! Auntie! (*Enter* ARÌNA, *dressed for wedding.*)

Arìna. What's the matter?

Agàfia. Is Ivàn Kouzmìch in your room?

Arìna. No, he must be here; he hasn't come into my room.

¹ The pious ejaculation used, with the sign of the cross, by strict members of the Orthodox Greek Church, on starting upon any enter-prise, great or small.

Fékla. Well, I know he didn't go through the hall, for I was sitting there.

Agàfia. But you see yourself he isn't here. (*Enter* KOCHARYÒV.)

Koch. What's the matter?

Agàfia. We can't find Ivàn Kouzmìch.

Koch. Can't find him? Has he gone out?

Agàfia. No, he hasn't gone out either.

Koch. What do you mean? Not here and not gone out?

Fékla. I can't think where he can have got to. I was in the hall the whole time; never left it for a minute.

Arìna. Well, he certainly didn't go out by the back stairs.

Koch. Well, but, the devil take it, he couldn't vanish without going out of the room! I expect he's hidden himself. . . . Ivàn Kouzmìch! Where are you? Leave off fooling! Come out, quick! There's no time for jokes; we ought to be at church by now! (*Looks into cupboard, and peeps askance under chairs.*) No making it out! But he can't have gone away; he can't possibly have gone away! He's here; there's his hat in the next room, I put it there on purpose.

Arìna. We'd better ask the girl, she was standing at the street door; perhaps she knows something about it. . . . Douniàshka! Douniàshka! . . . (*Enter* DOUNIÀSHKA.) Where's Ivàn Kouzmìch? Have you seen him?

Doun. Please'm, the gentleman jumped out of window. (AGÀFIA *screams and clasps her hands.*)

All three together. The window? . .

Doun. Yes'm. And if you please'm, when he was out he took a *drozhki* and drove away.

Arìna. Are you speaking the truth?

Koch. It's a lie! It can't be!

Doun. No, it's not then; he did jump out. And the

man as keeps the general shop saw him too. He took a
drozhki for ten kopecks, and he drove away.

Arìna (advancing to KOCHKARYÒV). I suppose, then,
little father, that you meant to play off a joke on us, to
make a laughing-stock of us? You've come here to disgrace us, is that it? Sir, I've lived for more than fifty
years, and I've never been put to such shame as this. And,
little father, I'll spit in your face if you call yourself an
honest man! You're a villain and a scoundrel if you call
yourself an honest man! To shame a girl publicly—before
every one! I—a peasant wouldn't do such a thing! And
you a noble! All the nobility you've got is good for
nothing but lies and cheating and rascally tricks!

(*Exit, furious, taking the bride with her.* KOCHKARYÒV
stands as petrified.)

Fèkla. Well. So this is the gentleman that knows how
to manage things! This is the way you get on without a
matchmaker! It's all very well to laugh at my suitors.
They may be draggletailed, and anything else you like, but,
whatever they are, they don't jump out of the window. I
don't have that sort, anyhow!

Koch. That's all nonsense; it can't be! I'll run after
him and bring him back. (*Exit.*)

Fèkla. Yes, bring him back, I daresay. Much *you* know
about marriages! If he'd run out by the door it would
have been another thing, but when the bridegroom pops
out of window all I can say is—I wish you joy!

CURTAIN.

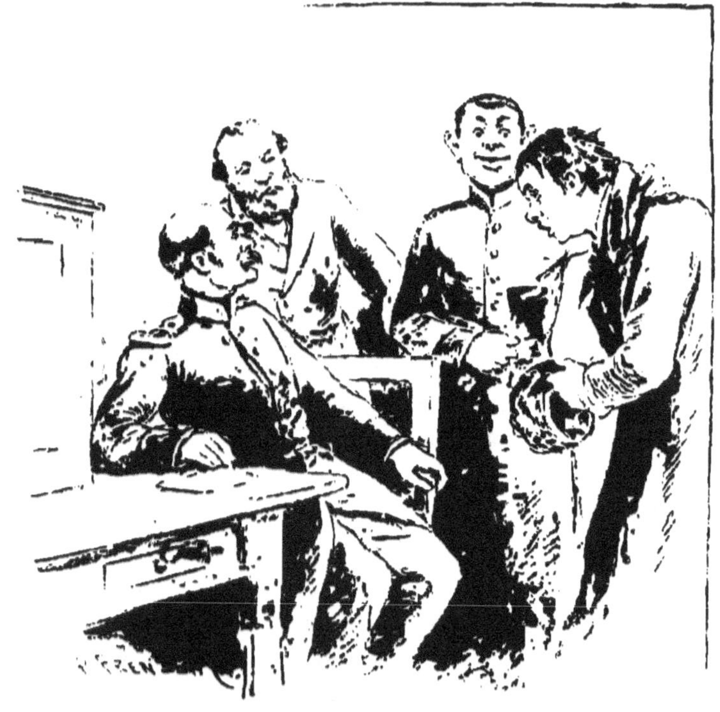

By GORBOUNÒV.

PERSONS.

THE POLICE INSPECTOR.
GRIGÒRIEV, *his servant.*
A SHOPKEEPER.
IVÀN ANÀNIEV, *a factory hand.*

TIME: *morning. The Inspector sits in his office reading documents.*

Inspector (reads). "Therefore, the Moscow Administration of Public Order——" Grigòriev!
Grigòriev. What is it, yer honour?

Inspector. Tell the cook to do me a herring with apple sauce.

Grigòriev. Yes, yer honour.

Inspector (*reads*). "To make all proper investigations——" (*Enter the* SHOPKEEPER.) Who's that?

Shopkeeper. It's only me, little father.

Inspector. And who are you?

Shopkeeper. An inhabitant of the town.

Inspector. What do you want?

Shopkeeper. I came, little father, to humbly beg a favour of you.

Inspector. Well, what now?

Shopkeeper. It's an odd business, little father.

Inspector. Odd? What sort of business?

Shopkeeper. Well, you see, it's this way—don't be angry, your honour, just take three silver roubles for your household expenses.

Inspector. Sit down, please.

Shopkeeper. Oh, I can stand, your honour; . . I don't mind standing.

Inspector. What's your business?

Shopkeeper. Your honour is aware that I have a 'ouse in your district, with a wooden fence. . .

Inspector. Yes.

Shopkeeper. Well, in that 'ouse I've got a factory—a weaving factory.

Inspector. Well?

Shopkeeper. Well, you see, sir——

Inspector. Sit down, sit down. . . . .

Shopkeeper. Don't trouble. . . . Well, on Saturday I was in the town, and I was kept a bit late. Well, I tore off home as hard as my legs would carry me— There! I thought, my wife'll be waiting—family matters, you know —and the tea'll all be kept about——

Inspector. Yes, yes, family matters. . . .

Shopkeeper. Well, there's a hand in my factory— Iván Anàniev——

Inspector. Well? I suppose he got drunk, or made a row, or something?

Shopkeeper. It's worse than that, sir—I'd 'ave put up with that—he's stolen my cutter.

Inspector. What's a cutter?

Shopkeeper. Why, you see, sir, it's a sort of thing, . . . for the stuff like that we weave, you know, in our line of business. . .

Inspector. Ah! I understand.

Shopkeeper. So I said to him : "Iván Anàniev, you come with me to the Police Inspector." And what d'you think he said? "I don't care for your Inspector," says he!

Inspector. What's that!—Grigòriev ! . . .

Shopkeeper. So I said to him : "What d'you mean?" I says ; "why, any gentleman can hit you over the head if he likes, and you can't do anything—let alone his honour the Inspector," says I.

Inspector. Grigòriev !

Shopkeeper. You see, your honour, people like us can't pass over things of that sort, 'cause why?—we should just lose all our capital. . . .

Inspector. Gri—gòriev !

Shopkeeper. And I do say, sir, that for us the Inspector . . . it's like this, you see, . . as if- —

(*Enter* GRIGÒRIEV.)

Grigòriev. What is it, yer honour?

Inspector. Blockhead !

Grigòriev. At your honour's service.

Inspector. Fetch Iván Anàniev here.

Grigòriev (*opening the door*). Kondràtiev ! Wheres' Iván Anàniev? Dost thou know who it is? Fetch him to the master. . . . Iván Ana—à—aniev !

(*Enter* IVÀN ANÀNIEV.)

Inspector.   What is your name?

Ivàn Anàniev.   Ha'nt got none; time to die soon.

Inspector.   What do you say?

Ivàn Anàniev.   Don't know nothin'.

Inspector.   Take him to the lock-up.

Ivàn Anàniev.   Koùzma Petròvich 'as jes' made it all up agin me, 'cause I wouldn't mix up in any o' his fine tricks.

Inspector.   Take him away.

Grigòriev.   Kondràtiev! . . .

Shopkeeper.   Thank you very much, sir.   Nothing more to be done, I suppose?

Inspector.   Just step into the other office and write out a formal statement.

Shopkeeper.   Certainly, sir. (*Exit.*)

Inspector.   Grigòriev!

Grigòriev.   What is it, your honour?

Inspector.   Give me my uniform.

Grigòriev.   Why, your honour, 'tis all mucky and spotty.

Inspector.   What!

Grigòriev.   *I* don't know nothing about it!

Inspector.   Can the spots be taken out?

Grigòriev.   Oh ay, your honour.

Inspector.   How?

Grigòriev.   I don't know.

Inspector.   I think with turpentine?

Grigòriev.   And *I* think with turpentine.

Inspector.   Only I'm afraid it'll smell.

Grigòriev.   'Twill stink, your honour.

Inspector.   I don't know, though—perhaps it won't.

Grigòriev.   Of course it won't, your honour! (*Brings back the uniform.*) 'Tis ready, your honour.

Inspector.   What?

Grigòriev.   Nothin'.

Inspector.   Does it smell?

Grigòriev.   'T stinks, your honour.

Inspector.   Badly?

Grigòriev.   Terrible bad, your honour.

Inspector.   I don't know—it's nothing to hurt, I think: one can't smell it.

Grigòriev.   Of course one can't.   Let me hold it, sir; there you be!

v.
he
  I
  Shi
says;
likes, a.
Inspecto
   Inspecto

BEFORE THE JUSTICE OF THE PEACE.

By GORBOUNÒV.

(The Justice's Court. Before the table stand two shopmen from the Apràksin market.)

The Justice of the Peace. You are accused of smearing mustard on the face of a waiter in the hotel Yàgodka.

First Defendant. We had a lark—that's true enough.

Justice. You broke the mirror.

First Defendant.   There—all that's paid for, and we have given the boy his due.

Justice.   Then you acknowledge yourselves guilty?

First Defendant.   Guilty?   What have I done wrong?   If I pay my money down——

Justice.   You were together?

Second Defendant.   Yes, your honour.

Justice.   Do you acknowledge yourself guilty?

Second Defendant.   Certainly not!

Justice.   It is stated in the accusation that you· —

Second Defendant.   I dare say!   I'd write you all the accusations you like for 2¾d.

Justice.   I cannot permit you to express yourself in this manner.

. ·ond Defendant.   I wasn't expressing anything at all!

Ɉ ɾe (to witness).   State what happened.

ɩ ·ss.   I dun'no wot ever money they're a-talkin' abo· ʅ never got no money!   They jes' come in, an' they was pretty well screwed, both on 'em, an' they ordered a stew, an' a big decanter, an' then a bottle o' sherry.   So when they got very tight, they began blusterin' away——

First Defendant.   If I smeared your ugly face——

Justice.   Silence!

First Defendant.   Cert'nly sir, only he's tellin' a pack of lies!

Advocate.   I beg permission to put a question to the witness.

Justice.   Who are you?

Advocate.   Retained for the defence.

Justice.   Afterwards.

Witness.   Well, they was blusterin' away, an' then they set to an' began a-cruelly ill-usin' o' me.

Justice.   How "ill-using"?

Witness.   By the air o' the 'ed, y'r worship.

Justice.   Which of them?

Witness. Why, them there, both on 'em.

First Defendant. That's all rot.

Advocate. I beg permission to put a question to the witness.

Justice. I told you—afterwards.

Witness. Well, then they begins smearin' o' mustard all over me. One gent as was in the coffee-room, he up an' says, "This is dis—graceful," says 'e ; and they told 'im, "We've paid our money down."

Justice. Is this a true account?

First Defendant. Maybe ; I was screwed pretty tight ; I don't quite recollect. But, even if we did smear him a bit, what's there to make such a fuss about? It wasn't turpentine we smeared him with—and then, besides, we paid money down for it. Well, it's all one to me ; I'l' "guilty," if you like.

Justice (to Second Defendant). And you?

Second Defendant. We keep to our former statem.

Advocate. May I speak now?

Justice. You may.

Advocate. May it please y'r worship! The heartfelt repentance brought into court, in accordance with the new statute, dimin'shes. . . . The law permits of moral conviction, and I therefore beg you to judge my client by moral conviction. I deny—a—any guilt in this case. I have long served in the Administrash'n of Benevo——

Justice. Excuse me. In what condition are you?

Advocate. I beg y'r p—pard'n?

Justice. In what condition have you come here?

Advocate. In w w-what con-d-dish'n?

Justice. I must fine you three roubles. Please to leave the Court.

Advocate. Prompt, just, and merciful.

INCOMPATIBILITY OF TEMPER.

PICTURES FROM MOSCOW LIFE.

By. A. N. OSTROVSKY.

PICTURE I.

DRAMATIS PERSONÆ.

PRÉZHNEV, *an old man, completely in his dotage, official of high rank;
    has lost the use of his limbs; is wheeled about in a chair.*
SÓFIA IVÁNOVNA PRÉZHNEVA, *his wife, aged forty-five.*
PAUL, *a young man, her son.*
OUSTÍNA FILIMÓNOVNA PERESHÍVKINA, *an elderly woman, formerly
    PAUL'S nurse; now a kind of toady and hanger-on in several
    families.*

*A large drawing-room; very rich paper-hangings, grown old and
    shabby, peeling off the walls. Polished parquet, sunk and uneven.
    Windows, left, looking into garden. Door opening on wooden*

balcony, with pillars. At back of stage, a door leading to hall. Door, right, to inner rooms. In narrow niches, little marble tables with bronze legs; over them hang long narrow pier-glasses with gilded frames. Furniture old, heavy, with gilding rubbed off. Old bronze-work on tables. Glass chandelier with lozenge-shaped drops. Two or three ivy-screens. A general appearance of former luxury now become shabby.

SCENE I.

(PRÉZHNEV *asleep in wheel-chair beside window. Fur dressing-gown: white woollen rug over feet.* MADAME PRÉZHNEVA, *in elegant morning négligé, lies on sofa with a book.*)

Madame P. (lays down book). That is cruel! That dreadful! I would never have acted so! *Nous a femmes* . . we . . . oh! we believe, we trust blind' never analyse. No, I cannot finish this novel. A man of good birth, handsome, clever, an officer in the declares his love to her in such exquisite language, and she—she has the heart to refuse him! No; she is no woman! Woman is a weak creature of impulse! We live only through the heart. And how easy it is to deceive us! We are willing to make all sacrifices for the man we love. If men deceive us—which, alas! happens very often—the blame lies not upon us, but upon them. They, for the most part, are cunning and deceitful. . . . We women are so loving, so trustful, so ready to believe everything, that only after bitter (*meditates*)—yes, bitter—experience we realise the immorality of the beings we adore. (*Silence.*) But, no! Even after a betrayal, even after several betrayals, we are ready again to yield to impulse, to believe once more in the possibility of pure and honourable love! Yes! it is our fate! All the more so, when the whole thing takes place amid such poetical surroundings as in this novel: spring-time, flowers, a beautiful park, gurgling streams; he came to her attired for the hunt, the gun upon his shoulder, the hound at his feet, ah! But men. . . how often do they abuse the exquisite tenderness of our loving hearts; they care not to know how much we suffer through them, we poor women! (*Silence.*) Of course there *are* women whose whole interest in life consists in vulgar, material considerations and household affairs. But that is prose, prose! Nothing shall make me regard it as anything but prose. There are even women who discuss various learned topics as if they were men; but I cannot recognise their womanhood. They may be clever; they may be learned; but instead of a heart they have a lump of ice. (*Silence.*) When such ideas come into my mind, I always think of Paul. Oh! how successful he will be with women! It is a joy to me in anticipation! How sweet is that thought for a mother! Oh! children! children! (*smells vinaigrette and rings bell. Enter footman.*)

Footman. Did madame ring?

Madame P. Has your master come in yet?

Footman. No, madame.

Madame P. When he comes, say I wish to see him.

Footman. Yes, madame. (*Exit.*)

Madame P. He is such a sensitive, nervous boy! He has inherited my temperament. He should be watched over and tenderly cared for. But what can I do? I have no fortune! After receiving such a high-class education, he is reduced to the necessity of serving in a Government office! All those head-clerks . . . They do wear such extraordinary coats! . . . and he is so nervous, so nervous! . . . I believe that they all persecute him out of envy.

(Enter PAUL.)

Paul (irreproachably dressed in summer costume, with an exhausted and somewhat affected air). Bonjour, Maman!

Madame P. (*kisses his forehead*). *Bonjour*, Paul! Where have you been?

Paul (*sits on sofa*). Where! In that charming place to which it pleased you to send me.

Madame P. What can we do, Paul?

Paul. I have come home on foot in this dreadful heat!

Madame P. It is charmingly cool in this room.

Paul. Yes; but what is it like in the winter? All the walls are damp-rotted; the floor is sunk in.

Madame P. Yes, my dear one; our affairs are in a very bad condition.

Paul. Your affairs! What affairs have you? There's papa only half alive; and you, too, have had your day, and finished it. Lo; k at *my* position!

Madame P. I know, my dear one. I can underst how hard it is for you!

Paul. Hard! I should think so! Listen to; it's *Maman.* By birth, by education, by the circle in w move—in fact, by everything—I belong, every inch of hat to the best rank of society.

Madame P. Oh, yes!

Paul. And what is wanting? It is shameful, infamous! A fortune! And, indeed, what does it matter that I have no fortune? All the same, I ought to live and do like other people. Am I to go and register myself as an artizan? A cobbler, perhaps! All because I have no fortune! That amounts to an absurdity.

Madame P. We had a fortune once, Paul.

Paul. I know you had. And where is it now? I know more than that. . . . I know that you squandered it.

Madame P. Ah, Paul! do not blame me! You know that we women are so weak, so confiding. Before your father's illness we were considered very wealthy people; we had a fine estate in the Simbirsk country. He knew how to manage all those things. Afterwards, when he was struck down with paralysis, I lived not at all luxuriously, only respectably.

Paul. How much did Mons. Péché cost you? Confess, *Maman!*

Madame P. Oh! my dear one, he was indispensable for your education. Then I went abroad twice. But I never ran into any heavy expense. And suddenly I was informed that I had spent all the fortune, that we had nothing left. It is dreadful! In all probability it was our stewards and bailiffs that were to blame for the whole thing.

Paul. Canaille!

Madame P. What can we do, my dear one? People are so wicked, so cunning; and you and I are so confiding!

Paul. It's you that are confiding, *Maman.* If they got my hands, I would tell them quite another story! two, . . . (*Makes gesture with his hand.*) There's else to be done with those creatures. It's good m to get a thrashing sometimes. It really makes me angry; just because of these scoundrels I have to go every morning, on foot, to a miserable office of which I need never have heard; and then either walk home, or jolt along with a wretched cabman. I cannot live in the same fashion as all these copying-clerks that I have to sit side by side with. They buy onion-pies at the costermonger's, and stand eating them at the street door. *They* can do that sort of thing—they are made that way—but *I* can't. Now, you see, I am in debt to every one—to the cabman, to the tailor, to Chevalier: all our set go to Chevalier, and all the young barristers. . . . You can hardly expect *me* to eat onion-pies! And now, I've got to go through an examination in some District Institution. It's dreadful! You see, if I had a fortune, I should never even hear of all these things—Law Courts, and District Institutions, and copying-clerks, with their onion-pies! What do I want with them all?

Madame P. Yes, yes, I understand. . . . With your sensitive nature. . . . You are so nervous!

Paul. I really don't know what to do! If there were a chance, I should have no scruples about cheating some one at cards.

Madame P. Well indeed, in your position——

Prèzhnev (waking up). Paul, have you been to the theatre lately?

Paul. Quite lately.

Prèzhnev. Who plays the marquises now?

Paul. No one has done for some time.

Prèzhnev. I used to play marquises very well once.

(Madame Prèzhneva *rings. Enter* Footman.)

Madame P. Wheel your master out on to the balc and take some old newspapers and read aloud to (*Footman takes newspapers and wheels Prèzhnev balcony.*)

Paul. Then there's my amiable uncle. Just becau been a judge somewhere, he puts on superior airs : " want too much," he says. What do I want? Have I ever asked for luxury and extravagance? I only want what is necessary, what a man in my set cannot do without. Surely that is plain enough. But no; my kind uncle tells me, "You have no right to want all these things, because you have no fortune." Why! is it my fault that I have no fortune? What sort of logic is that?

Madame P. No logic at all; it's absurd.

Paul. He says, "You ought to work!" Many thanks! Your humble servant! I'm not a horse, I suppose.

Madame P. Your uncle has no refinement.

Paul. No, *Maman;* it is a tragedy.

Madame P. A tragedy, indeed, *mon cher!*

Paul. And a terrible one! There's no need of murder and poison to make a tragedy.

Madame P. Do you know, Paul, I think the best thing would be for you to marry.

Paul. I've no objection. But whom should I marry?

Madame P. Ah, that is the question. I know you well, Paul. Why are you so highly educated? Why have you such a sensitive nature? It will make you unhappy all your life long There is no mate for you! To win your love and make you happy, a girl would need too many virtues.

Paul. You perhaps imagine, *Maman*, that domestic felicity has attractions for me? I'm not a child; I am twenty-one. That is too Arcadian! (*Bursts out laughing.*) I simply want money.

Madame P. None the less, my dear one, I know your character; I know that you would not care to marry any sort of person.

Paul. Any one you like; I want money in order to be *comme il faut*; in order to play my proper part in society— in a word, to do that for which I am fitted. I do not know how to save up money; I only know how to spend it with elegance and dignity. For that I have all the necessary gifts. I have tact, I have taste, I am fitted to take a leading position in society.

Madame P. Still, my dear—— (*Enter* FOOTMAN.)

Footman. Pereshívkina asks to see madame.

Madame P. She always comes at the wrong time!

Paul. We shall have time to talk afterwards.

Madame P. Let her come in. (*Exit* FOOTMAN. *Enter* PERESHÍVKINA.)

Madame P. What is it, Oustínya Filimónovna?

Pereshívkina (*kisses* PRÍZHNEVA *on the shoulder, and then stands a little back.*) I came to ask after your health, little mother: I never forget my benefactors.

Paul. Well, old vinegar face, where have you come from?

Pereshivkina. Ah, Mr. Paul, you're always full of your jokes !

Paul. She actually expects one to talk seriously with her !

Pereshivkina. I have a friend, little mother, who makes dimmy-tule. (*Paul laughs.*) Laugh away, little father ; it's a fine thing to laugh at an old woman. . . . So I thought perhaps you'd like to buy some ; I get it cheap. It's capital quality, and very wide. Shall I bring you some ? You won't get it for the same price down town.

Madame P. Very well ; I'll look at it.

Paul. How much money have you hoarded up, old hag ?

Pereshivkina. " Old hag," now, is it !

Paul. Why, dear me ! You're not thinking of getti· married, are you ?

Pereshivkina. It's not right of you, sir, to speak t like that ! I'm an old woman ; and I have carried y it's my arms.

Paul. She's going to get offended now ; that'll that ?· next thing.　　　　　　　　　　　　　　　　　　he

Madame P. Let her alone, my dear.

Pereshivkina. Never mind, little mother, never mind. Let him do as he likes, he was always such a one to joke. When he was quite a little fellow he set my cap on fire behind.

Paul. Ah ! so you haven't forgotten.

Pereshivkina. Not I. Why, you burnt off all my hair, and even my face got scorched. But you needn't laugh at me, sir. Maybe I shall come in useful to you yet.

Paul. Why, what use can I make of you ? Stick you up in the kitchen garden for a scarecrow ?

Pereshivkina. Maybe I can do you a better service than that, Pàvel Petròvich—who knows ? Little mother, you won't get angry with my nonsense, will you ? Maybe, after all, I shall say something worth hearing before I've done.

Madame P. Well, what is it?

Pereshivkina. There's a lady I know—Serafima Kàrpovna, her name is. She always allows me into her house. You see how it is, little mother. Her people are in trade, but she's been married to a very grand gentleman—Mr. Aslàmevich. He was an official, you know. Why, little mother, he was a general once.

Paul (laughing). How did that happen?

Pereshivkina. Why, this way, sir. The general where he served was away for a holiday, so he was general for a whole month.

Paul. I daresay! Well, let's hear some more lies.

Pereshivkina. It's the truth I'm telling you, sir. They were only married one year, and now she's been a widow more than a year. . . . But you won't be angry with me, mother?

Madame P. Well, go on!

Pereshivkina. She's just a beauty to look at; and very and kind—and then so modest! It's quite wonderful. And she's saving, too, and doesn't throw away her money on dresses and foolery.

Paul. That's to say, she's miserly.

Pereshivkina. No, no, not miserly, only saving—just a careful housewife. Now, you see, the dowry that she had when she was married all belongs to her. She's got a hundred and fifty thousand in money alone.

Paul. A hundred and fifty thousand!

Pereshivkina. I saw it myself, sir. She's got all the notes in her dressing-case; I saw her count it. Dear me, what a silly old woman I am! You'd much better tell me to hold my tongue, or it'll get me into trouble. She's a good woman, and she's been kind to me, but all the same she's not the first thing in the world to me. I don't want you to be angry with me because of her.

Madame P. and *Paul.* Never mind: go on, go on!

Pereshìvkina. Well, I'll tell you, if you wish it. You see, little mother, it's like—well, you know how it is with women. . . . She's young, and she's been a widow for over a year, and so you see . . . and don't think I'm telling you lies—I'd count it a sin. I always wished you well, madame; I haven't forgotten! Of course, I'm only a poor woman, but all the same, I don't forget kindnesses. And if ever I can do you a service——

Paul. There, there! (*With an impatient gesture.*)

Madame P. Well, but go on.

Pereshìvkina. Yes, little mother. Well, you see, she's a near neighbour of yours—it's the white stone house on the left-hand side. Pàvel Petròvich often passes.

Madame P. Well, what of that?

Pereshìvkina (whispers). She's fallen in love.

Madame P. What?

Pereshìvkina (louder). She's fallen in love. Yes; it's quite true.

Madame P. Well, what is there wonderful in that? You're very simp.., my good woman. How could she help falling in love with him? She's not the only one!

Pereshìvkina. Oh! of course, of course, ma'am. Only, you see, she's rich.

Paul (sings). "La Donna e mobile."

Pereshìvkina. "Oustìnya Filimònovna," says she, "I'm in love." So I asked her, "With who, little mother?" "You look," says she, "he'll pass in a minute." So I looked out of the window, and there was Pàvel Petròvich going past, and she says to me, "That's he," says she. You could have knocked me down with a feather.

Paul (sings). "La Donna e mobile."

Pereshìvkina. Of course Pàvel Petròvich must look at her himself, and see whether he likes her. And if you feel any doubt you might go to the Warden Council and see that the money's all right; there's no harm in making sure.

Love's all very well, but money's money. You see, it's for all your life.

Paul (goes up to his mother). *Maman.* I'm going for a walk.

Madame P. Good-bye, my dear. (*Kisses his forehead.*)

Paul (whispers). Try your hardest. (*Exit.*)

Madame P. You see, my dear Oustinya Filimonòvna, it's not a very great stroke of fortune for my Paul that some Madame Aslàmevich has fallen in love with him. However, if he sees her she may possibly take his fancy. . . . Of course, for my part, I shall make no difficulties, although she's only from the merchant class. . . . All I care for is his happiness. (*Rises.*) Come with me : I'll tell the servants to give you some tea. . . . Only I beg you to behave with discretion.

Pereshivkina. Little mother, I'd as soon—— (*Exeunt.*)

PICTURE II.

DRAMATIS PERSONÆ.

Karp Kàrpych Tolstogoràzdov, *merchant; short, fat, grey haired.*

Oulìta Nikìtishna, *his wife; an elderly woman, without any noteworthy characteristics.*

Serafìma Kàrpovna, *Tolstogoràzdov's daughter; widow; tall, slender, remarkably handsome; walk and gestures of boarding-school girl; often meditates; sighs and lifts her eyes to heaven when she speaks of love; also when she counts her money; and sometimes without any reason.*

Matryòna, *maid-servant; distant connection of the Tolstogoràzdov's, a young girl; plump, exquisitely white skin, red cheeks, black eyes and brows. Costume: Pelisse, ornamental chemise, with muslin sleeves, and coins woven into plait of hair.*

First Coachman, *Tolstogoràzdov's.*

Second Coachman, *Serafìma's.*

Courtyard, gallery of house, right. Garden in back-ground. Stables, &c., left. Two doors : one into cellar, one into hay-loft.

Scene I. In Courtyard.

(First Coachman *sits on cellar steps. Enter* Matryóna.)

First Coachman (*sings, falsetto*).
> " In my youth I knew of naught but pleasure,
>   Gold had I to spare and give ;—
>   Now my joys are vanished with my treasure,
>   As a wretched slave I live."

Matryóna. The master and mistress have waked up ; you might carry in the samovar, Ivànych.

First C. Oh ! you're a fine lady, I suppose. Why, you've got so fat that one can't pinch you anywhere ; just as if you'd been hammered on an anvil. (*Sings.*)
> " Who has known a captive's sorrow ?
>   Who shall tell its bitterness ? "

Matryóna. Talk about me being fat ! Why, your own cheeks are blown out like wind-bags ! Can't you take in the samovar when I ask you?

First C. Come again to-morrow. (*Sings.*)
> " In my youth I knew of naught but pleasure,
>   Gold had I to spare and give——"

Matryóna. Wait a bit ! I'll tell Oulita Nikitishna that you're an idle fellow, and one never can get you to do any-thing.

First C. I'm the coachman ; do you understand that ? I have my own work to do. And what are you ? A beggarly fine lady ! If you go so fine, you'll freeze your stockings. So you can just carry the samovar yourself.

Matryóna. Why, the thing weighs twelve stone, man ; how can a girl carry it?

First C. All I have to say is—it's not my business.

Matryóna. Then you're a brazen, shameless fellow ! A girl may break her back, for all you care !

(*Lifts samovar with great difficulty, and carries it to gallery, turning her head away from the steam.*)

First C. (*calls after her*).   Don't romp in your earrings, the gilding will come off!

MATRYONA: "THEN YOU'RE A BRAZEN, SHAMELESS FELLOW!   A GIRL MAY BREAK HER BACK, FOR ALL YOU CARE."

Matryóna (*going up steps: looks back*).   Impertinence! (*Puts samovar on table.*)

First C. (sings).

"Who has known a captive's sorrow?
Who shall tell its bitterness?"

Enter on gallery KARP KÀRPYCH *and* OULÌTA NIKÌTISHNA.
COACHMAN *stops singing, and exit.*)

SCENE II. ON GALLERY.

(KARP KÀRPYCH *and* OULÌTA NIKÌTISHNA *sit down at
table.*)

Oulìta (makes tea). Moiré antique is all the fashion now.
Karp. What do you mean by moiré antique?
Oulìta. It's a kind of material.
Karp. Well, it's all one to me.
Oulìta. Yes; I was only thinking. . . . Supposing Serafimochka were to marry, I really think I'd have a dress made of it. . . . All the ladies are wearing it.
Karp. And you call yourself a lady?
Oulìta. Well, what else am I?
Karp. You might have found out by now that I can't bear to hear you call yourself a lady. I hate the word!
Oulìta. What's the matter with the word? There's nothing—(*hesitates*)—nothing to be ashamed of.
Karp. If I don't like it, that's enough, I suppose!
Oulìta. Well, Serafimochka's a lady, anyway.
Karp. Of course she is! She's had learning; and she was married to a gentleman. But what are you? You were always a goodwife like any other. And now, just because your husband's got rich, you must be a lady! Climb on your own feet if you want to be so high!
Oulìta. No, no! But all the same . . . you know——
Karp. If I tell you to hold your tongue, that's enough. (*Silence.*)
Oulìta. When was that battle fought?

Karp. What battle?

Oulita. Why, lately, you know. Don't you remember?

Karp. And what about it?

Oulita. Such a lot of common soldiers got made into officers.

Karp. Why not? They weren't women. Everybody gets a fair reward for his services.

Oulita. But, do you know, there's a pedlar woman that comes here; and she says that, when her nephew passes his examination, she'll be made a noble too.

Karp. When the sky rains potatoes!

Oulita. But they say there are countries where they have women for soldiers.

Karp (laughs). Life Guards, no doubt! (*Silence.*)

Oulita. They say it's sinful to drink tea.

Karp. What do you mean by that?

Oulita. Because it comes from a heathen country.

Karp. Heaps of things come from heathen countries.

Oulita. No; it's quite true; now, bread grows on Christian soil, and we eat it at the proper time; but when do we drink tea? People go to mass, and we sit drinking tea; now its vesper-time, and here we are drinking tea. So you see it's a sin.

Karp. Well, then, drink it at the proper time.

Oulita. Yes; but still——

Karp. Yes; but still, hold your tongue. You haven't much of a headpiece, but you're very fond of talking. Just hold your tongue! (*Silence.*)

Oulita. How lucky our Serafimochka is! She married a gentleman, and that made her a lady; and now that she's a widow, she's still a lady. Supposing she should marry a prince now, perhaps she'll be a princess.

Karp. Only through her husband.

Oulita. Well, now, if she were to marry a prince, what should I be? Surely, something; she's my child.

Karp. It's enough to addle one's head to talk half an hour with you! I wanted to think about business, and here you keep worrying me with your chattering and non-sense. Life isn't long enough to hear all you women have got to say; I think the quickest way will be for you to hold your tongue! (*Meditates. Silence. Enter* MATRYÒNA, *hurriedly.*)

Matryòna. Oulìta Nikìtishna! Little mother! Serafìma Kàrpovna has come.

Oulìta. Goodness gracious! (*Rises hastily, and exit with* MATRYÒNA.)

Karp. If one didn't manage one's women by fear, there'd be no doing anything with them at all. They've got their own business; and yet nothing will satisfy them but to interfere in other people's. And to see the way a woman will get round her husband, to make him tell her all his affairs and secrets, and work on him with her beauty and her cunning ways, and make eyes at him; and it's all nothing but ruin and destruction. And if you tell them your affairs, they interfere, and lead you astray, and make you do everything their way instead of your own. Many men have gone to ruin through women. Of course, a young, inexperienced man can be led away by their beauty; but when a man has reached years of discretion, and grown serious and wise, a woman's beauty is nothing to him at all, it only disgusts him.

SCENE III. IN THE COURTYARD.

(*Enter* FIRST *and* SECOND COACHMAN.)

Second C. Why, there's no comparing it; you're a thousand times better off. If you knew what my mistress is like! She's more of a Jew than a lady; she measures the very oats out herself. (*Exeunt into stable. Enter on gallery* OULÌTA, SERAFÌMA, *and* MATRYÒNA.)

SCENE IV. ON GALLERY.

(KARP KÀRPYCH. OULÌTA sits down at her place and pours out tea. SERAFÌMA, in hat and cloak, with parasol and green gloves. MATRYÒNA places on table a figured china cup which she has brought from the room, and stands a little way off.)

Serafìma. Good evening, papa. (*Goes up to him. They kiss.*)

Karp. Good evening. Sit down, my girl.

Serafìma (*sits down*). And where's my brother, Onesime?

Karp. Where's Onesime? Off on the spree. He's been playing the devil for five days.

Serafima. And Anna Vlàsyevna?

Karp. Well, you see, whatever we do, we can't make Onesìme leave off drinking. So your mother has sent your sister round to the prisons to give out white bread; so perhaps God will forgive us.

Oulìta. Yes, yes; I sent her to take round white rolls to the prisoners. . . . You know they've most of them got into trouble for nothing. . . .

Karp. Oho! For nothing? They're to rob and murder to their heart's content, and not get locked up for it!

Oulìta. Well, but the robbers and murderers are in the great prison; what do people get put into the jail for?

Karp. For debt.

Oulìta. It's all very well to talk about debt; they say Kòn Kònych is in jail for interest.

Karp. For what—interest?

Oulìta. Yes, indeed; for interest. And it's not right! What a man borrows, he should give back; but interest is a sin.

Karp. Going to begin your chattering again, now! (OULÌTA *pours out tea;* MATRYÒNA *carries cup on tray to* SERAFÌMA; *she takes it with her gloves on.*)

Oulìta. Serafìmoushka, you'd better take off your hat and cloak; and you might as well unlace your dress at the back; there are no strangers here. Matryòna will do it for you.

Serafima. Oh! mamma, how *can* you? I don't feel the heat. I just came to you for a minute to ask your advice.

Karp (blowing on his saucer). What about?

Serafima. I want to marry.

Oulìta (clasping her hands). Good gracious!

Karp. Well, why not? Why shouldn't she? You might do worse. . . .

Oulìta (shaking her head, and folding both hands on her breast). My beauty!

Karp. Who is the man? I should like to hear that.

Serafima. He's quite a young man, papa; he serves in the Law Court; and, I ought to tell you, he's not well off. I wouldn't marry a poor man, only that I am so very much in love with him. (*Raises eyes to heaven; sighs, and meditates.*)

Oulíta (*clasping her hands*). Dear heart!

Karp. And who is he?

Serafima. His name is Prèzhnev. He's a noble, of good family; and may get a good situation. I've thought it over; you see, I have my own fortune. If I am careful with the money, there will be enough for me and a husband. I am willing to deny myself many things rather than live without him. (*Raises eyes to heaven, and sighs.*)

Karp. Perhaps there's something remarkable about him?

Serafima. I haven't heard of anything at all.

Karp. Well, Serafima, my girl, remember one thing: you're a cut-off twig; I shan't give you any more money; so mind you don't run through what you've got.

Oulíta. The other one was old; but you say this one's young, so very likely you may have children; you must keep the money for them.

Serafima. With my character, I can't squander my money. (*Gives cup to* MATRYÒNA.)

Karp. Hm!——You say he's young; and you're a widow, not a girl; I doubt you'll feel a bit ashamed before your husband; he'll just make a fool of you and get hold of your money.

Serafima (*takes cup from* MATRYÒNA). Do you think that men love only for money? (*Raises eyes to heaven, and sighs.*)

Karp. Why, what did you suppose? Everybody knows that.

Serafima (*suddenly waking out of meditation*). I won't give him any money.

Karp. That's right; that's capital; you do as I told you.

Serafima. Of course I will, papa. You needn't think I'm going to be silly.

Karp. We're going to have a wedding too, soon. Matryóna was found in the garden with one of the shopmen; so I'm going to marry them. (MATRYÓNA *hides her face in her sleeve.*) I shall give him a thousand roubles, and have the wedding at my cost.

Oulíta. It's all very well for you to get up weddings; you just want a chance to have a drunken spree.

Karp. Well, what now?

Oulíta. Nothing.

Karp (*sternly*). No; you say what you mean.

Oulíta. Nothing; really nothing.

Karp (*very sternly*). No; I will have you speak out; I want to hear.

Oulíta. There's no use speaking when you never listen.

Karp. What should I listen for? It's not worth while when *you* talk. Ah-h-h-, Oulíta Nikítishna! (*Threatens with his finger.*) You were told to hold your tongue! I want the lass to feel what I'm doing for her; and here you come in with your chattering! . . . (MATRYÓNA *hides her face with the other sleeve.*) She's only my second cousin twice removed, and yet I give her a dowry. I'm the benefactor of all my kindred. There's another little one; I shall take her in Matryóna's place, and bring her up, and settle her in life. (*Silence.*)

Oulíta. Are you quite sure he will love you, my dear?

Serafima. Why not, mamma? There's nothing objectionable in my character. The only thing is . . . when I was at boarding-school they used to say that I had no comprehension of music whatsoever, and that I was dreamy, and given to meditating about nothing; and then, I'm very fond of sweets — perhaps he won't notice that though.

There is one thing more : I'm very bad at counting silver money——

Karp. Oh. that's nothing ! You'll soon get into it.

Serafima. Perhaps he won't like my being economical; but then, how could I manage otherwise? I only try to live within my income, and not run into my capital. What should I be without capital? I should have no value at all !

Karp. Of course not !

Serafima. And I know how to add up interest—on paper : I was taught that at boarding-school. I can't do it without paper, though. (*Meditates.*)

Oulita. What are you thinking about, child ? . . . Why, what a silly I am ! It's not much wonder that you think, poor girl ! Such a change in your life ! And there's no telling beforehand how it'll turn out.

Serafima. No, mamma, it's not that. I've just been buying some ribbon—seven ells at eighty kopecks, paper money ; and I was just thinking how much that would be in silver money, and how much change I ought to have from three roubles. (*Takes out purse and looks into it.*)

Karp. Rouble sixty kopecks—one rouble forty change.

Serafima. Are you sure, papa?

Karp. Why, bless the girl, what else could it be ?

Serafima (puts back purse). All right.

Oulita. Are you sure he doesn't drink ?

Karp. There you are again ! Everybody drinks nowadays.

Oulita. I mean, you'd better ask what he's like when he's drunk.

Karp. Ah ! that's another matter !

Oulita. Because, you know, some people are so quiet in drink that it really doesn't matter. It's just as if they weren't drunk.

Serafima. All right, mamma ; I'll ask. I must go now.

Oulìta. Oh, no! You mus'n't, indeed; stop a bit. You're so fond of sweet things. . . . We've got some splendid fruit. Run and fetch it, Matryòna; it's on my bedroom window-sill. (MATRYÒNA *goes out, comes back with fruit, offers it to* SERAFÌMA, *and then places it on table.*) Take some, dear child; take some. Won't you have some liqueur?

Serafìma. Really, mamma!

Oulìta. Have a glass of beer, darling.

Serafìma. You know I never drink it.

Oulìta. Well then, mead?

Serafìma. I can't, really.

Oulìta. Jam, then?

Serafìma. I'll have some jam.

Oulìta (*taking keys out of pocket*). Go to the store-room, Matryòna, and bring me two kinds.

Serafìma. And tell my coachman to bring the carriage round.

(MATRYÒNA *crosses stage, and exit.*)

Oulìta. Have some more fruit, Serafimoushka. (SERAFÌMA *takes some.*) Won't you have any, Karp Kàrpych?

Karp. What next? As if I were going to eat all sorts of rubbish now! Put some aside for me, and have the rest cleared away. I'll eat an orange with my brandy. (OULÌTA *eats fruit. Silence.*)

SCENE V. IN THE COURTYARD.

Matryòna (*crosses stage with two plates, goes up to stable-door, and pushes it with her foot*). Here, you ragamuffins! (*Enter* COACHMEN *from stable.*) Bring the horses round; Madame wants to go.

Second C. You see, at that time, my master was angry with me about something, and wanted to sell me for a soldier.

First C. Bless my soul!

Second C. So you see, my dear fellow, I'd got my head just full of the war, and never talked about anything but war with every man I met. And I got so worked up in my feelings like, that I was ready to go at the Circassians themselves.

First C. I've got a neighbour here, a friend of mine; he's an officer's servant, and he was with his master in the Hungarian campaign; and you should just hear what he can tell about the Austrians!

Second C. What about them?

First C. Why, my good fellow, they told him beforehand, with the Frenchmen standing by—there were Frenchmen, you know—"Do you think you can stand against me? If I choose, I'll tear you in pieces."

Second C. And they can do it too!

First C. Ah! that they can!

Second C. Because they're so strong, you see!

First C. Nothing can stand against them. It's like when they had the militia . . . eleven *vershkov* high, and could lift fifteen *poods*. And there they'd advance on you! Then, bang, bang, bang goes the big drum, and they all shout, Forwards! March! Treason! And there they come on and on, and what can you do?

Second C. In course they must get the better of them; that's plain.

First C. You see, the one that wins, that'll be which ever is strongest.

Matryóna. I'm perfectly tired of hearing you. You're fine soldiers . . . do your fighting sitting by the oven. War can't be such a very dreadful thing after all.

First C. (glances sideways at MATRYÓNA *with absolute contempt).* Brazen hussy!

Matryóna. Madame's waiting; do you hear?

Second C. (hangs whip on right arm. and gives left hand to First C.). Good-bye!

First C. Good-bye, my lad! (*Exit behind house.* MA-
TRYÒNA *goes on to gallery.*)

SCENE VI. ON THE GALLERY.

Oulìta. Serafìmoushka! I'd almost forgotten! There's
one more thing you must certainly do; now mind you
don't forget. When you've found out all about your lover,
and are sure he's not a spendthrift, or a drunkard, or a
gambler, go to the wise woman, Paràsha. You must go
in quietly, and ask: "Will God's servant, Serafìma, be
happy with God's servant"——what's his name?
Serafìma. Paul.
Oulìta. "With God's servant, Paul?" And whatever
she tells you, do accordingly.
Karp. Don't you do anything of the kind.
Oulìta. Look here, Karp Kàrpych, I always obey you
in everything; but this is not your business; it's woman's
business! Don't listen to him, Serafìmoushka; do as I tell
you. I'm your mother; I shan't advise you wrong.
Serafìma. Very well. (*Rises.*) Good-bye, mamma;
good-bye, papa. (*Kisses them.*)
Karp. And listen here! You tell your lover that, if he
behaves to me respectfully and properly, I'll give him a
good fur cloak; and if he doesn't, I'll take it away again.
(*Exeunt.*)

PICTURE III.[1]

DRAMATIS PERSONÆ.

PAUL.
SERAFÌMA, *his wife.*
MADAME PRÈZHNEV.
A PERSON UNKNOWN, *a friend of Paul, middle-aged, with Greek profile and gloomy expression of face.*
A MAID-SERVANT.
A FOOTMAN.

(A richly-furnished study. PAUL sits at the table writing. Enter FOOTMAN.)

Foot. Pàvel Petròvich, the tailor and carriage-builder are waiting.

Paul (turning round). Send them off!

Foot. They won't go, sir.

Paul. Then tell them to come next week.

Foot. I told them; but they won't go.

Paul. You surely don't expect me to come out and speak to them myself? Tell them anything you like. You see I'm busy. You're always disturbing me; be off with you!

Foot. There's a gentleman that asks to see you too, sir.

Paul. Turn him out too.

(The person unknown comes in at the door. The FOOTMAN sees him, and exit.)

Unknown. Turn Nature out at the door, she'll come in at the window.

Paul (rises). Oh! my dear fellow: I didn't know it was you; I really beg your pardon.

Unknown. No; you didn't know. *(Inspects Paul from head to foot; then begins examining the room.)*

[1] Interval of one month between the Second and Third Pictures.

Paul. Indeed I didn't know. You don't suppose I should have refused to see you?

Unknown (sits down). There, that'll do, that'll do.

Paul. Won't you have a cigar?

Unknown (smiling ironically). A cigar? And when am I to have the money?

Paul. Very soon now.

Unknown. Which do you mean by that—now? or very soon?

Paul. Soon; quite soon.

Unknown. You'll pay it soon? (*Looks intently at* PAUL.) And supposing I don't believe you?

Paul. How can you help believing, when the document is in your hands?

Unknown. That's just it! The date in the document is up; and all this is not yours, but your wife's.

Paul. That's all the same.

Unknown. No; not all the same.

Paul. Well, then, what do you want?

Unknown. I'll tell you. Either you give me all the money to-morrow, or else we'll re-write the document.

Paul. Certainly. We'll re-write it now if you like.

Unknown. No; we'll re-write it to-morrow; only then your wife must sign her name as security.

Paul. What for?

Unknown. Oh! well, the broker will know what for; otherwise I shall simply go to law. (*Rises.*)

Paul. All right; all right.

Unknown. Mind, then, to-morrow. (*Goes to door.*) You're not thinking of getting out of it anyway, are you? You can't do that with me. (*Exit.*)

Paul. This sort of thing is really quite annoying! Here I am, as rich as you please, and yet I can't get any money. I shall have to ask my wife for it; it's all the same now whether the money is her's or mine; we have everything in common. It's even better that it should be in my hands. And what is the use of my putting it off so long? I only get more and more entangled.

(*Enter* SERAFÌMA. PAUL *writes.*)

Serafìma. Leave off, Paul! Don't write! (*Embraces him. He leaves off writing.*) I am so happy! so happy! What have I done to deserve such happiness! (*Meditates.*) I have abundance of everything; I have such a dear husband! (*Kisses him.*) So handsome! so clever! only one thing distresses me : you are out so much. Now that we are married, you ought to be always with me; I believe I should love you still more then.

Paul. It's impossible, my love; I have the office.

Serafìma. Are you going to-day?

Paul. Yes; it's time for me to start now.

Serafìma. Take me with you.

Paul. Where? To the Senate House?

Serafìma. Yes; why not?

Paul. What things you say! How could I ?

Serafìma. It's always, " I can't " with you ! You simply don't love me ; that's why you don't want to take me. If you loved me, you'd take me ! You'd say to every one, " This is my wife." You'll never have cause to be ashamed of me ; I was educated at a boarding-school.

Paul. If you don't believe me, ask any one you like whether men take their wives to Government offices.

Serafìma. They don't take us because they don't love us ; they would take us if they did. If you men loved us as we love you, you'd fulfil every whim we have. We're ready to do everything in the world for you ; and you don't care to do the merest trifle for us.

Paul. I, too, am willing to do anything you ask; only this is impossible.

Serafima. Well then, at least do me one kindness: don't go to-day; stop with me.

Paul (shrugs his shoulders). All right, if you like!

Serafima. No! Do you really mean you won't go?

Paul. I won't go, if you wish me not to.

Serafima. Dear Paul! How good you are! How you spoil me! What is there in the world I wouldn't do for you! Now tell me—tell me what you would like! you must tell me! (*Caresses him.*) Ask me for anything you like—anything—anything in the world! Come now, tell me what you would like; I'll drive straight into town and buy it for you.

(*Enter* MAID-SERVANT.)

Maid. If you please, ma'am, the dressmaker has come.

Serafima. Paul, dear Paul! I will come back in a minute. (*Exit.*)

Paul. What extraordinary fancies she has sometimes! I really can't make out whether it's from stupidity or from love for me. For that matter, it's a very good thing that she's so much in love with me. The idea of her asking me what I want! What I want? Why, money, of course. It seems it's quite a true saying that women's hearts are much tenderer than ours. I confess I used not to believe that; but now I see that, once love has taken a firm hold upon them, you can get anything you like out of them. . . . And then, she's so pretty! Even if you look at it from quite another point of view—it's delightful, there certainly is nothing else to be said about it. . . . I'd better ask her for a big sum at once; I must take advantage of her momentary exaltation. (*Re-enter* SERAFIMA.) Ah! Serafima! I wanted to speak to you.

Serafima. And I wanted to speak to you, Paul.

Paul. Very well; what is it?

Serafima. No, you speak first.

Paul. No, you, Serafima.

Serafima. No, you.

Paul. I give the precedence to you, as a lady, Serafima.

Serafima. This is what I wanted to say, my Paul: you change your shirt every day; that is rather extravagant.

Paul. Are you gone off your head! You can't call that an extravagance, in our position! No; I wanted to talk to you about something altogether different.

Serafima. All the same, my dear (*kisses him*), we must think about economy; there's nothing unreasonable in that.

Paul. Forgive me, Serafima! I understand you, my love; indeed it is a good thing that you are economical in trifles. Trifles are an important matter in life. I am glad that I have found in you such a house-wife. But I want to speak to you about more serious business.

Serafima. About what, Paul? No, no, stop! Why should we talk about business? We haven't done talking about love, yet. We have nothing to do, now, as you didn't go to the office. Why should we talk about business? Let us talk about love! (*Sighs, and raises eyes to heaven.*)

Paul. We can talk about love afterwards, whenever you like; but I must speak about business now.

Serafima. Ah! Paul! you have stayed at home with me. Indeed I don't want to think of anything else now!

Paul. No, Serafima; I really must have a serious talk with you.

Serafima (*a little offended*). Well, what is it you want?

Paul. How do you wish to employ your capital?

Serafima. What a question! I don't want to employ it anyhow. It can stop in the Council,[1] and we'll live on the interest.

Paul. But the interest is very little, my love; we had better put the capital into circulation.

Serafima. Into what circulation?

Paul. We might buy an estate, for instance.

[1] Warden's Council.

Serafima. No, no, no! Not for the world! What estate?

Paul. Why, a village in some good fertile province—Orèl, or somewhere there.

Serafima. Not for anything on earth! The peasants won't pay; the village may burn down; or the crops will fail five years running; what should we do then?

Paul. Crops don't fail five years running.

Serafima. But they may do; you're not a prophet, you know.

Paul. Well then, let's buy a house and put in tenants.

Serafima. But the tenants won't pay.

Paul. How do you mean, they won't pay? One can prosecute if they don't.

Serafima. And if the house burns down?

Paul. We must insure it.

Serafima. Then invaders will come and destroy everything! No, no, not for the world!

Paul. Well, well, we won't talk any more about it.

Serafima. Think of it yourself; you're a young man still; we may have children.

Paul. Of course we shall have children; but what of that? The more money we get, the more there will be for the children.

Serafima. No, no; I don't want even to hear about it, or I shall only get miserable; you mus'n't put me out. What's the use of circulation? We can live as we are; we have enough of everything. (*Meditates.*) You are free to-day; you haven't gone to the office. . . . (*Embraces him.*)

Paul (detaching himself from her arms). No, Serafima; as you like, but I must have a talk with you.

Serafima (seriously). What now?

Paul. This, my dear: if you really love me, give me five thousand silver roubles. I need the money pressingly for a certain business. It is a very profitable business, Serafima;

I won't tell you what it is now ; but we may get the amount
doubled, or perhaps even more.   Indeed, I am almost sure
that it will be more.

Serafima.   Five — thousand — silver — roubles !   How
much will that be in paper money ?

Paul.   How should I know ?

Serafima. Stop ; I'll calculate it. (*Takes paper and pencil out of pocket and calculates.*) Ah ! ah ! (*Rushes away.*)

Paul. What can be the matter now ? What's frightened her ? I can't make it out ! Does she suppose I'm going to spend all my life in making love ? That's a good idea ! Is she miserly? or what is it ? I must find out which she loves best—me or money. If she loves me best, the matter can be set right. But if she loves the money best, I've run my neck into a halter.

(*Enter* MADAME PRÉZHNEV.)

Madame P. *Bonjour*, Paul !

Paul. *Bonjour, Maman !*

Madame P. (*sits down.*) I've just been into your wife's room. What is the matter with her? She's crying, and getting ready to go out.

Paul. We've had a little scene.

Madame P. Oh, Paul ! already ? So soon after the wedding ! Did you do anything to hurt her feelings? Woman is such a frail and tender creature.

Paul. Why the devil should I hurt her feelings? I only asked her for money.

Madame P. Were you gentle enough with her ?

Paul. Why, dear me, I've been spooning with her a whole month, like a turtle-dove. (*Bursts out laughing.*) I never once asked her for money till just now. First of all, she got as sentimental as you please : " Ask anything you like ; I'll do anything in the world for you ; I'll go straight to town and buy whatever you want." What should she buy me?—a china poodle? or a hussar in sugar? Well, directly I asked her for five thousand, she just screamed and ran away . . . and now she's in tears ! The deuce knows what to make of it !

Madame P. She has no heart, my dear. Women are

ready to give up everything on earth for the man they love. No, my Paul, she is no woman.

Paul. Oh, she's a woman all right enough; only she won't give the money.

Madame P. Oh, Paul! I am convinced that she will appreciate you in time, and will come to love you so much, so much (*with enthusiasm*) that she will entirely give into your keeping both herself and—and all her possessions.

Paul Yes; but she hasn't done it yet; and I can't wait.

Madame P. Wait a little, Paul! Think what bliss awaits you in the future. (*Enter* MAID-SERVANT *and gives* PAUL. *letter and pocket-book.*)

Paul. What is that?

Maid. Madame has gone away in the carriage, and told me to give you these. (*Exit.*)

Paul. A pocket-book! That's good! (*Puts it in pocket.*)

Madame I I told you so!

Paul. Now let's read the letter. (*Reads.*) "DEAR PAUL —Much as I love you, we must separate. My heart will bleed all my life; and I shall weep for you day and night. I wish to go and live with my papa, like a prisoner, and bewail my fate; and I shall sell this house. You will never see me any more. I love you with all my soul; but you showed me to-day that you love me for my money's sake. In our merchant class, it is not the custom to give away one's money. Of what significance shall I be, if I have no money? I shall be of no importance at all! If I have no money, and I love a man, he will not love me. But if I have money, and I love any one, he will love me, and we shall be happy. I made a pocket-book for your birthday, and embroidered it myself, and as I hoped that a present from me would be a great pleasure to you, I send it to you now. Don't ever come to my papa's house; he is very passionate, and will be very angry with you when he knows all about it; and I cannot conceal anything. Farewell, Paul! When you are in need of money I shall always be glad to give you help without letting my relatives know; but only small sums—a hundred roubles, not more. Be happy. I shall pass all my life in tears. Yours for ever, SERAFÌMA." What in the world is this? It's so extraordinary that I can't even believe it. I expect she's joking, or wants to frighten me. Let's see, though, what there is in this pocket-book. I daresay there's something in it. (*Takes out pocket-book.*)

Madame P. I am almost sure of it, Paul. No doubt she wanted to give you a surprise.

Paul. It's a charming little pocket-book. (*Opens and examines it.*) Empty!

Madame P. Look; perhaps there's a secret compart-ment.

Paul. Here's the secret compartment, but there's nothing in it either. (*Enter* FOOTMAN.) What do you want?

Foot. Sir, sir, I never heard of such a thing! They've taken away the fur cloak!

Paul. What fur cloak?

Foot. Yours, sir! Madame told us to put it in the carriage with her, and took it away. Anyoûtka and I held out as long as we could; but what could we do? I really don't know what to think of it!

Paul. Mamma, that's more than a joke.

Foot. It's a disgrace, sir! I've been in service for many years (*clasps his hands*), but I never saw such a thing, never! Paul Petròvich! Think of it!

Paul. There, get along with you!

Foot. And to have to say such a thing to people! It's enough to make one die for shame. I never heard of such a thing, *never!* (*Exit.*)

Paul. (*Sits down and looks fixedly at his mother*). *Maman!*

Madame P. Women have no hearts nowadays, no hearts at all.

Paul. Permit me, *Maman*, to thank you, now, for two things : firstly, for squandering my fortune ; and, secondly, for bringing me up in such a way that I am fit for nothing. I only know how to spend money. And where is the money to spend? Where? (*Passionately.*) Where is the money? Give it to me! You liked to see me, at eight years old, in a velvet tunic, dancing better than all the other children in Moscow, and knowing how to make love to the little girls. You liked to see me at sixteen, looking so well on horseback! You looked on proudly when I used to gallop about our ancestral fields with my tutor, your favourite! You enjoyed all that. After such an education, one must have money, if one would play a leading part in our society. Why did you squander everything? Where are our estates gone? Where are our peasants gone? What is to become of us now? Now, perhaps, you will have the pleasure of seeing me dismissed from the service, a vagrant, a card-sharper, and maybe even worse! What am I to do? I can't marry again, with a wife living! (*Covers his face with his hands.*)

CURTAIN FALLS.

A MADMAN'S DIARY.

October 3rd.

AN extraordinary circumstance happened to-day. I got up rather late, and when Mavra brought me my boots I asked her what time it was. Hearing that it was long past ten I dressed hurriedly. I confess I did not want to go to the Department at all, knowing beforehand what black looks I should get from the chief of our division. For some time he's taken to saying to me, "What ever sort of rot have you always got in your head now, man? Sometimes you tear about like a possessed creature; sometimes you muddle the papers so that the very devil couldn't make them out; you write the titles without capital letters, and leave out all the dates and numbers!" Hang the fellow! He's envious, of course, because I sit in the director's study and mend his excellency's pens. In short, I shouldn't have gone to the Department at all if I hadn't hoped to meet the treasurer, and, perhaps, get the confounded Jew to give me, anyway, a little of my salary in advance. I never came across such a creature! For him to ever advance one the money a single month—why, doomsday will come before that happens! You can beg him, entreat him—however hard up you are the old grey devil won't give it you. And yet at home his own cook boxes his ears. She does—everybody knows that. I can't understand what advantage it is to serve in the Department. There are no resources whatsoever. Now, in the Provincial Administration, or in the Common Courts, or Court of Exchequer—that's quite another thing; there sometimes you'll see a fellow squeezed up in the corner writing away, in a shabby old coat, and such a fright to look at, and yet see what a nice little villa he rents! You can't offer him a gilded china cup, for instance; he'll say, "That's a doctor's present." No, you must give him a pair of carriage horses, or a fine sledge, or beaver fur worth three hundred roubles. He'll look as meek as meek can be, and talk so sweetly—"May I trouble you to lend me your penknife?" and then he'll fleece you—till he leaves nothing but the shirt on your back. It's true, though, our service is more genteel—everything's so clean, the tables are of red wood, and all the directors say "you." Indeed, but that it's a genteel service, I'd have left the Department long ago.

I put on my old cloak and took my umbrella because it was pouring with rain. There was no one in the streets; I saw nothing but a few women with shawls over their heads and some Russian shopkeepers with umbrellas. There was no one of the upper classes about except an official like myself. I saw him at a crossing, and said to myself, "Aha! No, my friend, you're not going to the Department; you're running after the woman in front of you and looking at her ankles." What a set of brutes our officials are! They're just as bad as any officer; can't see a woman's hat at all without going for it. Just as I was thinking that, I saw a carriage driving up to a shop I was passing. I knew it at once; it was our director's carriage. "But he wouldn't be going shopping," I thought; "it must be his daughter." I stopped, and leaned against the wall; a footman opened the carriage door, and she sprang out like a bird. How she glanced round with those eyes and brows of hers! Heaven defend me! I am done for! And why ever should she drive out in this pouring rain?

And then people say that women are not devoted to
chiffons! She did not recognise me, and indeed I purposely muffled myself up, because my cloak was very muddy
and old-fashioned too. Now they are worn with deep
capes, and mine had little capes one above the other; and
the cloth wasn't good either. Her lap-dog didn't get in

"I LOOKED ROUND AND SAW TWO LADIES UNDER AN UMBRELLA, AN OLD LADY AND
A YOUNG ONE."

before the shop-door was shut, and was left out in the
street. I know that dog; it is called Medji. The next
minute I suddenly heard a little voice, "Good-morning,
Medji." Why! what the deuce! Who said that? I
looked round and saw two ladies under an umbrella, an
old lady and a young one; but they went past; and sud

denly I heard again, "Oh, for shame, Medji!" What the devil! There were Medji and the ladies' lap-dog smelling each other. "I say," thought I to myself, "I must be drunk!" And yet it is a rare thing with me to be drunk. "No, Fidèle, you are quite mistaken" (I actually saw Medji saying that). "I have been—bow-wow-wow— I have been—bow - wow - wow—very ill." Well, there now! I really was very much surprised to hear the lap-dog talking in human speech. But afterwards, when I thought it over, it didn't astonish me. Indeed, there have been many such cases in the world. It is said that there appeared in England a fish that said two words in such a strange language that the learned men have been three years trying to make out what it said, and can't under-stand it yet. And I remember reading in the newspapers about two cows that went into a shop and asked for a pound of tea. But I was very much more astonished when Medji said, "I wrote to you, Fidèle; Polkàn can't have brought the letter." Well! may I lose my salary if ever I heard in my life that dogs could write! It quite amazed me. Lately, indeed, I have begun to see and hear some-times things that nobody ever saw or heard before. "I'll follow that lap-dog," thought I, "and find out what it is and what it thinks." So I shut up my umbrella and followed the two ladies. They went along Goròkhovaya Street, turned into Myeshchànskaya, then into a carpenter's shop, and at last up to the Kokoushkin Bridge, and there they stopped before a big house. "I know that house," said I to myself; "that's Tvyerkov's house." What a monster! Just to think of the numbers of people that live there—such a lot of strangers, servant maids, and as for my fellow officials, they are packed together like dogs! I have a friend living there who plays the trumpet very well. The ladies went up to the fifth story. "All right," thought I, "I won't go in now, but I will mark the place, and take advantage of the first opportunity."

October 4th.

To-day is Wednesday, so I have been on duty in the director's study. I purposely went early, sat down and mended all the pens. Our director must be a very clever man—all his study is fitted up with bookshelves. I read the titles of several books, but they were all so learned, so fearfully learned, that they are no use for a poor fellow like me; they are all either in French or in German. And just to look at his face! See the importance beaming in his eyes! I have never even heard of his saying an unnecessary word. Only, you know, when you hand him a paper he will ask, "What's the weather like?" "Damp, your excellency." Yes; we are not up to his level; he's a statesman. Nevertheless, I have remarked that he is peculiarly fond of me. Now if only his daughter . . . Confound it all! Never mind; never mind; hush! I began to read *The Little Bee.* What a stupid nation the French are! On my honour, I'd take them and flog them all round. Well, I was reading a charming account of a ball, written by a country squire from Koursk. The Koursk squires write very well. After that I observed that it was half-past twelve, and that the director hadn't come out of his bedroom. But about half-past one there happened an occurrence that no pen can describe. The door opened, and, thinking it was the director, I jumped up with my papers; but it was—She; She herself! Holy saints! how she was dressed! All in white, like a swan, and so gorgeously! And how she looked! like the sunlight, I swear. She bowed to me and said, "Has papa been here?" Aï, aï, aï, what a voice! A perfect canary bird! "Your excellency," I would have said, "have mercy on me. But, if I must die, let me die by your august hand." But, the devil take it, all that would come on to my tongue was, "No, madam." She looked at me; she looked at the books; she dropped her hand·

kerchief. I rushed for it, slipped on the confounded
polished floor, and nearly broke my nose.   Still I managed

"SHE DROPPED HER HANDKERCHIEF. I RUSHED FOR IT, AND SLIPPED ON THE
CONFOUNDED FLOOR."

to get the handkerchief. Heavens and earth! What a
handkerchief! So fine; pure cambric; amber-scented;

exhaling the aroma of high rank. She thanked me, laughed just a little, so that her sweet lips hardly moved, and went away. I waited another hour, and then a lackey came in and said, "You can go home, Aksèntyi Ivànovich. My master has gone out." I cannot endure the footman class; they always lounge about in the ante-room, and don't so much as take the trouble to nod to you. Indeed, that's not all; once, one of these brutes had the insolence to offer me some tobacco without getting up. Why, can't you understand, you stupid flunkey, that I am an official, that I am of noble birth! Nevertheless I took my hat, put on my cloak myself (these gentry never think of helping one), and went out. At home I spent most of the day lying on my bed. Then I copied out some charming verses :—

> "An hour I had not seen my dearest,
>   That hour was as a year to me ;
> Oh life, how hateful thou appearest !
>   Oh let me die and cease to be ! "

They must have been written by Poushkin. In the evening I muffled myself in my cloak, went to her excellency's door-step, and waited long on the chance of seeing her for a moment coming out and getting into her carriage; but she did not come.

November 6th.

I have infuriated the chief of the section. When I came to the Department he called me into his room, and began talking after this fashion, "Now just tell me, my man, what you're after." "How? What? I'm not after anything," said I. "Now, think it over and be reasonable! Why, you're past forty; you ought to have come to years of discretion. What have you got into your head? Do you imagine I don't know all you're up to? Why, you are dangling about after the director's daughter ! Now just look at yourself, and think a minute what you are like.

You know you're a complete nonentity. You know you haven't got a farthing in the world. Look at your face in the looking-glass—how can you think of such a thing?" The devil take it! Just because he has a face something like an apothecary's drug-bottle and one little wisp of hair on his head twisted up into a barber's cock's-comb, and holds up his head and smears it with a bandoline stick, he thinks he must be over everybody. But I understand, I understand perfectly well why he's so angry—he's envious; very likely he has noticed the signs of special favour shown to me. But what do I care for him? How very important —a D.C.L.! He's got a gold watch-chain and pays thirty roubles for his boots—and the devil take him! Does he imagine that I am one of the common people; that I'm the son of a tailor or a corporal? I am a noble! I, too, may rise in the service; I am only forty-two—just the proper age to begin one's career. Wait a bit, my friend! Perhaps we shall be a colonel some day, or higher up than that even, by God's grace; and we'll have a better reputation than yours is. I should like to know what put it into your head that no one can be a decent fellow except yourself. Give me a fashionably cut dress-coat and a fine necktie like yours, and you won't be fit to hold a candle to me. I have no fortune, that's the trouble.

November 8th.

I went to the theatre. They played the Russian fool, *Filátka*, and I laughed heartily. Then there was some sort of vaudeville with very funny verses about lawyers, especially about a certain collegiate registrar. They were written in so free a style that I wondered at the censorship passing them; and about shopkeepers it was said, right out, that they cheat the public, and that their sons are dissipated and always trying to get into the nobility. There was a very comic verse about journalists—

that they are always finding fault, and so the author begs
the public to take his part. Very amusing things are
written nowadays. I love the theatre; whenever I have
a few pence in my pocket I can't resist going. Now, a
good many of our officials are regular pigs; they care no
more about the theatre than if they were peasants. Of
course, if you give them a ticket free, they'll go. One
actress sang very well. I thought of Her. . . . Oh! hang
it all ! . . . Never mind. . . Hush !

November 9th.

At eight o'clock I went to the Department. The chief
of the section pretended not to notice my entrance at all.
For my part, I behaved as if nothing had happened
between us. I looked over a lot of papers, examined
them; and went away at four o'clock. I passed the
director's house, but there was no one to be seen. After
dinner, I lay on my bed most of the time.

November 11th.

To-day I sat in our director's study and mended
twenty-three pens for him, and four pens for Her—aï,
aï—for Her Excellency. He likes there to be plenty of
pens. What a head he must have! He never speaks;
but I suppose he is always thinking over things. I should
like to know what he thinks about most, what is going on in
that head. I should like to see more closely the life of these
grand people; all their little conventionalisms and court
tricks: how they live and what they do in their sphere,—
that is what I should like to know. I have often thought
of getting into conversation with his Excellency; but my
confounded tongue won't do as I want; all I can say is
that the weather's cold or warm—not another thing. I
should like to have a look at that drawing-room that one
sometimes sees the door of open ; and at the room beyond

the drawing-room. How richly it is all furnished. What mirrors, what porcelain! I should like to see the part of the house where Her Excellency lives! Oh! I know where I should like to go! Into her boudoir, where stand all the little toilet-trays and boxes, and flowers that one dare not even breathe upon; and where her dress lies flung down, more like air than a dress. I should like to peep into her bedroom. . . . There must be wonders! There indeed must be Paradise! Only to see the footstool that she steps on when she gets out of bed, when she draws the little stocking on to that snowy foot . . . aï! aï! aï! Never mind; never mind. . . . Hush!

To-day, however, a kind of light broke in upon me; I remembered the conversation between the two lap-dogs that I heard on the Nevsky Prospect. "All right," thought I to myself, "now I'll know everything. I must intercept the letters of those horrid little dogs. Then, of course, I shall find out something." Indeed, I once called Medji to me, and said: "Now look here, Medji, we're quite alone; and, if you like, I'll lock the door, so that no one shall see. Tell me everything you know about your mistress—what she is like, and all about her. I swear to you that I will not repeat it to any one." But the cunning little dog put its tail between its legs, screwed itself all up, and went quietly out of the room as if it hadn't heard anything. I have suspected for a long time that dogs are far cleverer than people; indeed, I felt sure that they can speak, but for some sort of obstinacy. They are wonderfully politic; they notice everything a man does. No; whatever happens, I will go to-morrow to Tvyerkov's house, interrogate Fidèle, and, if possible, seize upon all Medji's letters to her.

November 12th.

At two o'clock in the afternoon I started to find Fidèle and interrogate her. I can't endure cabbage; and all the

little provision shops in Myeshchànskaya Street simply reek
of it; and then there's such a stench from the yard of
every house, that I simply held my nose and ran along as
fast as ever I could. And then those confounded artizans
send out such a lot of soot and smoke from their work-
shops, that really there's no walking in the street. When I
got up to the sixth floor and rang the bell, there came out
a girl, not bad-looking, with little freckles. I recognised
her; it was the same girl who had walked with the old
lady. She grew a bit red, and it flashed upon me at once
—"You want a lover, my dear." "What can I do for
you?" "I must have an interview with your lap-dog." The
girl was stupid; I saw at once she was stupid. At that
moment the dog ran out, barking. I wanted to catch her,
but the nasty little thing nearly snapped my nose off.
However, I saw her basket in the corner. Ah! that was
what I wanted. I went up to it, turned over the straw,
and, to my immense delight, pulled out a little packet of
tiny papers. Seeing that, the horrid little dog first bit me
in the calf of the leg; and then, realising that I had got
the papers, began to whine and fawn on me; but I said,
"No, my dear! Good-bye!" and rushed away. I think
the girl took me for a maniac, for she was terribly
frightened. When I got home I wanted to set to work
at once and read the letters, because my sight is not very
good by candle-light. But of course Mavra had taken it
into her head to wash the floor; these idiotic Finns are
always cleaning at the wrong time. So I went for a walk to
think over the occurrence. Now at last I shall find out
all their affairs, all their thoughts, all the wires they are
pulled by; these letters will disclose everything to me.
Dogs are a clever race, they understand all the political
relations; and so, no doubt, everything will be here—this
man's portrait and all his affairs. And no doubt there
will be something about Her, who . . . Never mind;

silence! In the evening I came home. I spent the time lying on my bed.

November 13th.

Now let us see! The letter is fairly legible; but, somehow or other, there is something a little bit doggish about the handwriting. Let's see :—

MY DEAR FIDÈLE,—I still have not been able to accustom myself to your vulgar name. Why couldn't they find a better name for you? Fidèle, Rosa, what bad taste! However, this is off the point. I am very glad that we have agreed to correspond.

The letter is quite correctly written; there are no mistakes in the stopping, or even in the use of the letter *yat'*. Why, the chief of the section can't write as well as that, although he talks about having been educated in the University. Let's see further on :—

It appears to me that to share our thoughts, feelings, and impressions with another is one of the greatest blessings in the world.

H'm. . . . That idea is cribbed from some work translated from the German; I can't remember the title.

I say this from experience, although I have seen little of the world beyond the gates of our house. My life passes peacefully and joyously. My mistress, whom papa calls Sophie, loves me passionately.

Aï! Aï! Never mind, never mind; silence!

Papa, too, often caresses me. I drink my tea and coffee with cream. Ah! *ma chère*, I must tell you that I cannot understand what pleasure there can be in the big gnawed bones that our Polkán devours in the kitchen. Bones are only good if they are from game, and if no one has sucked the marrow out of them. It is a very good idea to mix several kinds of sauce together, only there must be no capers or herbs; but I know nothing worse than the custom of rolling bread into little balls and giving it to dogs. Some gentleman, sitting at the table, who has been holding all sorts of nasty things in his hands, will begin rolling a bit of bread with his fingers, and then call you and put it in your mouth. It's impolite to refuse, so you eat it, with disgust, of course, but you eat it.

What the deuce is all this rubbish? As if they couldn't find anything better to write about. Let's look at the next page, perhaps it will be more sensible.

I shall have the greatest pleasure in informing you of all that happens in our house. I have already spoken to you about the principal gentleman whom Sophie calls papa. He is a very strange man.

Ah, now, at last! Yes, I knew it. They look at all things from a politic point of view. Let us see what there is about papa :—

. . . Strange man. He hardly ever speaks. But a week ago he kept on constantly saying to himself, "Shall I get it or not?" Once he asked me, "What do you think, Medji? Shall I get it or not?" I didn't understand anything about it, so I smelled at his boot and went away. Then, *ma chère*, a week afterwards papa was in the greatest state of delight. The whole morning long gentlemen in uniform came to him and congratulated him on something or other. At table he was merrier than I have ever seen him before.

Ah! so he's ambitious; I must take note of that.

Good-bye, *ma chère*! I run . . . &c. To-morrow I will finish the letter.
Well, good-morning, I am with you again. To-day my mistress, Sophie.——

Ah! now we shall see—something about Sophie. Oh! confound it! . . . Never mind! never mind! Let's go on :

My mistress, Sophie, was in a great muddle. She was getting ready for a ball, and I was very glad she would be out, so that I could write to you. My Sophie is perfectly devoted to balls, although she nearly always gets cross when she's dressing for them. I cannot conceive, *ma chère*, what can be the pleasure of going to balls. Sophie comes home from them at six o'clock in the morning, and nearly always looks so pale and thin that I can see at once they haven't given the poor girl anything to eat there.   I confess that I couldn't live like that.   If I didn't get my woodcock with sauce, or the wing of a roast chicken, I— really I don't know what I should do.   I like pudding with sauce, too, but carrots or turnips or artichokes are no good at all.

What an extraordinarily uneven style!   One can see at once it wasn't written by a human being; it begins all right and properly, and ends in this doggish fashion.   Let's see another letter.   This seems rather a long one.   H'm, and it isn't dated.

Oh, my dearest, how I feel the approach of spring!   My heart beats as if yearning for something.   There is a constant singing in my ears, so that I often raise one foot and stand for several moments listening at the doors.   I will confide to you that I have many suitors.   Oh! if you knew how hideous some of them are!   Sometimes there's a great, coarse, mongrel watch-dog, fearfully stupid—you can see it written on his face—who struts along the street and imagines that he's a very important personage and that everybody is looking at him.   Not a bit of it!   I take no more notice than if I didn't see him at all.   Then there's such a frightful mastiff that stops before my window.   If he were to stand on his hind paws (which the vulgar creature probably doesn't know how to do) he'd be a whole head taller than my Sophie's papa, who is rather a tall man, and stout too.   This blockhead appears to be frightfully impertinent.   I growled at him, but he took no notice at all; he didn't even frown.   He lolled out his tongue, hung down his monstrous ears, and stared in at the window—like a common peasant!   But do you imagine, *ma chère*, that my heart is cold to all entreaties?   Ah! no. . . . If you could see one young beau who jumps across the fence from next door!   His name is Trézor. . . . Oh, my dearest! what a sweet muzzle he has!

The devil take it all!   What rubbish!   And fancy filling up one's letter with nonsense of that kind.   Give me a man!   I want to see a human being, I demand that spiritual food that would satisfy my thirsting soul, and instead of that, all this stuff. . . . Let's see another page, perhaps it'll be better.

Sophie was sitting at the table sewing something. I was looking out of the window, because I like watching the passers-by. Suddenly a footman came in and announced, "Teplòv." "Ask him in," cried Sophie, and flew to embrace me. "Oh, Medji, Medji! if only you knew who it is: a Kammerjunker,[1] dark, and with such eyes! Quite black, and as bright as fire." And she ran away to her room. A minute afterwards there came in a young Kammerjunker, with black whiskers. He went up to the mirror, set his hair straight, and looked about the room. I growled and sat down in my place. Presently Sophie came in, looking very happy. He clinked his spurs and she bowed. I pretended not to notice anything, and went on looking out of the window, but I turned my head a little on one side and tried to overhear their conversation. Oh, *ma chère*, what rubbish they talked! They talked about how, at a dance, one lady had made a mistake and done the wrong figure; then about how a certain Bobòv, with a *jabot* on, looked very like a stork and nearly tumbled down; then about how a certain Lìdina imagines that her eyes are blue, whereas they are green —and so on. I cannot think, *ma chère*, what she finds in her Teplòv. Why is she so enchanted with him? . . .

It seems to me, too, that there's something wrong here. It's quite impossible that Teplòv could bewitch her so. What comes next?

Really, if she can like this Kammerjunker, it seems to me she might as well like the official who sits in papa's study. Oh, *ma chère*, if you knew what a fright he is! Exactly like a tortoise in a bag. . . .

What official can that be?

He has a most peculiar name. He always sits and mends pens. The hair on his head is very much like hay. Papa always sends him on errands instead of the servant. . . .

I believe that beastly little dog is alluding to me. Now, *is* my hair like hay?

Sophie simply cannot keep from laughing when she looks at him.

You lie, you confounded dog! What an abominable

---

[1] Gentleman of the Emperor's Bedchamber.

style ! As if I didn't know that this is simply a case of envy ; as if I didn't know it's an intrigue. It's an intrigue of the chief of the section. The man has sworn implacable hate against me, and now he does everything he can to injure me, to injure me at every step. Well, I'll look at just one more letter, perhaps the affair will explain itself.

MA CHÈRE FIDÈLE,—Forgive me for having been so long without writing ; I have been in a state of absolute intoxication. It is perfectly true what some writer has said, that love is second life. And then there are great changes going on in our house. The Kammerjunker comes every day now. Sophie is madly in love with him. Papa is very happy. I even heard from our Grigòrii, who sweeps the floors and almost always talks to himself, that there will soon be a wedding, because papa is very anxious to see Sophie married, either to a general, or to a Kammerjunker, or an army colonel.

Deuce take it all !. I can read no more. A Kammerjunker or a general ! I should like to become a general myself, not in order to obtain her hand or anything like that—no, I should like to be a general, only to see them put on all their airs and graces and show off all their Court ways ; and then tell them that I don't care a brass farthing for either of them. It really is annoying, confound it all ! I tore the silly little dog's letters into bits.

December 3rd.

It cannot be ; it's impossible ; there sha'n't be a wedding. What if he is a Kammerjunker ! That's nothing more than a title ; it's not a tangible thing that you can pick up in your hand. Why, his being a Kammerjunker doesn't give him a third eye in the middle of his forehead. After all, his nose is not made of gold ; its just like mine or anybody else's ; after all, he has it to smell with, not to eat with ; to sneeze with, not to cough with. I have often wished to understand what is the cause of all these differences. Why am I a Government clerk? And for what purpose am I a Government clerk? Perhaps I am really a count or a general, and only appear to be a Government clerk. Perhaps I myself don't know what I am. There have been so many cases in history : some ordinary man, not a noble at all, but some common artizan or even peasant, will all of a sudden turn out to be a great lord or baron, or what do you call it? Well, if a peasant can turn out like that, what should a noble turn out? Now, suppose I suddenly come in with a general's uniform on, an epaulette on the right shoulder and an epaulette on the left shoulder, and a blue ribbon across—what will my beauty say, then, ah? What will papa himself say, our director? Oh! he's a very ambitious man! He's a Freemason; I'm convinced he's a Freemason; he makes all sorts of pretences, but I noticed at once that he's a Freemason; if he shakes hands with you, he only puts out two fingers. And does anybody suppose that I can't be appointed governor-general this very moment, or a commissary, or something else of the kind? I should like to know why I am a clerk? Why particularly a clerk?

December 5th.

I spent the whole of this morning reading the newspapers. Most extraordinary things are going on in Spain. I can't even quite make them out. It is said that the throne is vacant ; that the statesmen in office are in a great dilemma, having to choose an heir apparent; and that this has resulted in disturbances. All this seems to me exceedingly strange. How can the throne be vacant? They say that some donna will succeed to the throne ; but a donna cannot be sovereign, it is quite impossible. There must be a king on the throne. They say there is no king ; but it cannot happen that there is no king ; a State cannot exist without a king. Undoubtedly there is a king, only he is

living incognito somewhere or other. It is very likely that
he is living there, only he is obliged to hide himself for
some family reasons, or on account of some dangers
threatened by neighbouring states—France and the other
countries. Anyway, there must be some reason.

December 8th.

I had quite made up my mind to go to the Department,
but was prevented by various causes and meditations. I
could not get the affairs of Spain out of my head. How is
it possible that a woman should become sovereign? It will
not be permitted. To begin with, England will not allow
it. And then the diplomatic affairs of all Europe; the
Emperor of Austria. . . . I acknowledge that these matters
have so upset and unnerved me that I have been utterly
unable to settle to anything the whole day. Mavra remarked to me that I was extremely absent-minded at table.
And indeed I believe that, while absorbed in meditation, I
threw two plates on to the floor and smashed them. After
dinner I went for a walk by the hill. I couldn't find out
anything worth knowing. Most of the time I lay on my
bed and meditated on the affairs of Spain.

Year 2000, *April* 48*th.*

This day is a day of great solemnity! There is a king
in Spain. He has been found. I am the king. It was
only to-day that I found it out. It suddenly flashed across
me like lightning. I cannot conceive how I could imagine
that I was a clerk! How could such a crazy notion get
into my head? It's a good thing that nobody thought of
putting me into a madhouse. Now all is open before me.
I see all as from a mountain summit. But formerly—I
can't understand it—formerly everything was in a sort of
fog before me. It seems to me that all this results from

people imagining that the human brain is situated in the head; that is not the case: it travels on the wind from the direction of the Caspian Sea. First of all, I announced my identity to Mavra. When she heard that before her stood the King of Spain she clasped her hands and half died of terror. The foolish woman had never seen a Spanish king before. However, I did my best to quiet her; and told her that I am not at all angry with her for sometimes cleaning my boots badly. Of course she is one of the common people, and you cannot talk to them of high matters. The reason she was so terrified was because she is quite convinced that all Spanish kings must be like Philip II. But I explained to her that there is no resemblance between me and Philip II. I did not go to the Department. The devil take the Department! No, my friends, you won't catch me now; I am not going to copy your nasty papers.

Marchober 86th,
Between Day and Night.

To-day our usher came to me to insist that I should go to the Department; he said it was more than three weeks since I had been there. I went, just for a joke. The chief of the section thought that I should bow to him and make excuses; but I glanced at him with indifference, neither too sternly nor too graciously, and sat down at my place as if I observed nothing. I looked round at all the rag-tag-and-bob-tail, and thought, "Oh! if you knew who is sitting with you. . . . Good heavens! what a fuss there would be! And the chief of the section himself would begin bowing and scraping to me just as he does now to the director." They laid some papers before me, telling me to make an extract; but I did not so much as touch them with a finger. A few minutes afterwards they all began bustling about, saying that the director was coming. Several of the officials hurried out, one after another, to present themselves to him; but I never moved. When he passed through our section they all buttoned up their coats; but I took no notice whatsoever. The director! What's he? Do they think I'm going to stand up before him? Never! What sort of director is he? He's a dummy, not a director; an ordinary, common dummy, like a dummy in a barber's shop, and nothing else at all. The most amusing thing of all was when they handed me a paper to sign. They thought I was going to write at the very bottom of the sheet, "Clerk So-and-so." I daresay! I signed, in the most conspicuous place, just where the Director of the Department signs, "Ferdinand VIII." It was worth while to see what a reverential silence there was! However, I just waved my hand to them and said, "You needn't trouble about tokens of allegiance," and went away. I went straight to the director's house. He was not at home, and the footman did not want to let me in, but I said something to him that made him just collapse. I went straight into Her dressing-room. She was sitting before the looking-glass, but started up and shrank away from me. I did not tell her, however, that I am the king of Spain; I only told her that there lies before her such happiness as she cannot even imagine; and that, in spite of the snares of our foes, we shall be together. I did not want to say any more than that, and therefore went away. Oh! what a wily being is woman! It is only now I have fully understood what woman really is. Up till now no one has ever known with whom she is in love. I am the first to discover it. Woman is in love with the devil. Yes, it is a fact. Physiologists write all sorts of nonsense; but really she loves no one and nothing but the devil. There, you see, she sits in the dress-circle with her opera-glass; do you think she's looking at that fat man with the star on his breast? Not a bit of it! She's looking at the devil behind his back. The devil is hidden in the fat man's coat. There! he is beckoning to her with his finger! And she'll marry him—she'll certainly marry him! All that comes from ambition; and the cause of ambition is a little blister under the tongue with a tiny worm inside it no bigger than a pin's head; and all that is the doing of a certain hairdresser who lives in the Gorokho-

"I SAID, 'YOU NEEDN'T TROUBLE ABOUT TOKENS OF ALLEGIANCE,' AND WENT AWAY."

vaya. I can't remember his name; but I know positively that he and a certain midwife are trying to spread Mahometanism throughout the whole world; and it is said that in France the greater part of the population has already accepted the Mahometan faith.

*No date at all ; the day was
without any date.*

I walked incognito along the Nevsky Prospect, giving no sign at all that I am the king of Spain. I thought it would be a breach of etiquette to disclose my identity to every one now, because, first of all, I must present myself at Court. The only thing that hinders me is the want of a Spanish national costume. I must get hold of some sort of mantle. I thought of ordering one, but the tailors are such absolute donkeys ; and then, besides, they have quite neglected their work and taken to speculating. And now they have gone in for paving the streets. I finally decided to make a mantle out of my new uniform, which I have only put on twice ; but, for fear these scoundrels should spoil my work, I decided to sit with the door locked, so that no one should see me make it. I snipped the uniform all to pieces with the scissors, because it must have quite a different cut.

*I don't remember the day, and
there wasn't any month. The
deuce knows what there was.*

The mantle is made and quite ready. Mavra shrieked out when I put it on. I cannot make up my mind, though, to present myself at Court yet. There is still no deputation from Spain ; and to present myself without a deputation would be a breach of etiquette. I think it would prejudice my dignity. I expect the deputies every minute.

Date 1.

I am amazed at the tardiness of the deputies ! What can be the cause of their delay? Can it be France? Yes ; that is a most objectionable country. I went to the post-office to inquire whether the Spanish deputies had arrived ;

but the postmaster was exceedingly stupid, and knew nothing about it. "No," he said, "there are no Spanish deputies here; but if you like to write a letter, we can forward it at the ordinary postage rate." The devil take it! What's the use of a letter? Letters are all nonsense! Apothecaries write letters. . . .

MADRID, *February* 30.

So I am really in Spain; and it all happened so quickly that I can hardly realise it. This morning the Spanish deputies presented themselves to me, and I got into the carriage with them. I was surprised at the great speed with which we travelled. We went so fast that in half an hour we reached the Spanish frontier. For that matter, of course there are railways all over Europe now; and the steamers go tremendously fast. Spain is an extraordinary country! When we went into the first room, I saw a lot of people with shaven heads. I guessed at once that they must be either grandees or soldiers, because they always shave their heads. I was very much struck with the behaviour of the Lord Chancellor, who led me by the hand; he pushed me into a little room, and said, " You sit here ; and if you begin calling yourself King Ferdinand, I'll knock that rubbish out of you." But I, knowing that this was nothing more than a trial of my constancy, answered firmly. Whereupon the Chancellor struck me on the back twice with a stick so hard that I nearly cried out, but restrained myself, remembering that in chivalry this was a custom on a man's entering any high office, and that the customs of chivalry are still in force in Spain. Remaining alone, I decided to occupy myself with affairs of State. I discovered that China and Spain are all the same country; it is only from ignorance that people suppose them to be different. I advise every one, as an experiment, to write " Spain " on a

piece of paper, and it will come out "China." I was profoundly grieved, though, at an event which is to happen to-
morrow. At seven o'clock to-morrow morning there will
occur a strange phenomenon : the earth will sit down on
the moon. The famous English chemist, Wellington, has
written about that. I confess that my heart throbbed with
anxiety when I pictured to myself the extreme delicacy and
fragility of the moon. The thing is that the moon is
generally made in Hamburg, and is very badly made. I
cannot understand why England takes no notice of the fact.
It is made by a lame cooper, who is quite evidently a fool,
and understands nothing about the moon at all. He puts
in tarred rope and cheap oil; and it makes such an awful
stink all over the earth that everybody has to hold their
nose. And this makes the moon itself so fragile that people
can't live on it at all; and nothing lives on it but noses.
That is the reason why we cannot see our own noses,
because they are all in the moon. And when I thought
what a heavy substance the earth is, and how, by sitting
down, it may crush all our noses to powder, I was so over-
powered by anxiety that I put on my shoes and socks, and
ran into the State Council Chamber, to give orders to the
police not to let the earth sit down on the moon. The
shaven grandees, whom I found in the Council Hall in
great numbers, proved to be a very sensible people; and
when I said, "Gentlemen, we must save the moon, for the
earth is going to sit down on it !" they all instantly rushed
to fulfil my royal wish; and many tried to climb up
the walls to get at the moon. But at that moment the
Lord Chancellor came in ; and when they saw him they all
ran away. I, as king, alone remained. But the Chancellor,
to my great amazement, struck me with his stick, and sent
me into my room. What an extraordinary power national
customs have in Spain !

'WHEN I SAID, 'GENTLEMEN, WE MUST SAVE THE MOON, FOR THE EARTH IS GOING TO SIT DOWN ON IT!' THEY ALL RUSHED TO FULFIL MY ROYAL WISH."

January in the same year ; follow-
ing after February.

So far, I cannot make out what sort of country Spain is. The popular customs and Court etiquette are altogether extraordinary. I can't understand them; I can't understand; I simply *cannot* understand. To-day they shaved my head, although I shouted at the top of my voice that I would not consent to be a monk. But what it was like, when they began to drop cold water on to my head, I cannot bear even to remember. I never suffered such a hell in my life. I got into such a state of frenzy that they could scarcely hold me. I can't understand the meaning of this strange custom. It's an utterly stupid and senseless custom ! Nor can I make out the foolishness of the kings who have not abolished it before now. Considering all the probabilities of the case, it occurs to me that I must have fallen into the hands of the Inquisition ; and the person whom I took for the Chancellor is, no doubt, the Grand Inquisitor himself. Only it is quite incomprehensible how a king can be subject to the Inquisition. It is true, that might happen through the influence of France, and especially of Polignac. Oh, that brute, Polignac ! He has sworn to persecute me to the death ; and now he hunts and hunts me down. But I know, my friend, whose puppet you are. It's the English that pull the wires. The English are great diplomatists ; they worm their way in everywhere. For that matter, all the world knows that when England takes snuff France sneezes.

Date 25.

To-day the Grand Inquisitor came into my room, but, hearing his steps approaching, I hid myself under a chair ; and not seeing me, he began to call out. First of all he called, " Poprìshchin ! " I held my tongue. Then, " Aksèntyi Ivànovich ! Government official ! Nobleman ! "

I remained silent. " Ferdinand VIII., King of Spain ! "
I was just going to put out my head, but I thought, " No,
my friend, you won't catch me that way. I know what
you are after : you'll be pouring cold water on to my head
again." However, he saw me, and drove me out from
under the chair with a stick. It's most extraordinary how
that confounded stick hurts ! Ah, well ! my last discovery
repays me for all. I have found out that every cock has a
Spain of its own hidden away under its feathers. The
Grand Inquisitor went away very angry, and threatening me
with some kind of punishment ; but I remained completely
indifferent to his impotent rage, knowing that he acts as a
mere machine, as the tool of England.

Da 34 *te. Month yrae*
February 349

No ; I can endure no more. Good God ! what things
they do to me ! They pour cold water on to my head !
They neither see, nor hear, nor understand me. What
have I done to them ? Why do they torment me so ?
Alas ! what would they have of me ? What can I give
them, I that have nothing ? It is too much ; I cannot bear
all this misery. My head burns, and everything whirls
before me. Save me ! take me ! Give me steeds swifter
than the hurricane. Come, come, my yamshchik ! [1] Ring,
my sledge-bells ! Bound, my noble steeds, and bear me
from this world ! On, on, that I may see no more, no
more ! See ! the heavens whirl before me ; a star gleams
in the distance ; the forest rushes past, with the moon and
the dark trees ; the blue mist is unrolled beneath my feet ;
and through the mist I hear the vibration of a string. On
one side of me is the sea, on the other side is Italy. . . .
Ah, and there are Russian cottages ! Is that my house in
the blue distance ? Is that my mother that sits beside the

[1] Sledge-driver.

window ?   Oh, mother, save thy wretched son !   Weep one tear over his fallen head !   See how he is wronged and tormented !   Clasp thy sad orphan to thy breast !   He is driven and hunted down !   There is no place for him on earth !   Mother, have pity on thy weary child ! . . . But *do* you know that the Dey of Algiers has a wart just under his nose ?

PORRIDGE.

By NIKOLAI USPÈNSKY.

A CART drove in at the gate of a provincial town with a village deacon[1] sitting in it, and in front, driving, his legs dangling over the shafts, a peasant in a *kaftan*.[2]

"Well now, sir, who's above the bishop?" the driver was asking.

"Above the bishop is the archbishop,"[3] answered the deacon. "It is all arranged on the model of the celestial hierarchy, that I was telling you about in the posting station."

"And is there any sort of man above the governor?"

"Of course there is. . . . Look here, Yeremèi; when we get to the inn, I'll go into the Consistorium, and you order dinner for yourself here; there is bread in the bag, so you needn't get any here."

"As your honour likes; of course I'll eat our own bread, as if I didn't know! 'Tis all the same to me. How much oats shall I take? I doubt 'tis terrible dear in these parts?"

"Take half a measure, not more; everything's dear hereabouts. That's why it's so dear to live in the town." . . .

---

[1] Assistant to a village priest in Russia.
[2] Long coat worn by Russian peasants.
[3] Metropolitan.

"Lord bless you, yes, sir, 'tis all so dear, so dear, that it is !"

When they reached the posting inn the deacon put on his ecclesiastical dress, and went to the Consistorium; the peasant, meanwhile, went straight into the kitchen, where the dinner was cooking.

On the fire was a huge cauldron filled with pieces of beef, boiling, and emitting clouds of steam; a workman in a cotton shirt was ranging on a shelf steaming wheaten loaves, and a woman was turning a whole leg of veal on the spit, and sucking her fingers between whiles.

The peasant held his breath as he looked.

Meanwhile there came into the kitchen several travelling merchants and well-to-do sledge-drivers in fur coats; they were smoking their pipes and talking about the forthcoming dinner.

At last the dinner was ready; Yeremèi sat down to table with the travellers.

During the dinner (which lasted for three hours) Yeremèi experienced a misty sensation in the head, and occasionally a pain in the stomach; but he continued eating just the same, though he still remembered the deacon.

On rising from table he sighed profoundly, said grace with peculiar fervour, and lay down on a bench, but he could not sleep. He kept thinking of how the deacon would appear before him, and say, "Well, have you had your dinner? How much is it?" . . .

Yeremèi began to regret that he had not left table directly after the *shchi* (cabbage soup).

Two hours later the deacon arrived. He called the peasant into the other room and began—

"Well, Yeremèi, it's time to go home. God be thanked, I have settled my business up all right, and had a bite of something at a friend's house. You've had dinner, I suppose?"

The peasant stood in the middle of the room, looking at the floor.

"Have you had dinner or not?" said the deacon, standing with the abacus [1] in his hand.

"Oh, ay, I had my dinner, . . . only 'tis something . . . if I hadn't eaten it. . . ."

"What do you mean?"

The peasant held his tongue.

"I don't understand; what did you have? Can't you tell me? I've got to pay the bill, you know. Well, what was there? I suppose you had something to drink?"

"Oh, ay, something to drink, I had."

"What was it—cider?" And the deacon lifted his hand to mark it off.

"Ay, sir, there was cider, of course there was. . . ."

"Plain cider? No, something in it, I dare say?"

"Ay, sir, . . . there was cider. . . ."

"Well, what else did they give you? Speak up, man! Why, we shall stand here all day! . . . What else was there?"

"Ah . . . well, sir, there was a kind of quaking jelly stuff, . . . sort of sloppy mess it was, . . . I don't rightly know. . . ."

"Doesn't matter to me whether it was sloppy or not; I shall have to pay for it just the same. Well, and after the jelly what? Shchi, no doubt. Did you eat shchi?"

"Oh, ay, I ate it up, sartain sure. . . ."

"Well, then?"

"Only, you see, sir, 'tis almost as if I hadn't eaten it, like . . ."

The deacon put on a stern expression and continued gravely—

"Well, and what did you have with the shchi? I sup-

[1] In provincial places in Russia it is customary to use an abacus in adding up accounts.

pose there was some kind of soup-meat with it, wasn't there?"

"Ay, ay, there were a wee bit, for sure . . . but 'twas terrible fat—terrible fat, it was. . . ."

"What's that to me? You ate it, I doubt, even if it was fat? Well, that's all, I suppose. Or perhaps you had porridge too?"

"No, there was something else . . . the porridge come arter that. . . ."

"What then? Some kind of soup? Yes?"

"Ay, ay, sir! That's just it . . . and all sorts of trotter things . . . mucky stuff it was. . . ."

The peasant scratched his head.

"Trotters! Well, you ate them, I suppose?"

"Ah . . . sir! 'Twas the weest bit I ate . . . tru·*ly*!"

"*What — the — deuce* do you think any one cares *how much* you ate? Well, get on ; porridge now, is it?"

Silence.

"There can't have been anything *more?* Something with the porridge, was it?"

" Ay, sir, seems like as if there was something else besides the porridge."

"Pudding, was it?"

"Something of that kind."

"And with what was the pudding served?

" Eh, sir, they always do put that fancy bread . . . cake stuff . . . you know, with pudding, but it was right old and hard, it were like a stone. . . ."

"H'm! and what did you have with the porridge?"

"Eh, no, the porridge come arter that. . . ."

" After what?"

"Ah . . fecks, sir, I don't rightly know . . . kind of mess . . . the Lord knows what. . . ."

" Well, what kind of thing?

"THE PEASANT SCRATCHED HIS HEAD.

The peasant began to help himself out by gesticulating with his hands.

"You know, sir, kind of . . . veal, isn't?   Veal . . . something of that like. . . . All white and flabby. . . ."

"Con . . . found the blockhead!   And you gobbled that up too, did you?"

"Of course, . . . but 'twas all burnt to a chip. . . ."

"Never mind that! . . . Well, *is* that all, at last?"

Silence.

"When are we coming to that porridge, I'd like to know?"

"The porridge come arter that."

"After what?"

Silence once more.

"Can't you speak?"

"Eh-h!   There was a turkey, or something of that like . . . I don't rightly mind what it was   . or maybe the mutton came first. . . ."

"Anything else?"

"There was honey; only 'twas in the comb. . . ."

"My stars!   The landlord 'll bring me in a fine bill for that!   Is that all?   Ah, no, the porridge!"

"No, no, the porridge come arter that."

The deacon flung down the abacus, and, plunging his hands into his pockets, began to pace the room.   The peasant moved away to the corner, so as not to disturb him.

Presently the innkeeper came in.

"Landlord," said the deacon, "what do I owe you for my man's dinner?"

"He had everything on the bill of fare, didn't he?"

"Well . . . I suppose he did."

"Then it comes to a silver rouble."

"Can't you make it a bit less."

"No, no, little father, we never bargain; we make all our

little profit off the oats ; the dinners cost us what we get for them."

The deacon discontentedly took a silver rouble out of his pocket. Yeremèi, meanwhile, stood in the corner, equally discontented.

They had passed the town boundaries and got out into the open country two versts back, but the deacon remained perfectly silent. Yeremèi, anxious to know whether his master was still angry with him, ventured a question—

"And is there any kind of body grander than the archbishop?"

The deacon turned his head away in silence.

A DOMESTIC PICTURE.

A SCENE FROM MOSCOW LIFE.

By N. OSTRÒVSKY.

DRAMATIS PERSONÆ.

ANTÌP ANTÌPYCH POUZÀTOV, *merchant, 35 years old.*
MATRYÒNA SÀVISHNA, *his wife, aged 25.*
MÀRYA ANTÌPOVNA, *Pouzàtov's sister, a girl of 19.*
STEPANÌDA TROFÌMOVNA, *Pouzàtov's mother, aged 60.*
PARAMÒN FERAPÒNTYCH SHIRYÀLOV, *merchant, aged 60.*
DÀRYA, *servant maid.*

*A room in Pouzàtov's house, furnished in glaringly bad taste. Portraits
hanging above the sofa; Birds of Paradise painted on the ceiling; bright-coloured window-curtains; bottles on the window-sills.
MÀRYA ANTÌPOVNA sits by the window with an embroidery-
frame.*

Màrya (singing softly as she works).

> " Black colour, sad colour,
> Yet for ever dear to me."

(Breaks off, stops working, and meditates.)

There! The summer's nearly over; here we have
September already, and you just sit cooped up within four
walls, for all the world like a nun, and don't dare to look
out of window. That's an inter*est*ing life for a young

"MARYA: "THERE! LOOK! OH! HE BOWED TO US! OH! THE WICKED MAN!"

143

lady! (*A pause.*) I daresay! It's all very well to shut us up and turn the key on us; but I know what we'll do! We'll ask leave to go to midnight mass at the convent, and then we'll put on our best things and go off to the park or somewhere. There's nothing for it, one *has* to do things on the sly. (*Goes on embroidering; a pause.*) I wonder how it is that Vasìli Gavrìlych hasn't passed by once to-day? (*Looks out of window.*) Sister! sister! There's an officer riding past! Sister! Quick! With a white plume!

Matryòna (runs into the room). Where, sister, where?

Màrya. There! Look! (*They look out.*) Oh! he bowed to us! Oh! the wicked man! (*They hide behind the window-curtains.*)

Matryòna. How handsome he is!

Màrya. Sister, let's sit here; perhaps he will pass again.

Matryòna. Oh! Màsha! how can you? You'll just encourage him, and he'll take to passing half-a-dozen times a day; and then we shall never be able to get rid of him. I know what these military men are. Why, there was that hussar that Anna Màrkovna encouraged so; he used to ride past, and she'd look out of window and smile at him; and do you know what he did, my dear? He rode his horse right into the hall.

Màrya. Oh! how disgraceful!

Matryòna. I should think so! Nothing happened, you know; but she was just the talk of Moscow. (*Looks out of window.*) Màsha! there comes Dàrya. Oh! what message will she bring?

Màrya. Oh! if mamma were to see her!

(*Enter* DÀRYA, *hurriedly.*)

Dàrya. Matryòna Sàvishna, little mother! I as near as anything got caught! I was just running upstairs, and who must come running slap against me but Stepanìda

Trofimovna! Of course I said I'd been to shop for a skein of silk. You know, she's up to anything. Why, only yesterday, our Petrùsha——

Màrya. Yes, yes! But what about *them?*

Dàrya. Yes, miss; they sent their respects. I went in, ma'am, and there was Ivàn Petròvich lying on the sofa, and Vasìli Gavrìlych on the bed. . . . Leastways, it was Vasìli Gavrìlych as was on the sofa, and they'd been a-smoking, ma'am, till you fair couldn't breathe.

Matryòna. Yes; but what did they say?

Dàrya. Well, they said, ma'am, if you please, that you was both of you to come this evening to Ostànkino at vesper-time. And he said, "Dàrya," says he, "tell them to be sure and come, even if it rains."

Màrya. Of course we'll go, sister!

Matryòna. All right. Run back again, Dàrya, and say we'll come.

Dàrya. Yes'm. Anything else, please'm?

Màrya. Yes, Dasha. Tell them to bring some books to read. Say the young ladies desired it.

Dàrya. Yes, miss; is that all? . . . Oh! ma'am! I clean forgot! I was to tell you to bring some Madeira with you; that was Ivàn Petròvich's orders. "It's so nice," says he, "in the open air."

Matryòna. All right.

Dàrya (comes up to MATRYÒNA *and speaks softly).* Matryòna Sàvishna, Vasìli Gavrìlych was saying to Ivàn Petròvich, "Of course," says he, "it's quite a different thing for you," says he. "Matryòna Sàvishna's a married woman . . . and, of course . . . But Màrya Antìpovna," says he, "she's a young girl . . . and it isn't . . . like as if, you know . . . and somehow or other," says he, "'tis a bad business. Why," says he, "for all I know, they may go and marry her to some shopkeeper with a beard; and then what's the use of my putting myself out?" says he.

"Of course that don't mean as I'm not"—there, you understand me, ma'am. . . . "But I'm a poor man," says he. . . . "I'd be glad enough to marry her," says he, "but," says he, "what's the use of my going poking my nose in?" It was Vasìli Gavrìlych as said this to Ivàn Petròvich, you know, ma'am. "It's quite a different thing for you," says he; "Matryòna Sàvishna's a married woman . . . any sort of thing can happen with an official, you know. . . . Winter-time," says he, . . . "Well, and a fine cloak of racoon fur. . . . Anyways"——

Matryòna. Oh! you silly girl! Why, you should have said——

Dàrya (listening). Little mother! it's the master hisself come in! (*Goes to the window.*) Yes, it is; he's going in at the door.

Matryòna. Well, then, you take the message while we're at tea.

Dàrya. Yes'm.

Voice in the ante-room. Wife! I say! wife! Matryòna Sàvishna!

Matryòna. What's the matter?

Antìp (enters). Good-evening, wife. Why, how you jump! Who did you think it was? (*Kisses her.*) Give us another kiss. (*Caressing her playfully.*)

Matryòna (shrinking away). That'll do, Antìp Antìpych! Let me alone! Oh! what a nuisance you are!

Antìp. But I want a kiss.

Matryòna. Oh! leave off, for goodness' sake!

Antìp. I daresay! (*Kisses her.*) What a jolly little wife it is! That's the sort of wife to have! (*Sits on the sofa.*) Do you know what, Matryòna Sàvishna?

Matryòna. What now?

Antìp. It would be jolly to have some tea now. (*Stares at the ceiling, and puffs.*)

Matryòna. Dàrya!

(*Enter* DÀRYA.)

Matryòna. Bring the samovar; and ask Stepanìda Trofìmovna for the keys. (*Exit* DÀRYA. *Silence.* MÀRYA *sits at her embroidery ;* MATRYÒNA *beside her ;* ANTÌP *looks about the room, sighing.*)

Antìp (*sternly*). Wife! come here!

Matryòna. What now?

Antìp (*striking the table with his fist*). Come here, I tell you!

Matryòna. Why, are you gone crazy?

Antìp (*drumming on the table*). What do you expect me to do with you?

Matryòna. Whatever can it be? (*Timidly.*) Antìp Antìpych?

Antìp. Eh? Frightened you? (*Bursts out laughing.*) No, my lass! It was only my little joke. (*Sighs.*) Can't we have tea?

Matryòna. In a minute. Why, bless my heart, you won't die! .

Antìp. Well, it's so dull to sit and do nothing.

Enter STEPANÌDA TROFÌMOVNA ; *then* DÀRYA *carrying the samovar.*)

Stepanìda. Lord, save us! You're in a mighty hurry, my girl! What are you rushing about like a wild thing for? Nothing is going to fall on our heads. And as for you, little father, you must be gone clean daft! How many more times in the day do you want to drink tea? This is the third time at home; and I doubt you had some down in the town too? (*Pours out tea.*)

Antìp. Well, dear heart! what does it matter? A fellow can't get tipsy on tea. Yes; I had some tea with Brioùkhov, and again with Sàvva Sàvvich. What harm is there in drinking tea with a jolly good fellow? I say, mamma, I did Brioùkhov out of a thousand roubles to-day. (*Takes teacup.*)

Stepanìda. What next, child! Why, you get fleeced yourself on all sides. You never keep an eye upon your shopmen ; you never look after the business. Why, Antìpoushka, what sort of business man are you? All you do is to sit from morning till night in a tavern and drink tea. Ah! dear, dear! it's just a grief to look at you; there's not a bit of method in you ; even *I* can't manage to keep order in this house. The samovar stands on the table till eleven o'clock in the morning; first the men have their breakfast and go off to the shop; then you get up and dawdle over your breakfast till goodness knows when; and then your fine lady here comes down. And as for going to mass before breakfast, why, you don't so much as cross yourselves, the Lord forgive you! Ah! Antìpoushka! if you'd give up your new-fangled ways and live as all respectable people should! You ought to get up at four in the morning and see that everything's in order, and go out into the yard and look after everything there, and go to mass. Yes, my dear, and rout your good lady here out of bed too, and tell her it's time to get up and look after the house ; that's what you ought to do. Yes, you needn't look at me like that, Matryòna Sàvishna ; I've said nothing but what's right and true.

Matryòna. I suppose you are going to begin and preach now !

Stepanìda. Ah ! little mother ! And what would become of the house if it wasn't for me? *You're* not much of a housekeeper ; you're too young yet, little mother ; you've a good deal to learn yet ! Why, just look at you—you don't get up till after ten o'clock—it's a shame to say it, my girl, but it's the Lord's own truth—and here I have to sit by the samovar and wait till you please to come down ; and I'm older than you are, madam. You're too much of a fine

lady, Matryòna Sàvishna, too much by a long way! It's
no use for you to give yourself airs, my lass ; you're naught
but a shopkeeper's wife, and you can't be a real lady,
however hard you try. Why, my good man, what's the use
of her dressing herself up, and hanging herself all over with
gew-gaws and furbelows like a heathen savage, and making
a sight of herself, the Lord forgive us our sins ! and rustling
about with a long tail like a peacock . . . why, it's a sin
and a shame, so it is! You can flaunt about in your
furbelows as much as you like, Matryòna Sàvishna ; but
you're none the more of a lady for that . . . You can't
make a silk purse out of a sow's ear.

Martryòna. Yes ; you'd like me to go about with an old
shawl over my head !

Stepanida. You've no call to be ashamed of your own
class, my girl.

Antìp. Why, heart alive ! Why shouldn't she dress
herself up fine if the money's there? There's no harm in
it. And as for being a lady, hang me if she isn't handsomer
than any lady when she's dressed in her best things ! By
your leave, mother, I don't think all these fine ladies are
worth the trouble of looking at. But just see what my little
wife is like. . . . That's to say, I mean, what a figure she's
got ! . . . and all that, you know.

Matryòna. Really, Antìp Antìpych, what things you do
say !

Màrya. I wonder you're not ashamed of yourself,
brother ! You always make one blush.

Antìp. What's the matter now? I haven't said anything so dreadful. Another day a man may say worse
things than that, and nobody cares. Why, the other day,
before his Excellency the General, such a word slipped off
my tongue, I was quite frightened myself; but what can
a fellow do? A word isn't a sparrow, that you can put salt
on its tail. And as for what you were saying, mother,

I stick to my point. My wife shall dress as fine as she likes; I don't care if she isn't a lady, all the same . . .

Stepanida. Yes; I know, my boy, *I* know. When she goes out with you dressed up like that, with a train two yards long, what do you suppose she's thinking about? Well, I'll tell you my son, she thinks—"Here have I got to put up with a great clumsy husband with a beard, instead of having a proper sort of beau that pomades his hair and puts scent on his handkerchief!"

Antip. Do you think she'd change me for any one else? A handsome fellow like me! (*Strokes his moustache.*) I say, wife, give us a kiss! (MATRYÒNA *kisses him with feigned tenderness.*)

Stepanida. Ah! my child! the enemy of man is cunning. Look at the way my poor dear husband and I lived. We were a happier couple than you are; and all the same he kept me in fear and submission, as a man should, the Lord rest his soul! However much he loved and cherished me, he always kept a little whip hanging on a nail in the bedroom, just in case of anything.

Matryòna. You're always making mischief between me and my husband! Why can't you let me alone?

Stepanida. You'd best hold your tongue, my good girl!

Matryòna. I'm to hold my tongue! What next! Anybody would think I was the dirt under your feet. I'm a merchant's wife of the first guild!

Stepanida. You and your guild! You needn't talk like that to me, my girl! I've had to do with your betters in my time. . . .

Matryòna. Even so, you've no right to shut me up. I'm not going to hold my tongue for anybody.

Stepanida. And what do you suppose I care? There! go your own way; it's all one to me; but when you drive me to it I must speak out; it's my way. I'm not going to make myself over again for your pleasure. (*Silence. They all sit and sulk.*) You've just spoiled my Màsha between you.

Antìp. I say, Màsha, shall I find you a husband?

Stepanìda. 'Twas time to think of that long ago. Seems to me you've clean forgotten that you have a sister; and she getting on, too.

Màrya. Really, mamma! Always "getting on," and "getting on"! I'm not so old as all that comes to.

Stepanìda. Don't try your fine airs on me, miss! I was married at thirteen; and you—I'm downright ashamed to tell people of it—you're twenty.

Antìp. Well, Màsha, shall I ask Kossolàpov?

Màrya. Well, really, brother! You know he smells of onions all the year round; and in Lent it's just dreadful!

Antìp. Well, then, Perepyàtkin; he'd be a fine lover. (*Laughs.*)

Màrya. You just pick out all the frights on purpose.

Antìp. Well, they're all right. I think they're very fine lovers, Màsha; first-rate lovers! (*Bursts out laughing.*)

Màrya (*almost in tears*). You're just laughing at me!

Stepanìda. Come, leave off your foolishness! I'm talking seriously, Antìp Antìpych! What do you mean by all this rubbish? As for you, my girl, don't be afraid; you shall have suitors enough to choose from. Bless my heart! You're not a gipsy beggar-wench; you're a marriageable girl with a position. Only you needn't think I'll let you marry a nobleman . . . I won't; so don't imagine it.

Antìp. Why, mamma, any one would think there are no decent folks among noblemen. Dear me! there are plenty. (*Laughs.*)

Stepanìda. Of course there are, little father! there are decent people in every class; only everybody should keep to their own. Our grandfathers were no worse than we are, and they weren't always trying to get in among the nobles.

Antìp. I don't see why you shouldn't marry her to

a noble. There's no harm in it; why should you mind?

Stepanìda. Eh! my lad! A real proper noble, that's worth having, wouldn't take her; he'd want at the very least a hundred thousand, or may be two or three; and as for the others, they might as well not be there at all for me. All they know how to do is to turn up their noses and give themselves airs, as much as to say, " I'm a noble, and you're common people!" And after all, they're nothing but a lot of dressed up beggars! Goodness gracious! As if I didn't know! Look at Lopàtikha,[1] she married her girl to a noble, without asking any respectable person's advice. I told her of it at the time. " Eh! Maxìmovna,"[2] said I, "' Don't try to drive in strange sledges.'[3] You'll remember my words when it's too late." Well, of course she began and answered me that she wasn't going to stand in her own child's way, and all that. " I only want the best," says she; "after all," says she, "he's a gentleman, not a shopkeeper; and maybe he'll get on in the service and get a handle to his name." And now, you see what's come of it! Ah! it's a poor tale when a frog will be a bull! There's many a slip 'twixt the cup and the lip! Half her dowry he's drunk away; and the rest he's gambled away, good man! (*Sighs.*) Yes; I was at the wedding; such a set out as they had at the dinner, Lord save us! " Where's the bridegroom?" said I. And what do you think, my lad? When I looked round, as it might be now, a nasty little slimy toad buttoned up into a tight jacket with the tails cut off, for all the world like a blind kitten that's been licked down. And there he was, wriggling and twisting about, like any heathen flibberty-gibbet—Lord

---

[1] Colloquial for " the wife of Lòpàtin."

[2] The Patronymic without the Christian name of the person addressed is a common colloquialism.

[3] A Russian proverb.

forgive us our sins!—as if he couldn't find a place to sit down. Nobody'd ever have known him for a bridegroom, that they wouldn't. He might just as well have been all hung on wires. I thought to myself when I looked at him, "You've made a fine choice, my friends!" (*They all laugh.*) But, dear heart! What am I talking about? Everybody knows that. And even if you do get one that isn't a drunkard—of course there are decent ones here and there—he'll only smoke you out of your own house with his tobacco; or else he'll bring deadly sin into your house eating meat on fast days. (*Spits.*) Good Lord! it's just sickening to think of. . . . No doubt there are good sensible people among them, that do their business properly; only all I say is, we and they don't belong together, and we're best apart. Now, a good, well-to-do shopkeeper, Màsha——

Antip. Plump and fresh-coloured, you know, Màsha, like me. That's the sort of fellow to love; not a dried-up scarecrow, eh, Màsha?

Màrya. Really, brother, how should I know? . . . (*Casts down her eyes.*)

Antip. How should you know? Well, anyway, Matryòna knows; I say, Matryòna, don't you think I'm right? Best have a shopkeeper, eh?

Matryòna. It's always the same talk with you.

Stepanìda. He's quite right, Màsha, my girl. At least there's some one worth kissing.

Màrya. Mamma! How can you! I declare I shall go away! Come, sister! (*Runs out of the room,* MATRYÒNA *follows her.*)

Antip. Oho! my lass; it's not much use to run away.

Stepanìda. You made her bashful, Antìpoushka; she's only a girl, you see.

Antip. Well, I don't mind if it's a merchant. Give her to a merchant, you may as well.

Stepanìda. (Moves nearer to him and speaks softly). By the bye, Antìpoushka, I heard from neighbour Terèntyevna that Paramòn Ferapòntych thinks of marrying again, and is looking for a wife. That's a chance we oughtn't to miss, you know. Of course I know he's getting old, and a widower, and all that; but he has plenty of money, Antì-poushka—heaps of money. And then, you know, he's respectable and religious, and a capital business man.

Antìp. Ye—es, mamma; only he's an awful cheat.

Stepanìda. Dear heart alive! What do you mean by a cheat, I'd like to know? He goes to church on all the holidays; and he always comes before any one else; he keeps all the fasts; and in Lent he doesn't even drink sugar in his tea, only honey or raisins. Yes, my dear, you might take example by him! And if he does play a trick some-times, like any business man, who's the worse for it? He's neither the first nor the last. Why, there'd be no trade with-out that, Antìpoushka. It's a true saying—"No lies, no sale."

Antìp. That's true enough! Why shouldn't one trick a chap if it comes easy? There's no harm in that. Only you see, mamma, . . . a man must have a bit of conscience sometimes. *(Scratches his head.)* After all, you know, . . . one must think of one's latter end. *(Silence.)* I know I can be as cunning as he is, when it comes in my way; but I always tell a chap honestly afterwards. I always say:— " Look here, friend, I fleeced you a little bit over such and such a business." Last year, for instance, I did Sàvva Sàv-vich out of five hundred roubles when we were settling up accounts; but I told him about it afterwards:—"Sàvva Sàvvich," said I, "you've let a nice little five hundred slip through your fingers; but it's too late now, friend," said I; "only another time keep your eyes open." He was a bit riled up about it; but we're the best of friends again. There's no harm in that! . . . Why, just lately I did that

German, Karl Ivànych, out of three hundred roubles. That was a good joke! Matryòna had been buying a lot of furbelows and things in his shop, and he sent me in a little bill for two thousand.

Stepanìda. What! I never heard of such a thing!

Antìp. There, that's no harm! Let her dress up if she likes! Well, so I thought to myself—"Surely I'm not going to give the German all that money. No, no," thought I, "he may wait till he gets it." So I gave him a little over three hundred roubles short. "The rest, mounseer, afterwards," says I. "All right, all right," says he, as polite as you please. So after that, of course he began nagging at me; every time I met him it was the same thing—"What about the money?" I got just sick of it; and one day, when I'd got my back up, that German must needs come along. "What about the money?" says he. "What money?" says I; "I paid you long ago, man; let me alone, for the Lord's sake!" Eh! there was my German in a rage! "That's dishonest," says he; "that's underhand dealing," says he; "it's written down in my books," says he. And I said to him:—"The deuce knows what you've got written down in your books; you'd have one always paying you." "Ah!" says he, "that's the Russian way of doing business; no German would do that. I'll go to law," says he. Well, what can you do with a man like that? It's for all the world like a sick man and his nurse! (*Both laugh.*) "All right," says I; "much you'll get from lawyering!" Well, he went to law; and of course I simply denied it. I stuck to my point, that I'd paid and knew nothing more about it. Oh! what a laugh we had over that German! He was just wild. "It's dishonest," says he. So after it was all over, I said to him—"Karl Ivànych, I'd have given you that money, only I couldn't spare it." You should have seen how our shopkeepers shook their fat paunches with laughing! (*Both laugh.*) For that matter, why should I pay up all his bill? That's too much of a good thing. They stick on any price they like; and people are silly enough to believe them. I'd do the same thing again if a man won't give credit. That's my way, mamma, and I see no harm in it. But Shiryàlov—he's no better than a Jew; he'd cheat his own father! It's true, mamma; and he'll look you right in the face and tell you lies—and then pretends to be a saint! (*Enter* SHIRYÀLOV.) Ah! Paramòn Ferapòntych, glad to see you; how do you do?

Shiryàlov. How do you do, neighbours? (*Bows.*) Antìp Antìpych! Good-evening, friend. (*They kiss.*) Little mother, Stepanìda Trofìmovna, good-evening. (*They kiss.*)

Antìp. Sit down, Paramòn Ferapòntych.

Stepanìda. Sit down, little father.

Shiryàlov (*sits down*). Well, little mother, and how are you getting on?

Stepanìda. Badly enough, little father; I'm getting old. And how goes the world with you?

Shiryàlov. Ah! little mother! last week I was taken bad all on a sudden. Good Lord! how sharply it did catch me; I was downright frightened, I can tell you. First of all, ma'am, I got a pain in my bones; I assure you, every little bone and joint ached of itself: just ached as if it would all go to pieces, ma'am. The Lord sends us these trials, little mother, as a chast'sement for our sins. And then, ma'am, it went into the middle of my back.

Stepanìda. You and I are getting old, little father.

Shiryàlov. I turned this way and that, on one side and the other; no use, ma'am; it would just leave off a minute, and then catch me again. It seemed to go right to my heart.

Stepanìda. Dear! dear!

Antìp. I say, Paramòn Ferapòntych, haven't you been going it rather too much with your chums?

Shiryàlov. No indeed, sir; I haven't had a drop of

liquor in my mouth ; not for over a month, Stepanìda Trofimovna ! That is, I don't say that I've given it up for altogether ; only for a little while. I won't say I'll never touch it again ; the flesh is weak, as the Holy Scripture says.

Stepanìda. Very true, little father !

Shiryàlov. I'll tell you what I think, neighbours ; I must have caught cold, somehow ; maybe going out in the street without buttoning my coat, or standing out in the garden in my shirt after dark.

Stepanìda. Yes, yes ; it's so easy to go wrong, little father ! Let me give you some tea, Paramòn Feràpòntych.

Shiryàlov (*bows*). Thank you, ma'am, thank you ; I've just had tea.

Stepanìda. Never mind, little father, have some more.

Antìp. With us, for company's sake.

Shiryàlov. Just one cup, then. (STEPANÌDA *pours out tea. He takes his cup and drinks.*) So this is what I did, ma'am. I thought to myself—" All this doctor's stuff is just rubbish ! it's nothing but stealing people's money." And I never have taken doctor's stuff, little mother ; it's a sin that I've never taken on my soul. So I thought to myself—" I'll go to the bath ; that's what I'll do." Well, I went to the bath, neighbour ; and then I sent out for a bottle of wine, and two or three red peppers, ma'am ; and I had them mixed in properly ; then I drank one half and made the bath-man rub me down with the other half ; and when I got home I had some punch ; and at night, ma'am, I came out all in a sweat ; and that threw it off.

Stepanìda. Yes, yes, little father ! My Antìpoushka always takes punch if he's not well.

Antìp. That's good stuff for every sort of illness, friend ; you remember my words. (SHIRYÀLOV *puts down cup.*)

Stepanìda. Take another cup.

Shiryàlov (*bows*). Thank you, no more. Very grateful, Stepanìda Trofimovna.

Stepanìda. Without ceremony, little father. (*Pours out tea.*) How's your business getting on?

Shiryàlov (takes cup). Thanks be to God, Stepanìda Trofìmovna, fairly well. I've only one trouble : my Sènka's gone to the bad altogether. I can't think what I'm to do about it ; it's a real trial and affliction.

Antìp. Wild oats, I suppose?

Shiryàlov. Worse than that, Antìp Antìpych, worse than that ! I wouldn't mind if he'd take to drinking; he couldn't throw away so much on that ; but he runs over head and ears into debt. Ah ! little mother ! what are young people coming to nowadays?

Stepanìda. You've no one to blame but yourself, Paramòn Feràpontych ; you've regularly spoiled the boy ; you should have broken him in when he was a child, it's too late now. He should have gone into town with your shopmen, and learned to keep his eyes open and bring in money.

Shiryàlov. Ah ! little mother ! you see, he's my only one. In these days a young man has to get into society. It was very different when we were young : we whipped our tops until we were eighteen ; and then our elders took and married us and started us in business. Nowadays, a young man that's had no schooling gets called a fool ; the world's grown so wise ! And then you see, neighbour, God has blessed us ; we've a tidy little fortune. What would people say if I couldn't manage to give an only son learning, with all my capital ? I don't want to be worse than my neighbours. One's always hearing that So-and-So's sent his boy to a simminry and another's sent his to the Commercial 'Cademy. So I sent my Sènka to a simminry, and paid my money down for a year in advance. And if you'll believe it, ma'am, before three months was up, he cut an' run ; so I thought I'd eddicate him at home ; and I got a tutor, cheap. But I'd nothing but ill luck, ma'am; the tutor turned out wild, and Sènka took to wheedling money out of his mother and going off on the spree with his tutor, now to the drink-shops, now to the gipsy wenches. . . . Well, of course I turned the tutor out o' doors; and now I'm left to get on with my Sènka how I

SHIRYÀLOV: "LAST WINTER HE SPENT THREE HUNDRED ROUBLES ON GLOVES ALONE—*THREE HUN—DRED* ROUBLES!"

can. Dear Lord! dear Lord! how wicked the people are grown nowadays!

Antip. He seems to have taken after his father!

Shiryàlov. And indeed you wouldn't believe what he costs me: a hundred here, two hundred there; just lately

I paid his tailor a thousand roubles; it's dreadful to think of; I don't wear out a thousand roubles' worth in ten years. I don't know how it is; he can't be content with a waist-coat that's just a waistcoat and a coat that's just a coat. Ah! it must be a judgment on me for my sins! (*Almost in a whisper.*) Last winter he spent three hundred roubles on gloves alone—*three hun—dred* roubles!

Stepanìda. Dear! dear! dear!

Antìp. Wh—whew!

Shiryàlov. The worst of it is that they give him credit everywhere; they know that I can pay. He owes four thousand now in some restaurant or other. No fortune in the world would stand that sort of thing. (*Drinks tea; silence.*) By the bye, Antip Antipych, did I tell you the joke?

Antìp. What joke?

Shiryàlov. About the Armenian.

Antìp. No; what is it?

Shiryàlov. Eh! It's as good as a play. (*Laughs, moves his chair nearer, and speaks in a whisper*). Last year, my good sir, this Armenian came to the town with silk to sell; and he got playing ducks and drakes with his money, just like my Sènka. People began to talk about him in the town—you know how . . . and I'd got I O U's of his for fifteen thousand. It's a bad business, thinks I. There was no getting rid of them in the town; everybody smelled a rat. Just about that time our manufacturer turned up; his factory's in a town some way off, you know. I went straight to him, before he'd heard about it; and what do you think, sir? Got rid of them all in a lump!

Antìp. Well, and what was the end of it?

Shiryàlov. Just twenty-five kopecks. (*Laughs.*)

Antìp. No? Really? That's capital! (*Laughs.*)

Shiryàlov. But Sènka's not like that; no, no, sir, not that sort at all. Verily the Almighty chastises me in my son! He keeps company with the Lord knows what sort of rag-tag-and-bobtail (*puts down cup*), with people not fit to speak to. . . .

Stepanìda. Another cup?

Shiryàlov. No more, little mother, no more.

Stepanìda. Without ceremony——

Shiryàlov. Can't, little mother, can't, indeed. (*Bows.*)

Stepanìda. As you like; but there's plenty more.

Shiryàlov. Can't, really. (*Rises and bows.*)

Stepanìda. Dàrya, clear away the tea. (DÀRYA *enters, clears away tea, and goes out*). Good-bye, little father.

Shiryàlov. Good-bye, little mother. (*They kiss.*)

Stepanìda. Don't forget to look in on us.

Shiryàlov. Always a pleasure, ma'am; always a pleasure.

Antìp. I say, mamma, let's have some brandy in; and a bite of something, and a bottle of Madeira, or something of that kind. Let's have a drink, neighbour, eh?

Shiryàlov. Eh! Antìp Antìpych, that would be too much trouble.

Antìp. Not a bit of it; there's no trouble. (STEPANÌDA *goes out.*)

Shiryàlov. Yes, neighbour; he keeps away from home; he never goes near the shop. What does he care how his father has to get the money? It's time I should have a little rest in my old age. But I've no one to depend on. The other day I went and served in the shop myself; I hadn't done it for fifteen years. "I'll just go and show my lazy louts how to do business," said I to myself. And would you believe it, sir—— (*Draws his chair nearer. Wine is brought in.*)

Antìp. Have a drink, neighbour! (*They drink.*)

Shiryàlov. There was a piece of stuff that was left on hand. Two years ago the price of it was two roubles forty the *arshin;* but this year they'd marked it eighty kopecks. Well, sir, as I sat in the shop there came in two ladies, and asked for some stuff for blouses to wear in the house. "Certainly, ma'am," says I. "Mìtya, bring that last new material. Here's a fine stuff," said I. "And what's the price?" said the lady. "Two and a half roubles it cost me," says I; and profit—what you please, ma'am." "I'll give one rouble eighty," says she. What do you think of that, Antìp Antìpych? One rouble eighty. "Oh! no, ma'am," says I; "I couldn't possibly let it go for that." Well, they haggled a bit, and said they'd give two roubles. Hear that? Two roubles! (*Laughs.*) "How much do you want?" says I. "Twenty-five *arshin.*" "Can't do it, ma'am," says I; if you'll take the whole piece, I don't mind letting it go at two roubles." You see, the thing was that I didn't dare touch the stuff. (*Laughs.*) I was afraid to lay a finger on it. For anything I knew, it might be all rotten inside. Well, my ladies talked it over, and took the whole piece. You should just have seen how the shopmen stared. (*Laughs.*)

Antìp. Why, that's capital! That's first-rate! Have a drink, neighbour. (*They drink.*)

Shiryàlov. But Sènka's not that sort; oh, no! Sènka's not that sort at all. (*Sighs.*) My good sir, he goes to the theatre every blessed day. He knows everybody there; he's made friends with them all; every sort of rabble comes dangling after him. What do you think! The other day I called in at Ostolòpov's. "Just give me that money," says he. "What money?" says I. "For the shawl." "What shawl?" Why, that your son bought." I thought to myself: "What in the world can he want with a shawl?" Of course, I knew I shouldn't get the truth out of *him*, so I began making inquiries; and would you believe it, sir, he's got one of these actress girls!

Antìp. Well, I never did! . . .

Shiryàlov. What would you have me do with him? That's more than I can stand; I'm ashamed to acknowledge him.

Antip. The fact is, that it's time to marry him. You must find the boy a wife.

Shiryàlov. Wait a bit, Antip Antipych; that's not the worst of it; the worst is that there's no end; it's just like pouring water into a sieve. It's a shawl to-day, it'll be a sable cloak to-morrow; and for all I know a furnished house next day; and then a carriage and pair; and then heaven knows what; its worse than the horse-leech!

Antip. Very true.

Shiryàlov. And you know, when a man gets entangled with *them*, he's like one blind. That sort of company is just *ruin*, Antip Antipych.

Antip. You're right there; a man loses his head altogether. There's only one thing to do, neighbour—to get him married quick.

Shiryàlov. It's easy to say, "Get him married"; but how am I to do it?

Antip. How are you to do it? Well, of course, I don't mean that you should tie him hand and foot. Just hunt up a girl with a nice little dowry, you know; and I doubt he won't kick at it. Why should any one mind marrying? It's nothing but a pleasure!

Shiryàlov. Why, who do you think would have him? No one but a mad woman would marry such a rake!

Antip. You think the girls care for that? Bless my soul, that's nothing! Why man, young bachelors are always like that. Do you remember what I was like as a bachelor? I used to drink, and sow my wild oats, and be up to all sorts of larks. My poor father just gave me up for good and all. You talk about theatres! We didn't go to theatres, we used to be off to the dancing saloons, or to the gipsies at Grouzìna; and go on spree, drinking, for a fortnight at a time. Why, the factory hands at Preobrazhènskoye nearly murdered me over a wench; all Moscow knew about it. None the less I got Matryòna Sàvishna. All that's stuff and nonsense ; that doesn't matter.

Shiryàlov. Ah ! it's all very well to say, " Marry him, and find a girl with a dowry." Why, my dear fellow, now that he hasn't got any money, he carries on like mad ; but if once he were to get money into his hands, heaven knows what he'd do—he'd play old Harry with everything.

Antìp. He'd set the money in circulation. (*Laughs.*)

Shiryàlov. No, sir ; the thing I think of doing is to put a notice in the newspapers. Like this you know : " I entrust no commissions to my son ; and have no intention of paying his debts in future." Then I'll sign it : " Manufacturer-Counsellor-Merchant-Temporarily-of-the-First-Moscow-Guild, Paramòn, son of Ferapònt Shiryàlov."

Antìp. Yes ; that's not a bad idea.

Shiryàlov. And another thing I think of doing to punish him, is to get married myself and cut him out.

Antìp. Yes, why not ? Marriage is a good thing.

Shiryàlov. It's just possible, you know, that the good Lord will hear my prayers and send me a son and heir to comfort my old age. I'll leave everything to him. The other is like a stranger to me ; and my heart turns away from him. Only think of it ; if I were to leave the fortune to him, what would he do ? He'd just squander my money, the sweat of my brow, among his tailors and his actress wenches !

Antìp. Well then, marry ; there's no harm in that. Have you got any girl in particular in your eye ?

Shiryàlov. No, friend ; that's just my trouble.

Antìp. Would you like me to find you one ? Let's have a drink first of all. (*They drink.*)

Shiryàlov. Are you in earnest ?

Antìp. Quite. Why shouldn't I find you one ?

Shiryàlov (looks keenly at him). You're fooling me !

Antìp. What should I fool you for ? I haven't got far to look, man ; I've got a marriageable sister.

Shiryálov. What did you say? Eh-h-h!

Antip. Didn't that occur to you? Well, you are a simple minded fellow!

Shiryálov. My dear lad, of course I thought of it. (*Lowers his eyes.*) But I doubt she wouldn't care to have me.

Antip. What next. Why shouldn't she? Never fear, she'll have you.

Shiryálov (*drops his eyes lower*). She'll say: "He's old."

Antip. Old? What does that matter? There's no harm in that. Never fear, she'll have you. And then, my mother's fond of you. Why, what more can the girl want? A good respectable man: why shouldn't she have you?— quiet and peaceable in his cups. . . . By the bye, you are quiet in drink, aren't you? You don't get fighting?

Shiryálov. As quiet as any innocent babe, Antip Antipych. Whenever I get a drop too much, it just sends me off to sleep; I never get rowdy and wild.

Antip. You didn't used to come to blows with your first wife, did you?

Shiryálov. Never, so help me, God!

Antip. Very well then, why should she object to a decent fellow? Never fear, she'll have you. You can send the matchmaker. There now, let's drink health and happiness to you. (*They drink.*)

Shiryálov. Antip Antipych, you're my benefactor, my —I'll tell you what: we've had a little drink here; come to me and we'll make a regular jolly night of it. There's more room in my place, and there are no women-folk, and we'll fetch in the factory hands to give us a song.

Antip. All right. You go on and get everything ready, and I'll come in a minute; I'll just get my cap. (SHIRYÁLOV *goes out.*)

Antip (*alone, winks*). What a beast it is! And such a sly fox! To see the doleful ways he puts on. It's all poor Sènka's fault. It's very well for you to talk, my man, you've just got a sweet tooth in your old age. Well, for my part, I don't care; it's all one to me. But I know one thing, Paramòn Feràpòntych; when it comes to the dowry, who'll get the best of who—that's quite another matter. Mamma and I are not quite so green as you think. (*Goes out.*)

(MATRYÒNA *enters, showily dressed;* DÀRYA *follows her.*)

Matryòna. Has Antìp Antìpych gone out?

Dàrya. Yes, ma'am.

Matryòna. Off on the spree! What a nuisance it is He'll disappear for two or three days now!

(MÀRYA *enters, in her best clothes.*)

Màrya. Come along, sister! Do you know how I got leave?

Matryòna. How?

Màrya. Said I wanted to go to vespers! (*They burst out laughing; and exeunt.*)

"*LA TRAVIATA*"

(AS DESCRIBED BY A SHOPKEEPER).

BY GORBOUNÒV.

ONE day I was out for a spree with my man Jack, that serves in the shop, you know, and we passed a stone theatre.   Jack went up and began reading the advertisement bill that they'd got stuck up, and says he, " I can't understand this ; 'tisn't written plain in our talk."   Well, a gent came by and Jack says : " Please, mister, what's written here ? "   So he read it.   " *Frou-Frou*," says he.   " And what does that mean ? "   " Oh," says he, "that's foreign for any real good thing."   " Really now ! thank you kindly, sir. . . . Mister Policeman, you belong in these parts ; perhaps you can tell us what sort of thing a *frou-frou* is ? " " You'd better go to the ticket-office," says he ; " they'll tell you all about it there."   So we went to the ticket-office and asked for two tickets, right up top, as high as you can go. " For which performance ? "   " *Frou-Frou*."   " This is the opera here," says he.   " Oh well, it's all one to us ; give us two tickets ; we don't mind what you show us.   Now Jack ! Hurry up ! "   So we went in and sat down and these I-talian actor-folk were singin' away as hard as they could go.   First of all, they were sitting at dinner, eating and drinking and singin' about how they was havin' a jolly time and was quite satisfied.   Then Mrs. Patty poured out a

glass of claret and gave it to Mr. Canzelari, an' says she : " Have a drink, won't you?" So he drank it off and said : " My dear, I'm in love with you!" " You don't mean it?" "True." " Then if so," says she, "you can go off about your business and I'll sit and think over my life, because that's the right and proper thing for a woman to do when she thinks of takin' a sweetheart." So Mrs. Patty sat and thought over all her life, and then another man came in. " Look here, ma'am," says he, " I haven't the pleasure of knowing your name, but I've come to talk to you about my lad ; he's got himself into hot water, and now he's hiding in your house. Just you kick him out." " Let's go into the garden, sir," said she, " it's nicer talking in the open air." So out they went into the garden, and there she says to him, says she: " I tell you what I'll do, sir ; I'll write and give him a piece of my mind, and I'll give it him so plain that he won't come hanging about me any more, because I don't hold with wildness and bad ways myself." So then we went out into a sort of passage place and had some apples to cool our throats, for it was that hot that I was just stifled. When we got back again I says to Jack : " Now, mind you look at it and see all they do." " I'm a lookin'," says he. " What's going to come of it all ? " " Why," says he, " the young man's come back to her— silly fellah—to make his a-pologies and tell her it was none of his doin', an' his gov' or made the whole think up." So then she up an' says to him : " You've not done the genteel thing by me ; you've put me to the blush before all these people ; but all the same," says she, " I'm over head and ears in love with you ! An' there's my photygraph for a keepsake, an' I'm very sorry," says she, " but it's time for me to die." . . . She just went on singing for another half-hour, and then she gave up the ghost.

A SEVENTEENTH CENTURY LETTER FROM EMS.

By GORBOUNÒV.

M OST Orthodox Tzar! Thy faithful slave strikes the
earth with his brow before thy glory! In this present year (377) received I the letter which Thou didst deign

to write to me. In that letter is it written : "Go thou, oh Iván, and journey through the towns of the realm of Germany, and look upon the folk that dwell therein and write of them to me, thy great master. And thou shalt take with thee much goods and riches. And when thou journeyest through the towns of the land of Germany, so shalt thou neither rob nor steal, nor shalt thou drink of strong drink to be drunken therewith, but thou shalt speak with the men of Germany ; softly and fair shalt thou speak with them, and shalt give answer in soberness and truth, and in the fear of my displeasure, that I chastise thee not in my wrath. And if any man that is a chieftain among the men of Germany shall ask of thee for what need has thy mighty lord sent thee hither, thou shalt say unto him : ' For State matters of great moment.' And gifts shalt thou not give unto him. And if any man of Germany shall ask of thee help, so shalt thou give unto him food that he may eat and coins that he may have wherewithal to drink, even three pennies unto every one."

Therefore, oh Most Orthodox Tzar, by Thy command did I go out from the borders of the land of Muscovy in the month of May, on the seventeenth day of the month, even the day of the memory of the holy Saint N.N. And on my right hand I beheld the wide sea, and ships thereon, and by the sea standeth the town which is called Königsberg. And in the olden days that town and land were ruled over by the King of Poland, but now all these men of Poland are become changed into Germans, and are commanded to live after the fashion of the Germans, but to believe in the Catholic faith, even as their fathers before them. Yet if any man of them shall turn to the Lutheran faith, to that man shall be shown much honour. And the town of Ems is but a little town, and it standeth in the mountains, and the water therein is alive, and the water hisseth and bubbleth, and the water floweth from a stony

mountain and many trees grow thereon.   And if any man
have a sickness in his entrails, or an evil, or any unsound-
ness, then the doctors in their wisdom look upon his sickness and command him that he drink the hissing waters,
and that he sit in them naked.   But the men of the land of
Muscovy drink not of the water; they drink much Rhine-

wine and are whole and sound.   And the wine of the
Rhineland is good, and every day do I drink to Thee, Most
Orthodox Tzar.   And in that town is built a great stone
hall, and a German sitteth therein and turneth a foolish toy
like a wheel.   And the German is small of stature and fair.
And around the German is a mighty multitude of people

from far-off lands, both Jews and Jesuits, and maidens and matrons and aged women, and an evil folk of thieves and robbers, and they lay coins of gold and silver before the German, and the German gathereth up the coins and turneth his wheel, ceasing not. And in the doorway is the sound of trumpets and the beating of drums and the playing of instruments, to tempt the people that they fall away from righteousness.

BY N. USPÈNSKY.

AN elderly gentleman, sitting on the verandah of his house, called to a workman who was passing with a water-cart—

"Hi! Prokòfyi! Prokòfyi!"

The cart stopped.

"Are you deaf?"

"The wheels makes such a noise, Grigòryi Naòmich; one can't hear anything. They wants greasing."

"Oh, they're all right. What have you got there? water?"

"Yes, sir."

"From the pond?"

"Yes, sir."

"All right," said the master after a moment's pause, "you can go."

A soldier came up to the verandah.

"Wish your honour good-day!"

"Who are you?"

" From Verkhogliàdov in the Merkoùlovsky district ; perhaps you know it ?—by the river Kostra . . ."

" What d' you want ? "

" I'm looking for a place, sir, as doorkeeper, or bailiff."

" What have you been up till now ? "

" Well, when I served in the army, I used to be postillion for the commander ; then, in Mouràvki, I was cook for the examining magistrate. I'm a Jack-of-all trades, your honour—gardener, whipper-in, cook—anything you like ! "

" Can you break stones ? "

" Why, no, your honour, I can't do that kind of work ! "

" Why? "

" Well, you see, the army life breaks a chap down so ; I was in a line regiment, not in the guards, and a man never gets over that."

" Oh, you're healthy enough, I can see that, and yet you want to do such little fiddling work ! What sort of career is it to be a bailiff or a whipper-in?" . . .

"Surely, your honour, it's better than stone-breaking ! "

"I think stone-breaking a very fine occupation. . . . H'm. . . . Have you recommendations from your former employers ? "

" No, your honour."

" I can't take you without a character, my good man."

"Yes, sir, you're quite right, sir."

" Perhaps you're some good-for-nothing fellow—a thief or drunkard for all I know. . . ."

" Just so, your honour."

" You must bring me a character."

"Yes, sir ; good-morning, sir."

The soldier went away. Presently the steward came up to his master and announced—

" If you please, sir, a strange gentleman came while your honour was asleep ; he calls himself a village schoolmaster."

" Where is he now ? "

" Sitting in the office."

" Let him in."

There came on to the verandah a sunburnt man of about forty, in a nankeen coat and high boots. The master of the house offered him a chair.

" Who are you ? "

" Schoolmaster from the Pobiràkhinsky district, from the village of Bezzùbov. I humbly venture to trouble you with a request ; can I not obtain some kind of situation ? "

" I don't want a schoolmaster," said the owner of the house.

" I can take other situations. I have heard that you are looking for a clerk ? "

" Why did you leave your situation in Bezzùbov ? "

" The school was destroyed by fire."

" Long ago ? "

" On All Soul's day. The cause is not known—the whole village was burnt down."

" Yes, one is constantly hearing of fires nowadays. A village close to us has been burnt down too. . . . Alow me to ask, though, how did you become a teacher ? "

" After completing my education I lived in my brother's house in the village of Khmyèlnoye. I did not work, but he supported me. Then I took a situation as tutor in a country gentleman's house at Ogoùrtzov, at a salary of two roubles a month. But I did not stop with him long, and while there I served chiefly as coachman. . . ."

" But why ? "

" Because my pupil did not like studying, and his parents let him have his own way, and employed me temporarily as coachman. . . ."

" That's strange ! "

" I did the work properly ! I had no choice. . . ."

" How much did you get for it ? "

" Nothing ! only board and lodging, and a cast-off

dressing-gown that the gentleman gave me. In that dressing-gown I went back to my brother, and he said : ' What are you hanging about here for, doing nothing? can't you set to and learn something, if it's only singing— you might get to be choir-master in time." So I began to study singing, and then my brother got tired of hearing me. ' Confound it all ! ' he said, ' I'm sick of this ; go home to father.' Well, then I went home. Of course my people abused me :—' Always hanging about in the way ! We've had enough of this ! ' What would you have me do, sir, when I couldn't get a situation anywhere? I thought one time of going into a monastery ; but just then I got a letter from my brother, telling me to come to him. I went, and he said, ' The prince's steward wants to start a choir. You must engage yourself as choir-master.' I asked him how did he suppose I was to do that when I don't know how to sing myself? But all he would say was : ' Don't be afraid ! you'll learn in teaching your class.' So I took the post. They gave me a tuning-fork——"

" May I ask," interrupted the gentleman, " whether you were attired in the dressing-gown ? " . . .

" No, in my mother's cloak ; the dressing-gown was worn out. . . . It was a short cloak, . . . home-made. . . ."

" Well, and how did you get on ? "

" Very well. There was quite a fair choir. My brother sang tenor ; Iván Alexèyich (at the present moment a teacher of patrology and hermeneutics) bass ; then there were a few more volunteers. We got perfect in ' Kol Slàven,'[1] and two sort of . . . a . . . choral part-songs, ' Vzýde ' and ' Polozhìl yesi.' The steward was quite surprised at us ; he was a critic in musical matters ; and he wrote a letter to Moscow, to the prince, about a salary for the choir-master. Meanwhile we began to practice : ' Kto Bog ? ' and ' Kheruvìmskaya Razòrennaya '[2] . . . All of a

---

[1] Russian hymn.   [2] Russian sacred songs.

sudden the prince wrote back, 'I don't want a choir; I am going away for my health.' . . .

"So after that I got appointed at the village school at Bezzùbov. The people there are very poor; many of the peasants used to sleep in their ovens in winter-time. One day the priest came into a cottage to bless the household; he looked round, and there was no one there, so he began to sing the *tropar*.[1] Suddenly the people crawled out from the oven and came up to kiss the crucifix. . . . A good many of my pupils went about begging. For all that, though, a great gentleman from St. Petersburg passed through our village, and he said the people were not averse to education—really."

"Do you mean that ironically?" asked the master of the house.

"Oh dear no!"

"Of course, even a poor man may desire education; just take the case of Lomonòsov: he was a peasant and became an academician."

"Exactly so."

"Well, what else did the great gentleman from St. Petersburg remark?"

"He said that it would be a good thing for our administration to introduce a uniform for the scholars."

"A capital idea!" exclaimed the master of the house; "there ought to be discipline in a school. Without discipline no institution can exist. H'm . . . What subjects were taught in your school?"

"We used the New Testament in the Russian and Slavonic tongues, a hundred and four selections from the Old and New Testaments, the 'Elements of Christian Doctrine,' 'Examples of Piety,' and the Breviary, for the children to learn by heart; the first hour's division[2] of the

---

[1] Special canticle on a Saint's day.

[2] In the Greek Church the psalms are divided up into a kind of rosary.

Thirty-third Psalm, and the Book of Six Psalms, with 'All that has breath.' " . . .

" Is that all ? "

" No, we had a library, containing the following books:

"Selected Passages from Schreck's 'Universal History.'"

"The Programme for Acceptance into the Military Service."

" Food for the Mind and Heart."

The Psalter, without red lettering.

The Breviary, with red lettering.

A work of Glinka, entitled, " Hurrah."

" The Life of St. Prokopius the Natural."

" Reader for the People."

" Domestic Conversations."

" The Clever Reader."

And a few others."

" The books are good," remarked the gentleman ; " I'll order ' Domestic Conversation ' and the ' Clever Reader ' myself. How long did you retain your post ? "

" Eight years. I received no rise in my salary for the whole time. One day the inspector came, and he asked me, ' How long have you been teaching here ? ' ' Eight years,' said I. ' Has your salary been raised ? ' ' No,' said I ; ' I receive the minimum salary.' ' Why is that ? ' ' I don't know.' Then he turned to the chief of the district and said, ' The teacher is to receive a rise in his salary.' The inspector observed, too, that the school-house garden was neglected, and ordered it to be put to rights, saying, 'that it would then have a favourable moral influence on the minds of the scholars, who would, in time, become agriculturists.' "

" I agree with him. The bad tendencies must be restrained in these people from the very tenderest years."

" 'The inspector ordered flowers to be planted in the garden——"

"H'm, in my opinion that is superfluous.   He should have had birch trees planted; that would have influenced the pupils more favourably."

"There were birch-trees already——"

"Ah! Birch trees are as valuable as the 'Clever Reader' and 'Domestic Conversations.'   Are you married?"

"I SHOULD HAVE LIKED TO MARRY."

"I should have liked to marry, but I was afraid to.   The parish clerk of Ogoûrtzov offered me his sister-in-law in marriage.   I knew her—she was a first-rate girl.   I went to see her."

"Was she clever?"

"A-a! Really, sir, I don't know whether she was clever or not."

"But you talked with her?"

"Oh yes, of course! I said, 'We are acquaintances, Olga Mitrevna.'"

"Oh yes," she said, "I am quite aware of that."

"I have been brought here," said I, "to ask you in marriage."

"Indeed!" said she.

"Do you know where I have seen you? At a christening at Ogoùrtzov," said I, and she answered—

"Yes, I remember. And you are from Khmièlnoye?"

"Yes," said I.

"Ah! the scenery is pretty round there."

"And that was about all her cleverness! . . . Her father kept on begging me to marry quickly, because a man can't live properly without some one to keep his house. 'We shall get on much better together,' she used to say. . . . So we stayed up till dawn, singing and dancing."

"Sacred songs?"

"No, sir, various—sacred and secular."

"Well, and did your betrothed sing?"

"No; afterwards, when I left her—she sang that romance —you know—

> "'Twas my fault for thus betraying
> All too soon my love to thee ;
> Now thou hast beheld my weakness,
> Ah! thou hast forsaken me.'"

"That's to say, you jilted her?"

"I don't know— anyway, I hadn't anything to keep her on."

"H'm—so you say the school burned down?"

"To the ground."

"And are all the books and things burnt too?"

"No; they were saved. The fire was in the day-time, and our people had time to get the books out."

"That's good. So I suppose it will soon be built again, and you can go on being teacher?"

"I don't wish to take that work."

"Why not?"

"I'm sick of it! You wouldn't believe me, I've often thought of putting an end to myself."

"So you prefer to be a clerk?"

"Yes, sir."

"H'm'm—I am sorry that I can't help you; it's true that I've just dismissed my clerk, but I don't want another. You see, in these times one must look after everything oneself. I do all my accounts myself. Now, I have a vacancy for a bailiff, but you wouldn't care for that . . . the salary is so small . . . three roubles a month."

"That is very little," said the teacher.

"There you see! and I don't want a clerk. Besides, I can't understand why you don't wish to be a teacher."

"I can't stand it, indeed I can't!"

"It's true that the root of learning is bitter, but, you see, the fruits are sweet. . . . No, I would advise you to disseminate instruction among the people. . . . At the present time, when education has become a positive necessity, we ought all of us to assist in the work, to the limit of our powers. For my part, I am quite willing to do what I can. I will make a donation of books to your school. Here! Aliòshka! Fetch the hamper that stands under the ante-room sofa."

The footman brought in a hamper of books, gnawed all over by rats.

"Now," said the gentleman, "here's a book for you: 'Nature's Vengeance,' a capital book; I've forgotten what it's about. Ah! and here . . . 'The Oath, taken at the Holy Sepulchre.' . . . In fact, you can have the whole

"THE FORMER TEACHER, IT IS SAID, HAD HANGED HIMSELF."

183

lot. When your new school is built, kindly range all these works in your library with an inscription : ' Presented by Mr. Yàkov Antònovich Svinooùkhov,[1] the squire of Prokhòrovka.' Posterity will remember me. . . . I am very glad that fortune brought you here, otherwise my books would have lain by uselessly, but now they will do good ; and not to one generation only, but to future ages. . . . Hi ! Aliòshka. Tell the man to harness a horse and conduct these books and the schoolmaster with them to the village of Bezzùbov."

* * * * * *

Two months later the new school was built. The educational library had been enriched by the following works, the gift of Mr. Svinooùkhov :—

> " The Correspondence of the Nobility of Hell."
> " Hunting with the Hounds."
> " The Russian Theatre."
> " Nature's Vengeance."
> " The Works of Bulgarin."
> " Political and Moral Fables."
> " *The Moscow Gazette.*"
> " A New Latin Alphabet."
> " Words to Scholars, Concerning the Attributes of True Wisdom."
> " A Guide to Didactics."
> "A Short Dissertation upon the Rules of True Wisdom."

&c., &c.

Nothing was wanting, except a teacher. The former teacher, it is said, had hanged himself.

' Literally " Pig's ear."

THE RECOLLECTIONS OF ONÉSIME CHENAPAN.

"Une triste histoire. Souvenirs d'un voyage dans les steppes du Nord," par Onésime Chenapan, ancien agent provocateur, ayant servi sous les ordres de Monseigneur Maupas, Préfet de Police, 1853. Paris : Librairie nouvelle, 1 vol.

From " Opinions of distinguished foreigners concerning Pompadours,"—(Appendix to " Pompadours and Pompadouresses.")

By "SHCHEDRÍN" (SALTYKÓV).

I TAKE up my pen to show how one rash step may ruin a man's whole life, destroy all the fruits gained at the cost of long-continued humiliation, and turn to dust all hopes of further advancement in his special career—nay, it may even rob from a man his dearest earthly right—the right to be called a faithful son of the holy Roman Church !

All this was brought upon me by a worthless being who called himself a Pompadour; he did it simply, calmly, without an instant's hesitation, leaving me without even the faintest hope of obtaining any recompense whatsoever for all the losses he caused me !

Oh, young man ! Thou who readest these tear-stained pages, consider them and ponder deeply. And if ever, in the Closerie de Lilas, or any other such place, thou meetest with a man called a Pompadour, flee from him! For the name of that man is frivolity and hardness of heart!

*   *   *   .   .   .

In the year 1852, not long after the famous *coup d'état* of December, chance brought me together with the Prince de la Klioukwà, a man still young although a little *taré*, a man whom I, seeing only his personal appearance and cheerful manners, should never have guessed to be a high official. It appeared, however, that such he was.

We met in one of the Parisian *cafés chantans* which I frequented in the exercise of my professional duties, as these agreeable places were the favourite resorts of those mistaken young people who failed to show due unconditional confidence in the changes of December 2nd. Here also were to be found many foreigners, acquainting themselves with Paris from the point of view of the *dolce far niente*.

Our conversation began *à propos* of the song, "Ah! j'ai un pied qui r'mue," which at that time had just come into fashion, and was charmingly sung by Mdlle. Rivière. It appeared that my neighbour (we were sitting at the same table, in leisurely enjoyment of our *petits verres*) was not only a fine connoisseur of *genre*, but himself performed admirably the principal pieces of the *Cascade* repertoire. I cannot explain how it was, but, to my sorrow, I experienced a kind of blind, unreasoning attraction towards this man, and, after not more than a quarter of an hour's conversation, I frankly acknowledged to him that I was an *agent provocateur*, honoured by the peculiar confidence of Monseigneur Maupas. To my astonishment, he not only did not start up to strike me (as mistaken young people almost invariably do), but he even held out both his hands to me, and, in his turn, informed me that he was a Russian, occupying in his native land the rank of Pompadour.

"I will explain to you afterwards," said he, observing the perplexity expressed in my face, "what constitute the attri-

"WE MET IN ONE OF THE PARISIAN *CAFÉS CHANTANS.*"

butes and jurisdiction of a Pompadour's office; at present I will only say that no other meeting could cause me such pleasure as this meeting with you. I was just seeking to make the acquaintance of a good, thoroughly reliable *agent provocateur.* Tell me, is your business a profitable one?"

"Monseigneur," I replied, "I receive a regular salary of 1,500 francs a year, and, besides that, as encouragement, extra pay for every denunciation."

"Why . . . that's not bad!"

"If I were paid by the line, though only at the rate of the newspaper penny-a-liners, it would really be not bad; but the thing is, monseigneur, that I am paid by the job."

"But, no doubt, at Christmas or Easter there are some little perquisites?"

"No, monseigneur. All the perquisites go to Monseigneur Maupas, and his most gracious Majesty the Emperor Napoleon III. The only addition to the salary I told you of consists in a special sum, reserved for cases of mutilation and fatal injuries, which are very common occurrences in my profession. On the 2nd of December I literally presented the appearance of a mass of flesh streaming with blood, so that in one day I earned more than a thousand francs!"

"A thousand francs . . . *mais c'est très joli!*"

"But I have an aged mother, monseigneur! I have a maiden sister, whom I do my utmost to settle in life!"

"Oh! *quant à cela* . . . the deuce take them!"

This exclamation was very noteworthy, and should have served as a warning to me. But it pleased Providence to darken my reason, doubtless in order that I might drain to the very dregs the chalice of bitterness which this terrible man was to bring to me.

"Well, and now tell me, has it ever happened to you—in the exercise of your functions, *s'entend* — to open other people's letters?" he continued, after a momentary silence, which followed his exclamation.

"Very often, *excellence !*"

"Understand my idea. Formerly, when letters were fastened down merely with sealing-wax, when envelopes were not gummed at the edges, it was quite simple, of course. All that was necessary was to insert a thin wooden needle, roll the letter upon it and draw it out of the envelope. But now that the envelope presents an unbroken, impenetrable surface, what is one to do? I have repeatedly tried the use of saliva, but I confess that my efforts have never once been crowned with success. The persons who received the letters have always observed it and made complaints."

"And yet nothing is simpler, *excellence.* Here, in such cases, we take the following course : we approach the letter to boiling water and hold in the steam that side of the envelope on which are the gummed edges, until the gum melts. Then we open it, take out the letter, read it, and replace it in the envelope; and there remain no signs of indiscretion."

"So simple—and I never knew! Yes, the French are in advance of us in all respects ! Oh, generous nation ! How sad that revolutions so often disturb thee ! Et moi, qui, à mes risques et périls, me consumais à dépenser ma salive! Quelle dérision !"[1]

"But does the opening of other people's letters appertain to your . . . attributes, monseigneur ?"

"Everything connected with internal policy appertains to my duties, especially the opening of private letters and the exaction of *nedoimki.*[2]

---

[1] And I, at what risks and perils, go and waste myself expending saliva ! What folly !

[2] Extorsion des *nédoymkàs*, une espèce de peine corporelle, en

"Do you know, my new friend, that you have helped me out of a very great difficulty?"

He pressed my hand warmly, and was so generous as to invite me to supper with him at the Café Anglais, where we passed the time in the most agreeable manner till almost morning. Finally, he very amiably proposed that I should accompany him to his native Steppes, where, according to him, a highly advantageous career was open to me.

"You will travel with me, and at my expense," said he; "your salary will amount to four hundred francs a month; besides that, you will live with me and receive free board, light, and fuel. Your duties will be as follows : to teach me all the secrets of your profession and to find out all that is said about me in the town. And, in order to attain my purpose more easily, you will frequent society and the clubs, and there abuse me right and left."

I was bewildered and delighted. Oh, ma pauvre mère! Oh, ma soeur, dont la jeunesse se consume dans la vaine attente d'un mari ! . . .[2]

Yet, notwithstanding my agitation, I observed a certain inconsistency in his proposition, and instantly remarked it to him.

"Permit me to make one respectful comment, monseigneur," said I. "You were so kind as to say that I should live in your house, yet at the same time you desire me to malign you. Although I fully understand that the latter measure may be one of utility (for ascertaining the direction of public

vigueur en Russie, surtout dans le cas où le paysan, par suite d'une mauvaise récolte, n'a pas de quoi payer les impôts.—*Chenapan*.[1]

[1] Mr. Chenapan has made a slight mistake. *Nedoìmka* is the Russian word for debt; but he is so far right that " recovery of nedoìmki " is the expression officially used for the extortion of taxes from a starving population, and that such extortion is very often accomplished by means of " une espèce de peine corporelle."—*Translator*.

[2] Oh, my poor mother! Oh, my sister, wasting her youth in the vain hope of a husband !

opinion), still, would it not be better if I were to live, not in your house, but in a separate lodging—just in the character of a distinguished foreigner living on his income?"

"That's of no consequence," he replied, with a fascinating smile. "Please do not disturb yourself about that. In our Steppes it is a customary thing to foul your own nest; when you eat a man's bread, you're supposed to abuse him." . . .

I decided.

Parting with thee, oh, my beloved France, I felt that my heart was torn in pieces!

Oh, ma mère!

Oh, ma pauvre sœur chérie!

But I said to myself, "Oh, ma belle France! If only the Steppes do not swallow me up, I will scrape together a small capital, and will set up in Paris a matrimonial and divorce agency. Then shall nothing ever separate us more, oh, beloved—oh, incomparable native land!"

Looking forward to that longed-for moment, I decided to give up all my salary to my poor mother. For myself, I intended to live on casual gains, of which, by the exercise on my part of a certain amount of skill and inventive capacity, there would certainly be no lack.

On the journey the prince was exceedingly obliging. He always permitted me to sit at the same table with him, and gave me good food. Several times he attempted to explain to me in detail in what consist the "attributes of a Pompadour"; but I must confess that these explanations produced on me no other effect than complete bewilderment. This bewilderment was still further increased by the fact that during these explanations his face wore so ambiguous an expression that I never was able to make out whether he was speaking seriously or romancing.

"The Pompadourical profession," said he, "is almost a superfluous one, but just that very superfluity is what gives to it the *piquante* significance which it has in our

country. It is unnecessary, and yet it is . . . you understand me?"

"Not quite, monseigneur."

"I will try to express myself more clearly. A Pompadour
has no special business; it would be better to say *no* business," he added, corrrecting himself. "He produces nothing,
manages nothing directly, and decides nothing. But he has
internal policy and time to spare. The former gives him
the right to interfere in the affairs of others; the latter
enables him to vary that right without limit. I hope that
now you understand me?"

"Pardon me, *excellence*, but I am so imperfectly initiated
into the wire-pulling of the policy of the Steppes that there
is much which I cannot comprehend. Thus, for instance,
why do you *interfere* in other people's affairs? Surely all
those 'others' are servants of the same bureaucratic principle of which you are a representative. For, in so far as I
understand, the constitution of the Steppes——"

"First of all, we have no constitution whatever. Our
Steppes are free—as Steppes should be—or as the hurricane
that sweeps across them from end to end. Who shall
control the hurricane? I ask you, What constitution can
attain to it?"

He interrupted me so sternly that I became somewhat
embarrassed and felt it necessary to apologise.

"I expressed myself badly, monseigneur," said I; "I used
the word 'constitution' in quite another sense from the one
you were pleased to give to it. According to the opinion
of scientific men, any state, when once *constituted*, by that
very fact declares itself to have a *constitution*. It is a
matter admitting of no doubt that there may be constitu-
tions which are pernicious, and others again which are
useful——"

"All that is very fine, but I beg of you not to employ in
our conversations the hateful word 'constitution'—never!

Entendez vous : jamais ! Et maintenant que vous êtes averti, continuons."

I therefore explained that I could not understand of what use the interference of one set of bureaucrats in the affairs of another set could possibly be. I was just going to add : "Possibly you share? In that case . . . I understand. Oh, comme je comprends cela, monseigneur !" But, not being, as yet, *quite* intimate with my illustrious friend, I refrained from that remark. Apparently, however, he guessed my secret thought, for he grew as red as a boiled lobster, and exclaimed, in an agitated voice—

"I protest with all my soul ! Do you hear—I protest !"

"But, in that case, I really do not understand what is the purpose of this constant interference."

"You are stupid, Chenapan !" (Yes, he said that to me, although at that time he was still very polite to me.) "You don't understand that the more interference there is on my part, the more right I attain to the notice of the higher authorities. If I put down one revolution a year, that is well ; but if I put down two in a year, that is excellent ! And you, who are in the service of the greatest of suppressors of revolutions—you cannot understand that ! "

"I understand—I understand that very well, monseigneur. But I confess I had supposed that the condition of your country——"

"All countries are in the same condition for a man who desires to attract to himself the attention of the authorities —*vous m'entendez !* But that is not all ! I have my personal *amour-propre*. . . . *Sacrebleu !* I have my internal policy ; I have my prerogatives ! I wish to introduce my view—*sapristi !* I wish that people should act in harmony with my views, not in contradiction to them. It is my right ; if you like to put it so, it is my caprice. You lay a responsibility on me ; you demand of me this and that . . . allow me, too, to have my caprice. I hope that this does not amount to any monstrous pretentiousness on my part ? "

" But the law, monseigneur? How can you reconcile caprices with the law ? "

" La loi ! Parlez moi de ça ! nous en avons quinze volumes, mon cher ! "[1]

Here our conversation broke off. Although the administrative theory expressed in the last exclamation of my interlocutor was quite new to me, still I acknowledge frankly that the coolness with which he spoke of the law pleased me. Monseigneur Maupas had often said to me, " In case of need, *mon cher*, even the law can alter," but he said it softly, as if afraid that any one should hear. And now suddenly—this clearness, this daring, this *élan*—how could one fail to be charmed by them ! The Cossacks are a bold race altogether, and inclined to see enemies where we, people of an older civilisation, see only protection and surety. These people are absolutely fresh, and are free from all those prejudices which burden the life of a Western. They look upon the so-called "moral duties" with the most easy-going cheerfulness, but, on the other hand, no one can compare with them in matters of physical exertion ; and as for their activity at table, with the bottle, with women—there they are undoubtedly the first warriors in the whole world. I, for instance, have never once seen my amphytrion drunk, although the quantity of liquor consumed by him before my eyes is, indeed, hardly credible. Never once did he lay down his arms before the enemy, and all the effect that wine ever produced on him consisted in a change of colour and a certain extra animation in romancing.

I am none the less bound to acknowledge that the significance of Pompadours in Russian society continued to appear to me wanting in clearness. I could not conceive

[1] " The law, good gracious, we have fifteen volumes of law ! "

that there could exist anywhere an administrative caste, the duties of which should consist in *hindering* (I consider the word " intervene " too serious for such an occupation), and

"I CANNOT REMEMBER HOW THE CEREMONY WAS PERFORMED."

which, when reminded of the law, could answer, " 'Pristi ! nous en avons quinze volumes ! " For the rest, I ascribed my doubts, not to my own want of comprehension, but rather to the prince's incapacity to formulate his thought clearly. It was evident that he himself did not understand in what his administrative *rôle* consists ; and this is quite comprehensible if we remember that in Russia up to the present time[1] the corps of cadets are regarded as the nurseries of the administration. In these institutions the pupils are put through a detailed course of study in only one science, which bears the name of " *Zwon popéta razda-waiss* "[2] (the prince was in an exceedingly merry humour when he told me this long name, and I am convinced that in no other European country is there a science with such a name) ; the other sciences, without which it is impossible to get on in any human society, are passed over more than superficially. It is, therefore, not in the least surprising that persons who have received such an education prove incapable of expressing their thoughts coherently and consequentially, but get along how they can with such senseless exclamations as " Sapristi ! " " Ventre de biche ! " " Parlez moi de ça ! " and so on.

Only when the inhospitable Steppe received us in its stern embrace, that is to say, when we arrived at our destination, did I even to some extent realise what my exalted amphytrion meant by his prerogatives.

Until we entered the confines of that tract of country over which the Prince de la Klioukwà's Pompadourical sway extended, his conduct was in some degree moderate. He beat the drivers with a leniency of which I can only speak with the greatest admiration (as for his behaviour when abroad, of that I need not speak—it was the very pink of courtesy). But no sooner did he see the boundary-post

[1] 1853.

[2] Mr. Chenapan has again made rather a muddle of his Russian. " Zvon pobièdy, razdavaïsia ! " (" Bells of victory, ring out ! ") is the opening line of one of Derzhàvin's pompous, servile, and essentially jingoish odes on the victories of Catherine II.—*Translator*.

which marks the beginning of his jurisdiction, than he drew his sword from its scabbard, made the sign of the cross, and, turning to the driver, uttered a cry of gloomy significance. We flew along like an arrow from the bow, and the remaining fifteen versts to the posting-station were taken at a gallop. He, however, considered that we were not going fast enough, for every five minutes he would encourage the driver with violent blows of his sword.

I was unable to understand the cause of his anger, but I have never seen any human being so enraged. I confess that I was very much afraid the axle-tree of our carriage would break, as, if that had happened, we should inevitably have perished. But to persuade him not to hurry the driver was impossible, for furious driving along the roads is one of those prerogatives to which the Pompadours most passionately cling.

"I'll teach him how to drive—*canaille!*" he repeated, addressing me, and appearing to enjoy the terror depicted on my countenance.

And indeed we travelled more than two hundred vests in twelve hours, and yet, notwithstanding this unheard of speed, at the stations he used to order the drivers to be flogged, remarking to me :

"C'est notre manière de leur donner le pourboire !"[1]

On arriving at the principal town we stopped at a large state building, in which we were absolutely lost, as in a desert. (The Prince had no family.) It was early morning, and I was dying for want of sleep; but he insisted on having the official reception at once, and despatched couriers in all directions with the news of his arrival. Two hours later the state-rooms of the house were filled with trembling officials.

Although prerogatives play an important part in our fair

---

[1] "This is *our* way of giving tips."

France, yet I could never have conceived of anything like what I saw here. Among us such words as "scoundrel" ("vaurien," "polisson" and—unfortunately—"Chenapan") constitute the severest reprimand which a guilty official can possibly deserve from an angry superior. Here, on the contrary, independently of plenteously-scattered personal insults, it is customary to add emphatic remarks concerning the genealogy of the person abused.

The prince was as scarlet as a boiled lobster, and hurried on from one subordinate to another, pouring out deluges of virulent abuse. He was especially hard upon a certain lame major, whom he ironically introduced to me with the remark, "This is my Maupas." I at first imagined that this un-happy man must have attempted to usurp the prince's power during his absence (which, of course, would have justified his wrath), but it appeared that nothing of the kind had happened. Up to this day I cannot explain to myself what was the cause of those grievous scenes which I witnessed on that memorable morning. The prince explained them to me as resulting from a desire to defend his prerogatives, but that reason appeared to me insufficient, as no one, apparently, had infringed those pre-rogatives. In a word, the official reception ended in a complete victory for my exalted amphytrion, who paced about the rooms, bridling like a spirited horse and proudly rejoicing in his easily-won triumph.

It was only at dinner that I began to feel at ease. It went off rather pleasantly, for there were present several favourites of the prince, young men, evidently very well educated. One of them, who had lately returned from St. Petersburg, very cleverly mimicked Mdlle. Paget,[1] at her *soirées intimes*, singing, "Un soir à la barrière." This song,

---

[1] A well-known French actress of that time in St. Petersburg.—AUTHOR.

though far from new, and almost gone from my memory, gave me the greatest pleasure.

That evening the prince introduced me to the lady of his affections, whom he had taken away a short time before from one of the local municipal counsellors.[1] This most charming woman produced on me a profound impression, which was still further strengthened when I felt under the table the pressure of her foot against mine. Her husband was present, and greatly amused us by his jests at the expense of betrayed husbands, from which category the simple-hearted man did not exclude himself. Some of these jests, under the mask of *naïveté*, were so biting that the Pompadour reddened and lost his temper; but his morganatic friend, apparently, was accustomed to such scenes, for she looked on as if she had been an unconcerned outsider.

Our merry supper was drawing to a close, when suddenly some one came running in to announce that a fire had broken out at the end of the town.

"That is capital!" said the Pompadour to me. "Vous allez me voir à l'œuvre!"[2]

But I, for my part, was far from glad, for I observed that the prince, for the first time in our acquaintance, was quite drunk. Whether the proximity of the object of his affections acted on him as a stimulant, or whether it was the direct result of the intoxication of power—be that as it may, he could hardly keep on his feet. It turned out, however, that even this was to his advantage. As a general rule, no fire ever occurred without his beating somebody, but on this occasion he slept through the whole affair, and only woke up when the flames were fully extinguished.

As we returned home he startled me so distressingly that

[1] Evidently a mistake; there are no municipal counsellors in Russia. —AUTHOR.

[2] "Now you'll see me at my business!"

my heart seemed to contract as under the influence of some
dark presentiment.

"Well, Monsieur Chenapan" (he did not even conceal
the insulting double meaning that he put into my name),
"how do you (*tu*) like my place?" asked he.

However deeply I was wounded by this deliberate jest,
and by his unceremonious "thou," addressed to a man who
was no subordinate of his, I nevertheless felt it wise to
submit.

"I am more than enchanted, monseigneur," said I.

"H'm! . . . . I should just like to see you not enchanted,
you hound!"

As he said that he laughed so strangely that I suddenly
understood—I was not a guest, but a captive!

Oh, ma France bien aimée! Oh, ma mère!

*   *   *   *   *   *

The prince very soon learned from me all the secrets of the
craft, but, as he became more sure and confident in them, I
fell lower and lower in his estimate. The first two months
he paid my salary punctually, but the third month he told
me right out that the whole of me was not worth two sous.
When I tried to move him with entreaties, referring to my
aged mother and my maiden sister, whose only treasure on
earth is her virtue, he not only refused to hear the voice of
generosity, but even permitted himself certain ambiguities
concerning the virtue of my poor dear sister.

While waiting till God should soften his heart, I was
forced to be content with receiving my board and lodging.
Yet even this much cost me bitter insults. They took away
my former bed and replaced it by a thing for which in our
sweet language there is no name. At table they constantly
mocked and jeered at me, and took to habitually calling me
"rascal." Unhappily, I was so imprudent as to let out on
one occasion that I had sometimes been beaten in Paris

"STROLLING ABOUT THE BOULEVARDS.

when fulfilling my duties, and by this needless frankness I, as it were, laid myself open to the most monstrous and outrageous jests, in which these people (who have no inventive capacity of their own) indulged at my expense. Moreover, at every meal they would purposely leave me without some particular dish (as a general rule, with a refinement of cruelty, they would choose whichever dish I liked best); and when I complained of hunger they would unceremoniously send me into the servants' hall. But what hurt me most of all was the fact that they insulted in my presence my most gracious sovereign and emperor, Napoleon III., and in his person my dear, beautiful France. Thus, for instance, they would ask me was it true that Napoleon (they purposely pronounced his name *Napoleòschka*—a contemptuous diminutive) sold geese in London? or was it true that he and Morny together had kept a house of tolerance in New York? etc. .... And all this frivolous jesting at the moment when the terrible Eastern Question stood before us! ....

So it went on until autumn. The cold weather began, but they neither put double windows into my room nor heated it. I was never of a rebellious temperament, but at the first cruel grasp of cold, even *my* self-abnegation broke down. Only then did I become fully convinced that the hope that God would touch the heart of my exalted amphytrion was a hope in the last degree illusory and vain. Gathering up my courage, I decided to brave the inhospitable Steppes and appealed to the prince to grant me the necessary sum to reach the banks of the Seine.

"I no longer demand the payment of what is due to me, monseigneur," said I; "the payment of what I have earned, far away from my beloved country, while subsisting on the bitter bread of exile. .... "

"You're wise not to demand it—Chenapan!" he remarked, coldly.

"I beg for only one favour. Give me a sufficient sum to enable me to return to my country and embrace my beloved mother."

"All right; I'll think it over . . . Chenapan !"

Day after day passed—still they did not heat my room, and still he thought. During that time I reached the last degree of prostration, and no longer complained to any one, but my eyes shed tears of themselves. If any dog had been in my position it might have aroused compassion—but he was silent !

Afterwards I learned that such things are called in the Russian language "jokes." But if these are their *jokes*, what must their cruelties be?

At last he sent for me.

"All right," he said; "I will give your four hundred francs, but only on condition that you become a convert to the Greek faith."

I looked into his eyes with amazement, but those eyes expressed nothing, save an inflexibility that admits of no reply.

I cannot remember how the ceremony was performed. . . . I am even not quite certain whether it was a *real* ceremony, and whether the priest's part was not played by the Pompadour's adjutant disguised.

Justice compels me to add, however, that, after the ceremony was over, he behaved to me like a *grand seigneur*, that is, he gave me not only the whole of the sum agreed upon, but also two beautiful, hardly-worn suits, and ordered that I should be driven free of expense to the boundary of the next Pompadourdom. My hope did not deceive me. God had touched his heart at last !

Twelve days later I had reached the banks of the Seine, and, graciously received back into the service by Monseigneur Maupas, was strolling about the boulevards, humming merrily—

" Les lois de la France,
  Votre Excellence !
  Mourir, mourir,
  Toujours mourir !"

Oh, ma France !
Oh, ma mère !

THE CROCODILE.

AN EXTRAORDINARY EVENT; OR, A PASSAGE IN
THE PASSAGE.

(*The true narrative of how a gentleman of a certain age and
a certain appearance was swallowed alive and whole by
the crocodile of the Passage, and of what were the
consequences.*)

By FÈDOR DOSTOYÈVSKY.

"Ohè Lambert! Où est Lambert? As tu vu Lambert?"

ON the 13th of this present month of January, 1865, at
half-past twelve in the day, Elyòna Ivànovna, the
spouse of my learned friend, fellow in office, and distant
connection, Ivan Matvyèich, desired to visit the crocodile
which is now to be seen for a certain price in the Passage.[1]
Ivan Matvyèich, having already in his pocket his ticket for
a foreign tour (it was more for interest than for his health
that he was going abroad), and therefore considering himself as off duty, and perfectly free for the whole morning,
not only did not oppose his wife's uncontrollable desire, but
even became fired with curiosity himself. " A splendid
idea," he said contentedly; "we'll go and see the crocodile. Before starting for Europe it is well to make oneself
acquainted with its native population;" and with these
words he took his wife upon his arm and instantly started

[1] The St. Petersburg Arcade.

off with her for the Passage. I, as usual, went along with them, in my character of family friend. I had never seen Ivan Matvyèich in a 'more cheerful mood than on that memorable morning. How true it is that we know not our fate beforehand! The moment we entered the Passage he went into raptures over the magnificence of the building, and when we reached the shop in which the newly arrived monster was on view, he even wished to pay the crocodile keeper the twenty-five kopecks for my entrance out of his own pocket—a thing which had never happened with him before. On entering we found ourselves in a small room, in which, besides the crocodile, were several cockatoos and a collection of monkeys in a separate cage in the background. To the left hand of the door, by the wall, stood a large tin tank, something like a bath, covered with a strong iron-wire netting, and at the bottom of it were two or three inches of water. In this shallow puddle lay an enormous crocodile, as still as a log, perfectly motionless, and appearing to have lost all his powers in our damp and, for foreigners, inhospitable climate. At first sight the monster aroused no particular interest in any of us.

"So that's the crocodile!" said Elyòna Ivànovna regretfully, in a sing-song voice. "I thought he would be . . . quite different somehow."

She probably expected him to be made of diamonds. The German exhibitor, at once keeper and owner of the crocodile, who had come into the room, looked at us with an air of the greatest pride.

"He's right," whispered Ivan Matvyèich to me; "for he knows that no one else in all Russia is exhibiting a crocodile."

I attributed this utterly senseless remark to the particularly pleasant humour that Ivan Matvyèich was in, as on the whole he was a very envious man.

"I think your crocodile is dead," said Elyòna Ivànovna,

piqued by the ungraciousness of the German, and turning
to him with a fascinating smile, intended to "vanquish this
boor"—a peculiarly feminine manœuvre.

"Oh, no, madame," answered the German in his broken
Russian, and, half-lifting the network of the tank, he began
to tap the crocodile on the head with a cane.

At this the perfidious monster, to show that it was alive,
slightly moved its paws and tail, raised its head and uttered
a sound resembling a prolonged snuffle.

"There, don't be cross, Karlchen," caressingly said the
German, whose vanity was flattered.

"What a horrid brute ! I am quite afraid of him," lisped
Elyòna Ivànovna still more coquettishly. "I shall dream
of him now at night !"

"But he not vill bite you at ze night, madame," gallantly
rejoined the German, and burst out laughing at his own
joke, though none of us answered him.

"Come, Semyòn Semyònich," continued Elyòna Ivànovna,
addressing herself only to me, "let's go and look at the
monkeys. I am awfully fond of monkeys ; some of them
are such little loves—but the crocodile is horrible."

"Oh, don't be afraid, my dear," Ivan Matvyèich called
after us, showing off his bravery before his wife. "This
sleepy denizen of the realm of the Pharaohs will do us no
harm ;" and he remained beside the tank. He even took
off one glove and began to tickle the crocodile's nose with
it, in the hope, as he afterwards confessed, of making it
snore again. The keeper, out of politeness to a lady,
followed Elyòna Ivànovna to the monkeys' cage.

Thus all was well, and there was no sign of coming misfortune. Elyòna Ivànovna was so much fascinated with the
monkeys that she appeared completely absorbed in them.
She uttered screams of delight, talked incessantly to me, as
if wishing to ignore the keeper altogether, and went into fits
of laughing over resemblances which she found in the

monkeys to her most intimate friends and acquaintances. I, too, was greatly amused, for there could be no doubt as to the likeness. The German did not know whether to laugh or not, and therefore ended by scowling. At this moment an appalling—I may even say supernatural—shriek suddenly shook the room. Not knowing what to think, I stood for a moment rooted to the spot; then, hearing Elyóna Ivànovna shrieking too, I turned hastily round— and what did I see! I saw—oh, heavens!—I saw the unhappy Ivan Matvyèich in the fearful jaws of the crocodile, seized across the middle, lifted horizontally in the air, and kicking despairingly. Then, one moment, and he was gone. But I will describe all in detail, for I was standing motionless the whole time, and observed the entire process with an attention and curiosity such as I do not remember experiencing on any other occasion. For, thought I in that fatal moment, "what if this had happened to me, instead of to Ivan Matvyèich; how very unpleasant it would be for me!" But to the point. The crocodile began by turning poor Ivan Matvyèich round in its horrible jaws feet fore most, swallowed first of all his legs; then let Ivan Matvyèich, who all this while was clutching at the tank and trying to jump out, protrude again a little, and sucked him back into its throat to the waist. Again it let him protrude, and gulped him down once more. In this manner Ivan Matvyèich was visibly disappearing before our eyes. At last, with a final gulp, the crocodile drew into itself the whole of my learned friend, leaving nothing behind. On the surface of the crocodile one could see how Ivan Matvyèich, in his uniform, completely passed down its inside. I was just going to cry out again, when suddenly cruel fate played another jest upon us. The crocodile swelled itself out (probably half stifled by the enormous size of the mouthful), once more opened its fearful jaws, and for the last time the head of Ivan Matvyèich, with a despairing expression on the face, was suddenly protruded from them. At that instant the spectacles dropped off his nose into the bottom of the tank. It seemed as if this despairing head appeared only in order to cast one last glance upon everything, and take a mute farewell of all the pleasures of this world. But it had no time to carry out its intention ; the crocodile once more gathered up its powers, gulped, and in a moment the head vanished, and this time for ever. This appearance and disappearance of a living human head was so dreadful, but at the same time, whether from the rapidity and unexpectedness of the event, or whether from the dropping of the spectacles from the nose, so funny, that I suddenly burst into a quite unexpected fit of laughter ; but realising that for me, in my quality of family friend, to laugh at such a moment was improper, I instantly turned to Elyòna Ivànovna, and said to her with a look of sympathy—

" It's all up now with Ivan Matvyèich ! "

I cannot even attempt to describe the agitation of Elyòna Ivànovna during the whole process. After her first cry she stood for some time as petrified, and stared at the scene before her, as if indifferently, though her eyes were starting out of her head ; then she suddenly burst into a piercing shriek. I caught her by the hands. At this moment the keeper, who until now had also stood petrified with horror, clasped his hands and raising his eyes to heaven, cried aloud—

" Oh, my crocodile ! oh, mein allerliebster Karlchen ! Mutter ! Mutter ! Mutter ! "

At this cry the back door opened, and " Mutter," a redcheeked, untidy, elderly woman in a cap, rushed with a yèll towards her son.

There began an awful row. Elyòna Ivànovna, beside herself, reiterated one single phrase : " Cut it ! Cut it ! " and rushed from the keeper to the " Mutter " and back to the keeper, imploring them (evidently in a fit of frenzy) to "cut" something or some one for some reason. Neither the keeper nor "Mutter" took any notice of either of us; they were hanging over the tank and shrieking like stuck pigs.

"He is gone dead; he vill sogleich burst, because he von ganz Tchinovnik eat up haf!" cried the keeper.

"Unser Karlchen, unser allerliebster Karlchen wird sterben!" wailed the mother.

"Ve are orphans, vitout bread!" moaned the keeper.

"Cut it! Cut it! Cut it open!" screamed Elyòna Ivànovna, hanging on to the German's coat.

"He did teaze ze crocodile; vy your man teaze ze crocodile?" yelled the German, wriggling away; "you vill pay me if Karlchen wird bersten; dass war mein Sohn, dass war mein einziger Sohn!"

"Cut it!" shrieked Elyòna Ivànovna.

"How! You will dat my crocodile shall be die?" No, your man shall be die first, and denn my crocodile. Mein Vater show von crocodile, mein Grossvater show von crocodile, mein Sohn shall show von crocodile, and I shall show von crocodile. All ve shall show crocodile. I am ganz Europa famous, and you are not ganz Europa famous, and do be me Straf pay shall!"

"Ja, ja!" agreed the woman, savagely; "ve you not let out; Straf ven Karlchen vill berst."

"For that matter," I put in calmly, in the hope of getting Elyòna Ivànovna home without further ado, "there's no use in cutting it open, for in all probability our dear Ivan Matvyèich is now soaring in the empyrean. . . . ."

"My dear," remarked at this moment the voice of Ivan Matvyèich, with startling suddenness, "my advice, my dear, is to act through the bureau of police, for the German will not comprehend truth without the assistance of the police."

These words, uttered with firmness and gravity, and ex-

pressing astonishing presence of mind, at first so much amazed us that we could not believe our ears. Of course, however, we instantly ran to the crocodile's tank and listened to the speech of the unfortunate captive with a mixture of reverence and distrust. His voice sounded muffled, thin, and even squeaky, as though coming from a long distance.

"Ivan Matvyèich, my dearest, and are you then alive?" lisped Elyòna Ivànovna.

"Alive and well," answered Ivan Matvyèich; "and, thanks to the Almighty, swallowed whole without injury. I am only disturbed by doubt as to how the superior authorities will regard this episode; for, after having taken a ticket to go abroad, to go into a crocodile instead is hardly sensible."

"Oh, my dear, don't worry about sense now; first of all we must somehow or other dig you out," interrupted Elyòna Ivànovna.

"Tig!" cried the German. "I not vill let you to tig ze crocodile! Now shall bery mush *publikum* be come, and I shall fifety kopeck take, and Karlchen shall leave off to berst."

"Gott sei Dank!" added the mother.

"They are right," calmly remarked Ivan Matvyèich; "the economic principle before everything."

"Dear friend!" I exclaimed; "I will fly at once to the authorities and complain, for I feel convinced that we can't settle this hash by ourselves."

"I also am of that opinion," said Ivan Matvyèich; "but without an economic remuneration it is hard, in our age of financial crisis, to rip open the belly of a crocodile, and, nevertheless, we are confronted with the inevitable question: What will the owner take for his crocodile? With this there is also another question: Who is to pay? For you know I have not the means."

“Couldn't you get your salary in advance?” . . . I began, timidly; but the German instantly interrupted—

“I not sell ze crocodile. I tree tausend sell ze crocodile, I four tausend sell ze crocodile! Now shall mush publikum come. I fife tausend sell ze crocodile!”

In a word, he carried it with a high hand; avarice and greed shone triumphantly in his eyes.

“I will go!” I cried, indignantly.

“And I! And I, too! I will go to Andrey Osìpych himself—I will move him with my tears!” wailed Elyòna Ivànovna.

“Don't do that, my dear,” hastily interrupted Ivan Matvyèich, who had long been jealous of Andrey Osìpych's admiration of his wife, and knew that she was glad of a chance to weep before a man of refinement, as tears became her very well. “And you, my friend,” he continued, addressing me, “you had better go to Timofèy Semyònych. And now take away Elyòna Ivànovna. . . . Be calm, my love,” he added to her. “I am tired with all this noise and feminine quarrelling, and wish to take a little nap. It is warm and soft here, though I have not yet had time to look about me in this unexpected refuge.”

“Look about you! Is there any light there?” cried Elyòna Ivànovna in delight.

“I am surrounded by impenetrable darkness,” answered the poor captive; “but I can feel, and, so to say, look about me with my hands. Good-bye! Be calm, and do not deny yourself recreation. You, Semyòn Semyònich, come back to me this evening, and, as you are absent-minded and may forget, tie a knot in your handkerchief.”

The respectable Timofèy Semyònych received me in a hurried and, as it were, somewhat embarrassed manner. He took me into his little study and carefully shut the door: “So that the children shan't disturb us,” as he explained with evident anxiety. He then placed me in a seat by the writing-table, sat down in an armchair, gathered up the tails of his old wadded dressing-gown, and put on an official, even severe expression, although he was not in authority over either Ivan Matvyèich or myself, but simply an acquaintance and fellow-official.

"First of all," he began, "remember that I am not an authority; I am a mere subordinate, like yourself or Ivan Matvyèich. I am an outsider, and do not intend to mix myself up with anything."

He evidently knew all, much to my astonishment. However, I told him the whole story over again, with all details. I spoke with emotion, for at that moment I was fulfilling the duty of a true friend. He listened without any great surprise, but with evident suspiciousness.

"Just imagine," he said, when I had done; "I always expected that this very thing would happen to him."

"But why, Timofèy Semyònych—the case is a most exceptional one?"

"Certainly. But during the whole term of his service Ivan Matvyèich has been leading up to this result. He's too nimble—yes, and too conceited. Always 'progress' and new-fangled ideas—and that's where progress ends."

"Well, but this is an altogether extraordinary occurrence; one can't put it forward as a general rule for all progressists."

"Yes, but that's just how it is. You see, all this comes of too much learning—it does, believe me, sir. People that have too much learning always will poke their noses everywhere, and particularly where they're not wanted. However, of course you know best," he added, in a half-offended tone; "I'm an old man, and not so well educated as you; I entered the service from a school for soldiers' children, and my fifty-years' jubilee was this year."

"Oh no, indeed, Timofèy Semyònych, how can you! On

the contrary, Ivan Matvyèich longs for your advice, for your guidance. Even, so to say, with tears."

"'Even, so to say, with tears.' H'm, indeed! Well, those are crocodile tears, and mustn't be too much believed in. Now, just tell me, what put it into his head to go abroad? And on what money? He has nothing, has he?"

"Only savings, Timofèy Semyònych," I answered, sadly, "from the last perquisites. He only wanted to travel for three months—to Switzerland—to the fatherland of William Tell."

"William Tell. H'm!"

"And to Naples, to see the spring there. He wished to see the museums, the life, the animals."

"H'm, animals? In my opinion all that is nothing but pride. What animals? Animals? Haven't we animals enough at home? We have zoological gardens, museums, camels. There are wild bears quite near to Petersburg. And now, you see, he went and tumbled into a crocodile."

"Timofèy Semyònych, for mercy's sake—a man in trouble —a man comes as to his friend, as to an elder relative, imploring advice, and you—reproach him. Have pity, at least, upon the unhappy Elyòna Ivànovna!"

"You are speaking of his wife? A charming lady!" remarked Timofèy Semyònych, evidently softening, and taking a pinch of snuff with much gusto. "A person of subtle refinement. So nice and plump, and the head just on one side—just a *leetle* on one side. Very agreeable—yes. Andrey Osìpych mentioned her again the day before yesterday."

"Mentioned her?"

"Mentioned her, and in the most flattering terms. 'Such a bust,' he said, ' such a glance, such hair! A sugar-plum,' he said, not a lady!' and he began to laugh. They are both young people still." (Here Timofèy Semyònych blew his nose loudly.) "And yet, you see, a young man, and what a career he's made for himself!"

"Yes; but this is quite another case, Timofèy Semyònych."

"Oh, of course, of course!"

"Well then, Timofèy Semyònych, how is it to be?"

"Why, what can I do?"

"Advise us, guide us, as a man of experience—as a parent! What shall we do? Go to the authorities, or——"

"To the authorities? On no account!" hastily exclaimed Timofèy Semyònych. If you want my advice, I say the first thing is to hush up the matter, and act in the character of a private person. It is a suspicious case, an unheard of case. The worst is that it's unheard of—there's no precedent—indeed, it looks very bad. So that the first of all things is caution. Let him stop where he is a bit. He must have patience, patience!"

"But how can he stop there, Timofèy Semyònych? Supposing he chokes to death?"

"Why should he? Didn't you tell me that he had made rather a comfortable arrangement for himself there?"

I repeated all over again. Timofèy Semyònych meditated.

"H'm!" he pronounced, holding his snuff-box in his hands; "in my opinion it will be even a very good thing for him to stop there a bit, instead of going abroad. He can think at his leisure; of course it wouldn't do to choke, and he must take measures for the preservation of his health. . . . I mean—he must take care not to get a cough or anything. . . . And as for the German, my personal opinion is that he is right—more so than the other side, indeed; because, you see, Ivan Matvyèich got into *his* crocodile without leave, and not *he* into Ivan Matvyèich's crocodile; indeed, so far as I remember, Ivan Matvyèich had no crocodile of his own. Very well, then, a crocodile constitutes private property, therefore without remuneration it cannot be cut open, as I take it."

" To save a human life, Timofèy Semyònych."

" Oh well, that's the business of the police. You should apply to them."

" But then, again, Ivan Matvyèich may be needed. He may be sent for——"

" Ivan Matvyèich needed? Ha, ha, ha! Besides, he is supposed to be on. furlough, therefore we can ignore the whole matter and suppose him to be looking at European lands. It will be another case if he doesn't turn up at the end of his furlough; then, of course, we must make inquiries."

" Three months! Timofèy Semyònych, for mercy's sake!"

" It's his own fault. Who asked him to poke his nose in there? I suppose the next thing will be there'll have to be a nursemaid hired for him at Government expense, and that's not stated in the regulations. But the main point is that the crocodile is property, therefore what is called the economic principle comes into play. And the economic principle is before everything. Now, the day before yesterday, at Loukà Andrèich's evening, Ignàtyi Prokòfich was talking about that. He's a capitalist, a business man, and he put it all so plainly, you know : ' What we want,' he said, ' is industry ; we have too little industry. It must be created. We must create capital ; that is, we must create a middle-class, we must create what is called a bourgeoisie. And as we have no capital, we must import it from abroad. In the first place, we must give full liberty to foreign companies to buy up our land in lots, as is the accepted custom now abroad. Communal property,' said he, ' is poison—it is ruin!' And you know he talked so hotly—of course, such men as he have a right to—men of capital; . . . and then, he doesn't serve. 'With communal property,' said he, 'neither industry nor agriculture will improve. What we need,' said he, 'is that the foreign companies should buy up as much as possible of our land in lots, and then divide, divide, divide it up into as many little pieces as they can'—and you should have heard how positively he said it: ' di-v-vide,' said he—' and then sell it for private property. That is—not exactly sell it, but let it. Then,' said he, 'when all the land will be in the hands of the foreign companies that will have been invited over, then, of course, the rent can be put up to any figure you like. The result of that will be that the peasant will work three times as much as now, for bare bread, and we shall be able to do anything we like with him. Undoubtedly he will feel, he will be humble and submissive, and will do three times the work for the same price. But now, with common property, what can you do with him? He knows he won't starve, and so he gets lazy, and drinks. And then, besides all that, money will come in, and capital will be created, and a bourgeoisie will grow up. Now, the English political paper, the *Times*, speaking of our finances, expressed the opinion that the reason our finances do not grow is, that we have no middle-class, no long purses, no submissive proletariat. . . .' Ah ! Ignàtyi Prokòfich speaks well ; he's an orator. He is going to send in a report to the authorities, and then have it printed in the *News*. That's a very different thing from Ivan Matvyèich and his verses. . . ."

"And what about Ivan Matvyèich ?" I asked, when I had let the old man talk to his heart's content. Timoféy Semyònych liked to talk this way sometimes, to show that he knew everything and was not behind the age.

"Ivan Matvyèich ? Well, that is just what I was leading up to. As you see, we are making efforts to attract foreign capital into the country, and now judge for yourself: the capital of the crocodile-keeper (a foreigner attracted here) has barely had time to become doubled by means of Ivan Matvyèich, and we, instead of protecting the foreign possessor of property, are aiming, on the contrary, to rip open the belly of the fundamental capital itself! Now, really, is that consistent?   In my opinion, Ivan Matvyèich, as a true son of the Fatherland, should even be glad and proud that, by the addition of himself, he has doubled, and maybe trebled, the value of the foreign crocodile.   That, sir, is an essential feature in the attracting of capital. If one succeeds, perhaps another will come with a crocodile, and a third will bring two or three at once, and capital will collect round them.   And so you get your bourgeoisie. People must be encouraged, my good sir."

"But, Timofèy Semyònych," I exclaimed, "you demand almost supernatural self-abnegation of poor Ivan Matvyèich!"

"And who told him to get into the crocodile? A respect-able man, a man holding a certain position, living in lawful wedlock, and suddenly—such a step? Now, *is* that con-sistent?"

"But the step was taken unintentionally."

"How should I know that? And then, how is the crocodile-keeper to be paid, eh? No, no, he had better stop where he is; he has nowhere to hurry to."

A happy thought flashed into my mind.

"Can't we manage it this way," said I. "If he is fated to stay in the entrails of the monster, and if, by the will of Providence, he remains alive, can't he send in a petition that he shall be regarded as serving during his sojourn there?"

"H'm; you mean, as on furlough, without salary?"

"No, I mean with his salary."

"On what ground?"

"As being on an expedition, on Government service——"

"What expedition? Where to?"

"Why, into the entrails—the crocodile's entrails. . . . So to say, to collect information, to study facts on the spot. Of course it is a new idea, but then it is progressive, and at the same time it shows care for education."

Timoféy Semyónych meditated.

" 'To despatch an official," he remarked, at last, " into a crocodile's entrails on a special commission, is, according to my personal opinion, absurd. It is not in accordance with the regulations. And then, what commission can there be to fulfil there?"

" Well, you know, natural philosophy—I mean the study of Nature on the spot, in the living organism. Natural science is all the rage now, and botany and all that. . . . He could live there and give information. . . . Well, for instance, about the digestion . . . or even the general habits. For the obtaining of facts."

"That is to say, in the department of statistics. Well, I'm not strong on that point, and then I'm not a philosopher. You say—facts; as it is, we're crowded out with facts, and don't know what to do with them all. And then these statistics are dangerous things."

" How so?"

"Very dangerous. And, moreover, you must admit that he will have to communicate his facts while lying down at his ease. How can a man be on Government service while he's lying down? That, again, is an innovation, and a dangerous one; and for that, too, there is no precedent. Now, if there were even *any* sort of precedent, then, in my opinion, it might be possible to arrange a commission."

" But up till now live crocodiles have not been brought here, Timoféy Semyónych."

" H'm, yes." . . . He meditated again. " There is some truth in your argument, and it might even serve as a basis for the further development of the case. But again, on the other hand, if with the introduction of live crocodiles Government servants begin to disappear, and then, in conisderation of the fact that it is soft and warm inside there, begin to demand commissions to live there, and then spend their time lying down, you must acknowledge it'll be a bad example. You see, if it were so, every one would be wanting to get paid for nothing. Well, good-bye; I must go to Nikifor Nikiforych; are you coming?"

"No, I must go back to the captive."

"Ah, yes, to the captive. Oh-h-h! That's what frivolity leads to!"

When I reached the Passage it was about nine o'clock, and I had to enter the crocodile-room by the back door; for the German had shut up his place earlier than usual. He was walking about at his ease in a greasy old coat, and was evidently three times more self-satisfied even than in the morning. It was plain that he was troubled with no fears, and that "bery mush publikum" had come. "Mutter" came out, too, evidently for the purpose of keeping a watch upon me. She and her son often whispered together. Although the premises were shut up, the German took twenty-five kopecks as entrance-fee from me. That seems to me an excess of accuracy!

"You vill pay ebery time; ze publikum vill pay von rouble, and you vill pay twenti-fife kopeck, vy for you are von goot friend ob your goot friend, and I honour ze friend."

"Is he alive? Is my learned friend alive?" I cried, loudly, approaching the crocodile.

"Alive and well," he answered, as if from the far distance; "but of that afterwards. What news?"

Pretending not to hear the question, I began hastily and with sympathy to put questions in my turn. I asked him how he was, how he got on in the crocodile, and what the inside of a crocodile is like. But he interrupted me irritably.

"What news?" he shouted, in his squeaky voice, which sounded now peculiarly unpleasant.

I related to him all my conversation with Timoféy Semyònych, to the minutest detail. In relating it, I tried to express that I was somewhat hurt.

"The old man is right," said Ivan Matvyèich; "I like practical people, and can't bear sentimental milksops. Sit down anywhere—on the floor if you like—and listen to me:

"Now, for the first time, I have leisure to think out how to improve the lot of all humanity. Out of the crocodile shall come forth light and truth. I shall now invent a new theory, all my own, of new economic relations—a theory of which I can be proud. Up till now my time has been occupied with the service and with the frivolous amusements of the world. Now I shall overthrow everything and become a new Fourier. But to the point. Where is my wife?"

I told him how I had left Elyòna Ivànovna; but he did not even hear me out.

"I build great hopes upon her," he said. "From next week she must begin to throw open her drawing-room every evening. I feel sure that the keeper will sometimes bring me, together with the crocodile, into my wife's brilliant salon. I will stand, in my tank, in the splendid reception-room and shower around me witty sayings, which I will think out beforehand, in the mornings. I will confide my projects to statesmen, with poets I will speak of verse, with the ladies I will be amusing and fascinating (though strictly moral), and I shall have the advantage of being quite inocuous for their husbands. To the rest of society I will serve as an example of submission to fate and to the will of Providence."

I confess that, though all this was something in Ivan Matvyèich's usual style, it came into my head that he was feverish and light-headed. This was the ordinary, every-day Ivan Matvyèich twenty times magnified.

"My friend," I asked him, "do you hope for a long life?

Tell me about yourself: are you well? How do you eat, sleep and breathe? I am your friend, and indeed you must acknowledge that the case is altogether supernatural, therefore my curiosity is altogether natural."

"Idle curiosity and nothing more," he answered, sententiously; "but you shall be satisfied. You ask : How am I domiciled in the entrails of the monster? In the first place, the crocodile, to my great surprise, turns out to be completely hollow. Its interior consists of what appears to be an enormous empty sack, made of gutta-percha. If it were not so, think yourself, how could I find room in it?"

"Is it possible?" I exclaimed in utter stupefaction. " Can the crocodile really be quite empty?"

"Quite," severely and dogmatically affirmed Ivan Matvýeich. "In all probability it is so constructed in accordance with the laws of Nature herself. The crocodile has only jaws, furnished with sharp teeth, and, in addition to the jaws, a rather long tail ; and in reality that is all. In the middle, between these two extremities, is an empty space, enclosed in something which resembles indiarubber, and which, in all probability, is indiarubber."

" But the ribs, the stomach, the intestines, the liver, the heart?" I interrupted almost crossly.

"There is nothing, absolutely no-th-thing of the kind, and probably there never was anything of the kind. All those things are the idle fancies of frivolous travellers. Just as you swell out an air-cushion with air, so I now swell out the crocodile with my person. It is elastic to an incredible degree. For that matter, this hollow formation of the crocodile is fully in accordance with natural science. For supposing, for instance, you were commissioned to construct a new crocodile, the question would naturally present itself to you : What is the fundamental characteristic of the crocodile? The answer is plain : To swallow people. How should this aim—the swallowing of people—be attained in the construction of the crocodile? The answer is still plainer : Make him hollow. The science of physics has long proved that Nature abhors a vacuum. According to this law, the interior of the crocodile must necessarily be empty, in order that the crocodile may abhor a vacuum and may therefore swallow everything that comes to hand, so as to fill itself up. And this is the only reasonable cause that all crocodiles eat men. Now, the construction of man is different : for instance, the emptier is a human head, the less desire it feels to fill itself up ; and this is the only exception to the general rule. All this has now become to me as clear as day ; all this I have comprehended out of my own intellect and experience, being, as it were, in the entrails of Nature, in Nature's retort, listening to the beating of her pulse. Even etymology agrees with my theory, for the very name of the crocodile implies devouring greed. ' Crocodile,' ' *crocodillo*, is an Italian word—a word contemporary, it may be, with the ancient Egyptian Pharaohs, and evidently derived from the French root, *croquer*, which means : to eat, to devour, or in any way to use (any object) for food. All this I intend to explain in my first lecture to the audience which will assemble in Elyòna Ivànovna's salon, when I am carried there in my tank."

"My dear friend, don't you think you had better take a—a cooling medicine ? " I involuntarily exclaimed. " He's delirious, delirious ! " I repeated to myself in horror.

" Fiddlesticks ! " he replied, contemptuously ; " moreover, in my present position that would be not altogether convenient. For that matter, I knew you would begin to talk about cooling medicines."

"Ivan Matvyèich," said I ; "it is hard to believe all the wonders you speak of. And do you mean to tell me that you really, really intend never to dine any more ? "

" What silly things you think about, you frivolous rattle-pate ! I tell you of great ideas and you . . . Know then, that I am sufficiently nourished with the great ideas that illumine the night which surrounds me. For the rest, the good-natured keeper of the monster has talked the matter over with his kind-hearted mother, and they have decided together that every morning they will introduce into the jaws of the crocodile a curved metallic tube, something like a shepherd's pipe, through which I am to suck coffee or broth with white bread soaked in it. The tube has already been ordered from a neighbouring shop, but I consider that this is superfluous luxury. I hope to live, at the least, a thousand years, if it be true that crocodiles live so long (by the by, you had better look that up to-morrow in some book on natural history and let me know, for I may have made a mistake and confused the crocodile with some other fossil). One consideration alone somewhat disturbs me. As I am dressed in cloth and have boots on my feet, the crocodile is, evidently, unable to digest me ; moreover, I am alive and resist the digesting of myself with all my force of will ; for, naturally, I do not wish to turn into what all food turns into, as that would be too humiliating. But I fear one thing : in the course of a thousand years the cloth of my coat (which, unfortunately, is of Russian manufacture) may decay, and I, remaining without clothes, may then, notwithstanding all my indignation, begin to be digested ; and, although by day I shall not permit—shall not under any circumstances allow this,—by night, in sleep, when man is deprived of his free will, I may be overtaken by the most humiliating doom of a mere potato, pancake, or slice of veal. The thought of this drives me to frenzy. If only on this ground the Revenue law must be changed in order to encourage the importation of English cloth, which is stronger, and therefore will resist nature longer in cases of persons tumbling into crocodiles. I shall take the earliest opportunity of communicating this idea to some statesman, and also to the political critics of our St. Petersburg daily papers. They can cry it up. I hope that this will not be the only idea they will take from me. I foresee that every morning a whole assembly of them, armed with editorial twenty-five kopeck pieces, will crowd around me, to catch my thoughts upon the telegrams of the day before. In short, the future appears to me in quite a rose-coloured light."

" High fever, high fever ! " I whispered to myself.

" But, my friend, what about liberty ? " I asked, wishing to hear all he had to say upon that point. " You see, you are, as it were, in a dungeon, whereas man should enjoy freedom."

" You are stupid," he replied. " Savages care for independence, but wise men love only order, and there is no order ——"

" Ivan Matvyèich, have a little pity on me !"

" Silence ! Listen ! " he screamed out in his rage at being interrupted. " My spirit has never soared so high as now. In my narrow retreat I have but one fear : the literary criticism of the big magazines, and the gibes of our satirical papers. I fear that frivolous visitors, fools, envious persons, and nihilists generally, may hold me up to ridicule. But I will take measures. I await with impatience to-morrow's expression of public opinion, and, above all, the criticisms in the newspapers. Be sure and tell me about the papers to-morrow. But enough ; you are probably sleepy. Go home, and don't think of what I said about criticism. I am not afraid of criticism, for it is in a critical position itself. It is sufficient to be wise and virtuous, and you are certain to be raised upon a pedestal. If you do not become Socrates you will become Diogenes, or perhaps both at once, and that is my future vocation as regards humanity."

" Your friend is von bery clefer man," remarked the German to me in an undertone, as he came up to let me out ; he had been listening attentively to all our conversation.

"By the by," said I ; "so as not to forget ;—how much would you take for your crocodile, in case any one should think of buying it ? "

Ivan Matvyèich, hearing this question, awaited the answer with interest. It was evident that he did not wish the German to take too little ; at any rate, he uttered a very peculiar grunt when I put the question.

At first the German would not even listen ; he grew quite angry.

"No man not shall to buy my own eigener crocodile ! " he cried furiously, reddening like a boiled lobster. " I not vill ze crocodile to sell ! I for ze crocodile von million thaler to take not vill ! I von hondert treety thaler to-day from ze publikum take, and to-morrow ten tausend thaler take, and zen von hondert tausend thaler every day to take vill. I not vill sell."

Ivan Matvyèich even sniggered with pleasure.

Controlling my indignation, coldly and calmly—for I was fulfilling the duty of a true friend—I suggested to the crazy German that his calculations were not altogether correct : that if he were to take 100,000 a day he would soon exhaust the population of St. Petersburg, and then would get no more money, that life and death are in God's hands, that the crocodile might somehow burst, that Ivan Matvyèich might fall ill and die, &c., &c.

The German meditated.

"I to him from the apotheke drops vill bring," he said, after thinking it over, "and your friend shall not die."

"Drops are all very well," said I : "but also consider that a law-suit may be started. Ivan Matvyèich's wife may demand her lawful husband. You intend to get rich, but do you intend to settle any pension upon Elyòna Ivànovna ? "

"No, vot for I intent?" exclaimed the German, sternly and decidedly.

"No, vot for ve intent!" repeated the mother, angrily.

"Very well, then; would it not be better for you to take now, at once, a definite and certain sum, if even a moderate one, than to plunge into uncertainty? I consider it my duty to inform you that I put the question not from idle curiosity."

The German took his mother for consultation into the corner where stood the cage containing the largest and most hideous monkey of the whole collection.

"Now you'll see," said Ivan Matvyèich to me.

For my part, at that moment I was burning with the longing, firstly, to cudgel the German soundly; secondly, to cudgel the mother still more soundly; and thirdly, to cudgel Ivan Matvyèich most soundly of all for his boundless conceit. But all this was as nothing in comparison with the greedy German's answer.

After discussing the point with his mother, he demanded in exchange for his crocodile: 50,000 roubles in tickets for the latest internal loan lottery, a stone house in the Goròkhovaya Street, with a pharmacy of his own, and, in addition, the rank of a Russian colonel.

"There, you see!" cried Ivan Matvyèich, triumphantly; I told you so! Except for the last absurd demand to be made a colonel, he is perfectly right, for he thoroughly understands the present value of the monster he exhibits. The economic principle before all!"

"Gracious heavens!" I exclaimed, turning furiously to the German. "What do you want to be colonel for? What feat have you performed, what service have you done, what military fame have you attained to? Why, you must be mad to say such a thing!"

"Mad!" shrieked the offended German; "no, I am von very clefer man, and you are von very sheep-head! I haf merited ze colonel, vy for I did show ze crocodile, and in him von life Hof-rath sit, and no Russian not did show von crocodile, and in him von life Hof-rath sit. I am von wunderbar clefer man, and I to be colonel much vill like!"

"Good-bye, Ivan Matvyèich!" I cried, quivering with rage, and almost ran out of the house. I felt that in another moment I should not be able to answer for myself. The wild hopes of these two idiots were simply unendurable. The cold air refreshed me and somewhat calmed down my indignation, and at last I took a sledge, drove home, undressed, and threw myself upon my bed.

Meditating, over my morning cup of tea, upon all the occurrences of the preceding day, I decided to go at once to Elyòna Ivànovna, on my way to the Department, as, indeed, I was bound to do in my character of domestic friend.

In a tiny room adjoining her bedroom, and called the "little drawing-room" (though their "big drawing-room" was little enough), on a little fancy sofa beside a little tea-table, in a half-ethereal morning *néglige*, sat Elyòna Ivànovna, sipping coffee out of a little cup, in which she dipped the minutest of rusks. She looked distractingly pretty, but also, I thought, somewhat pensive.

"Ah, it is you, bad boy!" she said, greeting me with an absent smile; "sit down, you frivolous person, and drink some coffee. Well, what did you do yesterday? Were you at the masked ball?"

"Were you? I never go . . . and then I spent the evening visiting our captive."

"Who? what captive? . . . Ah, yes, of course! Poor fellow! Well, how is he? Very blue? By the by, I wanted to ask you . . . I suppose I can claim a divorce now?"

"Divorce!" I ejaculated indignantly, and nearly upset

my coffee. " It's that black-whiskered fellow," I said to myself, inwardly fuming.

There existed a certain person with black whiskers (he served in the Building Department) who had taken to visiting at the house rather too often, and who greatly amused Elyòna Ivànovna. I acknowledge that I detested him, and there could be no question that he had already contrived to see her, either here or at the masked ball, and had been talking all sorts of nonsense to her.

" Well, you know," Elyòna Ivànovna began hastily, as if she had learned her speech by heart, " very likely he'll stop in the crocodile all his life, and never come back at all, and what's the use of my sitting here and waiting for him ? One's husband ought to live at home, not in a crocodile ! "

" But then this is an unforeseen case," I began, in very natural agitation.

" No, no, no! I won't hear anything ! I don't want to ! " she cried out, suddenly firing up. " You always oppose me, you horrid wretch ! There's no doing anything with you, you never will advise one ! Why, even strangers have told me that I can get a divorce now, because Ivan Matvyèich won't get his salary."

I began to relate to her all the plans expressed by Ivan Matvyèich the day before. The idea of the evenings at home pleased her greatly.

" Only I shall want heaps of new dresses," she remarked ; " and so Ivan Matvyèich must manage to send me a lot of money, and as soon as possible. . . . Only . . . only, you know," she added, meditatively, " how about his being brought to me in a tank? That is absurd. I don't want my husband to be carried in a tank. I shall feel ashamed before my visitors. I don't want that . . . no, no."

" By the by, did Timofèy Semyònych call on you yesterday evening ? "

"Oh, yes ; he came to console me, and do you know, we played at trumps all the time. When he lost, he had to give me sweets, and when I lost I had to let him kiss my hands. What a rogue he is ! And do you know, he very nearly went to the masked ball with me. Really !"

"He's bewitched," I replied ; "and whom can't you bewitch, you sorceress !"

"Oh, there, if you're going to begin with your compliments ! Look here, I want to pinch you before you go. I've learned to pinch most frightfully. There ! What do you think of that ! Oh, by the by, did Ivan Matvyèich often speak of me yesterday evening ?"

"N—n—no, not very often . . . in fact, he thinks more just now of the destinies of humanity, and wishes to ——."

"There, there ! Let him think ! You needn't finish ; I'm sure it's something awfully dull. I shall run in and visit him some time. I'll be sure and go to-morrow. Only not to-day ; my head aches, and there will be such a lot of people there. . . . They will say, 'That's his wife,' and I shall feel confused. . . . Good-bye. In the evening shall you be there ?"

"With him, of course. He asked me to bring him the newspapers."

"Oh, that's capital. Go to him, and read aloud to him, and don't come to me to-day. I am not well, and perhaps I shall go out to some friends. Well, good-bye, you bad boy."

"That black-whiskered fellow is going to be there this evening," I thought to myself.

At the Department I of course made no sign that I was devoured with such cares and responsibilities. I soon observed, though, that several of the most progressive daily papers were on that morning passing unusually quickly from hand to hand among my fellow officials, who read them with exceedingly grave faces. The first which fell into my

hands was the " Listòk," a paper without any special tendency, but on the whole very humanitarian—for which it
was generally despised in our set, although much read.   It
was with a certain surprise that I read the following :—

" Yesterday our vast capital, enriched with its magnificent
buildings, was filled with extraordinary rumours. A certain
N., a well-known gourmand of the highest spheres of
society, wearied, no doubt, of the cuisine of our first-class
restaurants, entered the building of the Passage at that part
where an immense crocodile, just brought to the capital,
was on view, and demanded that the latter should be pre-
pared for his dinner. After bargaining with the keeper, he
instantly set to work to devour him (that is, not the keeper,
an exceedingly peaceable German with a taste for accuracy,
but the crocodile) alive, cutting off juicy morsels with a penknife and gulping them down with extraordinary speed.
Gradually the whole of the crocodile disappeared into his
fat paunch, and he even set to work upon the ichneumon,
the constant companion of the crocodile, probably supposing
that it would be equally delicious. We have no objection
at all to this new product, already long familiar to foreign
gastronomists. We have even prophesied this beforehand.
In Egypt the English lords and travellers go out in regular
parties to catch crocodiles, and eat the monster's back in
the form of steaks with mustard, onion, and potatoes. The
French followers of Lesseps prefer the paws, baked in hot
ashes, though, indeed, they do this merely to spite the
English, who make fun of them. Here both dishes will
probably be appreciated. We, for our part, gladly welcome
this new branch of industry, of which our great and varied
fatherland is so much in want. After the disappearance of
this first crocodile into the interior of the St. Petersburg
gourmand, it is probable that, before a year passes, they will
be imported by hundreds. And why should crocodiles not

be acclimatised here in Russia?   If the water of the Neva is too cold for these interesting foreigners, we have reservoirs within the capital and streams and lakes without. Why, for instance, should crocodiles not be reared at Pàrgolov or Pavlòvsk, or in Moscow, in the Prièssnensky pools or the Samotyòk?   While providing a delicate and wholesome food for our refined gastronomists, they would also afford amusement to the ladies strolling past these pools, and would serve for our children as a lesson in natural history.   The skin of the crocodiles could be made into étuies, travelling-trunks, cigarette cases, and pocket-books, and perhaps many a thousand roubles—in the greasy notes for which our commercial classes have so strong a predilection—would find its way into crocodile-skins.   We hope to often return to this interesting subject."

Though I had felt a presentiment of something of this kind, the blunders in this article quite upset me.   Turning to the fellow-official sitting opposite me, I observed that he was watching me and holding in his hand the paper *Vòlos*, as if waiting to hand it on to me.   He silently took the *Listòk* from my hand, and replaced it by the *Vòlos*, in which he had marked a particular article.   This is what I read :—

" It is a matter of public notoriety that we are a progressive and humane people, and are trying to catch up Europe in this respect.   But, notwithstanding all our efforts and the energy of our newspapers, we are still far from mature, as is shown by the disgraceful occurrence which took place yesterday in the Passage, and which we had already prophesied.   A foreign entrepreneur comes to St. Petersburg, bringing with him a crocodile, which he at once begins to exhibit to public view in the Passage.   We made haste to welcome this new branch of useful industry, of which our great and varied fatherland is so much in want.   Yesterday, at half-past four in the afternoon, there appeared in the foreigner's shop a personage of enormous corpulence and in an intoxicated condition, who paid the entrance-fee and instantly, without any warning, forced his way into the jaws of the crocodile, which was, of course, constrained by the instinct of self-preservation to swallow him, in order not to choke. Tumbling headlong into the interior of the crocodile, the unknown instantly fell asleep. Neither the cries of the foreign owner, nor the shrieks of his terrified family, nor the threat of an appeal to the police have any effect. From the entrails of the crocodile resounds only laughter, and the unhappy mammal, forced to swallow so enormous a body, sheds copious floods of tears. 'An uninvited guest is worse than a tartar'; but, in disregard of the proverb, the insolent visitor refuses to come out. We do not know how to explain such barbarous incidents, which bear witness to our backwardness, and disgrace us in the eyes of foreigners. The happy-go-lucky Russian temperament has led to a worthy result. We would ask : What did the unwelcome guest desire? A warm and comfortable dwelling? But there are in this city many fine houses, with cheap and exceedingly comfortable apartments, with Neva water laid on, staircases lighted with gas, and often with a porter hired by the landlord. We would also draw the attention of our readers to the savage brutality of such treatment of a domestic animal ; the foreign crocodile is, of course, unable to digest so enormous a mass at once, and now lies, frightfully swollen and in intolerable agonies, awaiting death. In Europe inhuman treatment of domestic animals has long been punishable by law. But, notwithstanding our European lighting-system, our European pavements, our European house-building, we are still far from having shaken off our ancient prejudices :—

  " ' The houses may be new, but the prejudices are old.' "

---

  ¹ A quotation from Griboyèdov.

Nay, even the houses are not new—at least, the staircases of them. We have already several times mentioned in
our columns that on the north side of the river, in the house
of the merchant Loukyànov, the bottom steps of the wooden
stairs are rotten, fallen in, and a constant danger to his
servant, the soldier's widow Afimia Skapidàrova, who is
often obliged to carry water or firewood up this staircase.
At last our warnings have proved true ; yesterday evening,
at half-past eight o'clock, Afimia Skapidàrova fell through
the staircase with a soup tureen and broke her leg. We do
not know whether Loukyànov will mend his staircase now ;
Russians are always wise when it is too late ; but the
victim of this Russian has perhaps already been carried to
the hospital. In the same way, we still persist in maintain-
ing that the dvorniks, who clean the wooden pavements of
the Wyborg district of this town, have no right to splash the
legs of the passers-by, but should shovel the mud into heaps,
as is done in Europe, where boots are cleaned," &c.

" But how's this?" said I, looking in stupefaction at my
neighbour ; " I never heard of such a thing ! "

" How so ? "

"Why, my dear sir, instead of pitying Ivan Matvyèich,
they pity the crocodile ! "

" And why not ? A mere animal—a *mammal*—and we
have pity even for it ! Which way are we behind Europe
after that, eh ? They're very tender to crocodiles in Europe
too, you know. Ha, ha, ha ! "

And my neighbour buried himself in his papers and
spoke not another word.

I put the *Volos* and *Listòk* into my pocket and took, in
addition to them, all the back numbers I could find, for the
evening recreation of Ivan Matvyèich, and, although it was
still early, slipped away out of the Department in order to
visit the Passage, to look on, if only from the distance, at

what was taking place there, and to overhear various expres-
sions of opinions and views. I was convinced that there
would be a tremendous crowd, and drew up the collar of
my cloak to hide my face, for somehow I felt a little bit
ashamed — so unaccustomed are we to publicity. But I feel
that I have no right to dilate upon my personal, prosaic
feelings in presence of so extraordinary and original an
event.

The Steam Chicken

(A Story fit to be printed only in the Christmas holidays.)[1]

By GLYEB USPÈNSKY.

ALTHOUGH I cannot protest against the above observation, which very truly characterises this little sketch, I am bound to remark that the title—" A Story "—given to this production by the editor in question, is entirely out of character with both the subject under discussion and the manner in which that subject is treated. The sketch contains no coherent story at all, nor is it founded upon any story in real life. A group of people were simply discussing " *the soul*," and one of the disputants, a poultry-farmer on a journey, delivered a kind of lecture upon the subject, bringing forward some very interesting facts concerning gallinaceous psychology. That is all.

This is how it happened :—

I got tired of waiting for my train in the stuffy little general waiting-hole of the most microscopic station on the whole N—— Railway, so I went out to sit and smoke on the platform. It was getting on for eleven o'clock on a warm, dark autumn night. The only light on the platform

---

[1] The observation of a certain editor.

came from three small paraffin lamps, placed at long distances from one another, and giving so little light that I was quite unable to see clearly the group of dark human silhouettes collected on the platform close to me, and, like myself, waiting for the train. I could see several black shadows, but it was impossible to form an idea what sort of people they were. The conversation that they were carrying on together was, however, distinctly audible in the motionless silence of the dusky, sultry night.

Unfortunately, this conversation was of a most gloomy character. It referred to an unusual misfortune which had happened early that morning at a neighbouring station, and had been a subject of general conversation along the whole line. A certain publichouse keeper, well known to every one connected with the railway, had thrown himself in front of the train. He had been a confirmed drunkard for some years, and had arrived at absolute beggary.

"You see, mates, towards the last he went off his head altogether," said one of the black silhouettes, whom, from the glittering of his badge when he moved, one could guess to be the railway watchman. "He tried to do it five times before . . . but he always got frightened. He'd run up to the train and then begin to yell. . . . The train would come thundering along, and he'd just scream with terror, and yet he'd run on, throwing up his hands. 'Ah!—ah!— ah!—ah!' and yet he'd run at it. . . . He was mortally scared, and yet he couldn't let it alone! . . . God always saved him; the good Christian people didn't want to let him die; . . . they'd catch him and take him home by force; . . . they put him in the hospital. . . . Well, it seems this time he was too sharp for them." . . .

"Did he call out? Did any one hear?"

"They said afterwards that somebody yelled like a wild thing. They say they heard something crying and screaming. . . . But, you see, it was night-time; it was quite dark

. . . every one was asleep. . . . No, it was God's will, that's plain!" . . .

"The devil's will, you mean. In such business as that, it's the devil that's lord and master, not God!" said a voice from the group of silhouettes.

"True! true!" muttered several voices; and a short silence followed.

The conversation was an unpleasant one; the subject under discussion was gloomy and fearful, and the people seemed ill at ease in talking of it. But maybe for that very reason they were unable to free themselves from the haunting idea, and enter into the ordinary small talk of chance-met passengers. Unpleasant as it was to think and talk of a suicide, the conversation about it started afresh.

"They do say it was all his wife's doing that he got like that; he took to drinking because of her."

"Did the silly fellow care more for his wife than his soul?"

"Ah! but then, you know, . . . she ran away from him —and he got lonely without her—and so——"

"Ran away! Why, the devil take her, let her run away as far as she likes; there are plenty of women to be got!"

"Plenty of women, but only one soul!"

"He'll have to answer for his soul to God in the next world!" . . .

"Ah! the soul! the soul!" . . . said the watchman, with a sigh; and the conversation would probably have broken off if the young assistant-stationmaster had not suddenly appeared beside the group. No one had heard him come up on account of his indiarubber goloshes.

He was a very cheerful young man; he had just got his situation, just got married, just put on his new uniform, and naturally felt that now he was "decently set up." He stopped, as he was sauntering past, to smoke a cigarette with the group, and, for want of anything to do, cheerfully threw in a word.

"What's the talk about? What soul?"

He had accidentally caught, in passing, the word "soul"; his thoughts were altogether at the other end of the earth from any stray conversations ; he was going merrily home to his young wife and his boiling samovar, and was altogether thoroughly contented with himself.

"Why, we were just talking about the misfortune that happened to-day . . . about the publican." . . .

"Well, what about him ? "

He struck a match on his coat-sleeve, hardly listening to what was said.

"We were just talking, sir ; that's all. . . . You see, the poor fellow's lost his immortal soul."

' " What soul ? "

The cigarette lighted suddenly, and scattered little sparks all round.

" What soul ? What nonsense are you talking ? "

" Why ! your honour ! his soul ! "

" The man was simply a drunkard ! It's all nonsense ! "

" But what about the next world ? "

" What's the use of talking rubbish ? Don't get drunk, and you won't be run over. . . . The deuce knows what they'll say next—a soul ! "

His young wife and his boiling new samovar occupied his thoughts so completely that they made his whole conversation merry, and gave it a tone of "all fiddle-sticks ! " Having uttered his few remarks in a cheerful manner, he walked away, also in a cheerful manner, along the platform, and flung back at the group of silhouettes one last word—

" Twaddle ! "

He then disappeared in the darkness, humming "Strielochka."

"No, it isn't twaddle!" rather decidedly remarked one of the silhouettes; and his dark figure moved forwards, hiding all the other silhouettes. "It's anything but twaddle —a soul is!"

The appearance of the cheerful stationmaster had somehow driven away the gloomy thoughts of the group, and, not finding at the moment any pleasant theme for conversation, they did not support the unknown orator by any positive announcement at all. But their silence in no way put him out of countenance, and he continued, in an impressive tone of voice—

"Twaddle! It's easy for him to talk! . . . The man simply doesn't believe in God—he's a Nihilist, that's what he is! . . . If he believed in God he wouldn't dare to talk like that. . . . I used to be no better than a dead log myself until I got conviction. . . . What can any of us understand? We know how to say our prayers; we know how to put candles before the altar; but what do we know about the wisdom of the Lord? . . . And yet, if the Lord God should call me now to the lot, first of a fish and then of a hen, and should give me a talent and allow me to enter into it, I tell you, mates, I understand all about it now! . . . Yes! There is a soul, mates! there is indeed! . . . That's what I say—it's true; it's not twaddle!"

The audience had at first some difficulty in understanding what this poultry-farmer was talking about. The most incompatible images and ideas had got so mixed up together in his speech—God, the soul, a fish's lot, a hen's lot—all this was too hard for the silhouettes to digest at once. Somebody tried how it would do to make one of the stock remarks of the Russian citizen in difficulties: "Of course it is!"—one of those phrases which will serve for an answer at a pinch, but have no meaning in particular (though they are constantly used in commerce); but he said it in a timid whisper, and relapsed into silence.

The silence was, however, of short duration. A pleasanter topic had been started, and the conversation grew lively.

"I don't quite understand—allow me to ask, do hens have souls?" slowly and deliberately inquired one of the silhouettes, with the evident intention of starting a long discussion. "Kindly explain to me on what you base that opinion. A soul is bound to be Christian; and there is surely nothing said in the Holy Scriptures about hens' and fishes' souls." . . .

"I grant you there is really nothing about it in the Scriptures ; but I, you see me, Selivèrstov, poultry-farmer—*I* tell you—yes ! You can believe me or not, as you like, but I assure you that when I get to really understand the affairs of fishes, and especially of poultry, then I began to believe in the Almighty Creator. Up till then I was just a dead log ! You can think what you like. Yes ! . . ."

There was great animation in the tone of the poultry-farmer's voice, but it was evident that the immensity of the theme which so deeply interested him rendered his position embarrassing and perplexed him in speaking.

"Yes," he continued, repeating the words he had already said, "it was through the poultry that I grew to recognise the wisdom of God. You must make what you can of that."

There was a short silence.

"And do poultry have souls?" inquired one of the silhouettes, in a tone of evident irony. The poultry-farmer hesitated a moment, then, as it were, gave himself a little shake, plucked up his courage, and growled, in a deep bass—

"They do !"

"What ! Hens have souls?"

"Yes, sir."

This answer was evidently given in blind recklessness,

and the poultry-farmer, seeing that he could no longer draw back, continued loudly and rapidly—

"I tell you, positively, I would swear it before the Lord Himself—fowls do have souls, may I die to-night if they don't! There!"

Silence.

"They do!" cried the poultry-farmer again.

Once more there was silence.

"Yes! They do, indeed they do!"

"There! there! friend. . . . It strikes me, my man, that you . . . you know. . . ."

"Not, 'you know,' at all! What's the use of 'you know'? It's the truth I'm telling you; not 'you know.' . . . Now I'll just catechise you, and you see if you can answer me."

"Why shouldn't I be able to answer you? If you talk like a human being, I'll answer you like a human being."

"You didn't suppose I was going to bark at you?"

"Well, if you don't bark, I won't cry: 'cock-a-doodle-doo!' . . . Fire away!"

"Very well, then; if you can answer me, I'll put questions to you. . . . First of all: we were just talking about the destroying of souls. . . . Now, tell me, why did the publican throw himself under the train?"

"'Twas the devil's doing, and nothing else," again interposed the decided voice from the group of silhouettes, before the person addressed had time to answer.

"Of course it's the devil's doing, I know that," said the poultry-farmer; "but what I want to know is, on what pretence this same devil got him to go under the wheels; that's what I want to know!"

"Why, you heard what was said—that he got cut up about his wife," answered the other speaker. "Got upset about a woman, took to drinking, and of course any sort of thing can come of the drink. . . ."

"So that, if you look into the matter, it appears like as if the first cause was trouble?"

"I s'pose so. . . ."

"Very well, then; now you explain. What part of him did the wheel go over?"

"I don't know; you'd better ask him. . . . I say! Mikhàilych! where did the wheel go over the publican?"

"It cut him right across the body," answered the watchman—"like this."

"And of course it went over his back and all?" demanded the poultry-farmer, like a regular expert.

"Of course it smashed every bit of him that came under it. . . ."

"That's all right! Now, allow me to ask you, When you say that it happened 'from trouble,' tell me whereabouts in him was the trouble—was it in his back, or his body, or anywhere in his bones?"

This question appeared to the audience so amazingly incongruous, that, after a short silence, several persons went off into fits of laughing; and the interlocutor of the poultry-farmer, evidently not wishing to continue such an idle conversation, remarked—

"Eh! friend! if one wants to talk with you, one must hang a cloth tongue in one's mouth; one's own would soon get wagged off. . . . Your head's so empty, that one can hear the wind whistle through it, even on a close night like this! . . . The trouble was in his inside."

"Do you mean the trouble about his wife was in his inside?"

"There! shut up with your foolery!" exclaimed the other, irritably; "I never heard a fellow rattle off such stuff! . . ."

"All that is because you haven't got any gift of reflection."

"Reflection be hanged!"

"Supposing a soldier's foot is cut off, that means it was his foot that was bad, not his back or his inside. Supposing my hand is cut off, it must have been my hand that was bad, and not my ear or my nose. . . . Very well, then ; if a man goes and breaks his back under a railway train from grief, I should like to know where was his grief—in his back, or in his inside ? "

Silence.

"Now, you see, that's just the whole point. . . . The trouble was in his conscience, in his soul—not in his bones or his ribs. . . . That's why you should say : ' He's lost his soul,' instead of saying ' Twaddle,' as that grand gentleman said. . . . It was his soul that was ill ; and it was his soul that went to pieces under the train. . . ."

"It's the devil's work, and nothing else," obstinately growled the unseen bass in the group of silhouettes.

"The devil's work ? Of course it's the devil's work ! Only, the devil doesn't pull you under the train by your leg, but by your conscience, by your soul. That's just the whole thing. No, no, mates ! There is a soul, there is indeed ! . . ."

"And what about the hen's soul ? " began again the man who had just broken off his conversation with the poultry-farmer.

"Hens have souls too. . . . It was a hen's soul that brought me to my senses. . . . You see my hamper of chickens over there ? "

The hamper was probably standing somewhere on the platform, though it could not be seen in the darkness.

"Well, what about it ? "

"Very well, then ; I thought I'd take our women in once more with a steam-chicken ; but they were too sharp for me. I thought I'd trick them, you see, and pay them for their eggs with a steam-chicken, but I had tried it once too often—they would not take it."

"WELL, I LOOKED, AND I THOUGHT TO MYSELF, 'HOW DID ALL THAT FIRE GET INTO
THAT LITTLE GLASS GLOBE.'"

"Why?"

"Because the steam-chicken has no soul! He has no soul at all, and so he doesn't breed. That's just the whole thing. I work on a steam-chicken farm. Well, you see, at one time we used to exchange steam-chickens for eggs. We'd give a woman a cock and hen—for that matter, it was quite worth our while to give a cock and two hens for a dozen or a dozen and a half eggs. . . . We could always raise ten or fifteen out of two or three dozen; so we made our profit. At first the women took them and it was all right—and of course it was better for us than paying in money. But after a bit we couldn't get anybody to take them; all the women came and made a row about it: 'Your machine-hens won't lay!' And there you are! It's no use, whatever you do; they *won't* lay! And it's just the same with fish. All those machine-raised fish —you know, you can rear them artificially now—but they won't breed. . . . Now, just you think of that—the wisdom of it! The temperature's there—'cause, you know, it's done with hot water and steam—but there's no soul!"

"But it can run about, your machine-chicken—can't it? and eat?"

"It runs about and it eats, but it hasn't any reason. . . It doesn't know how to think about life. . . ."

"Strikes me, my man, you're gone off the hooks! . . ."

"Off the hooks or not, there's not much sense in your talk either. . . . Runs about! What's running to do with it? There's your steam-engine runs, better than any horse; but just you go and tell it: 'Turn to the left,' 'Stop at the publichouse,'—d'ye think it'll turn? . . . Runs! 'Tis all the same thing as the 'lectric light. I've got a neighbour that's lamplighter in a theatre, and he said to me, 'Just look, this is the new fire they've invented!' Well, I looked, and I thought to myself: 'How did all that fire get in that little glass globe ('twas made just like a flower) and not break it?' So I said to him, 'Why doesn't the glass crack with all that fire?' and my neighbour just burst out laughing. 'It's a very dreadful sort of fire, that is,' said he; 'just you spit at it and see how it will hiss.' Well, I spat at that tulip-flower, and it never hissed at all. 'How's that?' says I. 'Why,' says he, 'that fire's just a made-up fire; it's a heathen fire; it's as cold as ice. . . . Just take hold of the tulip.' I took it, and it really was like ice. But it's fire all the same. . . . Now, how's a man to know after that what's God and what's Mumbo Jumbo? . . . It's just the same with the machine-fish and the steam-chicken—they've got a temperature, but they haven't got a conscience! There you see; it was the same with the publican: it was his conscience that ached; and if he went and broke his back, it wasn't his back that felt bad because his wife ran away—it was his soul."

"You put the cart before the horse again, my man! Why doesn't the steam-hen lay?"

"She doesn't lay because she's a machine invention, a creature of temperature, not a creature of God. A steam-hen has nothing but temperature; but a real hen has a conscience. That's why she lays. She lays because she's capable of mental reflections and considerations. There aren't any mental reflections in temperatures, but there are in souls! . . ."

" Are there?"

" Of course there are !"

" And were you ever in a madhouse? "

" Never, thanks be to God !"

"Glad to hear it! I was just thinking, perhaps they hadn't looked after you properly and kept the door locked. . . ."

" No one can talk sense to a fellow like you, without being taken for a madman. . . . What do you know about souls?"

"As much as you know about hens' consciences, I dare say!"

"I know all about them!"

"Do you?"

"I tell you, yes! I understand the whole soul of a hen! What's the use of your cackling? Just you answer me one thing: Do you know how to make a hen sit?"

"No, I don't; and it's not my business; I'm a wood merchant."

"Then, if it's not your business, hold your tongue and listen. . . . The hen, my man, is none too fond of sitting. . . . All she cares for is just to lay her egg, and then go off again to the café-restaurant to lark about with the cocks, and sing songs, and make love. . . . Why, you may have a hen so frivolous that if you keep her three days on the eggs with a coop over her, you can't make her sit on them; she just wriggles away to one side; she thinks to herself, like any fine lady, 'If I take care of the children myself, I may spoil the shape of my bust, and no one will love me!' . . . And she wriggles away into a corner; and there the poor eggs lie, out in the cold. . . . Well, then, when you take off the coop,—up she jumps and off she runs, and clucks and cackles for all the farmyard to hear; and complains of how she was shut up and ill-treated; and the cock comes running up at her bidding to take her part; he's sorry for her, you see! And off they go into the bushes, to the Islands,[1] to the Arcadia, and masked balls. Why, some hens are so larky that one doesn't know how to manage them! So this is what the women do with a gay hen of that kind: they make little balls of bread, and dip them in spirits and give them to her. . . . The gay young hen eats them and gets tipsy; then they stick her on the eggs and put a coop over her. . . . Of course while she's

[1] The Islands in the Delta of the Neva are recognised places for fast amusements. The Arcadia is a well-known music-hall there.

"TO THE ARCADIA AND MASKED BALLS."

249

asleep she doesn't think about dancing and masked balls ; and by the time she wakes up, she's got familiar like with the eggs. . . . Then, you know, the eggs get warm from her, and she feels the warmth of the eggs. . . . And when you take the coop off she can't get up ! She knows as well as any one that it would be fun to go off on the spree ; she hears the cock calling her, and singing romances ; she knows he's going off to the Islands ; and yet she can't get up, her conscience won't let her ! She's learned to pity her little ones ; her soul has waked up. . . . And there she'll sit, till she sits all the feathers off her body, and the flesh gets raw ; she'll sit till she aches all over ! And why ? Because of her conscience ! . . . Her conscience puts all kind of thoughts into her head. She thinks about how she lived before she was married (she has so long to sit, you know, she has plenty of time to think), and how she went off on the spree, and what she saw, and how the cock came up to her (she'll remember every feather on his body a hundred times over), and how it all happened, and then how she fell ill, and then how her baby was born, and how she cried when it was born—she'll think over all that while she's sitting. . . . Now, you see, all these thoughts go out of her soul into the chicken's soul, like ; and the chicken begins to think and feel as she does. . . . He gets all his soul from the hen, while he's the least bit of a thing,—and ideas, and everything. . . . They're just like little seeds, no bigger than a pin's head, just stuck about here and there in him ; and then of course they grow with him ; and by the time he's a grown-up fowl, they're grown-up thoughts. . . . No, no, mates ! it isn't a temperature of fifty degrees, or whatever it is, that does it ; it's a soul speaking to a soul ! . . . It's all the same with people. If a woman with child gets frightened at a fire, and beats her head with her two hands, her child is born with marks on its head—it's just the same thing here. The hen thinks it over, and sighs, and remembers all her youth, and everything that happened afterwards; and all that enters into the chicken's soul. . . . Why are so many cocks hatched? Because the hen thinks so much about the cock, of course; she remembers all his feathers. . . . Everybody knows that if a peasant goes to the priest, or the *starshinà*,[1] or the village clerk, he always take a cock for a present. The hens think a great deal about cocks. So, you see, all these thoughts and cares pass from the hen's soul into the chicken's; and the chicken gets to understand that it will have to be young and unmarried, and then that cocks will come, and it will have to lay eggs. . . . All that passes into its soul while it's in the egg. . . . But there is nothing of all that in hot water; there's nothing but temperature in it. . . . Do you suppose temperature thinks about a hen's life? Do you suppose temperature thinks about cocks?—about how tired it is of sitting, but how it must keep on for the baby's sake? It doesn't think about anything at all! And that's why the chicken comes out without any soul, or mind, or conscience, and doesn't care for anything. . . . It's just like with the 'lectric light—it can't make the grass grow. . . . That's what God is! . . . It isn't twaddle, mates; don't you believe it! A soul's one thing, and a make-up's another. No, no, it isn't twaddle; it's a thing that takes a lot of understanding!"

"I don't know," remarked the other man, indifferently; "it's a bit too learned for me. . . . Seems to me like as if there aren't any other souls except Christian souls. . . . And as for a hen's conscience, I don't know about that . . . don't see it at all!"

"That's just what I say: you don't know."

The discussion was evidently finished. But as the train had not yet come, and no one had anything to do, the com-

[1] Village syndic.

pany would have found it a little awkward to let the conversation drop at the conclusion of the poultry-farmer's speech. Every one felt (as is the case at the meetings of learned societies) the need of *some* kind of answer or continuation. After a moment's silence, therefore, one of the silhouettes (I think, from his voice, it was the one who had laid the suicide of the publican to the devil's account) suddenly remarked—

" You talk about inventions—you're right there ; there's no end to what they've invented nowadays ! One day, when I was in Petersburg, I was going along the Isàkievskaya Square, and there was a grand sledge driving past, with a beautiful horse ; it must have cost thousands, for harness and everything was splendid ; and the driver was just like a figure in a picture. And what do you think, mates ! they'd got stuck on to that driver, just here like— it's as true as I live . . . just in this place. . . ."

" Where ? "

" Here, I tell you ! . . . It's the truth. What do you think he'd got stuck on ? . . . A watch ! . . ."

" Stuck on to him there ? "

" A great watch, half as big as my hand. . . . That's so the gentleman in the sledge can always see it. I should have felt ashamed, if I'd been the driver."

" I suppose the gentleman was so grand he couldn't take the trouble to unbutton his coat."

" I s'pose he wanted to know, to a second, how long he was driving ; his time must have been precious ! I dare say he had a lot of business."

" Well ! " interposed the poultry - farmer, contemptuously ; " if that's what you call an invention ! There are inventions of quite another sort nowadays, my friend ! People are getting too clever to live with their inventions.'

The tone in which these words were uttered plainly

showed that the poultry-farmer was an ordinary hard-up peasant who found a difficulty in paying taxes.

"When I lived, as a merchant's driver, in Moscow, my master used to pay me two roubles to go from Nikòlsk to Nìzhegorod. . . . 'Only make haste,' he would say; 'I want to know if the goods have come in.' . . . But nowadays he can just mumble something into a pipe, and it goes along a wire, and there you are. . . . You can talk on a wire to people in Nìzhegorod, or Smolensk, or anywhere you like; and as for us poor drivers!" . . .

"That's what they call a telephone," remarked the poultry-farmer.

"Agafòn, or Falalèï, or anything you like . . . all their inventions only make it worse for us poor peasants. Wherever we go, there are always inventions in the way, taking the bread out of our mouths! But it's all one to the tax-gatherer."

All the gloomy images called up by the tragedy of the morning, and all the fantastic ideas suggested by the lecture on souls, were put out of everybody's head by this peasant's comment. His remark had brought back the thoughts of all the group to the realities of life; and thus put an end to this conversation of chance-met strangers, in the right and proper manner—the manner in which, in our days, all kinds of discussions end, no matter how they begin.

THE STORY of A KOPECK.

BY

S. STEPNIAK.

PUBLISHED BY THE SECRET PRESS.

AH, my lads! it was a fine, free life in Russia when there were neither landlords nor priests nor fat shop-keepers.

But that didn't last long, the old men say, for the devil saw that the peasant was getting the better of him ; there was no stealing or lying on earth, because every one lived happily ; and the devil began to think—how could he spoil the race of men. Seven years long he thought, never eating, drinking, or sleeping—then he invented the priest. Then he thought seven years more—and invented the barine.[1] Then he thought seven years more—and invented the merchant.

Then the devil was pleased, and chuckled till all the leaves fell off the trees.

So the devil sent priest, barine, and merchant to the peasant. But the silly peasant, instead of shaking them off, clothed and fed them and let them ride on his neck.

So from that time on there were no more good days for the peasant ; priests and barines and shopkeepers tore him in pieces.

Not with knives or swords they wounded him, but with a copper kopeck. When the sun rose he thought : Where shall I get a kopeck? When the sun set he thought, Where shall I get a kopeck?

Then the peasant prayed to his Mother Earth : " Oh, Mother Earth, tell me where to get a kopeck."

And the Earth answered, muttering . " In me is thy wealth."

The peasant took a spade and began to dig. He dug all the day long, and a second and a third day. He dug a deep, deep pit, but still there was no kopeck. He dug through the soil and came to sand, through the sand and came to mud. He dug and dug and baled out the water. At last he came to clay. His spade was all spoiled, and yet there was no kopeck. Then he began to dig with his hands, and dug and dug ; then he came to stone and could dig no further.

[1] Landlord and Serf-owner (corruption of the ancient word "boyàrin ").

The peasant fell down on the breast of his Mother Earth, and asked her why she had jested with him so bitterly. Suddenly he saw ; under a clod lay a copper kopeck. It was all green and spotted with damp, and as rough as the earth itself.

The peasant seized it, kissed it, wrapped it up and put it in his breast. Then he crawled out to God's daylight and went home with his kopeck.

As he went the birch tree with her thick tresses greeted him and asked—

" Peasant, peasant, why is thy clothing like a fishing-net ? "

" I have gained a kopeck," he answered.

" Thy kopeck costs thee dear," said the birch tree, shaking her locks.

He went on further and the forest bird asked him—

" Peasant, peasant, why art thou all roughened and blistered like oak-bark ? "

" I have gained a kopeck."

The bird whistled and flew away, saying to herself, " I'm glad I'm not a peasant."

He walked on, and the river fish asked him—

" Peasant, peasant, why art thou as thin as a herring ? "

" I have gained a kopeck."

The fish said nothing, she only whisked her tail and dived right down to the river-bed to get away from the world, for fear she should be made into a peasant too.

The peasant walked on and met a priest, so he took off his cap and went to receive his blessing. The priest saw that the peasant was coming home from work, so that he very likely had a kopeck ; and the priest thought he would like to have that kopeck himself. So he came up to the peasant and said—

" Open your mouth."

The peasant opened it.

"Put out your tongue."

He put it out. The priest put his hand in his pocket, took out some bread crumbs and sprinkled a little on the peasant's tongue. What was left he put by for another time.

"Now give me your kopeck," he said.

The peasant gave it him and went home.

"Well," said his wife, "did you get a kopeck?"

"Yes."

"Where is it?"

"I gave it for the kingdom of heaven," he answered.

"Thanks be to God," said his wife; "and now come to dinner."

They said grace and sat down to dinner—fir-bark and rain-water. When they had finished the peasant gave thanks to God for these earthly blessings, and lay down to rest.

Meantime the priest went home, thinking what he should do with the peasant's kopeck. He thought and thought; at last he said, "I know!" and called the *Ponomàr*.[1]

The Ponomàr not only sang in the choir; he was not too proud to drive bargains too.

So the Ponomàr came, and the priest said to him—

"Look here, long-mane! It's a fast to-day, so I've had no meat. Here's a kopeck for you; roast me your sucking-pig, and see you don't blab to any one, or I'll tear your hair out. But if you manage it properly I'll give you the tail to pick."

The Ponomàr went away. "What next, Fat-paunch," he thought. "No, no! You can pick the tail yourself, and I'll fatten up the sucking-pig and sell it to the *Arkhie-rèy*[2] himself."

And he took the kopeck to the village shopkeeper, and said—

"Look here, gossip, here's a kopeck for you; give the

---

[1] The village bell-ringer.   [2] Bishop.

priest a sucking-pig for it and me a hive of honey for my trouble."

The shopkeeper laughed, but he took the kopeck. "I'll go to the peasant," he thought.

So he went to the peasant and showed him the kopeck.

"Do you see this kopeck?" he said. "Well, you give me for it your sucking-pig and a hive of honey and a wolf-skin for a coat."

"All right," said the peasant, "I'm well rested now."

First of all he gave the shopkeeper his sucking-pig, that he had kept for a holiday—the greatest holiday in the year.

"Well, never mind," he thought. "When my little son that lies in his cradle now grows up we'll have a proper holiday."

Then he took a slice of bark-bread, put a knife into his boot, and went to the forest. He walked on, sniffing; does it smell of honey anywhere? No, not a bit. He went on and on; he had eaten his bread, and had to live on roots and acorns, and still no honey. At last he smelt it faintly in the distance, and went on till he came to a great lime-tree, with the bees swarming round it. But see! a huge bear was standing by the hollow trunk, and just going to put his paw in.

"Oh, Lord!" cried the peasant, "surely he is not going to take the honey from me!"

He drew out his knife and rushed at the bear; the bear turned round, drew himself up grandly, and came to meet him. The peasant hastily tore off a lot of fine birch twigs, twisted them round his left hand, and took the knife in his right.

They met. The bear put out his paw, but the peasant warded him off with the left hand, and with the right plunged the knife up to its handle right into his heart. Then he sprang back sharply, but unluckily he got tangled in a branch, so that the bear was able to catch him, and they met in a hand-to-hand fight. First the bear hugged him and nearly broke his bones; then he hugged the bear. The blood rushed from the wound, and Mishka fell down dead.

The peasant rubbed himself a little after the bear's embrace, and thought: "God is merciful even to peasants! If He had not sent me the bear I should have had to go hunting for a wolf heaven knows how long; but now, perhaps, the shopkeeper won't mind taking a bear's skin instead of a wolf's."

He skinned the bear, took the honey, and went home with his prize. But when the shopkeeper saw the bear-skin he shook his head and said—

"A bear-skin instead of a wolf-skin! What will you give into the bargain?"

"Why, what can I give?" said the peasant; "my breeches?"

"All right."

The peasant took off his breeches and gave them to the shopkeeper; then he received his kopeck and took it to the barine to pay off his debt for last year's cattle-drinking tax; no doubt it was the barine's prayers that made the water flow in the river so that the peasant's cattle could drink.

As he went the peasant looked at the kopeck that he held in his hand. It had passed through many hands, and was no longer so rough and rusty as when he had given it to the priest for the kingdom of heaven. It was the same kopeck, but the peasant did not recognise it, and said: "All right. This is a nice kopeck, much cleaner than my old one. I'll give it to the barine now; it won't soil his honour's hands."

So he went up to the manor-house, took off his cap and stood at the gate. But as ill luck would have it the barinya was looking out of the window to see whether a young officer was coming, and when she saw the peasant without breeches she cried out—

"Ah! ah! I shall die!" turned up her eyes, fainted away, and dropped on the carpet, only just kicking a little.

The servants ran to tell the barine that the barinya was graciously pleased to see a peasant without breeches and is dying. The barine rushed out and stamped his foot at the peasant and shouted at him, but when he heard that the peasant had come to pay the tax he got quiet. He graciously took the kopeck, and just wrote a note and gave it to the peasant.

" Here, my man," he said, "just take this note for me to the *Stanovòy*." [1]

The peasant took the note, gave it to the Stanovòy, and was just going when he looked at the Stanovòy and stopped short. The Stanovòy was clenching his fists and grinding his teeth and panting with rage.

"How dare you!" he shouted to the peasant; "you clown! how dare you insult the lady?"

The peasant tried to explain, but it was no use; the Stanovòy grew more furious than ever.

"What? You want to deny it, you hound! I'll send you to Siberia! I'll flay you alive!"—and so on, and so on. And he flew at the peasant as if he wanted to toss him or jump into his mouth.

The peasant's wife heard the row, caught up a cock, ran to the Stanovòy and dropped at his feet.

"Little father!" she cried, "there is a cock for you. Take it, and welcome, but don't kill my good man, or I and all the children will starve."

The Stanovòy almost choked with fury.

"A cock! How dare you offer me a cock! I've served God and the Emperor for twenty years as Stanovòy and

---

[1] District Police Inspector.

never suffered such an insult yet. Bring me your goat at once, or I'll have your cottage pulled down!"

There was nothing for it; they brought him the goat. The Stanovòy grew calm and ordered the peasant to be only flogged and then let go free. The peasant went home and told his wife to make him new breeches, because he must soon go to work in the barine's garden to pay off a debt, and perhaps the barinya might see him again.

The barine was walking about the manor thinking what he should do with the kopeck. At last he sent for the peasant.

"Look here, friend," he said, "you said you wanted fire-wood. There's a stick in the kitchen-garden that you may have, only you must do an errand for me. You must go to my friend, Saffròn Kouzmich—he lives only five hundred versts off—and tell him that I send him my compliments, and ask him to visit me."

"All right," said the peasant.

So he went to Saffròn Kouzmich. He walked and walked and walked. At last he got to the place and gave his message.

Saffròn Kouzmich came at once, for he and our barine were great friends; when they were young they had served the Tzar together. So he came to visit the barine, and they played for the kopeck. Saffròn Kouzmich won it, and drove away very merry and sang all the way home. But our barine was very angry, so he called the *Sòtsky*[1] and told him to collect taxes from the peasant.

The Sòtsky came to the peasant and asked for the taxes.

"Where am I to get the money from?" asked the peasant.

"Where you like. But you must get it somewhere, or the barine will send for the Stanovòy again."

The peasant scratched his head. However, there was

[1] Inferior police official, who collects taxes.

nothing for it, he must get the money.   So he went to look for work.   He went everywhere, and could find no work. At last he came to the same gentleman who had won the kopeck, and asked him for work.   The gentleman called his steward.

"Is there any work?" he asked.

"Certainly," said the steward, "the dam is broken down, and must be mended at once.   But it's very dangerous work, for the workman may get carried away by the water, and besides, it's just under the mill-wheel.   It will do nicely for this peasant; any peasant will jump into the fire, let alone the water, for a kopeck."

"Very well," said the gentleman.

The steward went to the peasant and said—

"Mend the mill-dam, and just build a cottage for me, because I took your part and got you the job.   You shall have a kopeck.   Only mind you do the cottage first, for we are in the Almighty's hands, and you may get drowned."

"All right," said the peasant.

He took an axe, cut down some trees, dragged them to the steward's yard and built a cottage.   The steward came and looked—a capital cottage.

"Very good," he said, and gave the peasant a glass to smell, out of which he had drunk vodka two days before.

"Thank you," said the peasant.   "That was very kind."

Then he went to mend the dam.   The water was seething like a boiling pot.   He got the job done at last, but the water swept him down right under the mill-wheel.

"He's lost!" thought the steward; "the kopeck he has earned remains with me."

But the peasant dived, and so got out of the water safe and sound, and the steward had to give him his kopeck. The peasant walked home with the kopeck, thinking—

"God be thanked!   Now the barine won't demand the

"'VERY GOOD,' HE SAID, AND GAVE THE PEASANT A GLASS TO SMELL, OUT OF WHICH HE HAD DRUNK VODKA TWO DAYS BEFORE."

tax for a week. I shall have time to do some work for my-self, and to rest enough for the whole year as well."

He went straight to the manor. All the court was strewn with juniper—every one was in black clothes, and there were two candles in the window.

"What has happened?" asked the peasant.

"The barine is dead," they told him.

The peasant burst into tears. "God rest his soul!" he thought; "he was a kind barine."

He asked for the barinya to take her the kopeck, but she

could not see him. She was broken-hearted about the barine, and a young officer was consoling her in her grief. So she would let no one in. The peasant went home, dug a pit in the cellar, and put his kopeck into it, just so that it should not get lost.

Some days afterwards, as he was going home, he heard some one sobbing. He looked round and saw a little girl sitting by the road and crying bitterly.

"What are you crying for, my lass?" he asked.

The child told him that her brother was very ill, so that a priest had to be called, to dip his finger in oil and rub it on the sick man's lips. The priest would not come for nothing, and they could not pay him.

The peasant laid his great rough hand on the child's head, ruffled her hair and said—

"Don't cry, silly child! I'll pay the priest."

The little girl thanked him and ran to the priest ; and the peasant went down into the cellar, dug out his kopeck, and brought it to the light. He looked at it and clasped his hands : he had recognised his kopeck—the same that with such toil he had won from the bosom of Mother Earth. Lying in the earth again, it had become just as green and rough as it was then. . . . And the peasant wept bitter tears of anger and grief, for he understood that all his labour had been in vain : he had gained nothing but this same kopeck, which had been his already. Now it must go to the priest again, and wander about the world once more, and every one into whose hands it fell would ride upon his neck. And if by chance it should come into his cottage again, he must only give it away once more, either to the barine or to the priest.

"*I will give no one my kopeck!*" the peasant decided.

He went to the neighbour's cottage, and saw that the

"'GIVE ME THE KOPECK! I'VE LISTENED TO ENOUGH OF YOUR NONSENSE!'"

sick man's lips were already smeared with oil, and in the middle of the room stood the priest, who had collected all kinds of things—cakes, eggs, flaxen threads—and was looking round to see what more he could get. He saw there was nothing more to give, and turned to the peasant.

"Well, now give me the kopeck."

"Oh, little father, little father!" said the peasant; "do not rob the Orthodox people!"

"You rascal!" cried the priest. "How dare you say such things to your spiritual father!"

"Little father, little father! From my very soul I say it;—do not rob the Orthodox people. Think what you are doing, little father!"

The priest caught up the baby's cradle, rushed at the peasant and cried—

"Give me the kopeck! I've listened to enough of your nonsense!"

The peasant answered, holding him by the hands—

"No, little father, go your way, and God go with you; I will not give you the kopeck. It would be a sin to encourage your sin."

The priest lifted up the tail of his cassock and rushed straight to the manor-house. He ran in and found the barinya with the officer. The officer was merry, as merry as could be, for he had just asked the barinya to be his wife, and she had consented.

"Why, little father, what's the matter with you?" he asked, laughing. "Has your wife been thrashing you?"

"My wife! That would be nothing serious; we could soon settle that. *The peasant has mutinied*, that's what has happened!" And he told them what the peasant had said.

"Well, you're a fine fellow to call yourself a priest! Your hair may be long, but your head's short enough! Couldn't manage a peasant!"

"Bring him to me," said the new barine to his lackey.

"I won't even speak ; I'll just look at him, and you'll see how tame he'll get ! "

The lackey went to fetch the peasant, and the barine twirled his moustaches and waited to show off his courage to the priest and the barinya. Presently the lackey came back with the peasant, and stood at the door.

"Bring him here !" said the barine; "let me look at him." And he glanced sideways, now at the priest, now at the barinya.

They brought in the peasant. The barine stood in the middle of the room, with his left arm a-kimbo, his right hand in his pocket, and his neck stretched out, clenching his teeth and rolling his eyes. The peasant looked at him, and got quite frightened.

"Little father !" he cried, "you must be ill ! Wait a minute, poor fellow, I'll bring you some water to drink ! "

Without waiting for an answer, he ran out into the yard, took off his greasy cap, filled it from the water-tub, and brought it to the barine.

"There, little father, drink ! "

But the barine sat blinking his eyes ; he was ashamed before the priest and the barinya. The barinya flew at the peasant ; she was almost ready to tear his beard out.

"How dare you bring the barine water in your filthy cap ?" she cried.

He emptied the water out of the window and asked the barine—

"What do you want with me ? "

The barine had recovered himself ; he leaned back in the armchair, put his hands in his pockets, and said—

"What are you mutinying for, my friend ?"

"Mutiny ? It's a sin for the priest to rob the people, and to encourage him is a sin too ; that's all !"

"What do you mean, my friend? Why, the priest is your spiritual father. Do you want him to live by his own labour, instead of yours ?   I suppose you'll say next that I ought to support myself too, instead of your working for me ! "

" You're no fool, even if you are a barine," said the peasant. " You have just guessed it ; I wont pay you either."

The barine started up as if he had been stung, rushed at the peasant and demanded the kopeck of him ; but it was no use, the peasant would not give him the kopeck.

The peasant went home, but officer, priest, and barinya sat thinking what they should do with him.   They thought and thought, and at last agreed to send a message to the Stanovòy, that the peasant had mutinied, and would not give up his kopeck, and that the Stanovòy must come and manage him.   The Stanovòy turned quite white when he read the letter.

" Heavens ! " he thought ; " my end is come, the peasant will murder me ! "

However, he was an official, and must go.   He put four pistols into his belt, mounted his fleetest horse and rode off. He rode slowly till he came to a hundred paces from the peasant's cottage, then started his horse at a furious gallop, and rushed past the cottage like a whirlwind, crying out—

" Give up the kopeck !   Give up the kopeck, you villain ! I will tear you in pieces if you don't ; I will sweep you off the face of the earth ! "   And he lashed his horse furiously.

There was a fearful hubbub in the cottage.   The peasant was not at home ; but when the Stanovòy made such a noise outside, the cow began to moo, the pig began to grunt, the sheep began to bleat, and the dogs jumped over the fence and rushed, barking, after the Stanovòy.

" I am lost ! " he thought.   He dropped the reins, caught at the horse's mane and closed his eyes, so as not to see death, and the horse rushed on and knocked against a huge stone.   The Stanovòy was flung head over heels on to the ground, where he lay and thought : "I am killed ! God receive my soul !"

The dogs ran up, smelt him all over, and ran home again, wagging their tails. He lay still, waiting for death. He waited and waited, but it did not come; at last he opened one eye, then the other. Then he cautiously lifted his head and looked round. His horse lay beside him with its legs broken.

"Oh, Lord !" thought the Stanovòy, "what shall I do? The peasant will seize me and take me into captivity !"

He almost died of terror, but he plucked up his courage

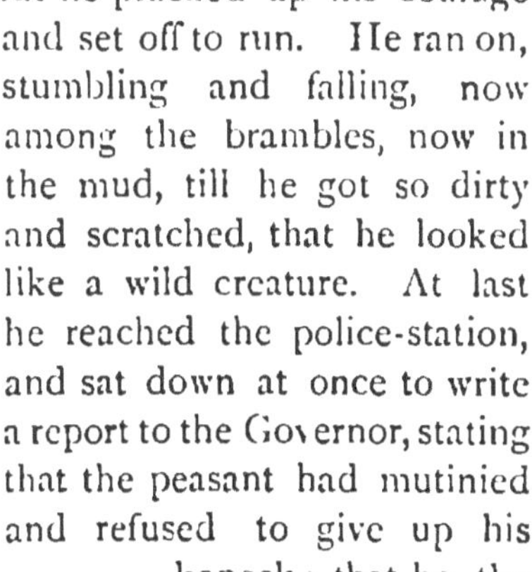

and set off to run. He ran on, stumbling and falling, now among the brambles, now in the mud, till he got so dirty and scratched, that he looked like a wild creature. At last he reached the police-station, and sat down at once to write a report to the Governor, stating that the peasant had mutinied and refused to give up his kopeck ; that he, the Stanovòy, had gone to persuade him ; but that the peasant would not listen, and in answer had bellowed like a whole herd of cattle. Then the peasant had loosed upon him a peculiar breed of dogs, which he had got for the purpose; these dogs were fearful to see—the size of calves—and ran like the wind. Then the peasant had flung a great stone at him, as big as a bull, and broken the forelegs of his horse.

The Governor read this report and said—

"The Stanovòy must be rewarded for his bravery with St. George's Cross!"

Then he ordered off a squadron of soldiers to fight the peasant. Early next morning the Governor, the Stanovòy, and the squadron of soldiers started off on their campaign against the peasant. In the evening they reached the wood where the peasant lived. The soldiers pitched their tent and lay down to sleep, and the officers met in the Governor's tent to hold council and decide how they should capture the peasant. Finally they agreed that a direct attack was dangerous, so they must wait till dawn, when the peasant would come out into the wood to wash in the spring, and then surround and seize him.

The next morning they surrounded the spring, and hid themselves in the bushes, so that the peasant should not see them. Just as he was going to stoop down and wash, they suddenly blew their trumpets and beat their drums and shouted on all sides of him.

"What can it be?" thought the peasant, rubbing his eyes. But the Stanovòy, fired with courage, rushed forwards, like one possessed, waving his sword and shouting to the soldiers—

"Courage, men! We will die for our father the Tzar, and for the Orthodox faith!"

Then he caught up a banner and cried—

"Follow me! hurrah!"

"Hurrah! hurrah! hurra-a-ah!" yelled the soldiers, and charged upon the peasant.

He tried to defend himself, but it was useless; in a

moment they seized him, tied his hands and led him to the Governor. But he had time to break several guns, and bite through two bayonets.

"Give up the kopeck!" shouted the Governor.

"I won't!" said the peasant.

So they put him in prison and tried him. They sentenced him, for the crime of mutiny and obstinacy, to receive twenty-five thousand lashes, and then to be sent back to his former habitation. Further (in order that he might not continue to hide his kopeck), to feed a squadron of soldiers, who should be billeted upon him until he gave up the kopeck. And for the bayonets that he had bitten through, and the Stanovòy's uniform that was spoiled, to pay costs.

The punishment was inflicted, and the peasant sent home. Then the soldiers arrived, and sat down to dinner.

The peasant killed them a sheep. They ate it and cried —"More!"

He killed a pig—"More! More!"

He killed a cow—"Why," they cried, "we are hungrier than before dinner!"

"If they go on like this," thought the peasant, "they'll end by eating me."

"Wait a minute, mates," he said; "I'll go to the bee-hives and get you honey."

"All right," said the soldiers.

He took his cap and ran out of the cottage.

"Now sit and gnaw logs for honey, accursed brood!" he thought; "and if you don't like that, try bricks instead, but I'll not feed you any more!"

And he went away into the deep, dense forest. He walked on for three days and three nights, till, in the evening of the third day, he came to wild thickets, where no human foot had ever trod. Then he sat down on a hillock, looked around him, lifted his left foot and took from under his ankle-straps his kopeck—that same kopeck for which he he had suffered so much. He looked at it and said—

"I have suffered many griefs for thee, my kopeck, since first I carried thee in my bosom, to bring down on me the birds of prey. I know that without thee I shall be still more unhappy; but they shall rather tear out my eyes than thou, my kopeck that I have toiled for, shalt go to serve my enemies!"

And he dug a pit and buried his kopeck. Then he lay down on the grave of his kopeck and thought in bitterness of spirit—

"*If thou hast no kopeck, lie down in thy coffin : if thou hast a kopeck, drown thee in the river!*"

And the peasant sighed heavily, heavily, and he fell down upon the earth and prayed, saying—

"Oh, Mother Earth! teach me, for I know not, what I shall do, that I may have not only sorrow and misery—that even in *my* life there may be bright days!"

And the peasant fell asleep.

Sunrise is wiser than nightfall. Next morning the peasant awoke, and, after pondering deeply, he broke off a strong bough, cut it with a stone and made a spade : with this he raised an earthen hut. And he covered it with brushwood, and filled the chinks with moss, and roofed it over. Then he closed the entrance with a stone and took up his dwelling there.

Time passed on, and a household grew up about the peasant, with fields and pastures and all things needful. There he dwelt and passed his days in peace and joy, praising God.

What then, my lads? If the good folk were but a bit wiser and would stand up for themselves and their own, maybe every man might live in peace and plenty, and never need to slip away and hide his head in the forest. Think of that!

THE DOG'S PASSPORT.

(TOLD BY A PEASANT.) [1]

WELL, you see, once there was a man with an old dog; and he took the old dog and turned him out of doors, he did. So the dog up and says: "Give me a passport that I lived with you." So the man wrote him a passport, and let him go his way—to the four winds. Well, the dog went his way, and at last he came to another man as hadn't got a dog; and he just hung on and begged him to let him bide. So the man took him, and he bided there one day, and two days,—and all at once he saw the cat. And it was a fine cat. And all their lives they two had never cast eyes one on the other. So the dog says—" Who are you?" and the cat says—" I am the cat, and I live here, and I look after the master . . . And who are you?" she says. " I am the dog," says he; "and I've got a passport; I live in the back-yard, and look after the master." " And where's the passport?" " Here it is, under my paw." " Give it to me; I'll hide it away safe, or you will be getting it all sopping wet when the rain comes." " Well," says the dog, "take it, but give it me back when I tell you." So those two were right good mates together. Only one night the cat

[1] The peasant is satirizing the Russian " Passport regulations," according to which it is a penal offence for a householder to take in any inmate who cannot show police certificates.

ran after a wee mousie, and she dropped the passport in the
old straw, and the gammer took it and burnt it up in the
fire, she did.   Well, then the gaffer took the dog and turned
him out of doors, because he hadn't got his passport; and
the dog called the cat.   " Give back my passport !"   " It's
gone," says she; " I lost it !"   And that dog, it just
flew at the cat, and tore it into little wee bits. . . . There
now! If the cat hadn't happened to have burnt the passport,
those two would have been mates like, and the dog would
have bided at home.   Only think of that!

THE DOG'S PASSPORT.

A Trifling Defect in the Mechanism

BY

GLYEB USPÈNSKY.

"WHAT I think about it is this: If a man is altogether innocent, there isn't any need at all to punish that man. But when you get a man that's either a criminal, or else what you may call a villain, or anything of that kind, then you should punish him. That's all."

The above reflections were uttered slowly, deliberately, and significantly, by the steward of the little steamer *Perch*, as he sat in his tiny crockery-filled pantry, cutting up a wheaten loaf into thin slices on the window-sill. The *Perch*, which travels once daily along the river Vȳdra, from the railway station to the little provincial town of M., is never very rich in passengers. Not many people care to sit for several hours at a stretch in the cabin, awaiting the moment when enough people shall have collected, "one at a time," to repay the owner of the *Perch* for the cost of the fifty-verst journey. Impatient passengers, instead of waiting for the steamer, prefer to drive in to M., or to go by the branch railway which runs from the main line to the next posting station. Thus the only passengers who travel on the *Perch* are those who are in no hurry, who do not care whether they reach the town to-day or to-morrow, and who, indeed, even prefer to travel in a leisurely manner and at their ease ; there is always so much room on the *Perch* that you can stretch yourself out at full length, undress, go to sleep—anything. This state of things is very convenient and profitable for the steward. The public saunters on to the steamer, in a gradual, indefinite way; and it is really not worth while ever to close the refreshment-bar, as it would have to be opened twenty times a day. This re-freshment-bar, being constantly before the eyes of passengers who have nothing to do and feel no desire to hurry anywhere, can hardly fail to be in demand. Sometimes a man will sit lazily looking at the various drinks exposed, and will finally say : "Here, just pour me out some of that; I don't particularly want a drink, but the bottle takes my fancy ; what's in it? Give me a glass." And once the refresh-ment-bar is resorted to, the passengers, who have been waiting so long for the little mosquito of a steamer to whistle, involuntarily slip into a chat ; somehow or other, all the people travelling on the *Perch* are sure to strike

up acquaintance together and enter into a general conversation.

This was the case on the present occasion. In the
second-class cabin about a dozen people of various kinds
were sitting or lying on the sofas beside the tables and the
bar window. There were two army officers, who, from their
appearance and conversation, might have been shopkeepers
in disguise, so feeble, effeminate, and altogether unmilitary
was their manner ; they were talking about their provisions,
about "comfort and good living," about the minutest of
injustices and intrigues—intrigues over hay, and soldier's
kvass, and one thing and another. There were shopkeepers,
artizans, and four money-lenders, evidently regular "skinflints," who sat apart, drinking tea together, and abruptly
snapping out broken phrases about their "business":
"Two six and six."—"One rouble five."—"And the goods?"
—"All right."—"Did you contract?"—"Yes," &c. . . .
In the intervals between these remarks they were affected
by sudden, loud hiccoughing, almost like a volley of guns
at a distance.

For some time the conversation among the passengers
rather flagged, and was in no way interesting. The officers
complained that every year they had to "make up out of
their own pockets," and boasted, each to the other, of their
irreproachable character. The "skinflints" alternately
snapped and hiccoughed; altogether, it was rather dull.
In reference to what topic the steward uttered the sentence
quoted at the beginning of this sketch I have no recollection.
I did not hear all the previous conversation, and do not
know what had made the steward feel it necessary to express
his opinion about punishment; but that opinion somehow
aroused in me a desire to listen further.

Having cut the bread into thin slices, and carefully swept
up the crumbs into his fat hand, the steward began to cut
thin slices of cheese, and continued, as gravely as before—

"That's my opinion. If a man's innocent and hasn't deserved any punishment, I should like to know why I should ill-use him?"

"Very true," remarked a shopkeeper, who was sitting with a bottle of beer.

"On the other hand," continued the steward, "if we come across a regular scoundrel, then most certainly the law should be obeyed."

"Of course it should. There's no need to pity a scoundrel."

"Then, again, you see, to punish a man is easy enough, there's nothing very clever in that; you just take him and put him in the lock-up, or give him a thrashing—you don't need much work for that, or much brains either. . . . But, first of all, you must find out, and go into the matter, and get to the root of it, and find out whether the man really is guilty or not; that's the great thing. Supposing you've flogged or locked up a man, and afterwards it turns out that he was innocent, what then? It's a bad business, that. But once you've made it out, and know all about it, then bury him alive if you like; that'll be all fair and lawful. . . . But to go and ill-use a man before you know what it is about yourself—any fool can do that. That's what I think. Will you have a sandwich?"

The plate of sandwiches was held out towards the two officers who were sitting next to the bar.

"I don't mind," half-reluctantly said one of them, adding, after a moment, "By the by, just pour me out a glass of that stuff in the green bottle; I'll try what it's like. . . . Won't you have some?"

"Well, I don't care if I do," said the other officer, still more reluctantly; "you can give me a glass."

For want of anything else to do, they began to eat and drink. The steward, for his part, started on some operation on a piece of ham, beginning by blowing on it, and continued—

"One ought to look into these matters, and not go into them at random. . . . Why, there are cases when, if you judge a matter properly, the man that everybody thought was a villain can prove his innocence. Before you go into it, you think he ought to be hanged; and then you go into it, and think about it, and he's done no wrong at all. But to go and punish a man without ever knowing what it's about—I say there's no justice in that at all! Why do they have law courts, and trials, and judges, and all that sort of thing? Why, because any jackass knows how to knock a man about for nothing; but you have to go into it first, and then say what's to be done. . . . Why, there's a lad that serves on this very steamer. He's been in trouble—he killed a man. Now, what's the law for that? Why, a halter, or underground mines! . . . That's so, isn't it? And yet the fellow's all right and straight. And why is that? Because they went into the matter, and made it all out. . . . There, I'll call the man himself, and he shall tell you about it."

He went out on to the landing at the foot of the winding staircase that led up to the deck, and shouted—

"Mikhàïlo![1] come here! Come here a minute! . . . He'll tell you himself. . . ."

Mikhàïlo appeared at once. He had evidently been gambling with some friends, for he was holding several greasy cards in his hand. He was a sturdy young fellow, with a peculiarly naïve, almost childlike face. He sprang as lightly as a bird down the iron steps, with his strong, bare legs sticking out from a pair of pink cotton trousers much too short for him, and stood before his master, with his belt unfastened, evidently in a hurry to go back to his game. His whole figure and the expression of his face showed that the game was in full swing and had reached an exciting point.

"What's up?" he asked, hastily.

[1] Colloquial for Mikhail.

"Come over here a minute."

"Tell me what you want. I can hear you from here."

"Come along into the cabin, you wooden figure-head! You'll have time to finish your game afterwards. Come and tell the gentlemen how you killed the old man."

"What the plague! . . . What did you call me for? I thought. . . . Is that all you've got to talk about? Catch me! . . ."

He turned back to the staircase, but the steward caught him by his shirt.

"Hold hard! What a jackass 't is! Can't you answer when you're asked civilly?"

"What's the good of going over all that nonsense again?"

"Who asked you to go over it? . . . I want you to tell the gentlemen how it happened. You lived with a wood-merchant then, didn't you?"

"No, I didn't. He'd only just taken me on that very day; and I'd never lived there at all——"

"All right; he'd just engaged you. . . . Well, what happened next?"

"Nothing at all happened next. . . . He engaged me, you see, to guard the timber. . . . He'd got a timber yard; 'twas worth hundreds and thousands. . . . He's a million-aire, he is."

"Where did it happen? Where does the merchant live?"

"'Twas in Moscow, sir. . . . I came straight up from the country to him. . . . How old was I? Don't suppose I was more than sixteen. . . . Well, he engaged me; and says he, 'Look here, boy, if you do your duty, I'll reward you for it; but if you go conniving with thieves, I'll let you know. I sha'n't say many words about it, but I shall just smash you into little bits. But if so be as you do your best, I'll raise your wages in a month. You keep your eyes open all night; don't go to sleep; and if you see a thief, just you punch his head!'   You see, sir, these here thieves were always stealing that man's timber; so, of course, I did as I was told—what else should I do?   A lad doesn't come up to town for his own pleasure.   If you get a place, you must try and do your best in it, and please your master, so that he'll raise your wages, and not swear at you or hit you over the head.   So I set my mind to do his bidding.   I chose a good cudgel—I pulled out a bit of timber, you know, a stout heavy sapling, with the root on.   Well, I cut and trimmed it and made it all nice; and when it got dark, I put on my coat and went out. . . . . It was in autumn, and a very dark night. . . . . So I walked up and down, up and down, and suddenly I heard some one move.   I called, and he didn't answer.   'He wants to hide,' thought I; so I went up and gave him a good one with my cudgel. It must have caught him sideways; then I hit again, straight down from the top, and he just gave a squeal like a hare. We-ell, after that, I went to poke him a little with the butt-end; I poked him a bit, but it was a dark night, and I couldn't see anything; I could only feel something soft, and it didn't give a sound. . . . Well, when I couldn't make him speak, I went to tell the master. . . . The master hadn't gone to bed yet. . . . So I came in, and I said, 'Please, I think I've done a mischief to a thief.   He was scrabbling about in the wood, and so I knocked him down. . . . And I can't make him speak,' says I; 'and he only squeaked a bit, like a hare.' . . . Well, so then the master called his coachman, and told him to take a lantern and go and see what had happened. . . . So we went. . . . Well, and after all, it was only a beggar. . . . But it wasn't my fault.   I was told to punch his head, and I did as I was bid.   Supposing he had stolen the timber, what then? Then I suppose I should have got——"

"There, shut up! . . . Tell your story, and don't argufy. What was the next thing?"

"The next thing was that when we looked at the man his head was all smashed in and his arm was broken. . . . Lord! it makes me feel creepy-like just to remember! . . . Well, we looked at him, and the coachman, he said: 'The master'll have to be told.' So I went to the master, and I said: 'Please, sir, I've smashed a man,' and I told him all about it.—'Surely he isn't dead!'—'Yes, that he is.'—And how he did swear at me! Then he told me to go and tell the police. So off I went to find a police-station. I hunted all over the place, and couldn't find one, hang it all! And when I did find one, everybody was asleep. However, I waited and waited, and at last somebody came out and asked me what I wanted. 'I've smashed a man,' said I, and so on. Well, I told him all about it—why not? I hadn't done any wrong. I didn't want to hit the man. . . . I told him everything. Well, he wrote it all down.—'And where's the cudgel?' said he.—'I left the cudgel in the kitchen,' said I.—'Go and fetch the cudgel,' said he; 'it'll be wanted.'—So I went and fetched it. Well, I gave them the cudgel. Then they put me into a dark room. In the morning they tied my hands and brought me into another room. Then they began asking questions. Well, whatever they asked me, of course I answered. Two months after, they had a trial. It was the same thing all over again:—'You killed him?'—'I did.'—'How?'—So I told them: 'First I banged him in the side, and then I banged him on the forehead.'—'What with?'—'A cudgel.'—You confess it?' —'Course I do.'—'You plead guilty?'—'Which way am I guilty? I was told to punch his head, and I punched it. . . . A servant's business is to do as he's bid.' . . . Well, they thought about it, and they judged about it, and they wrote, and they talked; and then they came out and said:— 'Here, you're not guilty; you be off!'—So I went. . . ."

"And the merchant?"

"Yes, they called up the merchant, too; but all he would

say was :—'Of course the timber had to be watched. All my capital's in timber. . . . It's always getting stolen. . . . The police are never there when you want them. . . . How was I to know he was going to keep watch that way?' . . . Well, and how was I to know who was there? I heard somebody scrabbling about, and I banged him. . . . So that's how it all ended: I wasn't guilty; nor the merchant wasn't guilty neither. . . . Only he was a regular Jew, he was—he wouldn't take me back again afterwards. He said :—'You set about your work too much in earnest. I only promised you six roubles, and you went and killed a man straight off; if I were to *pay* you your wages, the Lord knows what you'd do with your cudgel!' So he took a soldier, and gave me the sack. . . . Reg'lar Jew, he was! . . . Well, what else do you want?"

"Is that the whole story?"

"That's all. . . . Want anything else?"

"No, that's all; you can go."

The lad rushed up the steps like a whirlwind, and the steward started afresh upon his dissertation :—

"That's how it was," said he; "when you come to think of it, it seems as if the lad ought to be locked up; killed a man and smashed his head in—that's clear enough. But when they came to look into the case, and understood all about it, he turns out innocent. . . . That's just what I was saying: If so be as a man's really guilty, you've got to punish him; but, however much it looks as if a man was guilty, if you can prove him innocent, you should; and if you go and punish an innocent man, I say there isn't any justice in it. . . . That's what I think. . . ."

"Ye-e-es," remarked the shopkeeper, to whom the steward mainly addressed himself. Pouring out the remainder of his bottle of beer, he added: "Of course, it would really be fairer-like . . . to do so . . . that's true. Give me another bottle."

The steward uncorked a bottle, took the cork off the corkscrew, put it back in its place, came out of his bar, and brought the bottle to the shopkeeper. At that moment there rose from one of the sofas, pulling down a print shirt over an enormous paunch, another passenger, also a tradesman. He was a man of gigantic height, with a good-natured expression of face. He went up to the steward, and taking him by the shoulder, asked, with a slight smile—

"But the peasant, most respected sir, what about him? Is he guilty, or not?"

"What peasant?"

"Why, the one that came by his death—the old beggar-man. . . . Whereabouts are we to place him in the matter? You see, you can put it how you like, but we can't get over the fact that there's a man missing! He lived, and he walked about, and said his prayers, and all the rest of it, and all of a sudden he's not there. . . . What about him, then? What sort of position is he in?"

For a moment the steward was rather put out of counte-nance by this unexpected question, which greatly perplexed him. But his embarrassment was relieved by a general burst of laughter, in which he joined.

"Oh, that's what you're talking about! I thought you meant some other peasant. . . . Ye-e-es, that's a sort of thing that one may call sudden."

"That's just it!" continued the fat man; "that's always the way in these parts: everybody's innocent, and before you've time to turn round, somebody's given up the ghost in the middle of the scrimmage!"

"Yes, that's very true; it does happen sometimes," meekly assented the steward, going back into the bar; "it certainly happens sometimes."

"It does, sir. And more than that happens sometimes—I ought to know that! . . . After all, that old man had made a mess of it, in one way, by going and hanging about the timber-yard. You see, it wasn't altogether at random; people should keep away from timber. . . . But sometimes it'll happen this way: A man sits quiet, never mixes up in anything, fears God and honours his rulers, and does everything all right and proper, and all of a sudden, without either why or wherefore, people come and begin hitting him over the head and on the back, and boxing his ears, and knocking him down, and banging his head again, and giving him black eyes, and pitching him face downwards on the floor, and turning him over and kicking him, and poking his head into the gutter, . . . and then afterwards, here you come and say, ' nobody's guilty '! And it turns out that the man who stuck your head in the gutter is as innocent as a dove. And the man who dragged you about face downwards is not guilty either! . . . And then, at the end, the man that got all the knocks turns out to be innocent, too. . . . ' Go to your homes, good people; you're all innocent!' And all the same, when a man goes home, however much he's proved innocent, his nose is broken and his mug's all swelled-up, just as if—. Doesn't seem to me to make much difference, whether he's innocent or guilty; any-way, three teeth are knocked out of his jaw, and his arm's broken, and he's been shamed and disgraced, into the bargain. What's one to think about that, in your opinion?"

"Ah! yes," said the steward, quite subdued, and not even attempting to orate; "certainly that's not good manners."

"There you are! And yet nobody's guilty. . . . One says: 'I've got papers!' and the next one says; 'I've got papers!' and the third one's got papers, too. . . . But look here, my good sirs, I'd like to know what all this means! You've all got your papers, but I've got my own skin! I can buy all the paper I like for three kopecks, but I can't buy a new jaw anyway. . . . Seems to me there's a difference."

The giant tradesman spoke with evident excitement; he

gesticulated with his hands, grew red in the face, and finally, quite out of breath, sat down in the middle of his sofa.

"That's the sort of thing that happens, gentlemen!"

"Yes, it does happen, of course," assented one of the skinflints; "a man gets half smashed, and nobody's to blame."

"Exactly so," said the tradesman; maybe something of that kind has happened to you?"

But the skinflint only growled, lifted his saucer to his lips, and made no answer.

"Do you mean," said one of the officers to the giant, "that anything of that kind has happened to you?"

"Not only 'that kind,' but such a thing happened to me, that I think if I'd given way to my feelings I should have come to grief altogether. . . ."

"What was it all about?"

"That's just exactly what I can't tell you! . . . What did the lad smash the old man's head about? There you are —it's the same thing here. You see, it's a sort of thing——"

The giant broke off, and began more composedly :—

"The main reason. . . . First of all, I must tell you about my illness. You see what sort of a stomach I've got! . . ."

"You surely don't mean to say that a stomach could play any part in an affair of that kind?" interrupted one of the officers.

"Part! Such a part was played as I wouldn't wish to a Tartar!"

"Because of your stomach?"

"That's just the very reason that I can't explain the whole thing properly to you. I'll tell you just how it happened, from the beginning."

"Very interesting to hear!"

"Well, you see, it was this way : This same stomach of mine was the root of all the mischief. It began to swell up when I was a little child. There weren't any good doctors

in those days : and people of our sort went to wise women,
and soldiers, to be cured. We lived in the country, and
kept the mill—it was a big mill. Well, there was a sort of
barber fellow that set to work to cure me. He rubbed and
smeared me, and he gave me stuff to drink, and he pulled
me by the legs, and in fact he spoiled my inside altogether,
so that I've never got well of it to this day—I've got some
doctor's stuff with me this very minute. . . . Very well, . . .
I must tell you that I live, with my wife and children, near
Sousàlov—a district town it is—at the mill. I often go into
town. Well, about three years ago a new apothecary came
to the town, and I got to know him. So I thought : ' I'll
make friends with him, and perhaps he'll give me some help
about this stomach of mine.' Well, so I made acquaintance
with him. He was a good, kind-hearted young fellow. So
I told him all about it, and he thought it over, and gave me
a box of pills. ' You take these,' says he, ' and do as I tell
you.' And I wasn't to eat this, and I wasn't to drink that,
and so on ; he was very particular. So I began to take the
pills, and I got better ; and whenever I'd finished one box,
I had another. Only the next thing that happened was that
my inside got to want more and more of these pills : if ever
I was without them it just half killed me. At first a box
would last me a week ; but, after a bit, I'd finish it up in
one day. I went and talked about it to the apothecary.
He thought it over, and, says he, ' I'm afraid this is a bad
business' ; but, all the same, he risked it and went on. And
at last he began making such pills for me that he'd put three
doses into one pill, and when he rolled it up it would be as
big as a walnut. However, I took them, and they did me
no harm. All of a sudden, gentlemen, my apothecary leaves
the town. ' Where are you going?' said I. ' Can't get on
here,' said he ; ' no profit.' I was sorry to lose him ; he
was a good fellow, and then he'd helped me, too ; but there
was nothing for it—he went away. So I had to get on as

best I could, now with one doctor, now with another. So it went on for about a year and a half; and my wife and I thought we'd build a house for ourselves in the main-town.[1] . . . Because, you see, our children were growing up, and we had to put them to school. We wanted to do the best for them, and we're not badly off; thanks be to God, we've money to pay with. We thought and thought it over, and at last we went to the town, and bought a bit of land, and started building. I used to go into town to see after the building, sometimes for three days at a time, sometimes for five. I often used to go into Moscow to buy materials. The main-town is on the railway, and only eighty versts from Moscow; it isn't more than three hours in the train, so I found it cheaper to buy what I wanted in Moscow— nails and cramp-irons and all such things—for the house. Well, one day I was going into Moscow for things, and who should I meet in the train but my apothecary. . . . 'Ah! it's you, old fellow! How do you come here? Where have you been? Where are you going?' . . . We were right glad to meet again. Well, we got talking, of course; he told me about his affairs, and I told him about mine. He'd been in some other town, and hadn't got on there either ; and now he was going to Moscow. Then of course I told him how we were building a house. And after a bit we got talking of my illness. So I said to him : 'For the Lord's sake,' says I, 'help me like a good fellow; little father, give me some more pills ! I'm half killed.' 'All right,' says he, 'if you like. When we get to Moscow,' says he, 'I'll go into a chemist's and get all the things, and make the pills at home, and give them to you.' So we arranged where we were to meet. 'Come to the Patrikyevsky Tavern,' says he, 'the day after to-morrow. We'll have some cabbage salad together, and talk over old times ; and I'll give you the pills.' So that was all right. . ."

<hr>

[1] Principal town of any province.

The narrative was interrupted for a moment by the entrance of the young fellow who had just told about the manslaughter. He came running nimbly down the steps and stopped at the door.

"What do you want?" asked the steward.

"Nothing; I just came."

"I suppose you were beaten at cards?"

"I'll beat them some day," answered the lad, leaning against the lintel of the door, and rubbing one bare foot against the other.

"So that was settled," continued the narrator. "I went about Moscow and bought the goods, and arranged my business properly, and at the time we'd agreed on I went to Patrikyev's. I walked through all the rooms, but my friend wasn't there; so I sat down and waited, but he never came. I waited two whole hours, till at last I felt quite ashamed; so I ordered something, and ate it alone, and went away without him. Stupid-like, I'd forgotten to ask his address. 'I shall have to wait another day,' thought I, for I can't get on without the pills. So I stopped another night, and next day, at the same time, I went to the tavern again. Still he wasn't there! Well, there was nothing for it, I had to get back home. I didn't go straight home, I went into the town, because I had bought some things—bottles, and flasks, and one thing and another. . . . I thought I'd manage to put up for the night there; the stove was all finished in the kitchen, and the windows were put in; so I went to the house. I'd got a peasant there for a watchman —Rodiòn his name was; there were ten carpenters in the house; they were just going to bed. I came in and told Rodiòn to heat the samovar. I noticed that he looked at me in a queer sort of way. He did what I told him, and all that, but I could see there was something wrong; I couldn't rightly make it out. . . . He kept on looking at me. . . I told him—'Put down that box, and see you

don't set it too near the stove; for if it should get too warm
—the Lord forbid!' . . . Because you see, I'd got varnish
and spirit in the box. . . . Well, when I told him that, he
just opened his eyes and stared at me. First he stared at
me, and then he stared at the box. He stared, and stared,
and then he went away. I sat and waited a quarter of an
hour, but he didn't come back; so I went out into the
passage, and there stood the samovar, quite cold. 'I
wonder if he's gone for water,' I thought. I called, and
called, and he didn't answer. It was a wonderful sort of
business altogether. I went and got out some dried fish
(I'd brought two pounds of it from Moscow—good dried
sturgeon, at eighty kopecks a pound)—I got out some fish,
and cut a slice of white bread, and laid it on, and made a
sort of sandwich, you know, and crossed myself, and just
opened my mouth—the Lord make us truly thankful—when
all of a sudden there was such a crackling and howling and
blowing of whistles all round the house; and all the carpenters ran to the windows and stared like stuck pigs. . . .
I threw down my sandwich and ran to the door, and
knocked up right against a uniform. And there was
Rodiòn pointing at me, and saying 'That's he!' Seven
or eight of them caught hold of me and began to drag
me along; and I, of course, yelled and shouted, 'Hold
hard! What's the matter?'—'You'll be told there!'—
'Anyway, let me dress myself,' says I; 'it's autumn; it's
cold!'—'We haven't got any ladies!' . . . It was no
use, they'd got me tight. I didn't know what it was all
about; I couldn't make head or tail of it. And there they
began dragging me along. And there were the carpenters
and workmen and watchmen and doorkeepers—the Lord
defend us! And why, and what it was all about, I couldn't
get the hang of it at all. 'For mercy's sake,' I shrieked to
them; 'I'm a tradesman; I'm a householder; I'm a man
of property; I've got a wife and children!' . . . And all

the answer I got was : ' Yes, by one of the stations in
Moscow there were householders living, too, and they'd got
their wives.' . . . When the people heard that, oho ! you
should have seen how they squared up to me ! I saw it
was a bad business; I'd got into hot water, and no mistake;
and didn't even know what for. . . . When they said *that*,
I just felt my flesh creep. . . . I told them : ' I'm innocent !
May the lightning strike me dead if I . . . I've prayed for
him with tears . . . I'd give my life for him !' . . . I was
innocent before God ; and yet I just shook all over ! I
began thinking : 'Supposing there turns out to be some
evidence ! There may be something . . . God knows !
What will become of me then? What shall I do ?' My
very inside got cold. Then I began thinking : ' Heaven
defend us ! They'll take my wife too; and it'll kill her !
She'd die if they just looked at her ! What will she do
when she hears about it ?' In fact, I lost my head altogether, and got so I couldn't remember or think of anything ; I just went on and on, shaking all over, and with no
hat. . . . All of a sudden, what should come into my head :
' Supposing it's all a trick ? There was a case in Moscow,
at the Rogozhskoye cemetery ; they came in full uniform
and took a lot of money, and went away ; and then it turned
out that they'd been only thieves.' It just came into my
head, and it made my very heart jump; and I said to myself : ' Why, what a silly fellow I am to let them trick me
like that ! I left a lot of money in the house—over seven
hundred roubles. . . . What's the use of being such a fool?'
And directly that came into my head, I thought : ' I'll see if
I can't get myself out of the mess my own way ; ' and I
think, gentlemen, you can see for yourselves that I'm not
much like a baby in arms." . . . (The narrator here drew
up his gigantic form to its full height, squared back his
colossal shoulders, and, rolling up his sleeve, held out for
inspection a mighty fist.) . . . "I think I've got what you

may call means of defence. And here, at a time like that,
I seemed all at once to gather up strength all over my body.
I felt it rush into my neck and my chest and my legs; and
into my arm there went such an iron strength of will that I
just squared up, and made them see sparks enough to last
their life-time; and hit and hammered, and banged and
boxed, and punched their heads, and flattened their noses,
and squeezed their ribs . . . and when I looked round
there was an empty space all about me, and there I stood
alone in my shirt, like Minin and Pozhàrsky [1] in the Red
Square; and all the people kicking and wriggling about
like fish thrown up on the bank: there was one head-
downwards in a puddle; and another had got stuck fast in
the wattle-fence, and was kicking away and couldn't get out.
In one word, I had scattered the might of the devil till it
melted away like wax! So there I stood alone in the
middle of the battle-field, and said: ' What have you done
with me, you villains?' "

At this point in his story the giant was magnificent to
behold, but the lad who stood listening to him was still
more magnificent. When the miller told how he had
" hammered and banged," accompanying the narration with
appropriate gestures, the arms and legs and whole body of
the lad were continually in motion. He was utterly unable,
while looking at the miller, to refrain from imitating his
gestures. He kept squaring his elbows, and thrusting his
fist into empty space, and more than once came into col-
lision with the thin red-wood door of the cabin.

"What are you smashing the door for, you heathen idol?"
exclaimed the steward, severely. But though the lad
glanced round at the words, he evidently did not understand
them; and the miller, for his part, had worked himself up
into such a state of fury that he paid no heed to either the

---

[1] A famous group of statuary in Moscow.

lad or the steward or the audience, who could not refrain from smiling.

"'What have you done with me, you shameless scoundrels?'" he continued, frantically. "'What right have you? Do you think the law allows such things? Why, it's robbery and violence! Come near me if you dare! I'll kill you outright! I'll tear you in pieces! . . .' There I stood, blazing away at them, and never noticed that they were getting back their senses and coming at me again. Suddenly I looked back, and if there wasn't the whole squadron coming up behind me. . . . Up they came; and if you'd seen the way they rushed at me from behind, and the way they set off shouting—it's just a wonder I'm alive! . . . 'Ah! so we're attacked in the discharge of our duty! Ah! ah! ah! So that's what you go in for! . . . You've got a box! . . . If that's it, my lads, give the great hulking fellow what for!'"

Here the lad nearly choked with laughter, but restrained himself.

"'Hammer him black and blue! . . .' And what came next? . . . They blew their whistles, and sprang their rattles, and banged their truncheons, and fire seemed to come out of my head and out of my ears, and my neck was just like red-hot iron. . . . I heard some one say, 'There's an important telegram about him; he's got a box.' . . . And I shouted to them, 'There's varnish in it—varnish! . . .' 'Oho! Varnish! Pay him out, my lads, pay him out well!'"

At this point the lad could restrain himself no longer; he burst out laughing, turned to run out into the passage, and striking his head violently against the lintel of the door, literally tumbled down at the foot of the stairs in a fit of laughter. The narrator looked severely at him, but continued—

"And my friends, they *did* pay me out! They paid me

out in such a way that I lost my head altogether, and couldn't tell where I was or what was happening. I didn't even know whether I was alive or dead! I was just altogether——"

Here the narrator shrank down, let his arms hang helplessly, and began to speak in a kind of lifeless, almost abdominal voice.

"I could hardly move. . . . O Lord! . . . Holy Saints! . . . Holy Virgin! . . . I couldn't even speak or breathe. . . . And I don't remember whether I walked or whether they carried me. . . . I only know that I found myself in a dark place, and quite ill; all my bones ached, all my joints throbbed—I just lay and waited for death."

The narrator sank slowly down upon the sofa.

"Good Lord! it's dreadful even to remember, let alone—— Here, my good man, give me some lemonade and a glass of brandy."

He addressed the last sentence to the steward in a tone of exhaustion; but, suddenly changing his manner, turned to the lad, and said, somewhat irritably—

"I'd like to know what you find to laugh at! What's there to cackle about? Is there anything funny in an honest tradesman being half murdered? . . . Oh! of course it's funny to you! You're nothing but a baby, and anything can amuse you. . . He's a harmless child——"

Here the narrator turned to the audience.

But he can take a great club, for all that, and smash a man at one blow! And then he'll go back to his village as an innocent child, and hop about on one foot, and play skittles. . . . A fine sort of child you are! Pity no one's got time to thrash you nowadays!"

"Come now!" muttered the lad, in an injured tone, from the passage.

"What do you mean by 'come now'? Do you think I didn't see the way you cackled?"

“What are you hanging about here for?” interposed the steward, glancing at the lad, as he carried to the miller a tray with lemonade. “You've no business here. Be off!”

“Where am I to go?”

“Be off, I tell you! You've smashed all the doors here! Get along with you!”

The lad reluctantly lounged up the stairs, but instead of going away, sat down on the top step.

“I should like to hear,” said one of the officers, “what had become of your apothecary.”

The narrator drank some lemonade, wiped his beard and moustache, and continued—

“The apothecary? He was in a bad way. The poor fellow was tearing along the post-road with express horses. They rushed him along like mad, and he didn't know himself what for! ‘What it was all about,’ said he, ‘I can’t make out. I can't understand anything about it.’ Those are the very words he said to me afterwards. . . . ‘When I got to Moscow,’ said he, ‘I went and took lodgings, and settled my business, and bought some things, and made the pills’; but something or other kept him, so that he couldn’t come to the tavern to meet me. He missed seeing me, and he hadn’t got my address; so he packed up the box of pills, and wrote my name on the packet, thinking he’d send them off next day. Just as he had finished doing that—it was in the evening time—one of his friends came in and said—

“‘Let's go and hear the harp-playing girls outside the town.’

“‘All right.’

“So they took a *droshky*, and off they went. Well, of course they took some of these sewing-girls with them for company, as any bachelors would. . . . So they drank, and larked about, and enjoyed themselves; and my apothecary came home as drunk as a lord. As soon as he got in, he just threw himself down on his bed and snored. All of a sudden some one began banging and hammering at the door as hard as they could ; and as tight as he was, it woke him up. Well, he woke up and opened the door ; and in came that very same Mediterranean squadron.[1]

" ' Come with us, please.'

" ' Where to ? '

" ' You'll see.'

" ' But why, for mercy's sake ?   What about ? '

" ' You'll know when you get there.'

" My apothecary began blustering at them in his tipsy way ; but they only told him, ' It'll be the worse for you ; you'd better come quietly.'   So there was nothing for it ; he had to dress and go.   He thought he'd best hide those pills before he started ; but they asked him—

" ' What's that parcel ? '

" ' That ? ' says he ; ' oh, that's nothing ! '

" They saw he wanted to hide something from them, and caught hold of the parcel ; but he was afraid to let them have it.   Supposing any one should analyze the pills ! . . . There was poison in them, and his name was written on the box.   ' And I was afraid,' he told me afterwards, ' to leave them in the lodgings either.   Supposing anybody should take a fancy to them and swallow them, there'd be the devil to pay then ! '   So he tried to hide the box up his sleeve ; but they didn't give him the chance.   The end of it was that one of his visitors hit him on the shoulder, and the box tumbled out of his sleeve ; and they picked it up, and marched him away.   They took him to their central office ; and in less than half-an-hour's time some one came up to him, asked his name, bundled him into a *troika*,[2] and —off ! "

---

[1] A slang term for the gendarmes ; probably because their uniforms are " deeply, darkly, beautifully blue," like the waters of the Mediterranean.—TRANSLATOR.

[2] Equipage with three horses.

" What a disgraceful business !　How could such a thing happen ? " exclaimed one of the officers.　" It must have been some absurd mistake."

" Of course it was a mistake !　Things like that always are mistakes.　But who it was that made the mistake, that we don't know to this day."

" But no doubt it was afterwards proved to have been all nonsense."

" Certainly ; the truth came out, never fear.　Everything was made clear enough afterwards, though even now we don't understand anything about it. . . . My poor apothecary couldn't make out what it was all about.　He only just felt for his liver, to see if they hadn't squashed it to pieces ; and as for me, when I came to my senses, I couldn't make head or tail of the whole thing. . . ."

" And how was it all explained ? "

" Listen then ; I'll tell you all as it happened. . . . What they did with me, and where they put me, after that fight, I really can't rightly tell you.　I can only say one thing : I suffered enough from mortal fear, that's true, but they didn't do me any harm ; I'm bound to say they treated me kindly and politely, and altogether like real gentlemen. . . . I thought it would be worse ; but instead of that they soon began to look into it, and clear matters up."

" 'That's just what I say," interposed the steward ; " they should have looked into it first, and not go hitting people right and left."

" You're right there," assented the narrator ; " and it all turned out as you say. . . . When they called me up before the Member [1]—and there I was with my broken head all tied up in wet rags—he asked me—

" ' What's the matter with you ?　Are you ill ? '

" ' Why, your Excellency,' says I, ' they knocked me about so ! '

____
[1] Member of the Committee of Inquiry.

"'What!' he cried; 'how dare they? On what ground?'

"So I told him they said they'd got a paper.

"'Oh, the scoundrels!' and you should have heard him give it to them! He pitched into them hot and strong; and at last he turned round to me and said—

"'Just tell me what this is;' and he showed me the box of pills.

"At first I wouldn't let on that I knew anything about it, because I wasn't sure what might be up. I thought to myself, 'How should I know? Maybe the apothecary's got into some mess or other. These are dangerous times; I may get into trouble if I say I know him.' So I said, 'I don't know anything about it.' Then he asked me, 'Don't you know a person named Làptev?' (Làptev was the apothecary's name, you know.) And I said again, 'No, I don't!' Then he pulled out the canvas that the box of pills was done up in, and showed it to me, and there was written on the canvas—

"'*Ivàn Ivànovich Popòv. Packet from Làptev; price* 1 *rouble.*'

"'You are Popòv, aren't you?' says he.

"'Yes.'

"'And the packet is to you?'

"'It must be.'

"'Then you must know Làptev?'

"I saw I'd put my foot in it, and so I told him—

"'Very sorry, your Excellency—yes, I know him.'

"'Why didn't you say so at once?'

"'I was afraid to, your Excellency.'

"'What were your afraid of?'

"'I don't know.'

"'That's odd!'

"'I'm afraid of everything, your Excellency! They nearly killed me, and for the life of me I can't make out why!'

"Well, when I said that he began to laugh, and said—

"'Don't you be afraid; just tell me the truth.'

"'I'll tell everything I know,' said I. And he asked me—

"What did you want with poisoned pills?'

"'Poisoned! Which way poisoned?'

"'Why, there's poison enough in those pills to kill a man! A man! They would kill a horse! What did you want with them?'

"'I take them,' said I; 'my stomach's out of order.'

"'But they're poison!'

"'Not a bit of it! The Lord forbid! I've got into the way of it, little by little, and they do me nothing but good.'

"'H'm! And who made them?'

"'The apothecary, my friend.'

"'Tell me all about it.'

"So I told him all I knew. I said—

"'He promised to bring me the pills at Patrikyev's tavern, and he never came; and I don't know where he went.'

"'And where's your apothecary now?'

"'That,' said I, 'is more than I can tell your Excellency.'

"Well, he thought and thought, and he poked and poked over his papers; and then he rang the bell. And presently they brought in a young man; and his Excellency asked me—

"'Is this the gentleman who made your pills?'

"I looked at him, but it was quite a strange man.

"'No, sir,' said I; 'I never saw the gentleman in my life.' And the young man said the same thing. They showed him the pills, and he looked at them, and said—

"'I don't understand anything about it.'

"So then his Excellency poked and poked over the papers, and then he rang the bell, and whispered with somebody, and then with somebody else, and then he sent away the young man; and at last he said to me—

" ' Yes, there's been a mistake ; I hope you will not take it amiss.'

" ' God bless me !' said I ; ' I'm glad enough to be alive ! '

" ' You see,' said he, ' it was this way : we've got another Làptev, the young man you just saw ; and he's concerned in a very bad business. We thought that he had made those pills. And when the doctors declared that they were poison, we thought of course there might be. . . . Then, you see, the box was addressed in your name, and so we sent word to have you arrested, . . . and those blockheads of gendarmes went and played the very deuce.'

" ' Yes, indeed, your Excellency,' said I ; ' I shan't forget it in this life.'

" ' Well, really, you see, it can't be helped; they're stupid, ignorant men, and you know yourself what dangerous times we live in nowadays.'

" ' Yes,' said I, ' God knows the times are bad enough ! '

" Well, so after that I felt a bit encouraged ; and I asked him—

" ' Please, your honour, where is my apothecary ? '

" ' That's just the very thing I've got to find out,' said he. ' There seems to have been another mistake made over him.' And he began telling me about it. ' There must have been a muddle at the head office. . . . This young man's name is Làptev too, and he was to be forwarded on ; and it seems that, instead of him, they forwarded on your apothecary. . . . However, all that will be put straight.'

" ' And what's to happen to me now,' said I, ' if you please ? '

" ' You may go.'

" ' Go quite away ? '

" ' Wherever you like. It was nothing but an absurd mistake.' "

" Why, yes, of course," remarked the officer in a dignified

manner, but in a certain tone of relief; "that was to be expected."

"Yes," continued the narrator; "'a mistake,' says he. 'Ah, well,' thought I to myself, 'may the Lord be praised for that.' I just gathered up my coat-tails, and off I went —it was after dark—to the railway station. And when I got to that cursed town of ours, I drove through it hiding my face, and went straight to my own farmhouse. I didn't even go into the new house; and to this day I don't care to live in it, as I hope to be saved! If anybody cared to buy it of me, I'd sell it at their own price. Well, I got to the farm, and shut myself up under lock and key, and wouldn't let the workmen or clerks or any one come near me; I wouldn't even have my wife and children about me. I couldn't come to myself after it all; I wasn't fit for anything; it seemed as if I couldn't move a limb. I just ate and slept, ate and slept; that was all I cared to do."

"That's the way you took your recreation, I suppose," asked one of the skinflints.

"You're in too much of a hurry—recreation! Just hear what happened next."

"You don't mean to say anything more happened?" asked the officer.

"Oh, dear me! yes. You see, it was always one mistake after another; and we never could get to the root of the thing. You'll see how it all came out at last."

"And where was the apothecary?"

"You'll hear; only I must tell you from the beginning. The apothecary 'll turn up if you wait a bit. Well, you see, I stopped at the farm a month, eating and sleeping, and unstiffening my joints in the bath; and I left the house in town to my nephew to look after; and, my word, he did give those scoundrels a lesson! He's the lad to make the sparks fly! But all that doesn't belong to the story. Well, as I said, I stopped there a month, resting and coming to my senses, when one day, who should come riding up but a mounted gendarme ! My heart just leaped into my mouth ! Lord have mercy upon us sinners ! What could it be ? He handed me a paper—a summons to appear in court. 'What for ?'—'It says there.'—So I read the paper; it was a summons to appear and answer for insulting the police in the discharge of their duty. Very good; I read it, and signed my name. But it just made my heart burn—that was really *too* much of a good thing! What sort of duty do they call that? I'm hit over the head, and I'm responsible! I can't see much duty in promiscuous fisticuffing. 'No, no, my friends,' thought I to myself, ' I've had enough of this; you've played your little game, and that'll do. If his Excellency himself took my part, and let me go free as an innocent man, you needn't think you can get the better of me, not a bit of it !' I had a *troika* harnessed at once, went straight to the town, and telegraphed to Moscow for an advocate : '*Fisticuffing* versus *Fisticuffing*. *Prosecution*. *Will pay* 1,000 *roubles*.' And a fine kettle of fish they got ready ! So when the trial was to be, I went to Moscow with my wife. We got to the court quite early, before nine in the morning; and the trial wasn't to begin till twelve ; so we sat down in the porch to wait. All of a sudden up comes my apothecary. He came along dragging one foot after the other, all thin and shabby, for all the world like a beggar.—' Where have you come from ?' I asked him.—'That's more than I know myself; my health's gone to pieces; I've got rheumatism in both my legs; I'm half dead.'—And it was quite true; he had a cough, and couldn't get his breath. He sat down on the step with us, and I said to him : 'Well, well, friend ! your pills have cost me something ; I shall remember them, never fear !'—' D'you think they didn't cost *me* anything ?' says he.—And so he told me how it had all happened : how he missed me at the tavern, and all that I told you before.

' To this day,' he said, ' I haven't got back the use of my arm, since they hit me on the shoulder when they took away the pills.'

"HE CAME ALONG DRAGGING ONE FOOT AFTER ANOTHER."

" ' But why didn't you give up the pills ? '
" ' I was afraid to ; they were illegal pills. I made them for you, as a friend, because I know your temperament.'

So then I asked him how did the whole thing happen ; and he told me—

" 'That's just what I can't make out for the life of me. They tore off with me to the other end of the world; and then there came a telegram : '*Send him back ; it's the wrong man.*' So they brought me back ; and I began asking at the head office what it was all about. They poked and muddled and fussed over their papers, and at last they got to the root of the whole matter. And what do you think it was? What do you suppose was the cause of it all ?'

" 'How should I know? I've hardly got to the bottom of my own case yet.'

" 'Well,' says he, 'it was all because of that scoundrel Lipàtkin.'

" Lipàtkin, I must tell you, is a shopkeeper in our town ; he's just a regular bloodsucker, and nothing else. So I asked him what Lipàtkin could have to do with it ; and he said—

" ' When I had the business at Sousàlov, I hired rooms from him, and it was in the contract that I should repair the roof. Well, if you remember, I didn't get on ; and so I left the town and didn't repair the roof, because, you see, as I had paid beforehand, and went away four months before the time was up, I didn't see that I was bound to do it. I gave up my business, and off I went. But old Lipàtka[1] thought he'd screw some money out of me; so he hunted up some pettifogging notary and scribbled off a complaint to the Medical Department at St. Petersburg, asking to have apothecary so-and-so forced to pay, and all the rest of it. Well, in the Medical Department they didn't take the trouble to go into it; they just wrote off to the administration in my province. And when it got to the head office of the province, they mixed up one paper with another ; and they wrote to the district office : ' *Summon*

[1] Contemptuous diminutive of Lipàtkin.

the apothecary to explain.' So when the paper got to the district, I wasn't there, so they set to work and made up a third paper : ' *Find and forward apothecary.*' And off they sent it to Moscow. So in Moscow they hunted me up. As soon as ever I got to Moscow and handed in my passport to the police, of course they nabbed me. Well, then, of course there were those unlucky pills ; they wanted to take them away, and I wouldn't give them up, and tried to hide them. And so they began to suspect all sorts of things. And at last they got so muddled at the head office that they mixed everything up together, and somehow the devil got into the thing. And now that I've gone back to my lodgings, all my luggage is stolen, and I don't know what on earth I am to do.'

"So I asked him what he was there for ; and he said—

" ' Why, to answer that old bloodsucker's summons.'

" ' About the roof ? '

" ' Yes ; still that confounded roof. He wants thirty-four and a half roubles; but I shan't give him a penny. And I shall call him up for the four months' over-payment. I've begun a counter-suit against him. Two can play at that game, my fine fellow ! I've dug a little pit too ! When they've heard both our cases, you'd better come to my lodgings to rest.'

" Well, the law-suits began. First of all they heard the case of the apothecary and Lipàtkin, and found for the apothecary, and Lipàtkin didn't get a penny. So when that was done, they took up my case. Dear heart ! what a business it was ! I can tell you my great gun of a counsel hit the right nail on the head ; he didn't leave them a leg to stand on. At last the public prosecutor got up and said—' No,' says he, ' it's no use ; I give it up.' But mine never stopped ; he just went on hammering and blazing, and letting off fireworks at them ; and the end of it was they all got up and said : ' He's innocent ! ' And there you are."

"There's a statute about that," interrupted one of the skinflints : ' *In cases of reciprocal fisticuffing and mutual personal insults, all parties are innocent.*'

"That's just it. ' You're innocent,' said they, 'because the fisticuffing was reciprocal. You can go home.' So we went out into the street, all the lot of us : the Mediterranean squadron, and the carpenters, and the door-keepers, and I ; and there we stood in the street, fifty or sixty of us, like so many green geese. You see, it was a bit strange ; we'd been banging and slashing at each other like the biggest blackguards you could find ; and here we come out as innocent as new-born babes. So there we stood on the pavement, as dumb as any stocks and stones. All of a sudden up comes that knave Rodiòn, with his cap off."

" ' I've come to ask your honour's pardon.' .

"I should just think you had, after what you've done, you blockhead !'

" ' Well, I don't know, sir. . . . We were told to let the police know, because there was one of those papers. People like us only have to do as we are told. . . . Just pass it over this once, sir, and take me on again. . . . The Lord will reward you for it. . . . It's very hard on a poor man ; it all comes upon us.' Of course as soon as Rodiòn had done, a carpenter began—'Forget and forgive, sir. . . . You know yourself the times are so bad nowadays. . . . What could we do, when they said to us : " Mind you watch him carefully ; he's mixed up in a bad business !" Don't take it ill, sir.' . . . 'So it was you, was it, you blockhead, I asked, ' that got me into trouble ?' ' If you please, sir, it was all of us. But, if you please, sir, it seems. to me that we're pretty well quits ; for you've got a good-sized fist of your own, and you let us know it.'—Well, as soon as the carpenter had done, the gendarmes began : ' It was all a misunderstanding ; we're very sorry.' So I told them : ' It's all very well to be sorry ; but what did you give me so many bruises for?' 'Well,' said one, 'you laid my cheek open.' And then another put in : 'We only obeyed orders ; we had a telegram. . . . And you knocked me down, you know. . . . It was nothing but a misunderstanding. . . . We always . . . As you're a householder we're very sorry. . . .' Then it was just the same with the apothecary ; Lipàtkin came up and said : 'Let's make it up ; don't go to law against me.' And the clerk of the police-station began excusing himself : 'You know what troubled times we have nowadays ! If a fellow has to sit the whole day long, from morning till night, writing *Instantly*, and *Apprehend*, and *Produce*, it's not much wonder if he makes a mistake. . . . Such dangerous times !' . . . And they all came swarming. round me together : 'Such terrible times nowadays. . . . If it wasn't for the times . . . We're very . . . With the utmost respect. . . . Nothing but a mistake.' And bless you ! *I* understood that the blockheads only wanted to be treated all round ! You see, they'd all been so very painstaking ; and nobody was guilty ; and yet there was no drink going ! They thought I ought to have a glass with them. 'No, no ! my fine fellows,' says I, 'if you weren't such a set of dunderheads and blundering asses the times wouldn't be so dangerous. And the times would be very different too, if all you knaves had got a bit of conscience between the lot of you.' And I just walked away with the apothecary ; and not a drop of drink did any of them get."

"Is that all ? " asked the steward.

"Why, heart alive ! isn't it enough ? "

THE SELF-SACRIFICING RABBIT.

By "SHCHEDRÍN" (SALTYKÒV).

ONE day, a rabbit incurred the displeasure of a wolf.
You see, he was running along not far from the
wolf's lair, and the wolf saw him, and called out : "Little
bunny ! Stop a minute, dear !" But the rabbit, instead of

stopping, ran on faster than ever. So the wolf, with just three bounds, caught him, and said—

" Because you did not stop when I first spoke, this is the sentence I pronounce : I condemn you to death by dismemberment. But, as I have dined to-day, and my wife has dined, and we have stored up food enough to last us five days, you sit down under this bush and wait your turn. Then perhaps—ha ! ha ! ha !—I will pardon you ! "

So the rabbit sat on his haunches under the bush, and never moved. He thought of only one thing—how many days, how many hours would pass before he must die. He looked towards the lair, and saw the glittering eyes of the wolf watching him. And sometimes it was still worse ; the wolf and his wife would come out into the field, and stroll up and down close by him. They would look at him, and the wolf would say something to his wife in wolf language, then they would burst out laughing, " Ha ! ha ! ha ! . . ." And all the little wolf-cubs would come with them, and run up to him in p'ay, rub their heads against him, gnash their teeth. . . . And the poor rabbit's heart fluttered and bounded.

Never had he loved life so well as now. He was a highly respectable rabbit, and had chosen for a bride the daughter of a widowed lady-rabbit. At the moment when the wolf caught him by the neck, he was just running to his betrothed.

And now she, his betrothed, would wait, and think, " My squint-eyed one has forsaken me ! " Or perhaps—perhaps she has waited—waited . . . and loved another, . . . and . . . Or it may be . . . she, too, . . . playing, poor child, among the bushes, caught by a wolf ! . . .

Tears almost choked the poor fellow at this thought. " And this is the end of all my warrens in the air ! I, that was about to marry, had bought the samovar already, looked forward to the time when I should drink tea with sugar in it with my young wife,—and now, instead, what has befallen me ! . . . How many hours now till death ? " . . .

One night he fell asleep where he sat. He dreamed that the wolf had appointed him his special commissioner, and while he was absent, performing his duties, the wolf paid visits to his lady-rabbit. . . . Suddenly he felt some one touching his side; he awoke, and saw the brother of his betrothed.

"Your bride is dying," said he. "She heard of your misfortune, and sank at once under the blow. Her one thought now is, 'Must I die thus, and not say farewell to my beloved?'"

At these words the condemned one felt as though his heart would burst. Oh, why! How had he deserved his bitter fate? He had lived honestly, he had never stirred up revolutions, had never gone about with firearms, he had attended to his business—and must he die for that? Death! Oh, think what that word means! And not he alone must die, but she too, his little grey maiden-rabbit, whose only crime was that she had loved him, her squint-eyed one, with all her heart! Oh, if he could, how he would fly to her, his little grey love, how he would clasp his fore-paws behind her ears, and caress her, and stroke her little head!

"Let us escape," said the messenger.

At these words the condemned one was for a moment as if transformed. He shrank up altogether, and laid his ears along his back. He was just ready to spring, and leave not a trace behind. But at that moment he glanced at the wolf's lair. The rabbit heart throbbed with anguish.

"I can't," he said; "the wolf has not given me permission."

All this time the wolf was looking on and listening, and whispering softly in wolf language with the she-wolf. No doubt they were praising the rabbit's noble-mindedness.

"Let us escape," said the messenger once more.

"I can't," repeated the condemned.

"What treason are you muttering there?" suddenly snarled the wolf.

The rabbits stood as petrified. Now the messenger was lost too To incite a prisoner to flight—is that permitted? Ah! the little grey maiden-rabbit will lose both lover and brother; the wolf and the she-wolf will tear them both in pieces.

When the rabbits came to their senses, the wolf and the she-wolf were gnashing their teeth before them, and in the darkness their eyes shone like lamps.

" Your Excellency, it was nothing; we were just talking; . . . a neighbour came to visit me," stammered the condemned, half-dead with terror.

" Nothing! I dare say! I know you! Butter won't melt in your mouths! Speak the truth. What is it all about?"

" It's this way, your Excellency," interposed the bride's brother. " My sister, his betrothed, is dying, and asks, may he not come to say farewell to her? "

" H'm! It's right that a bride should love her betrothed," said the she-wolf. " That means that they will have a lot of little ones, and there will be more food for wolves. The wolf and I love each other, and we have a lot of cubs. Ever so many are grown up, and now we have four little ones. Wolf! wolf! shall we let him go to take leave of his betrothed ? "

" But we were to have eaten him the day after to-morrow——"

" I will come back, your Excellency. I'll go like a flash; I -indeed. . . . Oh, as God is holy, I'll come back!" hurriedly exclaimed the condemned. And, in order to convince the wolf that he *could* move like a flash, he sprang up with such agility that even the wolf looked at him admiringly, and thought—

" Ah! if only my soldiers were like that."

And the she-wolf became quite sad, and said—

" See that, now! A rabbit, and how he loves his she-rabbit."

There was nothing for it ; the wolf consented to let the rabbit go on *parole* with the stipulation that he should return exactly at the appointed time. And he kept the bride's brother as hostage.

" If you are not back the day after to-morrow by six in the morning," he said, " I'll eat him instead of you ; then if you come I'll eat you too ; perhaps, though, I'll—ha ! ha !— pardon you ! "

The squint-eyed one darted off like the arrow from the bow. The very earth quivered as he ran. If a mountain barred his way, he simply dashed at it ; if a river, he never stopped to look for a ford, but swam straight across ; if a marsh, he sprang from tuft to tuft of grass. Not easy work ! To get right across country, and go to the bath, and be married ("I will certainly be married ! " he kept repeating to himself), and get back in time for the wolf's breakfast. . . .

Even the birds wondered at his swiftness, and re-marked—

" Yes, the *Moscow Gazette* says that rabbits have no souls, only a kind of vapour, and there it goes."

At last he arrived. Tongue cannot speak, neither can pen write the rapture of that meeting. The little grey maiden-rabbit forgot her sickness at the sight of her be-loved. She stood up on her hind paws, put a drum upon her head, and with her fore-paws beat out the " Cavalier March " ; she had been practising it as a surprise for her betrothed. And the widowed lady-rabbit completely lost her head with joy ; she thought no place good enough for her future son-in-law to sit in, no food good enough to give him. Then the aunts and cousins and neighbours came running from all sides, overjoyed to see the bridegroom, and perhaps, too, to taste the good cheer.

The bridegroom alone was not like himself. While still embracing his betrothed, he suddenly exclaimed—

" I must go to the bath, and then be married at once."

“Why should you be in such a hurry?” asked the mother rabbit, smiling.

“I must go back. The wolf only gave me leave of absence for one day.”

Then he told them all, and his bitter tears flowed as he spoke. It was hard to go, and yet he must not stay. He had given his word, and to a rabbit his word is law. And all the aunts and cousins declared with one voice : “Thou speakest truth, oh squint-eyed one. Once given, the spoken word is holy. Never in all our tribe was it known that a rabbit was false to his word ! ”

A tale is soon told, but a rabbit’s life flies faster still. In the morning they greeted the squint-eyed one, and before evening came he parted from his young wife.

“Assuredly the wolf will eat me,” he said. “Therefore be thou faithful to me. · And if children shall be born to thee, educate them strictly ; best of all, apprentice them in a circus ; there they will be taught not only to beat the drum, but also to shoot peas from a pop-gun.”

Then suddenly, as though lost in thought, he added, remembering the wolf—

“It may be, though, that the wolf will—ha ! ha !—pardon me ! ”

And that was the last of him they saw.

— —　　　　— —

Meantime, while the squint-eyed one was making merry and getting married, great misfortunes were happening in the tract of country which divided him from the wolf’s lair. In one place heavy rains had fallen, so that the river, which the rabbit swam across so easily the day before, overflowed and inundated ten versts of ground. In another place King Aaron declared war against King Nikita, and a battle was pitched right in the rabbit’s path. In a a third place

the cholera appeared, so that quarantine was established for
a hundred versts round. And, besides all that, wolves,
foxes, owls—they seemed to lie in wait at every step.

The squint-eyed one was prudent; he had so calculated
his time as to leave himself three hours extra; but when
one hindrance after another beset him his heart sank. He
ran without stopping all the evening, half the night; the
stones cut his feet, the fur on his sides hung in ragged tufts,
torn by the thorny branches, a mist covered his eyes, blood
and foam fell from his mouth,—and still he had so far to go!
And his friend, the hostage, haunted him constantly, as
though alive before him. Now he stands like a sentinel in
front of the wolf's lair, thinking : "In so many hours my
dear brother-in-law will return to deliver me." . . . When the
rabbit thought of that, he darted on yet faster. Mountains,
valleys, forests, marshes—it was all the same to him. Often
he felt as though his heart would break; then he would
crush it down, by sheer force of will, that fruitless emotion
might not distract him from his great aim. He had no time
now for sorrow or tears : he must think of nothing but how
to tear his friend from the wolf's jaws.

And now the day began to break. The owls and bats
slipped into their hiding-places; the air became chilly.
Suddenly all grew silent, like death. And still the squint-
eyed one fled on and on, with the one thought ever in his
heart : " Shall I come too late to save my friend ?"

The east grew red; first on the far horizon the clouds
were faintly tipped with fire; then it spread and spread, and
suddenly—a flame. The dew flashed on the grass, the birds
awoke, the ants and worms and beetles began to move, a
light smoke rose from somewhere; through the rye and oats
a whisper seemed to pass—clearer, clearer. . . . But the
squint-eyed one saw nothing, heard nothing, only murmured
to himself again and again : " I have destroyed my friend,
—destroyed my friend !"

At last, a hill! Beyond that was a marsh, and in the marsh the wolf's lair. . . . Too late, oh squint-eyed one, too late ! . . .

With one last effort he put forth all his remaining strength, and bounded to the top of the hill. But he could go no further; he was sinking from exhaustion. And must he fail now? . . .

The wolf's lair lay before him as on a map. Somewhere far off six o'clock struck from a church steeple, and every stroke of the bell beat like a hammer on the heart of the agonized creature. At the last stroke the wolf rose from his lair, stretched himself, and wagged his tail for pleasure. Then he went up to the hostage, seized him in his fore-paws, and stuck the claws into his body, in order to tear him in two halves, one for himself, the other for his wife. And the wolf-cubs surrounded their father and mother, gnashing their teeth and looking on. . . .

" I am here !—Here ! " shrieked the squint-eyed one, like a hundred thousand rabbits at once ; and he flung himself down from the hill into the marsh.

And the wolf praised him.

" I see," he said, "that a rabbit's word can be trusted. And now, my little dears, this is my command : Sit, both of you, under this bush, and wait till I am ready, and afterwards I will . . . ha ! ha ! . . . pardon you ! "

CHOIR PRACTICE.

AT about six in the evening the singers assembled at
the choir-master's house. After rubbing their boots
on the mat in the hall, they went into the ante-room, which

contained an old rickety sofa, a wardrobe, and a fat chest of drawers. For want of room the out-of-door garments were flung in a heap on the sofa or chest of drawers. Here, too, there was a sort of mat on the floor, upon which the singers were expected to rub their feet. At the door leading into the inner room stood the choir-master himself—a man of about forty, of middle height, with an expressive face and short-cropped whiskers. He stood in his dressing-gown with a pipe in his hand, watching to see that the singers rubbed their boots properly. In the inner room, on the table, burned one tallow candle, dimly lighting up a large stove in the corner, a sofa, a piano covered with music, a red wooden cheffonier, several chairs, and a violin hanging on the wall. On the opposite wall hung a portrait of the Metropolitan Filarèt, a clock, and a starched shirt-front. The room was crowded and musty, smelling of stale tobacco, and when any one coughed, the lack of resonance became noticeable. On entering the room the singers bowed, blew their noses (we will not inquire how), and sat down silently. They came in not all together, but in little groups; and every time that the rubbing of boots and blowing of noses was heard in the ante-room, the choir-master would ask—

"Now, are you all here?"

Then a voice would answer from the dark ante-room—

"Not yet, sir."

"Trebles and altos, don't come in; stop outside till your boots are dry," said the choir-master, meeting at the door a fresh crowd of boys.

The trebles and altos stopped outside, and instantly began playing tricks. The tenors and basses either sat smoking or walked up and down the room talking together softly.

"Now then!" said the choir-master; "are you all here?"

"All here, Iván Stepànych."

" Koulìkov, give out Beriouzov's *Credo*."

The singers began coughing, straightening their neckties, jerking their trousers, and otherwise preparing for their work. One of the tenors, who served as assistant to the choir-master, handed round the music.

The boys, called in from the ante-room before they had had time to finish their tricks, continued pinching each other and treading on each other's toes after their parts had been handed to them. The choir-master scolded them incessantly, but it was evident that they had not much fear of him.

"Now then! Make haste and begin! Get to your places!" said the choir-master. "Koulìkov, have you tried through *The Gates of Mercy* with the trebles?"

"Yes, sir," answered the pale, curly-haired tenor. "Only I wanted to speak to you about Pètka; I simply can't do anything with him! He sings so flat that there's no bearing it. Indeed, he does nothing but put the others out."

"Pètka, how much more trouble am I to have with you? Take care, my boy; I shall have to take you in hand soon!"

Pètka, a jolly-looking, sharp-eyed treble, put on a serious face, and steadily perused his music.

"Place yourselves! Place yourselves!" shouted the choir-master, sitting down to the piano. "Who's that smelling of whiskey? Mirotvòretz, is that you?—For shame!"

"It's what I use to rub my feet, Ivàn Stepànych; I've caught cold, and I was advised to rub them with spirits."

"Caught cold, indeed! At the funeral yesterday, I suppose?"

"Yes, sir."

"H'm, so I see. . . . Your face looks drunk enough."

"No, sir . . . indeed . . ."

"There, there! Never mind! Gentlemen, you're

placed all wrong! Basses, don't you know you have to stand by the stove?"

The basses sullenly went across to the stove.

"And you, Pàvel Ivànych? One might as well talk to a baby as to you, for all the notice you take!"

Pàvel Ivànych, a gloomy, unshaven, deep-bass singer, stared meditatively at the ceiling.

"Pàvel Ivànych!"

"What?"

"What did I say to you?—And all you answer is, 'What?' Confound it all, man, where's your place?"

Pàvel Ivànych gazed meditatively at his music, and never moved.

"Ivàn Stepànych, Pètka's hitting me," whimpered an alto.

"Pètka!"

"Ivàn Stepànych, I didn't——"

"Hold your tongue before I come and make you. Now, then!"

The choir-master struck several chords.

"Now listen! You all begin *piano:* '*I believe in one God the Father Almighty,*' . . . recitative, you know; and mind every word is clear. The basses must get their vowels out well. . . . Pàvel Ivànych! Where are you looking?"

"I?"

"No, I, of course! What do you suppose I'm talking to you for? Oh! good heavens, what a life! Well now, you begin *piano;* and, trebles, mind you don't drag! Do you hear? '*By whom all things were made!*' All the parts break up here! *Sforzando:* '*By whom all things!*' . . . D'you understand? Pètka, look at me! '*And the third day He rose again, according to the Scriptures.*' . . . *Forte.* '*And sitteth on the right hand.*' . . . *Fortissimo.* . . . Do you understand what it means? Do you? '*From thence*

He shall come again with glory to judge both the quick and the dead.' . . . 'Think what it means—the earth, the heavens, everything, going to dust . . . and the last trumpet,—lightning,—thunder,—everything annihilated! . . . ' *Whose kingdom shall have no end.'* . . . At 'end' you have another *diminuendo*, and let the voices die away. You have to express all that great—how do you call it?—wisdom, and power, and eternity, . . . don't you see? Basses lead. Bring out all the tone you can ; it wants to be like three hundred voices here! Tenors, change tone ; take the octave! Trebles and altos : tra-la-la-la-la. . . . Stop !"

The choir-master had got so absorbed in describing how the Creed ought to be sung, that he had started up from the piano, and, imagining that it was really being sung as he said, began gesticulating and excitedly nudging the tenors, who edged away as far as they could. The basses, meanwhile, were taking snuff indifferently, while the trebles and altos, hiding their faces behind their music, were pinching each other and giggling. At last the singing began in good earnest ; they all coughed, shuffled their feet, mumbled a little, and suddenly burst out in a roar : "*I believe in one God the Father Almighty.*" . . . The choir-master stood in the middle of the room, with his eyes fixed on the ceiling, nodding his head and beating time with his hand.

"Stop ! Stop ! Not that way !"

The singing broke off.

"What do you want to roar like bulls for ? Basses ! Pàvel Ivànych, what did I say to you ? Anybody would think you were gone daft ! Koustòdiev, where are you looking ? And you a clerical![1] How can you behave so ?"

Koustòdiev, a burly, red-eyed bass, with stubbly hair

[1] Of the clerical class.

sticking up in disorder, frowned at his music and made no answer.

"It's no matter what one says to you people; you take not a bit of notice. I wonder you're not ashamed of yourselves; you're not children, I should hope—you might have a little sense! Why, you've got children of your own; it's pardonable in them," added the choir-master, pointing to the trebles and looking reproachfully at the basses.

Koustòdiev muttered something inaudible.

"What? Now then, begin again! Remember what I said: recitative: and, basses, don't roar!—Don't roar!" shrieked the choir-master when the singers began once more: "*I believe*." . . .

"Pàvel Ivànych, what are you bellowing for? Do you want to frighten us all?—Mìtka, don't snuffle!"

"*Very God of Very God, begotten, not made*." . . .

"*Legato!* Hold the note. . . . Break off! Basses, *crescendo*. . . . Ivàn Pàvlovich, as loud as you can. '*By whom all things were made*.' . . . What do you stop for? Oh, dear, oh, dear; what *am* I to do with you? Look this way, I tell you; look this way! I didn't tell you to look at *me;* there's nothing written on me!" cried the choir-master desperately, tapping the music.

The singers looked at him in a languid, careless way, and he began to lose his temper. Suddenly one of the, trebles pulled another's ear, which instantly resulted in a quarrel.

"Ivàn Stepànych," said one of the most troublesome, "I can't sing with Mìtka; he keeps on snuffling all the time."

"Mìtka!"

"Yes, sir!"

"What are you doing?"

"I haven't done nothing," replied the injured alto.

" Nothing! I'll give you what for, my lad! Come and stand over here; I won't put up with much nonsense, I can tell you! Oh, good Lord! what a dog's life! What do you come here for, if you please? To dance and sing comic songs, eh? Oh, heavens, how much more of it? . . . Pètka, find my pipe!"

Here the choir-master began tramping up and down the room, ruffling up his hair in front. The trebles all scrambled to pick up the pipe, and, of course, got fighting again ; the rest of the choir broke into little groups and talked.

"Confounded idiot!" muttered the stubbly-haired bass, rolling up a bit of music-paper into a cigarette. "He's a regular brute, that's what he is !"

In a corner sat two basses and a thin, consumptive tenor.

" I've sung through four services this blessed day," one of the basses was saying, "and I'm downright tired of it ; my throat's quite sore. First I sang at the early service, then in another church at high mass, then at vespers at the Holy Virgin's church, and then at a funeral. I got Kouznetzòv to come to the Holy Virgin's, and we had a rare lark with the deacon ;—I told him we would! I tell you, that deacon won't forget us in a hurry—the way we put him out! When he started on one note, we got on to another. You know, he always tries to take ' *Give ear* ' as high as he can, so as not to have to take the octave—his voice is fit for nothing ;—so when we started ' *Glory be to Thee* ' a whole tone lower, he was just done for. ' *For ever and ev*——' and there he stuck--couldn't get a word out for the life of him. And that scamp Kouznetzòv, there he stood saying his prayers as if it wasn't his doing a bit ; bowing and crossing himself, as pious as you please. I nearly died of laughing. Oh, and what a rage the priest is in—my word! After service the deacon came up to the chancel, and says he : ' Wait a bit, my fine fellow; I'll serve you a trick.' . . . But that's all nonsense. What can he do to him?"

"But what did the priest say?" asked the consumptive tenor.

"What's it to him? He said, 'I'm not going to take that deacon's part.' So you see, we can do as we like."

"Get to your places; make haste," interrupted the choir-master's voice. "Koulìkov! '*We sing to Thee.*' Trebles hold your tongues!"

The singers once more ranged themselves in order; the choir-master took his place at the piano.

"Do—mi—la. *Pianissimo.* One!"

"*We sing to Thee, we bless——*"

"Stop! How many times am I to tell you? What are you doing? What sort of thing do you call that? Now I ask you, what *are* you doing? Skvortzòv, what are you doing?"

Skvortzòv meditated.

"What am I a-doin'? I'm a-singin'."

"What are you singing "

"Sing to Thee——"

"And I tell you that you're hacking wood, not singing!"

Skvortzòv smiled.

"What's there to laugh at? There's nothing funny about it. Who's the first to ask for his salary? You. Eh—h—h —you clumsy sledge-hammers! How many times have I told you? Tenors, don't bawl, take your vowels properly. '*We-eee siiiiing toooo Theeeeeee !*' You always make it sound like, '*Wewewe sssssssingg tttto Ththththee !*' What sort of music do you call that? Begin again. '*We give thanks to Thee.*' Tenors, just touch the note and break off. Altos ought to ripple along like a brook. Trebles, die away."

At last they got into swing. The basses left off sledge-hammering, the trebles died away, the altos rippled, the

tenors "touched" their note and broke off, and the choir-
master accompanied. Suddenly, in the midst of the singing,
there resounded a smart box on the ear, given to one of the
altos for singing flat and not rippling properly, but that in

no way disturbed the music. The alto only blinked a little
and went on singing.

" *And we worship Thee*," roared the basses with the most
ferocious faces they could put on.

"*Oh-h-h Lo-o-rd,*" quavered the tenors, throwing back their heads and wagging their voices as a dog wags its tail.

"*And wee-e-e woo-o or-ship Th-ee-ee-ee,*" bellowed, like an ophicleide, the stubbly-haired bass, savagely rolling the whites of his eyes and looking ready to tear some one in pieces.

At this moment there was a knock at the door. The singing broke off again.

"Who's that?" shouted the choir-master, angry at being interrupted.

The deacon came in; a short, thick-set man of about forty-five, in a long-tailed coat, and with whiskers completely surrounding his face, after the fashion of anthropoid apes. He made a slow salute, and uttered the conventional salutation: "My respects."

"Ah, Vasìli Ivànych. Sit down, please. Won't you have a pipe?" The choir-master had suddenly become very amiable.

"Thank you, don't trouble, I have cigars. I am disturbing you, am I not?"

"No. We were just going through the old things, so as not to forget them. Sit down Vasìli Ivànych. Will you have some tea? I'll order it at once, in a minute."

The choir-master half-opened a door leading into a bedroom, thrust in his head and said softly to his wife, who was lying on the bed—

"Vasìli Ivànych has come. Think yourself. You know we can't——"

"Yes, you'll be inviting twenty people here next, and giving them tea," answered his wife.

"I didn't invite him; he came."

"There, there; get along with you."

"Well, but, really, you might——"

"Shut up!"

"All right, I won't, I won't really."

And the choir-master returned into the sitting-room, and sat down beside the deacon.

"Well, Vasìli Ivànych, and how are you getting on?"

"Pretty middling, thank you," answered the deacon, coughing.

"Won't you really have a pipe?"

"No, thanks."

"Ah, I forgot, you don't smoke pipes; and I have no cigars. Dear, dear, what a pity! And is your wife pretty well, and the children?"

"Very well, thank you."

"That's all right."

"And how's the reverend father?"

"The father? Oh, as usual, you know."

"Not well?"

"He doesn't like this place; there's such a lot of work, and at his age it's hard."

"Yes, yes, he's getting on. Yes, it's a pity."

Silence.

"Won't you have some whiskey?" suddenly asked the choir-master.

"Whiskey? Oh, no, thank you, no."

"As you like. I'll send for it, if you wish."

"Why should you—trouble?"

"Oh, its no trouble. I'll send, then."

The deacon coughed again, much as if a crumb had got into his throat, and carefully examined the ceiling.

"Fèkla!" called the choir-master rather timidly.

There was no answer.

Several minutes of embarrassing silence followed. The tenors and basses cautiously seated themselves round the walls, while in the bedroom the furniture creaked angrily; the boys whispered in the ante-room. The choir-master sat looking at the door, but, seeing that the servant did not come, muttered to himself: "What's come to her?" and went into the bedroom. There another whispered conversation began.

"Can't you understand?" exclaimed the choir-master, trying to impress upon his wife the necessity of sending for whiskey.

"There's nothing to understand. I know you're always glad of a chance to get drunk with anybody. What's the use of trying to fool me?"

"Sh-sh! How am I trying to fool you? Can't you see that my reputation may suffer?"

"From the drink? Yes, I should think so. Be off with you—be off!"

"Now, really, Màshenka, do be reasonable."

Presently the choir-master returned, and after him came the maid-servant, carrying a tray with a decanter and a plate of cucumbers.

"Ah-h! Put it down here, my girl. Vasili Ivànych, the first glass is yours."

"Won't you drink too?"

"You first; you are a guest."

"Properly, the master of the house ought to begin," said the deacon, modestly.

"No, no, you first, please. I'll drink afterwards."

"Well, if you will have it so. . . . "

The deacon drained his glass, drew a long breath, snuffed at a bit of bread, and began upon a cucumber.

"Yes, this music is a wonderful thing," began the choir-master, pouring himself out some whiskey. "It's a thing there's no comprehending. Won't you have another glass?"

"H'm. Well, I'm afraid it'll be too much."

"Oh, Vasili Ivànych, no!"

"Well, then, you begin."

And the former ceremony was gone through again.

"Your health!"

"Yours!"

The deacon drank another glassful and gazed meditatively at the cucumbers. The poor singers looked very miserable. The stubbly-haired bass stared gloomily at the decanter; the tenors tried to distract their minds from temptation by talking together, but the conversation halted.

"Koulikov!" said one.

"Well?"

"What time is mass to-morrow?"

"How should I know? What's it to you?"

"Nothing."

Another tenor was remarking to a friend—

"Look here, when you write out music, you ought to put the sharps bigger. I always get wrong."

"All right."

"I shall go home and get to bed," murmured one of the basses, yawning.

The boys in the ante-room had started some game there in the dark.

After the third glass the choir-master became sentimental and embraced the deacon.

*　　*　　*　　*　　*　　*

The whiskey was nearly all drunk—only two glassfuls were left. The choir-master, holding on to the table with one hand and leaning against the deacon, tried to snuff the candle, but could not. The deacon had got upon his dignity, and would listen to nothing.

"Vasìli Ivànych! Vasìli Ivànych!" cried the choir-master, frowning.

"No, I won't, then!" answered the irate deacon.

"Won't you, my friend? Oho! Very well, you remember that. I'll remind you of it; I'll remind you!" said the choir-master, threatening him with something unknown. Then, seeing that his menaces had no effect, he suddenly became affectionate. The deacon, pacified, drank another glass.

"There now! There's a good fellow! Kiss me, old man, and let's be friends. You and I are both . . . psalm singers . . . We ought to be friends . . . eh?" said the choir-master, tapping the deacon on the chest. "I'm not a common sort of man either, I can tell you; you needn't mind my looking a bit queer. . . . Just see what a wife I've got, eh? She's a civic councillor's daughter. D'you understand that?"

"'Course I do . . . 'tisn't a syntax . . . nothing much to understand."

"Ah! I tell you that woman's an angel. I'm not worthy of her. I feel myself I'm not. I've held an officer's rank for fifteen years, and I've got a medal belonging to me, but all the same I'm not worth her little finger."

An angry murmur came from the bedroom.

"There! D'you hear? She's angry. She doesn't like to be praised before people. She's modest. I tell you I never saw any one so modest. . . . You'll hardly believe it. . . . Why, sometimes, when we're alone——"

The sounds from the bedroom grew more threatening.

"Iván Stepánych, Missis is angry," said the servant, suddenly entering.

"Sh—sh! All right, all right, I won't," whispered the frightened husband. "I'm very sorry. I won't . . ."

The deacon got up to go home.

"Vasíli Iványch! Where are you going? Listen, my dear fellow." He took the deacon mysteriously into a corner.

"What should I listen to? That's all nonsense!"

"No, no. I'll send for some more. One of the boys'll run for it quick. She won't know. Secretly; d'you see? There's no difficulty Own money. . . . Just see there," and the choir-master pulled a rouble note out of his waist-coat pocket.

"Only do as I tell you! It's all according to law. . . . D'you see?"

The deacon nodded his head and laid down his hat. At
this the choir-master clapped him on the shoulder and
winked significantly.

" Pètia ! " he whispered, going into the ante-room, and
shaking a slumbering treble. " Pètia, make haste ! Like a
flash of lightning, you know — to the publichouse. Off with
you ! "

Five minutes later the choir-master was pouring out a
sixth glass for the deacon. It was only then that he suddenly
remembered the tenors and basses, who, not able to endure
this sight any longer, had in sheer desperation made up their
minds to go home.

" Come along, come along ! What are you afraid of ? "
said the choir-master, with a faint attempt to keep up his
dignity in the eyes of his subordinates. The singers started,
and one after another came up to the table. Koustòdiev
took a glass, looked at it, held it up to the light, and suddenly,
as if struck with a new idea, turned it upside down into his
mouth, without eating anything.

" Pàvel Ivànovich, and you ? "

Pàvel Ivànovich modestly declined

" Why ? "

" Thanks, I won't take any."

" Stuff and nonsense ! Why not ? "

" N—no, I . . . really—— "

" Rubbish ! "

" No ; you must excuse me. I have taken a pledge."

" When ? "

" More than a month ago."

" As you like."

Pàvel Ivànovich reddened and sat down ; the other singers
began to make fun of him. The choir-master, meanwhile,
had worked himself up to such a condition of temerity that
he no longer took any notice of the ominous symptoms of
an approaching domestic storm which were plainly audible

from the bedroom. By the time the second pint of spirit was finished the singers had arrived at the stage of walking unceremoniously up and down the room, and had begun to talk so loud that their conversation sounded remarkably like quarrelling. The room grew close and stifling, the candle began to flare, the deacon's cigar-smoke got into the people's eyes. The choir-master, holding the deacon by his coat-button, assured him for the tenth time (*à propos* of nothing) that his wife was an angel, and that but for her he should have come to utter ruin. The conversation then jumped with extraordinary rapidity back to music, and the deacon affirmed that C sharp major and G minor are the same, and that the whole thing depends upon how you breathe, and finally proved to demonstration that "all these composers" ought long ago to have been kicked down stairs. Notwith-standing all this, the choir-master once more went into the ante-room, waked Pétia, and sent him for a third pint.

"No, no; wait a bit! Just hear what I tell you!" yelled the choir-master, holding the deacon by the coat.

"All that's idle talk."

"No, no; I'll prove it," shrieked the choir-master. "See now! Where is my music got to? Ah, there now, I forgot to sent for the supper . . . Fékla!"

The angry face of the maid-servant appeared at the door.

"Fékla!" said the choir-master in a stern voice, trying hard not to stagger; "go and fetch some cucumbers."

"Missis told me not."

"Then you won't go?"

"No, I won't."

"Then you're a pig. I'll go myself."

"Go then! Missis'll give you what for."

However, after thinking it over, the choir-master decided not to go, and only shouted at her:

"Be off with you! Yah! Scandalmonger!"

"THE DEACON WENT HOME."

The servant went away. Presently a third pint was brought in and the basses and tenors once more crowded round the decanter. Suddenly the choir-master quite unexpectedly sat down at the piano, struck a few chords, and shouted: "Get to your places!" The sleepy boys came in from the ante-room, and the whole choir stood in a crowd together.

> See, the light is dying,
> See, the time is flying . . ." [1]

yelled the choir-master, hammering unmercifully on the keys.

> " The lasses went to the fields to play,
> Among the grasses and flowers gay" [1]

bellowed the choir.

> " Oh, my bonny blue kirtle!" [1]

howled the tipsy deacon, swinging his legs under the table.

"In the name of law and order!" shrieked the choir-master. " Basses, out with your tone! *Crescendo! Crescendo!* "

*   *   *   *   *

At about eleven o'clock at night the deacon was hunting for his galoshes in the ante-room. For a long time he could not find them; at last he stuck his foot into somebody's cap, which happened to be lying on the floor, and went home.

[1] Fragments of popular songs.

The Eagle as Mæcenas

A FABLE.

BY

"SHCHEDRÌN"

(SALTYKÒV).

A GREAT deal is written by various poets about Eagles; and always in praise of them. The Eagle has invariably a form of indescribable beauty, piercing vision, and a majestic flight. In fact, he does not fly like other birds, but "sails" or "soars" through the air; moreover, he can gaze upon the sun and battle with the thunders. Some writers speak of the magnanimity of his soul. For in-

stance, if you want to write an ode in praise of a policeman, it is quite essential to compare him to an Eagle.
Thus : " Like the majestic Eagle, Police-sergeant No.
So-and-so looked on the suspected person, seized him,
heard his explanation, and magnanimously pardoned him."

I, personally, long cherished a belief in these panegyrics.
I used to think : After all, it really is a grand idea ! " Seized
him and . . . pardoned ! ' Pardoned ! That was what
really fascinated me. Whom did he pardon? A mouse !
A miserable mouse ! And then I would rush off to some
one of my poetical friends to tell him of this new act of
magnanimity on the part of the Eagle. And my poetical
friend would strike an attitude, breathe hard for a moment,
and then . . . would become affected with the sea-sickness
of versification.

One day, though, the idea occurred to me : What did
the Eagle " pardon " in the mouse ? All that the mouse
had done was to run across the road on its own private
business ; and the Eagle saw it, swooped, squeezed it half to
death, and . . . pardoned it ! Why in the world did the
Eagle pardon the mouse and not the mouse the Eagle?

Well, I began to look about me and take notice of
things ; and the more I saw, the more muddled I got.
There certainly was something askew about the whole
business. In the first place, it is evident that the Eagle does
not catch mice for the purpose of pardoning them. In the
next place, even if the Eagle did pardon the mouse, I cannot help thinking that it would have been still better if he
had taken no interest in its affairs at all. And, finally, in
the third place, granted he is an Eagle—an Arch-eagle for
that matter—all the same he's a bird. Indeed, he is so
essentially a bird that, even for a policeman, a comparison
with him can be considered complimentary only in virtue of
a misunderstanding.

My present opinion concerning Eagles is as follows :—

Eagles are Eagles—and that is the long and short of the matter. They are simply carnivora, birds of prey; but, it is true, they have this justification: that Nature herself made them anti-vegetarians. As they are, moreover, powerful, long-sighted, agile, and merciless, it is perfectly natural that, whenever they appear, the entire feathered kingdom does its best to hide itself away. This is simply the effect of terror, and not at all of admiration, as the poets maintain. Eagles habitually live in solitary and inaccessible places; never exchange bread-and-salt with any one;[1] but live by robbery; and, when not engaged in burgling, go to sleep.

There turned up, however, a certain Eagle who grew sick of living in solitude. So one day he said to his mate: "It's a fearful bore to live in this fashion, *tête-à-tête*; if one does nothing but gaze at the sun the whole day long, it muddles one's head."

He set to work to meditate. The more he thought about it, the more it seemed to him that it would be very nice to live as the landed proprietors used to live in the old days. He could get a whole suite of servants and be as happy as the day is long. The rooks would provide him with scandal; the parrot would turn upside down and do tricks; the magpie would cook his porridge; the robins would sing songs in praise of him; the owls and night-jars would serve as watchmen and sentinels; and the hawks and falcons would bring him food. For himself he would keep no speciality but bloodthirstiness.

He thought and thought; and at last he made up his mind. One day he called a hawk, a kite, and a falcon, and said to them—

"Collect for me a staff of servants, such as the old land-lords used to have; they will amuse me, and I will keep them in order. That will be pleasant for me and good for them."

---

[1] The popular emblem of hospitality.

So the birds of prey flew off in all directions to fulfil the
Eagle's commands. No one can say they dawdled over
their business.   First of all they drove in a whole flight of
rooks, registered their names, and gave them out passports.
The rook, you see, is a fertile bird, and puts up with everything.   Its best quality is that it admirably represents the

peasant class : and everybody knows that if once you have
got the peasants settled, all the rest is a matter of detail and
quite easily managed. And they certainly managed beautifully.
The corn-crakes and mud-suckers were trained for an orchestra:
the parrots were dressed up for acrobats ; the white-feathered
magpie, being a notorious thief, was intrusted with the keys

of the treasury; and the owls and night-jars were put on duty as sentinels. In a word, the whole thing was arranged in a manner that would have done credit to any nobleman's establishment. Even the cuckoo was not forgotten ; employment was found for her as fortune-teller to the female Eagle; and a foundling hospital was instituted for orphan cuckoos.

But before the whole arrangement was fairly in working order the managing directors realised that something was wanting. For a long time they could not think what it could be ; but at last they remembered that in all high-class establishments Science and Art are supposed to be represented, and they had made no provision for either the one or the other. Three birds especially felt themselves aggrieved by this omission—the robin, the woodpecker, and the nightingale.

The robin was a smart little soul and had practised whistling since his fledgling days. He had received his earliest education in an ecclesiastical school; then he had served as regimental clerk ; and as soon as he had learned the rules of correct punctuation he had begun to edit, without preliminary censorship, a newspaper : *The Forest Gazette.* But, somehow or other, he could never get it right : whenever he touched upon a subject, it turned out to be *taboo ;* whenever he refrained from mentioning a subject, that subject particularly ought to have been mentioned ; and for all these mistakes he used to get hard knocks on his poor little head. So at last he decided : "I will enter the service of the Eagle ; all I shall have to do will be to sing his praises every morning ; and no one will punish me for that."

The thrush was a modest and studious person, who led a strictly solitary life ; he had no acquaintances (many even believed him to be a drunkard, like all very learned persons), but would sit for whole days alone upon a fir-branch,

cramming up information.   He managed to plod through a
perfect desert of historical investigations : "The Ancestral
Records of a Bogie," "Was the old Woman who rode on a
Broomstick married?" "What Sex should be ascribed to
Witches in the Register-Papers?" and so forth.   But, however hard the poor bird crammed, he could not find a
publisher for his pamphlets.   At last it occurred to him
too : "I'll engage myself as Court-Historiographer to the
Eagle ; perhaps he will print my investigations in rook's
dung !

As for the nightingale, he couldn't complain of the
cruelty of fate ; he sang so exquisitely that not only the
mighty fir-trees, but even the Moscow shopkeepers were quite
touched when they heard him.   All the world adored him ;
all the world held its breath to listen when he poured out
torrents of divine song from among the branches of some
silent grove.   But the nightingale was ambitious beyond
measure, and desperately given to falling in love.   He was
not content with making the forest ring with his wild
melodies, or filling sad hearts with the harmony of sound
. . . he kept on thinking how the Eagle would hang round his
neck a shining chain of ants' eggs, and decorate his breast
with live beetles, and how the female Eagle would appoint
secret meetings with him by moonlight. . . . In short, all
three birds gave the falcon no peace till he undertook to
speak on their behalf.

The Eagle listened attentively to the falcon's assurances
of the necessity of encouraging science and art; but did
not quite understand.   He sat sharpening his claws, and his
eyes flashed back the sunlight like polished gems.   He
had never seen a newspaper in his life ; he had never taken
the slightest interest in either witches or the old woman
who rode on a broomstick ; and about the nightingale he
had only heard that it was a little bit of a bird not worth
soiling one's beak over.

"I daresay you don't even know that Buonaparte is dead," said the falcon.

"Who was Buonaparte?"

"There you are!   And you certainly *ought* to know about that.   Supposing visitors come and begin a polite conversation ; they'll say : 'In Buonparte's days so-and-so happened' ; and you'll just have to sit and blink your eyes. That won't do."

They called in the owl as adviser, and she agreed with the falcon that science and art must be introduced into the establishment ; for they amuse Eagles, and it does ordinary mortals no harm to enjoy them from a distance either. Knowledge is light, and ignorance is darkness.   Any fool knows how to eat and sleep ; but just try and work out a problem; take the one about the flock of geese, for instance, that's a very different matter.   In the old days the clever landowners understood that ; they knew that forewarned was forearmed ; they were sharp enough to see which side their bread was buttered.   Just take the case of the finch : all the learning he has is how to draw water in a little bucket, and yet see what a high price he fetches just for that one trick !   "I," concluded the owl, "can see in the dark, and I am called wise for that ; now, you can stare at the sun for hours together without ever blinking ; and all people say about you is : 'That Eagle's a bit of a blockhead.'"

"Well, I have no objection to science," said the Eagle, rather snappishly.

No sooner said than done.   On the next day the "Golden Age" began in the Eagle's establishment.   The starlings set to work to learn by heart the hymn : "Let our youth be fed with science"; the corn-crakes and mud-suckers began practising the trumpet ; the parrots invented new tricks.   A new tax was laid upon the rooks, to be called "Public Instruction Tax."   A *Corps des Cadets* was founded

for fledgling falcons and vultures; and an Academy of
Science for owls. They even went the length of buying a
farthing alphabet apiece for the baby rooks. Last but not
least, the oldest patriarch among the starlings was appointed
poet-laureate, with the honorary title of " Vasili Kirilych
Trediakòvsky,"[1] and commanded to prepare for a public
competition with the nightingale, to be held on the next
morning.

At last the great day dawned. The newly-elected
flunkeys were admitted into the presence of the Eagle, and
the tournament of arts began.

The most successful competitor was the robin. Instead
of reciting his compliments, he read aloud an article, so
clear and simple that even the Eagle fancied he understood.
The robin said that people ought to live in happiness and
prosperity; and the Eagle remarked, "Exactly so." He
said that if he could make his paper sell properly he would
be quite indifferent to all other questions; and the Eagle
repeated, "Exactly so." He said that the life of a servant
is preferable to that of a master; for the master has many
responsibilities, whereas the servant lives under his master's
protection, free from care; and the Eagle again repeated,
"Exactly so!" He said that, in the days when he kept a
conscience, he could not get a pair of trousers to wear,
but, now that he had got rid of his conscience, he was in
the habit of putting on two pair at once; and the Eagle
once more repeated, "Exactly so!"

At last the Eagle began to get bored, and snappishly commanded: "The next one."

The woodpecker began by tracing the pedigree of the
Eagle back to the Sun, and the Eagle confirmed his state-
ments with the remark: "That's just what I used to hear
from poor papa." According to the woodpecker, the Sun
had three children: two sons, the Lion and the Eagle; and

---

[1] A flunkeyish poetaster at the Court of Catherine II.

one daughter, the Shark. The Shark misconducted herself; and her father, as a punishment, sent her to rule the depths of ocean; the Lion turned aside from his father's way, and the father made him ruler of the deserts; but the Eagle was a son after his father's heart, and the father kept him nearest to himself and gave to him the realms of air for a kingdom. But before the poor woodpecker had got through even the prosy introduction to his history, the Eagle called out impatiently: "The next one! The next one!"

Then the nightingale began his song, and made a mess of

it from the very first note. He sang of the joy of the flunkey hearing that God has sent him a master; he sang of the magnanimity of Eagles, and of their liberality in tipping flunkeys. . . . But, however desperately he tried to pitch his voice in the true flunkey tone, the art that dwelt within his breast somehow or other would not be controlled. He himself was a flunkey from beak to tail (he had even got hold, somehow, of a second-hand white cravat, and had ruffled up the feathers on his little head into a hair-dresser's curl), but his *art* refused to be confined within flunkey-ish bounds, and kept on bursting forth in spite of all his efforts. It wasn't any use for him to sing; he could not give satisfaction anyhow.

"What's that booby droning about?" cried the Eagle; "call Trediakòvsky!"

Vasìli Kirìlych was quite in his element. He chose just the same toadyish subjects, but gave so clear an exposition of them that the Eagle kept on all the time repeating—

" Exactly so! Exactly so!"

When the competition was over, the Eagle hung upon Trediakòvsky's neck a chain of ants' eggs, and flashed his eyes at the nightingale, exclaiming—

"Take away that scoundrel!"

Thus ended the nightingale's ambitious dreams. He was quickly hustled into a hen-coop and sold out of the way to the tavern "Parting Friends," where, to this day, he fills with sweet poison the hearts of tipsy "meteors."

Nevertheless, the work of public instruction was not abandoned. The fledgling vultures and falcons attended the gymnasium regularly; the Academy of Science began to publish a dictionary, and got half through the letter A; the woodpecker finished the tenth volume of "The History of Bogies." The robin, however, kept very quiet. From the first day he had felt an instinctive conviction that all this educational rage would come to a speedy and grievous end ; and apparently his presentiments were well founded.

The troubles began with a grave mistake on the part of the owl and falcon, who had accepted the management of the work of education : they took it into their heads to teach the Eagle himself to read and write. They taught him upon the easy and agreeable phonetic system ; but, notwithstanding all their efforts, after a whole year's training, instead of " Eagle," he signed his name " Agull " ; the result of which was that he could not get a single respectable financier to accept his bonds. The owl and falcon also made another great mistake : like all pedagogues, they never gave their pupil any peace. Every minute of the day the owl would follow at the poor Eagle's heels, screaming out, " B-b-b-b ; Z-z-z; D-d-d; K-k-k; " while the falcon as incessantly dinned into his ears that it is impossible to divide the prey one has caught without knowing the first four rules of arithmetic.

" Suppose you have stolen ten goslings, of which you have given two to the police-inspector's clerk, and eaten one yourself, how many have you left ? " asked the falcon, in a reproachful voice.

The Eagle was not able to work this problem, so he remained silent ; but anger against the falcon burned in his heart more and more fiercely with every day.

All this resulted in a condition of general tension, which was at once taken advantage of by intriguing adventurers. The ringleader of the conspiracy was the kite ; he enticed over the cuckoo, who took to whispering in the ear of the female Eagle—

" They are simply killing our dear master with their learning."

Whereupon the female Eagle began ironically calling her mate " Wiseacre ! Wiseacre ! " The conspirators next turned their energies to the business of arousing " evil passions " in the vulture.

One morning, just at dawn, and while the Eagle was still sleepily rubbing his eyes, the owl, as usual, slipped behind him and began her eternal buzzing in his ear—

"V-v-v . . . Z-z-z . . . R-r-r——"

"Oh! go away, you awful bore!" murmured the Eagle, wearily.

"Be so good, your worship, as to repeat B-b-b . . . K-k-k . . . M-m-m——"

"I tell you, for the second time, go away!"

"P-p-p . . . H-h-h . . . Sh-sh-sh——"

"For the third time, go away!"

"S-s-s . . . F-f-f . . . J-j-j——"

With the quickness of lightning the Eagle turned upon the owl and tore her in pieces. An hour later the falcon, knowing nothing of what had happened, returned from the morning hunt.

"Here is a problem for you," said he. "We have brought back 60 lbs. of game. Now, suppose we divide the game into two equal parts, one half for you and the other half for the remainder of the establishment, how much of the 60 lbs. will fall to your share?"

"All of it," replied the Eagle.

"No, no; answer proper y," persisted the falcon. "If it had been "all," I shouldn't have asked you!"

It was not the first time that he had set his pupil such problems; but on this occasion the tone in which the question was asked struck the Eagle as quite intolerable. All his blood boiled at the thought that, when he said "all," his slave should dare to answer "not all." Now, it is a well-known peculiarity of Eagles that, when their blood begins to boil, they become incapable of distinguishing pedagogical disquisitions from revolution. The Eagle acted accordingly.

Nevertheless, after finishing up the falcon, the Eagle announced—

" The Scientific 'Cademy is to stop as it is."

The choir of starlings once more repeated their hymn, " Let our youth be fed with science." But it was already plain to every one that the " Golden Age " was drawing to its close. In the near future darkness and ignorance were at hand, with their inevitable train—civil war and general confusion.

The disturbances began with the competition of two candidates for the post of the defunct falcon—the vulture and the kite. As the attention of the two rivals was absorbed exclusively in their personal interest, the affairs of the establishment were to some extent shoved aside and gradually fell into a neglected condition. In a month there remained not a trace of the " Golden Age." The starlings had grown lazy ; the corn-crakes played all out of tune ; the white-feathered magpie took to stealing right and left ; and the rooks got so hopelessly behindhand with the taxes that there was nothing for it but an " *execution.*" [1] Matters went so far that the servants began to bring the Eagle and his mate bad meat for dinner.

In order to exculpate themselves from responsibility in all this mismanagement, the vulture and the kite, for the moment, played into each other's claws, and threw all the blame upon education.

" Science," said they, " is undoubtedly a useful thing, but only under the right conditions. Our ancestors,'' said they, " managed to live without any science; and we can do the same."

And, to prove that all the troubles came from science, they set to work to hunt up conspiracies, and particularly conspiracies in which some book, if only a prayer-book, was concerned. There began a perfect rain of searches, police-investigations, and trials.

---

[1] " *Exckoützia,*" official term for wholesale flogging, in case of mutiny, or inability to pay taxes, among the peasantry.

" Drop it ! " suddenly rang through the aerial heights.

It was the Eagle who said that. The process of education broke off short. Throughout the whole establishment there reigned such dead silence that one could even hear the whispers of slander creeping along the earth.

The first victim of the new tendency of affairs was the woodpecker. Indeed, indeed the poor bird was not guilty ; but he knew how to read and write, and that was quite sufficient ground for an accusation.

" Do you know the rules of punctuation ? "

" Not only the rules of ordinary punctuation, but even those for extra signs, such as quotation marks, hyphens, parentheses ; on my conscience, I always put them right."

" And can you distinguish the feminine from the masculine gender ? "

" I can. I should not make a mistake, even by night."

And that was all. The woodpecker was chained and placed in solitary confinement for life in a hollow tree. On the next day, being devoured by ants, he gave up the ghost in his prison. His sorrows were hardly over when the thunderbolt fell on the Academy of Science.

The owls and night-jars, however, defended themselves sturdily ; they did not wish to be evicted from their cosy free quarters. They said that they followed scientific pursuits, not in order to popularise science, but to protect it from the evil eye. But the kite instantly demolished their arguments by asking—

" What's the use of having science at all ? "

This being an unexpected question, they could give no answer. They were then separated and sold to market-gardeners, who killed and stuffed them and set them up in their nurseries for scarecrows. The farthing alphabets were next taken away from the baby rooks, and mashed up in a mortar, to form a homogeneous mass of pulp, which was then made into playing-cards.

Matters grew worse and worse. After the owls and the night-jars came the turn of the starlings; then the corn-crakes, parrots, and finches. Even the deaf heath-cock was suspected of "a certain way of thinking," on the ground that he held his tongue all day and slept all night.

The staff of the establishment gradually dwindled away. At last there was no one left to serve the Eagle and his mate but the vulture and the kite. In the background there remained, of course, a crowd of rooks, who multiplied at a pace that was perfectly disgraceful; and the faster they multiplied the more their arrears of taxes accumulated.

Finally the kite and vulture, having no one else to intrigue against (of course you don't count the vulgar rooks), began to intrigue one against the other; and all on the ground of science. The vulture denounced the kite as reading the prayer-book in secret; and the kite invented against the vulture the slander that he kept the " New Song-Book " hidden in a hollow tree.

The Eagle began to grow uneasy.

But just at this moment an extraordinary thing happened. Finding themselves left without supervision, the rooks suddenly raised the question—

" By the by, what did the farthing alphabet say about all this ? "

And, without stopping to remember clearly what was said, they all left their nests in a body and flew away.

The Eagle started off to pursue them, but it was no use ; the indolent life he had been living had so enervated him that he could hardly flap his wings.

He returned to his mate, and uttered these words of wisdom—

" Be this a lesson to Eagles ! "

But in what exactly the " lesson " consisted—whether it were that education is injurious to Eagles, or that Eagles are njurious to education, or, finally, that each is injurious to the other—that he never explained.

THE WALTER SCOTT PRESS, NEWCASTLE-ON-TYNE.

NEW BOOKS

Life of Byron.   By Hon. Roden Noel.

"He (Mr. Noel) has at any rate given to the world the most credible and comprehensible portrait of the poet ever drawn with pen and ink."—*Manchester Examiner.*

Life of Bunyan.   By Canon Venables.

"A most intelligent, appreciative, and valuable memoir."—*Scotsman.*

Life of Burns.   By Professor Blackie.

"The editor certainly made a hit when he persuaded Blackie to write about Burns."—*Pall Mall Gazette.*

Life of Thomas Carlyle.   By R. Garnett, LL.D.

"This is an admirable book.   Nothing could be more felicitous and fairer than the way in which he takes us through Carlyle's life and works."—*Pall Mall Gazette.*

Life of Coleridge.   By Hall Caine.

"Brief and vigorous, written throughout with spirit and great literary skill."—*Scotsman.*

Life of Congreve.   By Edmund Gosse.

"Mr. Gosse has written an admirable and most interesting biography of a man of letters who is of particular interest to other men of letters."—*The Academy.*

Life of Crabbe.   By T. E. Kebbel.

"No English poet since Shakespeare has observed certain aspects of nature and of human life more closely; and in the qualities of manliness and of sincerity he is surpassed by none. . . .   Mr. Kebbel's monograph is worthy of the subject."—*Athenæum.*

Life of Darwin.   By G. T. Bettany.

"Mr. G. T. Bettany's *Life of Darwin* is a sound and conscientious work."—*Saturday Review.*

Life of Dickens.   By Frank T. Marzials.

"Notwithstanding the mass of matter that has been printed relating to Dickens and his works . . . we should, until we came across this volume, have been at a loss to recommend any popular life of England's most popular novelist as being really satisfactory.   The difficulty is removed by Mr. Marzials's little book."—*Athenæum.*

Life of George Eliot.   By Oscar Browning.

"We are thankful for this interesting addition to our knowledge of the great novelist."—*Literary World.*

Life of Emerson.   By Richard Garnett, LL.D.

"As to the larger section of the public, to whom the series of Great Writers is addressed, no record of Emerson's life and work could be more desirable, both in breadth of treatment and lucidity of style, than Dr. Garnett's."—*Saturday Review.*

Life of Goethe.   By James Sime.

"Mr. James Sime's competence as a biographer of Goethe, both in respect of knowledge of his special subject, and of German literature generally, is beyond question."—*Manchester Guardian.*

Life of Goldsmith.   By Austin Dobson.

"The story of his literary and social life in London, with all its humorous and pathetic vicissitudes, is here retold, as none could tell it better."—*Daily News.*

New York: CHARLES SCRIBNER'S SONS.

Life of Nathaniel Hawthorne.   By Moncure Conway.

"Easy and conversational as the tone is throughout, no important fact is omitted, no useless fact is recalled."—*Speaker.*

Life of Heine.   By William Sharp.

"This is an admirable monograph . . . more fully written up to the level of recent knowledge and criticism of its theme than any other English work."—*Scotsman.*

Life of Victor Hugo.   By Frank T. Marzials.

"Mr. Marzials's volume presents to us, in a more handy form than any English, or even French handbook gives, the summary of what, up to the moment in which we write, is known or conjectured about the life of the great poet."—*Saturday Review.*

Life of Samuel Johnson.   By Colonel F. Grant.

"Colonel Grant has performed his task with diligence, sound judgment, good taste, and accuracy."—*Illustrated London News.*

Life of Keats.   By W. M. Rossetti.

"Valuable for the ample information which it contains."—*Cambridge Independent.*

Life of Lessing.   By T. W. Rolleston.

"A picture of Lessing which is vivid and truthful, and has enough of detail for all ordinary purposes."—*Nation* (New York).

Life of Longfellow.   By Prof. Eric S. Robertson.

"A most readable little book."—*Liverpool Mercury.*

Life of Marryat.   By David Hannay.

"What Mr. Hannay had to do—give a craftsman-like account of a great craftsman who has been almost incomprehensibly undervalued—could hardly have been done better than in this little volume."—*Manchester Guardian.*

Life of Mill.   By W. L. Courtney.

"A most sympathetic and discriminating memoir."—*Glasgow Herald.*

Life of Milton.   By Richard Garnett, LL.D.

"Within equal compass the life-story of the great poet of Puritanism has never been more charmingly or adequately told."—*Scottish Leader.*

Life of Dante Gabriel Rossetti.   By J. Knight.

"Mr. Knight's picture of the great poet and painter is the fullest and best yet presented to the public."—*The Graphic.*

Life of Scott.   By Professor Yonge.

"For readers and lovers of the poems and novels of Sir Walter Scott, this is a most enjoyable book."—*Aberdeen Free Press.*

Life of Arthur Schopenhauer.   By William Wallace.

"The series of 'Great Writers' has hardly had a contribution of more marked and peculiar excellence than the book which the Whyte Professor of Moral Philosophy at Oxford has written for it on the attractive and still (in England) little known subject of Schopenhauer."—*Manchester Guardian.*

Life of Shelley.   By William Sharp.

"The criticisms . . . entitle this capital monograph to be ranked with the best biographies of Shelley."—*Westminster Review.*

Life of Sheridan.   By Lloyd Sanders.

"To say that Mr. Lloyd Sanders, in this volume, has produced the best existing memoir of Sheridan is really to award much fainter praise than the book deserves."—*Manchester Examiner.*

"Rapid and workmanlike in style; the author has evidently a good practical knowledge of the stage of Sheridan's day."—*Saturday Review.*

Life of Adam Smith.   By R. B. Haldane, M.P.

"Written with a perspicuity seldom exemplified when dealing with economic science."—*Scotsman.*

"Mr. Haldane's handling of his subject impresses us as that of a man who well understands his theme, and who knows how to elucidate it."—*Scottish Leader.*

"A beginner in political economy might easily do worse than take Mr. Haldane's book as his first text-book."—*Graphic.*

Life of Smollett.   By David Hannay.

"A capital record of a writer who still remains one of the great masters of the English novel."—*Saturday Review.*

"Mr. Hannay is excellently equipped for writing the life of Smollett. As a specialist on the history of the eighteenth century navy, he is at a great advantage in handling works so full of the sea and sailors as Smollett's three principal novels. Moreover, he has a complete acquaintance with the Spanish romancers, from whom Smollett drew so much of his inspiration. His criticism is generally acute and discriminating; and his narrative is well arranged, compact, and accurate."—*St. James's Gazette.*

Life of Schiller.   By Henry W. Nevinson.

"This is a well-written little volume, which presents the leading facts of the poet's life in a neatly-rounded picture."—*Scotsman.*

"Mr. Nevinson has added much to the charm of his book by his spirited translations, which give excellently both the ring and sense of the original."—*Manchester Guardian.*

Life of Thackeray.   By Herman Merivale and Frank T. Marzials.

"The book, with its excellent bibliography, is one which neither the student nor the general reader can well afford to miss."—*Pall Mall Gazette.*

"The last book published by Messrs. Merivale and Marzials is full of very real and true things."—Mrs. Anne Thackeray Ritchie on "Thackeray and his Biographers," in *Illustrated London News.*

Life of Cervantes.   By H. E. Watts.

Life of Voltaire.   By Francis Espinasse.

Life of Leigh Hunt.   By Cosmo Monkhouse.

Life of Whittier.   By W. J. Linton.

Life of Renan.   By Francis Espinasse.

Complete Bibliography to each volume, by J. P. ANDERSON, British Museum, London.

Cloth Elegant, Large 12mo,

Price $1.25 per vol.

LIBRARY OF HUMOUR.

EDITED BY W. H. DIRCKS.

Each Volume will contain from 50 to 70 Illustrations and from 350 to 500 pages.

IN each of these volumes the object will be to give an anthology of the humorous literature of the particular nation dealt with. France, Germany, Italy, Russia, Spain, and Holland will each have their respective volumes; England, Ireland, and Scotland will each be represented, as will also America and Japan. 'From China to Peru' the globe will be traversed in search of its jokes, in so far as they have recorded themselves in literature. The word Humour admits of many interpretations; for the purposes of this Series it has been interpreted in its broadest generic sense, to cover humour in all its phases as it has manifested itself among the various nationalities. Necessarily founded on a certain degree of scholarly knowledge, these volumes, while appealing to the literary reader, will nevertheless, it is hoped, in the inherent attractiveness and variety of their contents, appeal successfully and at once to the interest of readers of all classes. Starting from the early periods of each literature—in Italy, for instance, from the fourteenth century, with Boccaccio, Sacchetti, and Parabosco; in France with the amusing Fabliaux of the thirteenth century; in Germany from Hans Sachs; characteristic sketches, stories, and extracts from contemporary European and other writers whose genius is especially that of humour or *esprit* will be given. Indicating and suggesting a view and treatment of national life from a particular standpoint, each volume will contain matter suggestive of the development of a special and important phase of national spirit and character,—namely, the humorous. Proverbs and maxims, folk-wit, and folk-tales notable for their pith and humour, will have their place; the eccentricities of modern newspaper humour will not be overlooked. Each volume will be well and copiously illustrated; in many cases artists of the nationalities of the literatures represented will illustrate the volumes. To each volume will be prefixed an Introduction critically disengaging and marking the qualities and phases of the national humour dealt with; and to each will be appended Notes, biographical and explanatory.

LIBRARY OF HUMOUR

Cloth Elegant, Large 12mo, Price $1.25 per vol.

VOLUMES ALREADY ISSUED.

THE HUMOUR OF FRANCE. Translated, with an Introduction and Notes, by Elizabeth Lee. With numerous Illustrations by Paul Frénzeny.

"From Villon to Paul Verlaine, from dateless *fabliaux* to newspapers fresh from the kiosk, we have a tremendous range of selections."—*Birmingham Daily Gazette.*

"French wit is excellently represented. We have here examples of Villon, Rabelais, and Molière, but we have specimens also of La Rochefoucauld, Regnard, Voltaire, Beaumarchais, Chamfort, Dumas, Gautier, Labiche, De Banville, Pailleron, and many others. . . . The book sparkles from beginning to end."—*Globe* (London).

THE HUMOUR OF GERMANY. Translated, with an Introduction and Notes, by Hans Müller-Casenov. With numerous Illustrations by C. E. Brock.

An excellently representative volume.—*Daily Telegraph* (London).

"Whether it is Saxon kinship or the fine qualities of the collection, we have found this volume the most entertaining of the three. Its riotous absurdities well overbalance its examples of the oppressively heavy. . . . The national impulse to make fun of the war correspondent has a capital example in the skit from Juliu. Stettenheim."—*New York Independent.*

The Contemporary Science Series.

Edited by Havelock Ellis.

Crown 8vo, Cloth.   Price $1.25 per Volume.

I. THE EVOLUTION OF SEX.   By Prof. PATRICK GEDDES and J. A. THOMSON.   With 90 Illustrations.   Second Edition.

"The authors have brought to the task—as indeed their names guarantee —a wealth of knowledge, a lucid and attractive method of treatment, and a rich vein of picturesque language."—*Nature.*

II. ELECTRICITY IN MODERN LIFE.   By G. W. DE TUNZELMANN.   With 88 Illustrations.

"A clearly-written and connected sketch of what is known about electricity and magnetism, the more prominent modern applications, and the principles on which they are based."—*Saturday Review.*

III. THE ORIGIN OF THE ARYANS.   By Dr. ISAAC TAYLOR.   Illustrated.   Second Edition.

"Canon Taylor is probably the most encyclopædic all-round scholar now living.   His new volume on the Origin of the Aryans is a first-rate example of the excellent account to which he can turn his exceptionally wide and varied information. . . . Masterly and exhaustive."—*Pall Mall Gazette.*

IV. PHYSIOGNOMY AND EXPRESSION.   By P. MANTE-GAZZA.   Illustrated.

"Brings this highly interesting subject even with the latest researches. . . . Professor Mantegazza is a writer full of life and spirit, and the natural attractiveness of his subject is not destroyed by his scientific handling of it." *Literary World* (Boston).

V. EVOLUTION AND DISEASE.   By J. B. SUTTON, F.R.C.S.   With 135 Illustrations.

"The book is as interesting as a novel, without sacrifice of accuracy or system, and is calculated to give an appreciation of the fundamentals of pathology to the lay reader, while forming a useful collection of illustrations of disease for medical reference."—*Journal of Mental Science.*

VI. THE VILLAGE COMMUNITY.   By G. L. GOMME.   Illustrated.

"His book will probably remain for some time the best work of reference for facts bearing on those traces of the village community which have not been effaced by conquest, encroachment, and the heavy hand of Roman law."—*Scottish Leader.*

VII. THE CRIMINAL.   By HAVELOCK ELLIS.   Illustrated.

"An ably written, an instructive, and a most entertaining book."—*Law Quarterly Review.*

"The sociologist, the philosopher, the philanthropist, the novelist— all, indeed, for whom the study of human nature has any attraction—will find Mr. Ellis full of interest and suggestiveness."—*Academy.*

VIII. SANITY AND INSANITY.   By Dr. CHARLES MERCIER.
Illustrated.

"He has laid down the institutes of insanity."—*Mind*.

"Taken as a whole, it is the brightest book on the physical side of mental science published in our time."—*Pall Mall Gazette*.

IX. HYPNOTISM.   By Dr. ALBERT MOLL.   Second Edition.

"Marks a step of some importance in the study of some difficult physiological and psychological problems which have not yet received much attention in the scientific world of England."—*Nature*.

X. MANUAL TRAINING.   By Dr. C. M. WOODWARD, Director of the Manual Training School, St. Louis.   Illustrated.

"There is no greater authority on the subject than Professor Woodward."—*Manchester Guardian*.

XI. THE SCIENCE OF FAIRY TALES.   By E. SIDNEY HARTLAND.

"Mr. Hartland's book will win the sympathy of all earnest students, both by the knowledge it displays, and by a thorough love and appreciation of his subject, which is evident throughout."—*Spectator*.

XII. PRIMITIVE FOLK.   By ELIE RECLUS.

"An attractive and useful introduction to the study of some aspects of ethnograpy."—*Nature*.

"For an introduction to the study of the questions of property, marriage, government, religion,—in a word, to the evolution of society,—this little volume will be found most convenient."—*Scottish Leader*.

XIII. THE EVOLUTION OF MARRIAGE.   By Professor LETOURNEAU.

"Among the distinguished French students of sociology, Professor Letourneau has long stood in the first rank.   He approaches the great study of man free from bias and shy of generalisations.   To collect, scrutinise, and appraise facts is his chief business.   In the volume before us he shows these qualities in an admirable degree. . . . At the close of his attractive pages he ventures to forecast the future of the institution of marriage."—*Science*.

XIV. BACTERIA AND THEIR PRODUCTS.   By Dr. G. SIMS WOODHEAD.   Illustrated.

"An excellent summary of the present state of knowledge of the subject."—*Lancet*.

XV. EDUCATION AND HEREDITY.   By J. M. GUYAU.

"It is at once a treatise on sociology, ethics, and pædagogics.   It is doubtful whether among all the ardent evolutionists who have had their say on the moral and the educational question any one has carried forward the new doctrine so boldly to its extreme logical consequence."—Professor SULLY in *Mind*.

XVI. THE MAN OF GENIUS.   By Prof. LOMBROSO   Illustrated.

"By far the most comprehensive and fascinating collection of facts and generalizations concerning genius which has yet been brought together."—*Journal of Mental Science*.

New York: CHARLES SCRIBNER'S SONS.

XVII. THE GRAMMAR OF SCIENCE. By Prof. KARL PEARSON. Illustrated.

" The problems discussed with great ability and lucidity, and often in a most suggestive manner, by Prof. Pearson, are such as should interest *all* students of natural science."—*Natural Science.*

XVIII. PROPERTY: ITS ORIGIN AND DEVELOPMENT. By CH. LETOURNEAU, General Secretary to the Anthropological Society, Paris, and Professor in the School of Anthropology, Paris.

" M. Letourneau has read a great deal, and he seems to us to have selected and interpreted his facts with considerable judgment and learning."—*Westminster Review.*

XIX. VOLCANOES, PAST AND PRESENT. By Prof. EDWARD HULL, LL.D., F.R.S.

" A very readable account of the phenomena of volcanoes and earthquakes."—*Nature.*

XX. PUBLIC HEALTH. By Dr. J. F. J. SYKES. With numerous Illustrations.

"Not by any means a mere compilation or a dry record of details and statistics, but it takes up essential points in evolution, environment, prophylaxis, and sanitation bearing upon the preservation of public health."—*Lancet.*

XXI. MODERN METEOROLOGY. AN ACCOUNT OF THE GROWTH AND PRESENT CONDITION OF SOME BRANCHES OF METEOROLOGICAL SCIENCE. By FRANK WALDO, PH.D., Member of the German and Austrian Meteorological Societies, etc.; late Junior Professor, Signal Service, U.S.A. With 112 Illustrations.

"The present volume is the best on the subject for general use that we have seen."—*Daily Telegraph* (London).

IMPORTANT ADDITION TO THE SERIES.

Price $2.50.

XXII. *THE GERM-PLASM: A THEORY OF HEREDITY. By August Weismann, Professor in the University of Freiburg-in-Breisgau. With 24 Illustrations.*

"There has been no work published since Darwin's own books which has so thoroughly handled the matter treated by him, or has done so much to place in order and clearness the immense complexity of the factors of heredity, or, lastly, has brought to light so many new facts and considerations bearing on the subject."—*British Medical Journal.*

XXIII. INDUSTRIES OF ANIMALS. By F. HOUSSAY. With numerous Illustrations.

" His accuracy is undoubted, yet his facts out-marvel all romance. These facts are here made use of as materials wherewith to form the mighty fabric of evolution."—*Manchester Guardian.*

New York : CHARLES SCRIBNER'S SONS,

IBSEN'S DRAMAS.

Edited by William Archer.

12mo, CLOTH, PRICE $1.25 PER VOLUME.

" We seem at last to be shown men and women as they are ; and at first it is more than we can endure. . . . All Ibsen's characters speak and act as if they were hypnotised, and under their creator's imperious demand to reveal themselves. There never was such a mirror held up to nature before: it is too terrible. . . . Yet we must return to Ibsen, with his remorseless surgery, his remorseless electric-light, until we, too, have grown strong and learned to face the naked—if necessary, the flayed and bleeding—reality."—SPEAKER (London).

VOL. I. "A DOLL'S HOUSE," "THE LEAGUE OF YOUTH," and "THE PILLARS OF SOCIETY." With Portrait of the Author, and Biographical Introduction by WILLIAM ARCHER.

VOL. II. "GHOSTS," "AN ENEMY OF THE PEOPLE," and "THE WILD DUCK." With an Introductory Note.

VOL. III. "LADY INGER OF ÖSTRÅT," "THE VIKINGS AT HELGELAND," "THE PRETENDERS." With an Introductory Note and Portrait of Ibsen.

VOL. IV. "EMPEROR AND GALILEAN." With an Introductory Note by WILLIAM ARCHER.

VOL. V. "ROSMERSHOLM," "THE LADY FROM THE SEA," "HEDDA GABLER." Translated by WILLIAM ARCHER. With an Introductory Note.

VOL. VI. "PEER GYNT: A DRAMATIC POEM." Authorised Translation by WILLIAM and CHARLES ARCHER.

The sequence of the plays *in each volume* is chronological ; the complete set of volumes comprising the dramas thus presents them in chronological order.

"The art of prose translation does not perhaps enjoy a very high literary status in England, but we have no hesitation in numbering the present version of Ibsen, so far as it has gone (Vols. I. and II.), among the very best achievements, in that kind, of our generation."—*Academy*.

"We have seldom, if ever, met with a translation so absolutely idiomatic."—*Glasgow Herald*.

New York: CHARLES SCRIBNER'S SONS.